Hardy the Physician

Hardy the Physician

Medical Aspects of the Wessex Tradition

Tony Fincham

First published 2008 by
PALGRAVE MACMILLAN
Houndmills, Basingstoke, Hampshire RG21 6XS and
175 Fifth Avenue, New York, N.Y. 10010
Companies and representatives throughout the world

PALGRAVE MACMILLAN is the global academic imprint of the Palgrave
Macmillan division of St. Martin's Press, LLC and of Palgrave Macmillan Ltd.
Macmillan® is a registered trademark in the United States, United Kingdom
and other countries. Palgrave is a registered trademark in the European
Union and other countries.

ISBN-13: 978–0–230–20317–4   hardback
ISBN-10: 0–230–20317–5   hardback

This book is printed on paper suitable for recycling and made from fully
managed and sustained forest sources. Logging, pulping and manufacturing
processes are expected to conform to the environmental regulations of the
country of origin.

A catalogue record for this book is available from the British Library.

Library of Congress Cataloging-in-Publication Data
Fincham, Tony, 1952–
   Hardy the physician : medical aspects of the Wessex tradition /
      Tony Fincham.
         p. cm.
   Includes bibliographical references and index.
   ISBN 0–230–20317–5 (alk. paper)
      1. Hardy, Thomas, 1840–1928 – Knowledge – Medicine. 2. Literature
   and medicine. 3. Physicians in literature. 4. Diseases in literature.
   5. Medicine in literature. 6. Wessex (England) – In literature. I. Title.

   PR4754.F47 2008
   823′.8–dc22

                                                                      2008015907

10   9   8   7   6   5   4   3   2   1
17   16   15   14   13   12   11   10   09   08

Printed and bound in Great Britain by
CPI Antony Rowe, Chippenham and Eastbourne

To Mary,
Rebecca, Guy,
Clara and Harriet

who have all endured so much Hardy for so long!

Contents

List of Illustrations and Tables

Illustrations

Tables

Acknowledgements

A section of Chapter 3, 'The (mad)Woman in the Attic', and a shortened version of Chapter 5 have previously been published in *The Thomas Hardy Journal*. I am grateful to the editor, Claire Seymour, both for their initial publication and permission to republish them here.

I am grateful to The Wellcome Trust for permission to reproduce the illustration of Laennec's wooden stethoscope, and to Dorset County Museum for permission to reproduce the photo of the The Hardys at Max Gate.

Special thanks also to all those who have supported me in my literary quest thus far – particularly at the Hardy Society: Jim and Helen Gibson – and in the early days, Christina Rogers and Jenny Ford. And at Tonbridge – 'Mr Ford' and Bruce Hugman. At Unikent, Helen Wheeler, Agnes Cardinal, Michael Irwin, Rod Edmond and my brother Ken, the historian. Also, Angela Faunch in Document Delivery and Lilian Swindall at the DCM. Medically, my gratitude to Roger Higgs and Iain McGilchrist, and to my colleagues and patients in Yalding. Finally, I owe an incalculable debt to Frank Fincham who, through Paul, gave me a genetic inclination which I was unable to resist.

Abbreviations

AI	Hardy, Thomas, *An Indiscretion in the Life of an Heiress*, Oxford University Press, Oxford 1994
AL	Hardy, Thomas, *A Laodicean*, Penguin, Harmondsworth 1997
BE	Hardy, Thomas, *A Pair of Blue Eyes*, Penguin, Harmondsworth 1998
CL	Hardy, Thomas, *Collected Letters of Thomas Hardy*, ed. T. Purdy, R. Little and M. Millgate (7 vols), Oxford University Press, Oxford 1978–98
CM	Hardy, Thomas, *A Changed Man & Other Tales*, Macmillan, London 1962
CP	Hardy, Thomas, *The Complete Poems*, ed. J. Gibson, Macmillan, London 1976
DR	Hardy, Thomas, *Desperate Remedies*, Penguin, Harmondsworth 1998
ED	Hardy, Emma, *Diaries*, ed. R. Taylor Carcanet, Manchester 1985
EL	Hardy, Florence, *The Early Life of Thomas Hardy*, Macmillan, London 1928
FM	Hardy, Thomas, *Far from the Madding Crowd*, Folio, London 1985
FN	Hardy, Thomas, *Hardy's 'Facts' Notebook*, ed. W. Greenslade, Ashgate, Aldershot 2004
GT	Hardy, Thomas, *Under the Greenwood Tree*, Folio, London 1988
HE	Hardy, Thomas, *The Hand of Ethelberta*, Penguin, Harmondsworth 1997
JO	Hardy, Thomas, *Jude the Obscure*, Folio, London 1992
LH	Hardy, Emma and Florence Hardy, *Letters of Emma and Florence Hardy*, ed. M. Millgate, Clarendon, Oxford, 1996
LI	Hardy, Thomas, *Life's Little Ironies*, Oxford University Press, Oxford 1996
LN	Hardy, Thomas, *Literary Notebooks of Thomas Hardy Volumes I & II*, ed. L. Bjork, Macmillan, Basingstoke, 1985
LY	Hardy, Florence, *The Later Years of Thomas Hardy*, Macmillan, London 1930
MC	Hardy, Thomas, *The Mayor of Casterbridge*, Penguin, Harmondsworth 1978
ND	Hardy, Thomas, *A Group of Noble Dames*, Alan Sutton, Strood 1983

QC   Hardy, Thomas, *The Famous Tragedy of the Queen of Cornwall*, Macmillan 1923

RN   Hardy, Thomas, *The Return of the Native*, Oxford University Press, Oxford 1998

TD   Hardy, Thomas, *Tess of the d'Urbervilles*, Folio, London 1988

TM   Hardy, Thomas, *The Trumpet-Major*, Folio, London 1985

TT   Hardy, Thomas, *Two on a Tower*, Penguin, Harmondsworth 1999

TW   Hardy, Thomas, *The Woodlanders*, Penguin, Harmondsworth 1998

WB   Hardy, Thomas, *The Well-Beloved*, Penguin, Harmondsworth 1997

WT   Hardy, Thomas, *Wessex Tales*, Wordsworth, Ware, 1999

Supporting works

DNB   *Dictionary of National Biography*, on CD-ROM Version 1.1, Oxford University Press 1995

OED   *Oxford English Dictionary*, Clarendon, Oxford 1933

THJ   *Thomas Hardy Journal*, various years

THSR   *Thomas Hardy Society Review*, various editions

THYB   *Thomas Hardy Year-Book*, various years

SA   *Scientific American*

Introduction

When the present has latched its postern behind my tremulous stay,
    And the May month flaps its glad green leaves like wings,
Delicate-filmed as new-spun silk, will the neighbours say,
    'He was a man who used to notice such things'?

                                                                    (CP 553)

I treat Hardy himself less as a real person than as a text. By Hardy,
I always mean 'Hardy', the larger text woven by the writer's or the
speaker's words in all the discrete texts assembled under that name.

                                                            (Garson 1991: 4)

This book is an exploration of the medical aspects of Thomas Hardy's
written works – his fiction, poetry, drama, autobiography, correspondence and non-fictive writings – with three principal intentions. Firstly,
to shed new, or at least differently diffracted, light onto Hardy's understanding of the human condition. Secondly, to use the medical and
psychological descriptions of the 'man who used to notice such things'
to generate fresh understandings of nineteenth-century medicine and
our twenty-first-century attitudes towards it; particularly at that interface between the physical and the psychological, which is Hardy's
home ground. Thirdly, and somewhat tentatively, to uncover attitudes
towards healthcare and healing which are likely to be of benefit to
doctors and patients in this new century.

   Why Hardy? Because Hardy was an astute observer of the human
condition, both in sickness and in health; a man with a poet's unique
gift for transferring clearly and concisely to paper not only his innermost thoughts and feelings, but also the symptoms and signs which he
observed in suffering humanity around him.

By 1887 Coventry Patmore had already realised the potential value of Victorian fiction to future historians:

> from Jane Austen to Thomas Hardy, we have had scores of 'fictions' which are only fictions in form; the substance being the very reality of contemporary life ... the student of 1987, if he wants to know anything really about us, will not find it in our poets or our philosophers or our parliamentary debates, but in our novelists ...
>
> (Cox 1970: 146)

Hardy's life spanned the period in which medicine changed from a healing art based on ancient and unprovable doctrines to an interventional science based on objective measurements. Despite this revolution in medical thinking, Hardy remained consistent in his deeply sympathetic holistic approach to human pathology and to his enduring belief that psychological factors outweighed physical in both the aetiology and the therapeutic management of illness.

In this study, I reinterpret Hardy's texts in the light of both contemporary (nineteenth-century) and current (twenty-first century) medical knowledge, balancing this 'hard' science against the 'soft' concept of medicine as an art – a magic blender of the physical and the psychological. This is not to deny that scientific advance – the germ theory of disease, safe anaesthesia and surgical asepsis – has brought much benefit to mankind. The issue here is more that of the price – in human and environmental terms – at which this has been achieved and of what can be done in this new century to redress the balance.

This medico-literary approach to Hardy is a two-way process – the interpretative skills used in the consulting room are a valuable tool in approaching literary texts and, conversely, the critical exploration of literary texts is of value in understanding the multiplicity of ways in which patients present fragmented stories to the doctor and the different ways in which the physician can help to gather this unsorted information into a coherent narrative. In my exploration of Hardy and medicine, I have dwelt particularly on the complex cross-fertilisation between Hardy's own experiences of illness and that of his fictional characters; here 'the horizons and landscapes' of his 'partly real, partly dream country' (*FM* xvii) are seen to blur, amalgamate and then separate and reform like the patterns in a kaleidoscope.

For Hardy, the boundaries between fiction and reality are quite as indistinct as are the boundaries between the psyche and the soma. Both form an integral part of the same whole, which constitutes that complex construct known as man. These are the same boundaries, which tend to disappear when analytical techniques are applied to the medical consultation. My method in this study has been to use interpretative psychotherapy, as pioneered in England by Michael Balint and subsequently refined by the Institute of Psychosexual Medicine, to explore Hardy's Wessex.

Balint stressed the importance of the 'inner consultation' or psychological subtext in the GP's surgery, whereby non-verbal clues – such as the patient's gait, mode of dress, eye-contact and the doctor's emotional response to them – are given equal significance in reaching a diagnosis as the words she chooses to utter in presenting her complaint to the doctor. In this holistic approach, what the patient says is seldom as important as what she does not say.

In this book I am also working at another boundary; namely the interface between medicine which is narrative-based and that which is founded on evidence-based science. The roots of narrative medicine stretch far back into the history of the healing art. Hardy claimed that the productions of his pen were:

> Simply an endeavour to give shape and coherence to a series of seemings or personal impressions, the question of their consistency or their discordance ... being regarded as not of the first moment.
>
> *(JO* xix)

This definition of literary intent would fit comfortably on the shoulders of the traditional General Practitioner attempting to mould the patient's presenting narrative (series of seemings) with the 'objective' signs (personal impressions) into a tentative diagnosis. This book, inevitably reflecting the material on which it is based, is hence constructed out of the interaction of a series of symptoms or seemings with a series of interpretative signs or personal impressions. My particular personal medical interests, experiences and preoccupations have inevitably also directed the text – rural General Practice, dispensing, obstetrics, holistic medicine, psychosexual problems and the concept of 'an improper emotional relationship' between two consenting adults all stamp their mark. Hardy's 'series of seemings' owe a not inconsiderable debt to his literary progenitors, most especially *Tristram Shandy* where Sterne uses a seemingly discursive and erratic text to brightly illuminate the human condition. It is a technique that passed through Hardy, the 'proto-modernist' into modernism and beyond.

In my first chapter, 'Obsextrics', I briefly consider Hardy's own experiences of birth, female health, women, subfertility and contraception, most especially where these issues are reflected in his fiction. I look at the high maternal, neonatal and infant mortality rates in Wessex and then explore two particular obstetric case histories – Lucetta (Le Sueur-

Templeman-Farfrae) and Barbara of the House of Grebe – placing them in the context of contemporary medical knowledge. I also consider nineteenth-century methods of birth control, ignorance of which is an important aetiological factor in many of his tragedies.

In the next chapter, 'Hardy and Illness', I examine medical aspects of Hardy's life, especially his personal experience of physical illness and also that of Emma and Florence Hardy. In working through this subject, I have treated Hardy's autobiographical *Early Life* and *Later Years* as literary texts; extending this treatment to his published *Collected Letters* and also *The Letters of Emma and Florence Hardy*. I begin this account with an exploration of Hardy's serious illness of 1880/81; then consider the colds and 'influenza' which troubled him so much in his later years, revisiting these in the light of twenty-first-century understanding, and follow through with an exploration of ophthalmic problems, Emma's lameness, Gout, Cholera and Typhoid. In this chapter there are two distinct but closely interwoven narratives; firstly, the narrative of Hardy's fictional characters and his poetry and, secondly, the 'real' narrative of his own life in sickness and health and that of his two wives and his family.

Chapter 3, 'Endgames', continues this theme with an investigation of Heart Disease both in the fiction and as suffered by Hardy and Emma; then giving consideration to the second Mrs Hardy and that long disease – her life. I finally discuss Emma's proto-feminist retreat to her attic eyrie, both for the effect that this had on Hardy's own well-being and as a manifestation of 'The Interloper', or familial trait towards insanity, present in the Gifford family. Emma's mental health suddenly became topical last year because of a wholly unsubstantiated but widely publicized allegation that Hardy had infected her with Syphilis. My own conclusions are quite different and are based, at least, on a thorough medical analysis of all the available evidence.

In the fourth chapter, 'General Practice', I examine the role of General Practitioners in Hardy's Wessex – starting with Physician Vilbert and the still-thriving world of alternative medicine. I then explore the activities of a number of Hardy's fumblingly incompetent registered practitioners – for as many critics have observed, 'Doctors do not bring out the best in Hardy' (Gibson 1994: 123) – before concentrating on his GP hero, Edred Fitzpiers. I consider Fitzpiers in relation to the emergence of Medicine as a Profession in the nineteenth century and the particular issue of GP dispensing. I then compare him with his literary progenitors, especially Tertius Lydgate, before examining the medical practice and competence of these love-led men and analysing their transgressions in relation to that new institution, the GCMER.

The fifth chapter 'Psychosomatic Illness and Death', which is an analysis of the causes of morbidity and mortality in Hardy's Wessex, draws sharply into focus Hardy's fundamental belief in the primacy of psychological factors in the aetiology of illness. This chapter starts with a brief history of the twentieth-century 'scientific' development of psychosomatic illness, which I relate back to its nineteenth-century and traditional forebears. I then compare and contrast death statistics for Hardy's Wessex, late nineteenth-century England and late twentieth-century Kent (allowing mortality statistics from my own practice to enter this meld of fiction and reality). The focus then shifts to Egdon Heath, where the depressed lay down and die and young women are prone to bewitchment. The chapter closes with an investigation of violent death and suicide.

Chapter 6 is an analysis of Love in Wessex – that electro-emotive excitation, which I have labelled 'The Fitzpierston Syndrome', in honour of its two chief exponents. I construct a series of diagnostic criteria for this condition and examine these various aspects of love, in relation to nineteenth-century electrochemical theorisation and twentieth-century biochemical research. I also explore love in relation to the medieval romantic legend of Tristan and Iseult – Hardy's *Queen of Cornwall* – and love as illness, particularly its relation to Bipolar Affective Disorder. Finally, I return to the territory of *The Woodlanders* and *Jude*, with an examination of marriage and divorce in Hardy's Wessex.

In my final chapter, 'The Mind Diseased', I extend the links between the Fitzpierston Syndrome and Bipolar Affective Disorder into the creative triad 'the lunatic, the lover and the poet' (Shakespeare 1595: V.i.7). I examine the strong evidence base that Hardy suffered from a recurrent depressive tendency, or moderate psychopathology (Post 1994: 25), which correctly classifies as a cyclothymic personality disorder rather than full-blown Manic Depressive Illness (MDI/BAD). I relate this diagnosis to the poem 'So Various' and to *The Return of The Native*, where the heath itself becomes the embodiment of depression and the protagonists, six separate expressions of Hardy's personality and depressive illness.

A passage which Hardy recorded in his Literary Notebooks is particularly pertinent, when considering the utilisation of Hardy's life and works for a medical exploration of Wessex:

The poet does not perceive things: the poet perceives the hitherto unperceived relation of things.

(*LN* II / 2412)

Such – on a limited scale – is the aim of this book.

1
Obsextrics

Hardy's world is non-procreative; children are an embarrassment, an irrelevancy – worse – a sign of the curse over mankind.

(Thurley 1975: 168)

At 8 a.m. on the morning of Tuesday 2 June 1840, the recently married wife of a country bricklayer (1851 Census) lay 'near death's door' (*EL* 20) in the third stage of a prolonged and difficult first labour. The attending surgeon, concentrating his efforts on saving the mother, abandoned the apparently stillborn infant until the 'monthly nurse', the wife of an old militiaman, contradicted the doctor and rescued the babe exclaiming 'Dead! Stop a minute: he's alive enough, sure!' (*EL* 18). Thomas Hardy's survival of those perilous neonatal moments probably owed much to the long-running conflict between Physician Accoucheur and Midwife, as portrayed by Sterne 80 years previously in *Tristram Shandy* and documented by the Department of Health 145 years later in *Changing Childbirth* (Cumberlege).

The nurse scored a point off the doctor; Hardy survived for 87 years, long enough to create a lasting literary industry; his mother lived for 64 more years during which time she completed three further successful pregnancies despite nearly dying when Hardy was three years old of a 'dangerous miscarriage' complicated by 'brain fever' from which she emerged 'a changed woman, harder, sterner, altogether more assertive' (Millgate 1982: 20).

Thomas Hardy, 'the only one of the four who married' (*EL* 18), despite two wives and numerous well-beloveds, left no recorded offspring, being thus the direct opposite of Mr Penny's daughter Mrs Brownjohn who 'do know the multiplication table onmistakable well' (*GT* 7). Referring in his diary in August 1877 to the expected confinement of his dismissed servant Jane, whose bastard son Tom, subsequently died at two days of age, he recorded sadly 'Yet never a sign of one is there for us' (*EL* 153). Millgate notes the parallels between Jane's obstetric and neonatal experiences and those subsequently suffered by Tess and Sorrow (Millgate 1982: 191). As Pierre D'Exideuil observed 'the child plays no role in Wessex' except for 'poor Tess's offspring so speedily carried off and Jude's children all doomed to die' (D'Exideuil 1929: 70). In Hardy's fiction childbirth is indeed rare and the outcome usually disastrous.

The two fecund mothers discussed by the choir in *Under The Greenwood Tree* are an early indicator of this tendency, for although Mrs Brownjohn and Mrs Leaf between them bear 17 children, only four survive the neonatal period.

Obstetric mortality

Overall in Hardy's novels, 33 births occur to a total of 14 mothers; 20 infants are stillborn or die in the neonatal period, one dies as a child (Young Father Time) and eight are still alive at the end of the novel. The mothers do not fare much better as five die in childbirth or miscarrying; four others die before the end of their respective novels – and only three survive, wounded: Thomasin, Sue Bridehead and Arabella. The pregnancy rate is higher in the short stories but the statistics are equally grim, 30 births occurring to a total of 12 mothers, 14 infants are stillborn or die in the neonatal period, one dies in infancy and 15 survive to the end of the story. The mothers fare even worse – seven dying in childbirth and two more before the end of the tale – only three mothers survive. If a child survives the trauma of Wessex childbirth, there is a high probability of it being mentally and physically defective as exemplified by Thomas Leaf, an imbecile with 11 dead siblings, Christian Cantle (no moon, no man) and the four 'hipless shoulderless (motherless) girls' who are foisted on to the hapless Baptista Trewthen in 'A Mere Interlude'. The overall combined neonatal and infant mortality rate in Hardy's fiction is 62 per cent whilst the maternal mortality rate works out at 70 per cent. The actual national maternal mortality rate in the mid-nineteenth century, the period during which most of Hardy's fiction is set, was in the order of one death in 189 deliveries or 0.53 per cent according to the Seventeenth Annual Report of the Registrar General published in 1857 (Tyler Smith 1858: 614). Neonatal and infant mortality were taken very much as a fact of life in the mid-nineteenth century and therefore no statistics were recorded.

Whilst obstetricians strove to reduce the maternal death rate (representing about 3300 mothers annually in England), the thought of reducing perinatal mortality was still several generations away. This throw-away attitude towards infant and neo-natal mortality is illustrated by the rapid disposal of the first Elizabeth-Jane in *The Mayor of Casterbridge*, in which town, Lucetta's house boasts the convenience of adjoining 'the pool wherein nameless infants used to disappear' (*MC* 212). The Select Committee on Death Certification in 1893 heard evidence from Mr Athelstan Braxton Hicks, Coroner for South West London, about lying-in houses where: 'the newly-born child was dropped in a bucket of water, which prevented it from breathing, or that a wet cloth was clapped over it, which had the same effect ...' (HMSO 1893).

Hicks, son of the eminent Guy's Hospital obstetrician, lamented the difficulties of proving infanticide at inquest, juries being reluctant to convict a bereaved young mother. Detailed obstetric case histories are rare in Hardy's fiction; two, however, warrant further exploration – firstly, 'the dangerous illness of Mrs Farfrae' (*MC* 362) and, secondly, the sad case of Barbara Uplandtowers.

Eclampsia

Lucetta Le Sueur/Templeman/Farfrae dies from an eclamptic fit, precipitated by the stress of her public shaming in the skimmity-ride. In 1886, when Hardy was writing *The Mayor of Casterbridge*, the aetiology of eclampsia was even less well understood than it is today. Blood-pressure measurement was at this time very much in the experimental stage – so no link between the condition and hypertension had been established. In fact, the first reference to a 'Sphygmodynameter, an apparatus for measuring the pressure of the blood' dates from 1876 (OED: vol. X, 588).

The 'complication of albuminuria' in some cases of puerperal convulsion had first been noted by Richard Bright at Guy's in 1842, but its significance not understood (Barnes 1884: 383). Eclampsia gravidarum was considered to have two causes – firstly, *toxaemia* which was thought to be secondary to infection or poisoning (but not linked to the modern pre-eclamptic triad of hypertension, albuminuria and oedema) and, secondly, that it was '*psychical* in its character ... emotion (being) a very important cause of centric convulsion in the puerperal state' (Tyler Smith 1858: 500). Robert Barnes, whose detailed *System of Obstetric Medicine* was published by Smith

Elder in 1884, waxes lyrical on eclampsia as part of the female tendency to swoon:

> We may here venture to state a general proposition. The chief acts of reproduction in woman are marked by nervous phenomenon allied to convulsion. The orgasm of coitus, the vomiting, cramps and other phenomenon of gestation and labour itself are of this character.
>
> (Barnes 1884: 383)

There is no record surviving of where, or from whom, Hardy obtained medical advice concerning illness in his later fiction. The only clearly documented such reference is a letter from Dr George Brereton Sharpe, dated 21 January 1868, advising Hardy on the most appropriate mode of death for the heroine of his 'lost' novel *The Poor Man and The Lady*. It seems highly probable that he continued in this habit of obtaining appropriate medical advice throughout his writing career; certainly the illness and death of Lucetta follow closely the descriptions of eclampsia in contemporary textbooks. From 1875 onwards, Hardy was corresponding and mixing regularly during the London Season with some of the most eminent physicians and surgeons of the day.

Lucetta first appears in person near the mid-point of *The Mayor of Casterbridge* as a solitary dark figure, clothed in mourning – she stands by the grave of Henchard's first dead woman in anticipation of what she will soon become – his second dead woman. She is 'dark-haired, large-eyed, pretty' and 'undoubtedly French' (*MC* 221) – all characteristics which would tend to predispose to an hysterical personality. Shortly afterwards, she bursts into 'hysterical sobs' at the discovery that her calculating bid to attract Henchard by inviting Elizabeth-Jane to live in her house may have misfired. She dismisses the girl. Then dolled-up for Henchard but surprised instead by Farfrae, she complains to him of bitter loneliness; becomes tearful over her ideal of free love for servants, before denying non-existent rumours that she is a coquette. Farfrae, whose ignorance of women matches Henchard's, sheds tears as well. Henchard has previously described Lucetta to Farfrae, in their early days of confidence, as a girl 'terribly careless of appearances' with whom he enjoyed a sexual relationship in Jersey (*MC* 149). But 'clever Mr Farfrae' fails to make this link until Lucetta is dying.

In subsequent angry debate with Henchard, Lucetta tries to maintain her innocence whilst admitting only to 'a foolish girl's passion'.

However innocent the liaison, Lucetta manages not to fall pregnant by Henchard (whose potency was already proven) but is rapidly impregnated by Farfrae. She appears to have been the driving force behind the illicit affair – Henchard at the time being ill and sunk 'into one of those gloomy fits ... when the world seems to have the blackness of hell'. Lucetta, nursing him, then as always had 'feelings warm' and 'honestly meant to marry' (*MC* 149). The implication must be that foolish as she often was in Casterbridge, at home on the Continent, this woman of French extraction was wise enough to be readily supplied with French letters, particularly in view of her known enthusiasm for letters in general. Lucetta is a clear portrait of a histrionic personality for such people:

> are usually emotionally labile – sudden bouts of desperate gloom pass quickly and are replaced by some capricious infatuation or enthusiasm ... behaviour tends to be dramatic and the person is importunate ... the emotions are shallow – effuse demonstrations of feeling mean nothing and relationships are never stable.
>
> (Houston, Joiner and Trounce 1975: 36)

Almost her every appearance on the Casterbridge stage reinforces Lucetta's personality type. On Henchard's forcibly extracted promise of marriage, Lucetta falls back in a 'fainting state', the hysterical nature of which is confirmed by her 'seeming to wake from her swoon with a start' when Henchard points out to Elizabeth-Jane that Farfrae will then be free to marry her (*MC* 270). The pattern repeats itself – in her encounter with the bull, in her 'semi-paralysed state' and 'hysterical sobbing' on hearing Henchard read her old *billet doux* to the ever-ignorant Farfrae and her readiness to faint on Henchard's performance for the Royal Visitor. Her request in public to Henchard to return her old letters merits the epithet 'imprudence incarnate' (*MC* 316) and directly precipitates the skimmity-ride and her untimely death. Nearly all deaths in Hardy can be similarly interpreted as indirect suicide.

Hardy carefully conceals the fact that Lucetta is pregnant until shortly before the announcement of her death. After her initial collapse, the doctor merely states that 'a fit in her present state of health means mischief' (*MC* 354), but no information is given as to exactly what that state of health comprises. It is almost as if the pregnancy was added as an afterthought to give medical validity to Lucetta's death after an hysterical collapse. There is a possible early *double entendre* reference to pregnancy when, on Farfrae being elected Mayor, the narrator comments that 'fair Lucetta was the courted of the town ... But, ah! that worm i' the bud' – (*MC* 317), the reference here is to Henchard but there is a second 'worm i' the bud' – Farfrae's foetus which she will carry until it destroys her: closely paralleling his ability to creep 'into a maid's heart like the giddying worm into a sheep's brain' (*MC* 265). Toxoplasma or Farfrae's foetus – both parasites are equally destructive.

The scandal, which spread 'like a miasmatic fog through Mixen Lane and thence up the back streets of Casterbridge', soon erupted into the din of 'cleavers, tongs, tambourines, kits, crouds, humstrums, serpents, rams'-horns and other historical kinds of music' – an 'uncanny revel' of noise and laughter which causes Lucetta's features to grow 'rigid and wild'; 'with a wild laugh' she 'fell heavily to the floor' and then 'convulsed on the carpet in the paroxysms of an epileptic seizure' (*MC* 352–4). Quite appropriately, Barnes describes eclamptic fits as 'frequently preceded by ringing or buzzing in the ears, difficulty of articulation, nervousness and a sense of terror' (Barnes 1884: 388). Hardy skilfully links this clinical description of eclampsia with a realistic depiction of the ancient custom of the skimmity-ride and its physical effect upon its intended victim – a woman who has been foolish enough to give herself naturally in love – in such a way as to cause social disapprobation. He also beautifully melds together the social and medical consequences of trying 'to live and love at pleasure!' – the philosophy of life, which Lucetta had expounded to Farfrae on their first meeting (*MC* 233).

Thomas Graham, whose best-selling *Modern Domestic Medicine* was on the shelf at Max Gate, describes the symptoms of eclamptic convulsions as follows:

> Hurried respiration, headache, ringing in the ears, giddiness ... followed by quick repeated spasms of the face, eyes, arms, legs and indeed of the whole body ... the vessels of the neck are distended and beat violently and the patient is thrown into most frightful contortions. No force can restrain the woman and the distortions of her countenance are dreadful ...
>
> (Graham 1861: 234)

The patient passes from tonic to clonic fit, to coma, then remission. 'Whilst Elizabeth-Jane was undressing her she recovered consciousness but as soon as she remembered what had passed the fit returned' (*MC* 353). 'The interval of calm before another storm is of variable duration'

(Barnes 1884: 386). Hardy doesn't relate how the local doctor, 'who arrived with unhoped for promptitude', treated his patient nor what extra help was given by the second physician from Budmouth, who came in the small hours. Graham outlines the standard mid-nineteenth-century treatment, which involves the well-established triad of venesection, purgation and cooling the patient, followed by effecting delivery as rapidly as possible of the (usually dead) infant:

> From 16-20oz of blood may be drawn at once from the patient's arm and this may be repeated according to the violence of the fits and the strength of the patient ... the bowels should be emptied without delay ... at the same time, the hair of the patient should be shaved or cut off and rags dipped ... in the coldest water laid over it and frequently renewed. Dipping a bunch of feathers into a large basin of the coldest water and dashing it over the face and neck is another valuable remedy ...
>
> (Graham 1861: 235–6)

In the light of modern obstetric understanding, the venesection, which would lower the blood pressure, and the induction of labour, facilitated by the purgation, would probably be of benefit; the application of cold to the head and neck would most probably raise the blood pressure and be counter-productive. Lucetta, with head shaved, purged, bled and soaked in cold water, would not have been a pretty sight by the time Farfrae reached her side. Whether she died from the eclampsia itself (cardiorespiratory failure or cerebral haemorrhage) or more gradually from haemorrhage induced by the miscarriage is uncertain, but the implication of the narrative is that she gradually faded away, making the latter option the more probable cause of death.

Death by haemorrhage, aggravated by the Physician's treatment of venesection is unlikely to have allowed much opportunity for effective communication with Farfrae, particularly on the complex and sensitive issue of her relationship with Henchard. Hardy is certainly right therefore to speculate on what or how much she 'ultimately explained to him ... in the solitude of that sad night' (*MC* 363).

Noble dames

A Group of Noble Dames is undoubtedly the most fecund collection of females in all Hardy's fiction. This is a reflection of the issues with which Hardy is here primarily concerned – the discord between social convention and sexual passion, and its consequences in terms of the laws of property and inheritance whereby male stands above female, legitimate child over illegitimate. Even then, only five out of the ten *Dames* give birth; out of these five only the unfortunate Lady Mottisfont survives to tell the tale. The others succumb quite rapidly in the neonatal period to the injurious effects of childbirth or else waste away and die as a direct result of child-bearing/rearing. Barbara of the House of Grebe, once successfully suppressed by her husband's crude aversion therapy, is second only to Mrs Leaf in reproductive capacity for:

> Little personal events came to her in quick succession – ... in brief, she bore him no less than eleven children in the nine following years, but half of them came prematurely into the world, or died a few days old; only one, a girl attained maturity ...
>
> (*ND* 75)

At the end of this catalogue of obstetric disasters, Barbara herself, now 'completely worn out in mind and body' dies too – in Florence where she has been transported in a vain attempt to recover her health. The obstetric failure is also a deeply wounding social failure to provide the required son and heir. These failures directly mirror the degraded relationship between the contracting parties to the marriage. There is no love between Uplandtowers and Barbara – merely bloody-mindedness on his side and depressed indifference on hers. Barbara only begins to conceive once Uplandtowers has performed his crude and dastardly aversion therapy on 'one of those sweet-pea or with-wind natures which require a twig of stouter fibre ... to hang upon and bloom' (*ND* 65). Thwarted nature thus turns this pathological marriage into a stream of abortions, still-births and neo-natal deaths. In a manner absolutely characteristic of Hardy's fiction, Barbara does not conceive during her two-month passionate elopement with Edmond. Love fulfilled in Wessex begets neither joy nor offspring. As Hillis Miller shrewdly commented:

> The only permanent and (ironically) happy love relationships are those which are no union at all, but for one reason or another prolong indefinitely the time before possession.
>
> (Hillis Miller 1982: 155)

Possession results neither in happiness nor in successful pregnancy. *Barbara of The House of Grebe* signals an attitude present in many of the short stories and in *Jude*, where sexual reproduction is effectively reduced to no more than an excretory function. The Darwinian psychiatrists who dominated the profession in the last decades of the nineteenth century promulgated this approach, as here Maudsley:

> Looking at the matter objectively ... could anything be more ridiculous than all this affectionate fuss about what is essentially an excretory product and comes into the world by excretory ways? Moreover, there is nothing nice in the process of parturition nor in the base services which the child exacts.
>
> (Showalter 1985: 124).

As is not infrequently the case, the psychiatrist appears here to be more mentally disturbed than his patients! This quasi-scientific Puritanism fitted well with Hardy's grim understanding of the nature of the organism. Barbara in love with 'one of the handsomest men who ever set his lips on a maid's' (*ND* 52) cannot conceive, nor can she conceive when first wedded by Uplandtowers; it is only once all sensibility has been battered out of her by his crude manipulations that the mechanics of reproduction grind into gear. Nature confirms in her cold indifferent irony that conception is an involuntary excretory function. But Hardy here, as always, is working on a number of different levels. In the early months of her marriage, Uplandtowers complains of Barbara's 'lack of warmth' for 'he had set his mind on a lineal successor' and 'he asked her what she was good for' (*ND* 65).

It is not until he finds her 'locked in an abandoned sexual embrace with the statue' which represents 'Edmond in all his original beauty – a specimen of manhood almost perfect in every line and contour', then takes her back in his bed 'shaken by spent sobs and sighs' that she conceives (*ND* 67, 69). Uplandtowers had previously noticed on his wife's face 'a sort of silent ecstasy, a reserved beatification' and discovered 'from her breathing that she was strangely moved' (*ND* 68). With the statue, Barbara attains the orgasm which was missing from marital coition and thus ovulates and conceives. Nineteenth-century medicine gave scientific endorsement to the ancient folk-belief that female orgasm was an indispensable part of conception. As James Copland states in his authoritative *Dictionary of Practical Medicine*: 'It is generally understood by females of all ranks in society, that indifference during intercourse or suppression of the orgasm will prevent impregnation ...' (Copland 1866: 323)

It was thus generally believed that female pleasure was an essential ingredient in fecundity and that a wife could not become pregnant by her husband if he failed to arouse her to orgasm. The twentieth-century view that Victorian women led a life of joyless inhibition and ignorance can thus be dismissed as unhistorical, but in its stead comes a sad reality of women denying themselves sexual pleasure in the belief that it will cause them to conceive. As Barbara with her statue so Ella, Hardys' *Imaginative Woman,* conceives with the aid of a photograph. Locked by 'the necessity of getting life-leased at all cost' (*LI* 8) into loveless marriage with a cold and indifferent gun merchant, Ella falls in love by proxy with a young poet who closely resembles Hardy in being 'a pessimist', 'who looks at the worst contingencies as well as the best in the human condition' (*LI* 11).

Ella's fetishistic infatuation feeds on his room, his books, his scribblings on the wall, his discarded clothing. With 'a serene sense of something ecstatic to come', she gets 'rid of superfluous garments' preparing to adore the as 'yet uncovered photograph' of a man with 'an unlimited capacity for misery' (*LL* 18) in what Terry Wright aptly describes as 'a positive orgy of eroticism' (1989: 98). Her ecstatic fantasies are rudely disturbed by the unexpected reappearance of her husband, who is seeking sexual relief ('I wanted to be with you tonight'). Being a Victorian Gentleman, he utters the code words for refusal ('Have you a headache?') but Ella is too insensible to grasp this lifeline.

Instead, she submits and is impregnated – to die nine months later giving birth to the fat 'infant for whose unnecessary life' she parted with her own (*LI* 31). Impregnation by statue is followed, in this instance, by impregnation by photograph. In the same quasi-scientific way in which orgasm was thought to be necessary for ovulation and conception, the genes of the man whose photograph was in the bed beneath the copulating couple find their way into the fertilised ovum. Robert Trewe, the object of Ella's desire, though never seen, never touched, dies without heir; his seed is all fruitless but his features live on in the gun merchant's youngest child. By a form of rampant Lamarckism called by Hardy 'a known but inexplicable trick of nature', 'the dreamy and peculiar expression of the poet's face' was transmitted 'upon the child's, and the hair was of the same hue' (*LL* 32). Put another way, the power of Ella's imagination was so strong that it amended the embryological development and subsequent physiognomy of the child. Such were her psychosomatic powers that she was also able to will herself to die 'pulseless and bloodless' in this fourth confinement, much against the statistical odds. Death in Hardy is almost always the triumph of mind over matter.

After the fire, wispy Barbara, who is no Jane Eyre, has neither the mental strength nor agility to love the *écorche*, the mutilated human remnant to which her handsome Edmond is reduced. But once he is dead, and most particularly once he is physically resurrected in all his original beauty in purest Carrara marble, she is able to love and worship him with abandon. On one level, this is mere confirmation that her love was skin deep – as already implied by the fact that it was his image rather than his intelligent and affectionate letters that she required to sustain her during his absence abroad (*LI* 53). On a deeper level, Barbara is experiencing the power of death to renew love and raise it to levels of sublimity impossible whilst the beloved remains alive. This is an essential ingredient of Hardy's experience of love, one of the most pervasive themes of the poetry and a principal motif of *The Well Beloved*. In Hillis-Miller's succinct analysis: 'As death puts an infinite distance between lover and beloved, so it raises love to a mea-sureless intensity of longing' (Hillis-Miller 1970: 169).

A measureless intensity of longing allows Barbara psychological and psychosexual fulfilment but physically turns her into a brood mare, a battery hen trapped in a purposeless production line which can lead only to cachexia and her own certain death.

Most appropriately, it is the Old Surgeon who relates Barbara's history, with its clinical description of Uplandtowers' use of a crude form of Behaviour Modification Therapy to redirect her errant affec-tions. Hardy explains that Barbara is a 'delicate soul' with a heightened sensibility to visual imagery and as such is an ideal subject for the kind of aversion therapy planned by her husband. The first two exposures to the 'ghastly figure' result in fainting turns, her 'strange fascination' with 'this grisly exhibition', notwithstanding. Uplandtowers remains:

> Firm in enforcing his ferocious correctives ... he continued treat-ment until the nerves of the lady were quivering in agony under the vicious tortures inflicted by her lord to bring her truant heart back to faithfulness.

> (*ND* 73)

On the third occasion, she shrieks with hysterical laughter and then becomes insensible in 'an epileptic fit'. In the late nineteenth century, epilepsy was thought to be principally psychological in origin and the boundaries between a fit and a faint were even less clearly distin-guished than they are today. However, the fact that neurology and psy-chiatry were still part of the same discipline at the time that Hardy was writing allowed for diagnoses which fully incorporated both psychological and physical factors – a capacity which was lost in the twentieth century with its very clear division between physical and 'functional' illness. What Hardy is really telling us is that the attack on the third night was more profound than the preceding one. As such it represented 'the turn', the psychological denouement – for on recovery (and Uplandtowers had done all he could to restore her) – 'She flung her arms around him, and ... abjectly kissed him many times', declaring that she loved him and hated the statue (*ND* 74).

Hardy's description of this form of psychotherapy, published in 1891, more than 40 years before the technique was described in detail by medical practitioners and 60 years before it came into routine practice, can be seen as a prime example of Hardy's 'extraordinary insight into how the mind works' (Sumner 1981: 28). Hardy then puts the icing on the psychological cake by demonstrating how 'the cure became so permanent as to be itself a new disease'. The dangers of excess response or adverse counter-reaction to hypnosis and other dramatic psychological therapies are now well recognised, but were hardly common knowledge when Hardy was writing in this story in 1890. Hardy combined the astute observation of the 'man who used to notice such things' (*CP* 553) with a profound comprehension of the inner mechanisms of the human psyche.

Female pills

Hardy's understanding of the human mind and body is often much closer to a twenty-first-century understanding of the human organism than that of his late nineteenth-century medical contemporaries. Victorian doctors (and the same concept can be applied to doctors throughout history) were very much products of the society they served and on which they depended for their income; the attitude of the emergent profession towards sexual matters was therefore determined by the requirements of its (paying) customers. The nineteenth century was the great age of Science and Technology; the healing physician was suddenly clothed in a pseudo-scientific mantle; his ancient arts largely forgotten, his newly found scientific instruments and theories allowed him to interfere with the human psyche and soma with an unprecedented authority.

Because Victorian natural science was primarily concerned with taxonomy, the physician entered the sexual arena (and specifically the middle-class bedroom) as a great classifier turning insignificant aberrations, petty indecencies and minor perversions into a whole new pathology of eroticism; the foundation stone of which was undoubtedly Dr von Krafft-Ebing's *Psychopathia Sexualis,* first published in 1846 but remaining in print until the 1930s. Foucault aptly described this book as 'an orthopaedics specific to sex' (1979: 118), but to modern eyes it appears no more than a compilation of pornographic case histories, the nineteenth-century equivalent of *FHM*. Krafft-Ebing's titillating work is, however, central to the understanding of Victorian medicine and sexuality. Stephen Heath neatly summarises the position:

> It is not that the Victorians repress the topic of sexuality; it is on the contrary that they produce it, that with them the sexual becomes a problem that needs to be faced – thought about and investigated, explained and theorized, with medicine having the prime responsibility for this social task; over to the doctors, the sanctioned custodians of the body in their recently acquired professional respectability to furnish the treatises ...for the individual the sexual is then perceived as doubt.
>
> (1982: 16)

For Tess, it is doubt; for Jude and Sue, it is doubt – for Tom, it so often appears to be doubt. Deeply enwrapped in exciting and erotic theory, the medical profession failed to provide the practical support in sexual matters that was needed by nineteenth-century women and their male partners. Although contraception had been available in England since the Restoration and abortion practised since the Middle Ages, 'medical practitioners spent the better part of a century turning a deaf ear to appeals of the advocates of birth control' (McLaren 1978: 116). Until 1914, contraception was not a medical issue, despite the often fatal consequences of induced abortion:

> There she lay – silent, breathless, dead,
> Stone dead she lay – wronged, sinless, she! –
>
> ('A Sunday Morning Tragedy', *CP* 205)

and despite the fact that demographic studies reveal a steady decline in the birth rate from the census of 1861 onwards (Mason 1994: 53). Most revealingly, these studies show the highest decline in fertility to be amongst medical families. Despite evidence of the widespread availability of contraception during Hardy's lifetime, it plays no part in his fiction. When Sue informs Young Father Time that 'There is going to be another baby', he jumps up wildly and bursts out weeping:

> How ever could you, mother, be so wicked and cruel as this, when you needn't have done it till we was better off, and father well!
>
> (*JO* 330)

Sue, 'her bosom heaving', can offer no explanation so subsequently suicide and fratricide play the role better reserved for the condom. Whilst Sue is effectively destroyed by her sexuality, Arabella uses her body as a means of economic survival, trading her sexuality in her progress through life and through men. Despite Arabella's implied multiple sexual involvements, it is Sue who becomes recurrently pregnant. In her initial entrapment of Jude and in her subsequent capture of Dr Vilbert, Arabella seeks the quack physician's advice and makes use of his potions. Amongst the remedies for which young Jude had to find customers in order to obtain grammars were 'Physician Vilbert's golden ointment, life-drops and female pills' (*JO* 21). These 'French or Female pills were guaranteed to cure a suppression of the menses' (McLaren 1978: 81).

In other words, quack physicians openly marketed them as abortifacients because the medical profession declined to involve itself in such issues. The implication must be that Arabella, the worldly-wise pig-breeder's daughter, avoided pregnancy by the regular use of abortifacients. The use of such substances was thought to account for 'the low illegitimacy rate of the factory towns' (McLaren 1978: 81).

Even, Copland in his *Dictionary of Practical Medicine,* having dismissed abortion as 'a felonious act', gives a list of 'active emmenagogues as savine, ergot of rye, juniper, hellebore ...' and then recommends 'mechanical means to break the membranes' as the most efficacious method (Copland 1866: 5). Steven Marcus confirms that procured abortion seems to have been 'fairly easy to arrange in the England of that time' (Marcus 1964: 94). But not in Hardy's Wessex except for his last fictional heroine, that 'New Woman' Arabella.

A handful of heroic doctors stood up against the medical conspiracy of silence on these matters. In 1854, Dr George Drysdale published anonymously *The Elements of Social Science or Physical, Sexual and Natural Religion*. In this lengthy work he not only recommends regular sexual exercise as essential to the physical and mental well-being of both sexes from adolescence onwards, but also promotes the universal knowledge of 'the modes of preventative intercourse' without being too specific on their details (Drysdale 1875: 83, 375). This work, which is a breath of fresh air after Krafft-Ebing, ends with a meliorist statement, not far removed from Hardy:

> It is the dearest wish of my heart ... to help my fellow suffering men. I have a deep and abiding conviction that these evils are not insuperable; that the future of our race will be brighter than the past; and that what I have written has not been written in vain.
>
> (Drysdale 1875: 592)

There are clear echoes of this in the *Apology* with which Hardy introduces *Late Lyrics and Earlier*, summarised by him in the line from *In Tenebris II*: 'If a way to the Better there be, it exacts a full look at the Worst:' (CP 557). It was not until 1885 that an English doctor finally published 'a book that could be understood by most women at a price that would ensure it a place in even the poorest household' – namely sixpence. In *The Wife's Handbook* Dr Henry Allbutt of Leeds detailed 'matters of importance necessary to be known to married women'. Chapter VII of this work describes nine different methods of contraception. These include the sheath (with the address of the sole agent for high quality 'Patent Circular Protectors'), the cap ('in shape something like a round dishcover'), coitus interuptus ('hurtful to the nervous system in many persons'), the vaginal sponge and several forms of douching and pessary, plus 'the safe period' method which is in fact highly unsafe because it recommends 'avoiding connection from three days before the monthly flow until eight days after it' (Allbutt 1886: 46, 50). This method is based on the erroneous assumption that women were like bitches on heat, ovulating at the time of menstruation – the result of scientific canine studies in the 1840s (Laqueur 1990: 9). Although it encouraged women to enjoy sex at mid-cycle, it was claimed by 'Dr William Hitchman of Liverpool' to have only a '5 per cent failure rate'.

The medical profession could not cope with this degree of frankness about a problem, which was of major – and often life-threatening – importance to much of the population, so the General Medical Council prosecuted Dr Allbutt. At a disciplinary hearing in November 1887, the full Council of 26 eminent men resolved that:

> (a) He had published, and publicly caused to be sold a work entitled *The Wife's Handbook* in London and elsewhere, at so

low a price as to bring the work within the reach of the youth
of both sexes to the detriment of public morals.

(b) The offence is, in the opinion of the COUNCIL, 'infamous
conduct in a professional respect'

(c) The Registrar is hereby ordered to erase the name of Mr Henry
Arthur Allbutt from the Medical Register.

(GCMER 1888: 316–17)

The publicity generated by the GMC hearing at least ensured that
The Wife's Handbook sold in hundreds of thousands of copies over many
years – the slim volume reaching its fifty-fifth edition by 1921, the year
in which Marie Stopes opened Britain's first family planning clinic.
Contraceptive advice was therefore readily available in the last quarter
of the nineteenth century, albeit seldom from family practitioners.
Cost of devices was not a deterrent either, for by this time mass production had brought the price of condoms down from 10d, at which
price they were the province of the 'gentlemanly libertine', to as low as
a halfpenny each by the 1870s, making them 'freely available to the
working classes' (Mason 1994: 58).

Although Henry Allbutt failed in his attempts to gain reinstatement
on the Medical Register, this enterprising and far-sighted physician
(MRCP 1880), made a successful second career as medical author – his
subsequent publications including *Disease and Marriage* (1891), *Every
Mother's Handbook* (1897) and *Artificial Checks to Population: is the teaching of them infamous?* (1900). He remained, however, ignored and dis-
dained by the medical profession to the end of his life. This is in
sharp contrast to his first cousin, Professor Sir Thomas Clifford Allbutt,
credited as the inventor of both the clinical thermometer and the
ophthalmoscope. Up until the GCMER debacle in November 1887,
both Dr Allbutts were in practice at Park Square, 'the Harley Street of
Leeds' (Rolleston 1929: 20) – Henry at No. 24 and Clifford at No. 6.

By 1889 they were both gone and the Leeds Hospital for Diseases of
the Skin, at which Henry practised, had closed. Clifford had left his
Yorkshire practice due to 'fatigue' and accepted 'a commissionership in
lunacy' (DNB). It was in this capacity that he invited Hardy to spend
the day with him at 'a large private lunatic asylum in May 1891' (*EL*
309). Two years later, Clifford Allbutt was appointed Regius Professor
of Physic at Cambridge, receiving a knighthood in 1907 and being
admitted to the Privy Council in 1920. Like his cousin Henry, he was a
prolific medical writer, including a mammoth eight volume *System of
Medicine* (1896–9). Sir Clifford was, therefore, a distinguished man who

received every accolade possible for a member of his profession – in stark contrast to his cousin, cast off by his chosen profession in his prime. However, in the longer scheme of things, it was Henry not Clifford Allbutt whose writings and teachings had the greatest influence on the medical world, and were of the greatest benefit to humankind.

Hardy was closely acquainted with Clifford Allbutt, who he described as my 'bright-minded friend' (*CL* 3: 267). It is hard, therefore, to believe that Hardy, with his prying enquiring mind, did not have a working knowledge of contraception. As a young man in London, he freely admits to frequenting 'gay Cremorne' and 'those crowded rooms // Of old yclept 'The Argyle' ' (*CP* 217). Both these places are identified by Michael Mason as being 'patronized by high-class prostitutes' who 'sold themselves mainly to middle-to-upper class clients' as opposed to the less expensive girls on the street (Mason 1994: 102–3, 150). Confirmation of this fact is found both in Royston Pike and in *The Other Victorians* where Marcus quotes Walter from *My Secret Life* as noting: 'I have avoided Argyle or Cremorne and any other places to which whores resort' (Marcus 1964: 96). Of course, Hardy may have just gone there for 'Jullien's grand quadrilles'!

Hardy also was well versed in eighteenth-century literature, where references to contraception are not infrequent. Boswell in his diary for May 1763 records equipping himself in 'armour complete' (condom) before engaging 'a strong jolly young damsel' on Westminster Bridge (Boswell 1966: 278–9). Marcus has unearthed similar nineteenth-century fictional references. Here Eliza addresses Alfred in *Rosa Fielding* (1867):

> You really must cover your beautiful instrument with that sheath or condom, or whatever you call it. I have no notion of having a pretty white belly bow- windowed before marriage – indeed I shan't particularly care about it after marriage!
>
> (Marcus 1964: 234)

The voice of the 'New Woman' but never uttered – for Grundyian reasons – in these terms by Bathsheba or Eustacia or Sue Bridehead. But why didn't Alec d'Urberville or Charles Raye use a condom? Failing that, why didn't Tess or Anna procure an abortion? Contraception was very definitely not on the agenda in the 'shiftless house of Durbeyfield', where reliance was placed rather on the Wordsworthian 'Nature's Holy Plan' (*TD* 19), but both Alec and Raye were young men about town who should have been cognisant with such matters.

Dreamy unfruitful Edith can perhaps be forgiven for not knowing how best to deal with a servant's unwanted pregnancy. At least she acted more charitably than Tom and Emma who summarily dismissed the pregnant Jane (*EL* 153). In any case, with contraception and abortion there would have been no tragedy for Tess or Sue or Jude or Ella Marchmill or Elfride or any other of the many Hardyan heroines who suffered and died as a consequence of unwanted or inappropriate pregnancy. The lack of these options, which in the twenty-first century are taken so much for granted, forms an essential ingredient in the generation of many of Hardy's tragedies.

Speculation notwithstanding, there are no references to contraception in Hardy's fiction or in his extant public and personal writings. His concern naturally was more for his own subfertility or Emma's 'unfruitfulness' – a condition described by Thomas Graham, as 'a very serious evil', classified into three categories, namely:

1. The Barrenness of Impotency which may be organic or atonic.
2. The Barrenness of Mismenstruation – best treated by a diet of oysters, pigeons & lobsters.
3. The Barrenness of Irresponsibility and Incongruity i.e. personal aversion.

(1861: 141–51)

The third category seems sadly compatible with the image of Hardy busy writing *Time's Laughingstocks* in his study, whilst Emma sits alone and unloved poring over religious tracts in her garret bedroom. Hardy only twice makes direct written reference to this 'serious evil' – once in writing about Jane, the maid-servant and, secondly, in the poem *She, I, and They* where 'I was sitting, // 'She was knitting' beneath the 'portraits of our fore-folk' which suddenly sigh:

> That we should be the last
> Of stocks once unsurpassed,
> And unable to keep up their sturdy line.
>
> (*CP* 435)

We do not know which woman this raw heartfelt little poem refers to – but it is most probably Emma. In the 1920s the Hardys became acquainted with Dr Marie Stopes who had acquired a disused lighthouse at Portland Bill as a holiday home. Millgate has published three letters from Florence Hardy to Marie Stopes, in the first of which, dated

September 1923, Florence acknowledges how 'Sue Bridehead & her luckless children' might have benefited from Marie's pamphlets. She also reveals that Hardy 'would have welcomed a child when we first married, ten years ago', but that now 'the idea of my having a child at his age fills him with terror' (*LH* 203). Although Florence has a tendency to be indiscrete, she does not reveal here whether she and Tom were relying on Marie's pamphlets. If the Hardys were following Dr Stopes's advice, this was not the reason why Florence failed to conceive for Marie Stopes, still reliant on the incorrectly extrapolated canine experiments of the 1840s: told hundreds of thousands of readers that conception took place during or just after the period and that the mid-cycle was relatively safe (Laqueur 1990: 213).

Thus the champion of contraception was inadvertently promoting fertility by encouraging women to indulge in lovemaking at the time of ovulation. It was not until the 1940s that the correct time of human ovulation was finally determined.

The cause of the Hardys' infertility will never be known; there is no objective evidence to support Millgate's insinuations that Hardy was incapable of close physical contact nor Seymour-Smith's implication that it all must have been the women's fault. In her third and final letter to Marie Stopes, Florence praises Dr Stopes's novel *Love's Creation* but concludes, 'I don't much appreciate the love-making. I seem unable to enter into that: a lack of real feeling on my part I suppose' (*LH* 283). This has been taken as evidence that Florence suffered psychosexual difficulties but, in reality, it is no more than a comment on certain passages in an erotic novel, from a woman just eight months widowed.

In an earlier letter to Lady Hoare, Florence wrote, 'How eagerly a baby would have been welcomed in – Max Gate – years ago!' (*LH* 142). But just as contraceptives would have destroyed the tragedies, so children would have drawn the fangs of Hardy the novelist and poet; to function at full perceptivity, he needed to be like Jude – a self-alienated man. Hardy the family man would have been (in his own estimation, I suspect) like the married Somers producing work to please the middling critic in order to pay for his daughters' education – a man for whom 'strange conceits and wild imaginings were departed joys never to return' (*WB* 301). For as Hillis-Miller concludes, Hardy: 'was recurrently driven to enact in his own life a drama like that in his fiction and poems'. To Hardy, 'Life imitated art as much as art life' (Hillis-Miller 1970: 191).

As to the doctors, they remained the servants of their financial masters. They were happy to provide the middle classes with detailed and graphic classifications of varieties of fictitious sexual illness, mainly masturbatory, but denied the need for contraception or abortion. This did not become mainstream medical practice until after two world wars, a nationalised health service and a 'permissive society' made it financially lucrative. But as Zola described in *Fecondite* (1899), if the price was right Victorian doctors were willing to collude with wealthy patients in performing ovariotomy as a means of sterilisation and in excising pregnancies, conveniently misdiagnosed as 'ovarian cysts'. But for Hardy, the world remained essentially non-procreative; when children did appear they were signifiers of tragedy.

2

Hardyan Illness

A Wasted Illness
Through vaults of pain,
Enribbed and wrought with groins of ghastliness,
I passed, and garish spectres moved my brain
To dire distress.

And hammerings,
And quakes, and shoots, and stifling hotness, blent
With webby waxing things and waning things
As on I went

'Where lies the end
To this foul way?' I asked with weakening breath.
Thereon ahead I saw a door extend –
The door to Death.

It loomed more clear:
'At last!' I cried. 'The all-delivering door!'
And then, I knew not how, it grew less near
Than theretofore.

And back slid I
Along the galleries by which I came,
And tediously the day returned, and sky,
And life – the same.

(*CP* 152)

To his heartfelt regret, the 40-year-old Hardy recovered from this serious illness to live another 47 years. He continued in the habit of regularly writing poems expressing a preference to be dead rather than alive until the death of Emma in November 1912. It appears that reality of the death of a once well-beloved took the gloss off the psychological need to be a man unborn or at least 'The Dead Man Walking' (*CP* 217).

Hardy's life-threatening illness of the autumn of 1880 seems a reasonable starting point for an analysis of his experience of illness both personal and fictitious. Bearing in mind, Florence Hardy's assertion that there is more autobiography in a single poem than in the whole of his fiction, the poem *A Wasted Illness* merits close consideration. But firstly, what are the facts of this illness? The main source of such limited information, as is available, is *The Early Life* plus *The Collected Letters* and one or two items of correspondence written to, or about, Hardy at the time.

From *The Early Life,* we ascertain that during his visit to Cambridge in October 1880, Hardy 'felt an indescribable physical weariness' (*EL* 184). He took to his bed on 24 October and was visited first by Dr Henry Edward Beck, who lived opposite in Trinity Road, Tooting and was a graduate of Guy's Hospital (LSA 1840; MRCS 1841). Dr Beck diagnosed internal bleeding which was confirmed by the second opinion obtained from Alexander Macmillan's GP, Dr Arthur Shears (MD Edin 1864; MRCS 1863). Hardy was 'in considerable pain' for several weeks, but accepted the recommended treatment of being 'compelled to lie on an inclined plane with the lower part of his body higher than his head' rather than submit himself to 'a dangerous operation' (*EL* 187, 188). From this awkward position he started to dictate *A Laodicean* to Emma 'and continued to do so – with greater ease as the pain and haemorrhage went off' (*EL* 188).

Hardy's correspondence confirms that on 15 December he was still 'laid up with a troublesome malady' and, four months later in April 1881, admitted to still 'passing my days over the fire, with my feet on the mantelpiece' (*CL* 1: 84, 88). On 24 February 1881, Kegan Paul, the publisher, wrote to Hardy, informing him that he had discovered that the eminent Guy's physician, Sir William Gull, only charged five guineas for coming down to Clapham and continuing:

> I suppose therefore Sir H. Thompson only charges the same to go to Balham, and I hope you would have him in. It would be a good point to get quite free from the fear you had of some worse mischief, or if he does not free you from it to know it from one who can do so much and so well to set you to rights as he can.
>
> (Letter in *DCM*)

Presumably the Hardys could not afford five guineas for a domiciliary visit or, more likely, Sir Henry Thompson, the founding father of Urology in the United Kingdom, worked to a more inflated fee scale. Either way, he was not enticed out to Tooting and it was not until over two months later on 3 May, that Hardy, freed at last from his reclining position, called on Thompson at his house in Wimpole Street for an opinion.

No details of this consultation are extant, but it is apparent that Sir Henry did not recommend any form of surgical intervention. Seymour-Smith correctly notes that Thompson was a 'stone surgeon' and makes the reasonable presumption that Hardy was thought to have been suffering from a bladder calculus (Seymour-Smith 1994: 277). After this specialist opinion, Hardy appears to have gradually resumed a normal lifestyle.

Unlike Hardy's medical advisors in 1880/1, we have the benefit of that magnificent diagnostic instrument 'the retrospectoscope'. We at least know how the story concluded – in other words, that he lived until January 1928, ultimately succumbing to cardiac failure, the first signs of which did not apparently appear until June 1921. His general well-being in the interim was however punctuated by a number of documented episodes of:

> that same bladder inflammation you will remember me being laid up with for six months when I lived at Upper Tooting, which repeats itself at intervals of some years, as it has done now.
> (Letter to Gosse 14/2/1922, *CL* 6: 115).

Hardy's GP on this latter occasion, Dr Gowring, was much less relaxed about this episode, which he initially diagnosed as bladder cancer, telling Florence to prepare for Tom's imminent demise (*LH* 180).

In addition, following his severe illness in 1880, Hardy suffered recurrent attacks of acute rheumatism, many of which were sufficiently disabling that he was unable to write or to leave the house. In fact, Gittings suggested that Hardy abandoned the writing of fiction in 1896 not because of critical hostility to *Jude the Obscure*, nor because he was now financially secure, but rather because he was simply no longer physically capable of writing another novel (Gittings 1978: 121). Part of the difficulty in reaching a definitive diagnosis for this severe relapsing illness is the Victorian habit of never calling a spade a spade. Whilst Hardy was happy to find ways of doing this in his fiction, he avoided all indelicacy in his correspondence and in the two-volume *Life*, which he ghosted for Florence. The simple question that needs answering was what was the nature of the 'internal haemorrhage'? Was Hardy peeing blood? As both bladder stone and bladder cancer cause haematuria as a principal symptom, it seems likely that he was. This, however, is, of course, an external rather than an internal haemorrhage.

A true 'internal haemorrhage' in a man of 40 requiring protracted treatment by restricted diet is only likely to be a bleed from a gastric or duodenal ulcer. But if that was the case, there was no possible explanation for involving Thompson, whose field of expertise was limited to the bladder, the prostate and the male external genitalia. An attempt to solve the problem from the opposite angle by working backwards from the treatment prescribed has drawn a complete blank. Nowhere in contemporary medical texts – specialist, general or lay – can I find any recommendation that a patient should remain in a recumbent position with their feet elevated higher than their head for weeks – let alone months – at a time. Nor can the eminent medical historian Harold Ellis shed any light on the matter (personal communication). From the mid-twentieth century onwards, when the haemodynamics of the circulation began to be understood, elevation of the feet became a standard first aid measure in cases of shock. It is not a recorded recommended ongoing treatment for any medical or surgical condition in the latter half of the nineteenth century. It was however imposed on the Hardys both by Dr Beck, who was a GP of 40 year's standing, and by Dr Shears, who belonged to a different medical generation, having qualified 24 years later and in Edinburgh, which was at the time a centre of great medical excellence. No record survives of Thomson's opinion of this treatment regime or of his diagnostic opinion regarding Hardy, but what do survive are his extensive publications on urology, including his comprehensive *Clinical Lectures on Diseases of the Urinary Organs,* the fifth edition of which was published by J. & A. Churchill in London in the summer of 1879. Again, there is no mention of any such therapeutic regime anywhere in this or his other published works.

Sir Henry Thompson modestly describes himself as Surgeon-Extraordinary to H.M. The King of the Belgians (from whom he had once removed a stone); Late Professor of Surgery and Pathology to the Royal College of Surgeons of England; Emeritus Professor of Clinical Surgery and Consulting Surgeon to University College Hospital. As such, he was just the kind of doctor in whom Florence Hardy would subsequently have put an absolute trust; a Mayfair telephone number appearing to be her primary criteria for clinical excellence! In the preface to his *Clinical Lectures,* Thompson avers that the book is employed as a textbook at most of the medical schools of Europe and has been 'translated for the purpose into the French, German, Italian, Spanish & Russian languages' (Thompson 1879: Preface). He would have been mortified to discover that the copy of his *Clinical Lectures* held by The Wellcome Library was largely uncut until I took a knife to it in 2003!

Thompson was an all-rounder who came late to medicine, not qualifying until in his early thirties. He described his experiences as a medical apprentice and subsequent student at UCH in the successful novel *Charley Kingston's Aunt*, published by Macmillan in 1885.

Bladder calculus was a common condition in England in the early Victorian period. The only widely practised treatment for this painful debilitating condition was 'cutting for the stone' – a procedure which he describes in his *Clinical Lectures* as dating 'back to the Augustan era' and involving 'lateral operation by incision through the prostate' (Thompson 1879: 190). As a medical student, Thompson witnessed the high morbidity and mortality associated with this bloody form of surgery. Crushing the stone appeared to be a much safer method so he travelled to Paris to learn the technique from its pioneer, Civiale. Thompson subsequently modified the operation of lithotrity and improved the instrument with which it was performed, and within a few years:

> became the first specialist in urinary diseases in this country ... and after the successful operation on King Leopold, his name was well-known on the continent, patients coming to him from all parts.
>
> (Cope 1951: 53)

Thompson comes across both from Zachary Cope's biography and his own published writings as a thorough but dogmatic and obsessional man, who ultimately presented his collection of over 1000 bladder calculi in a cabinet to the Royal College of Surgeons, together with a detailed catalogue, published by Churchill in 1893, giving the history of each patient. (This unique collection of historic excreta was unfortunately incinerated by the Luftwaffe in 1940.)

Lady St Helier, 'the leading London hostess and active worker for social causes' (Millgate 1984: 572–3), who befriended Hardy and both his wives, described the self-confident Thompson as being 'like many enthusiasts, most intolerant of contradiction' (Cope 1951: 143). In effect, he was the typical strong-willed extrovert who traditionally has made the most successful surgeon. At the time Hardy consulted him, he was at the mid-point of the 20-year 'zenith of his professional career

... during this time he was the acknowledged authority on stone in the bladder and other urinary diseases' (ibid.: 52). If Sir Henry Thompson had believed that Thomas Hardy had a urinary calculus, there can be little doubt that that calculus would have rapidly found its niche in the catalogued collection, ultimately to be presented to the Royal College of Surgeons, and Hardy's name would have been added to the collection of the eminent on whom Sir Henry had operated. Both Thackeray and Dickens had been treated successfully by Sir Henry, but the Emperor Napoleon III had died in 1873 following an operation performed by him at Chislehurst, so the world of English literature must be grateful that the ebullient Thompson did not choose to explore Tom's bladder with his lithotrite. Instead, Thomson satisfied himself with taking a single photographic portrait of Hardy, which he claimed 'was preferred by the novelist's family to any other which had been taken' (Cope 1952: 88).

At the time Hardy originally consulted him, Sir Henry's enthusiasms included a new house in the country where 'the community of fowls' (*TD* 54) shared a purpose-built cottage with their human carers (echoes of 'The Slopes' at Trantridge) and astronomy, in pursuit of which he ultimately built his own brick observatory and dome, complete with '12-inch equatorial' (Cope 1951: 86) (echoes of *Two on a Tower*). Another of Thompson's great enthusiasms was ultimately to have a malign influence on Hardy for Sir Henry 'was the chief pioneer of the practice of cremation in Great Britain' (ibid.: 120). He was the founder President (for over 25 years) of The Cremation Society, in which capacity in 1879 he oversaw the building of the first crematorium in Britain – at Woking. As a doctor, Thompson was most concerned by the dangers to health of the noxious gases produced by the decomposition of a buried body. He claimed that the force of these gases was sufficient to burst open leaden coffins and published evidence demonstrating that:

in a single year an estimated 2,572,580 cubic feet of toxic gas is emitted into the atmosphere in London from soil over graves.

(Thompson 1901: 106)

On Saturday 14 January 1928, Hardy's body minus his heart, which had been extracted by Dr Nash-Wortham, Dr Mann's senior partner, was transported to Thompson's Crematorium at Woking and incinerated. Then, as Florence describes, 'the ashes were taken the same day to Westminster Abbey' (*LY* 267). This strange ritual was alleged to have had pre-historic origins as a 'means of preserving the heart from the flames' and as such might well have appealed to Hardy – as a source of ironic humour, if nothing else. But to return for the moment to 1880/1, Sir Henry, 'all that was eminent in European surgery' (*WB* 57), does not seem to have considered that Hardy had a bladder stone. In *Clinical Lectures,* Lecture XI is entitled 'Stone In The Bladder'. Thompson starts his lecture by stating the stone is most common from the age of 'about fifty-five to seventy-five' and that 'the most rare period is that of middle age' (Thompson 1879: 135); Hardy was 40 when he developed this illness. The symptoms of bladder stone, he summarises as 'urinary frequency', pain felt 'after passing water' 'at the lower part of the glans penis', 'muco-pus and also perhaps streaks of blood' in the urine. Exercise will tend to increase the likelihood of blood in the urine and also increase the pain. 'On the other hand, the bleeding caused by calculus is rarely considerable' (ibid.: 138–9). A very similar description is given by Graham in *Modern Domestic Medicine* (1864).

The pain which King Leopold described to Thompson was greatly exacerbated by laying down, so that the King slept standing upright in the Palace Bedchamber (Cope 1951: 39). If this was typical of bladder stone, then the recumbent treatment prescribed by Hardy's physicians would have served merely to aggravate his symptoms. Bladder stones are rare in the United Kingdom in the twenty-first century and there-fore given scant attention, a current textbook acknowledging that: 'Bladder Stones are endemic in some developing countries. The cause is unknown but dietary factors are probably important' (Kumar 2002: 627)

It is reasonable, therefore, to conclude that Hardy did not have a vesicular calculus. Firstly, because Thompson, a man whose mission in life was to detect stone, did not think that Hardy had one. Secondly, because Hardy was at the age at which bladder stone was least likely to occur. Thirdly, because Hardy's principal complaint appears to have been haemorrhage, which is not a major feature of calculus disease.

Finally, it is reasonable to presume that this haemorrhage was haematuria because of his General Practitioner's (or do I mean pub-lisher's?) referral to an eminent urologist. In *A Wasted Illness*, the poet is 'wrought with groins of ghastliness' – an expression certainly sug-gestive a urological disorder; in addition, he suffers 'hammerings, / And quakes, and shoots, and stifling hotness' blent 'With webby waxing things and waning things' which is a highly graphic accurate depiction of a fever with associated delirium. Ultimately, with 'weakening breath', he can take no more of 'this foul way' and seeks 'The all-delivering door' of death. (*CP* 152). A severe urinary tract infection, a pyelo-nephritis, would be likely to produce most of these symptoms, could continue for some weeks (but not the six month's of Hardy's illness) and recur again after many years' apparent good health. For a renal disease to continue so long and require such stipulations from his medical attendants implies an illness more serious than a mere urinary tract infection. The severely restricted diet which Hardy was prescribed and of which we have no details could well have been 'the diet of ... light farinaceous food and milk' (Physicians 1883/4: 152) recom-mended in Bright's Disease or, in twenty-first-century terminology, Acute Nephritic Syndrome (Kumar 2002: 606).

This illness most commonly starts with a prodromal 'streptococcal throat infection one to three weeks previously', consistent with Hardy's 'indescribable physical weariness' (*EL* 184). The patient then deterior-ates with haematuria, 'malaise, shivering, fever and ... pain in the loins and abdomen' (Houston, Joiner and Trounce 1975: 372); renal func-tion is severely impaired for a number of days, then 'a diuresis occurs, the temperature settles, the oedema subsides' and the blood and pro-tein begin to disappear from the urine (ibid.: 373). The disease is the result of 'immune complex formation' in response 'to a Lancefield Group A Beta-haemolytic streptococcus of a nephritogenic type' (Kumar 2002: 606). Acute Bright's Disease is associated with a tendency to joint involvement – patients often suffering recurrent symptoms of a rheumatoid-like arthropathy affecting the small joints; an association completely consistent with Hardy's already detailed recurrent episodes of disabling arthritis which followed his severe illness in 1880/1. In modern terminology, this arthritic link probably constitutes a form of Lupus Syndrome.

In addition, post-streptococcal immune complexes have long been recognised to effect the heart either directly as in Rheumatic Fever or indirectly through cardiac failure secondary to renal insufficiency. In 'A Wasted Illness', Hardy complains of 'weakening breath'; in addition, a contemporary portrait reputedly shows him to have oedematous hands. Both these symptoms are suggestive of cardiac involvement, although they may merely indicate renal insufficiency and/or anaemia. In Hardy's 'well-marked' copy of *Modern Domestic Medicine*, 'Acute Rheumatism' is described as commencing with 'languor and chilliness, succeeded by heat, thirst, restlessness', a tachycardia and haematuria and accompanied by 'pain, inflammation and fullness, usually about the larger joints and muscles' (Graham 1864: 648). Graham counsels against venesection but still recommends in cases of severe cardiac involvement that 'eight leeches should then be applied at once ... over the region of the heart'. The mainstay of his treatment is a mixture of calomel and opium.

Graham's description of the symptoms of this condition takes just over a page of his large book – his advice on treatment extends over nearly eight pages which must reflect a deep insecurity amongst Victorian doctors over the appropriate treatment of this group of serious illnesses. Whenever multiple treatments are available for a condition, it almost invariably means that none of them are particularly efficacious. It may therefore seem easier to forgive Hardy's physician's for making him keep his feet on the mantelpiece for six months, even at the price of the failure of *A Laodicean* to fulfil its complex initial promise.

A further cloud over these already muddied waters is the existence of a letter from Edmund Gosse to Hardy dated 16 December 1917. This appears to be in reply to a letter sent from Hardy to Gosse five days previously, in which Hardy complains of rheumatism caused 'by my working with a pickaxe in the garden!' (*CL* 5: 234). Gosse, who describes himself as 'your affectionate old friend', commiserates with Hardy, then adds:

> I also am in bed but I have not been digging in the garden. I have, like Falstaff, 'a great whoreson cold'. I think it is rather amusing to be obliged sometimes to spend a day in bed, and regard life horizontally. More than one day of it is a bore. Do you remember me coming to visit you in bed when you had the jaundice? Wasn't it at Tooting or somewhere then. You were dictating the 'Laodicean', I think. I see you now in my mind's eye.
>
> (Letter in *DCM*)

This is the only mention of jaundice in this context. Surely if Hardy had been jaundiced, he would have remembered it and recorded it, with the other details of what at the time was an extremely worrying illness, in *The Early Life*? On the other hand, Gosse's details – the year, the book, the place, the treatment – are all correct; and Hardy in his account didn't even mention the presumed haematuria so was definitely showing a reluctance to be too frank about his symptoms.

If Hardy really did suffer from a febrile illness with jaundice, internal haemorrhage and haematuria, which he believed he had acquired from spending too long in the water, then there is only one likely explanation, namely Leptospirosis icterohaemorrhagica. This potentially fatal illness is due to a spirochaete contracted from the urine of infected rats. Hardy's medical advisors could certainly be forgiven for failing to diagnose this infection in 1880 because it was not first described until 1886 when Weil published a paper detailing 'a severe illness consisting of jaundice, haemorrhage and renal impairment' (Kumar 2002: 80), the illness which is now commonly referred to as Weil's Disease. After a prodromal febrile illness, 'patients progressively develop, hepatic and renal failure, haemolytic anaemia and circulatory collapse' (ibid.: 80). As well as haemolytic anaemia, the infection can cause 'haemoptyis, haematemesis and melaena' (Houston, Joiner and Trounce 1975: 522) so there would have been multiple reasons for Drs Beck and Shears to suspect 'that Hardy was bleeding internally' (*EL* 187). If Gosse was correct in remembering the jaundice, then Hardy did very well to survive an infection, which in the twenty-first century 'even with full supportive (intensive) care' has a mortality rate of 10 per cent to 20 per cent (Kumar 2002: 80). Small wonder then that Death appeared 'The all-delivering door!' (*CP* 152). The same door through which Horace Moule had voluntarily stepped by slitting his throat in his rooms at Cambridge, seven years previously. Hardy had revisited Cambridge in October 1880, just before the start of his serious illness and was, perhaps at last coming to terms with the death of his friend and mentor. This long suppressed grief, plus the stresses of his increasingly unhappy and infertile marriage and his failure to repeat the success of *Far from the Madding Crowd* were undoubtedly the psychosomatic soil which allowed the seeds of infection to take root, but the evidence does not support Ralph Pite's contention that 'Essentially, Hardy had a breakdown' (Pite 2006: 253). If that were the case, he would have failed to meet serial deadlines for *A Laodicean* and would not have maintained a lively correspondence from his demeaning head-down position; haemorrhage is seldom psychosomatic.

Whatever the cause of this illness, one of its most lasting effects was the Hardys' decision to abandon London as a place of permanent residence – the second time Tom had been forced back to Dorset from the metropolis on the grounds of ill-health. Although from a creative viewpoint it was a major advantage for him to be back near Egdon Heath, he continued at times to play the role of medical exile:

> I was obliged to leave town after a severe illness some years ago – & the spot on which I live here is very lonely.

> (14/4/89) (*CL* 1: 190)

URTI (upper respiratory tract infections)

Both *The Life* and *The Collected Letters* are full of reference to minor illnesses, particularly coughs, colds and influenza. Very frequently these illnesses are described in great detail and the source of infection – most often exposure to cold or wet but at times a named individual from whom the infection was acquired – identified. Thus he fell ill because of 'the uncertain weather' (*EL* 201), 'standing in a high wind' (*CL* 2: 153), 'the change of weather from tropical to polar' (*CL* 2: 221), 'invariable London influenza' (*CL* 3: 2) – a recurring problem, 'incessant rain' (*CL* 3: 90); 'damp weather' (*CL* 4: 36), 'being bitterly cold in a motor-car' (*CL* 4: 258), 'a rainy walk' (*CL* 4: 320) and somewhat exceptionally 'a mysteriously caught cold' (*CL* 6: 42). Hardy blamed his *Wasted Illness* on being 'apt to stay too long in the water' whilst 'bathing every day' on holiday in Normandy in August 1880 (*EL* 181).

Hardy also records at times the names of those who have caught colds from him or with him. The annual attacks of (London) influenza from which he appears to suffer are commonly associated with post-influenzal debility. His definition of influenza appears to differ little from modern-day lay definitions of 'the 'flu' which medically appear interchangeable with the common cold; as, herewith, Thomas Graham:

> There are *two species* of this complaint, *common cough* or *cold;* and the *epidemic cough,* or *influenza.* The epidemic cough or influenza, differs from the common cold in the suddenness of its attack, the severity of its symptoms … the fever is most strikingly depressive. Indeed, influenza may be considered as a catarrhal fever, followed by extraordinary depression of the nervous energy for several weeks after the fever has ceased.
>
> (Graham 1864: 361)

Was Hardy just a man neurotically over-conscious of minor illness, which he 'perhaps over-obsessionally chronicled' (Gittings 1978: 147) in his correspondence – or is there some deeper meaning here? This topic warrants more detailed exploration: firstly, because colds and chills are the commonest cause of mortality throughout Hardy's fiction and, secondly, because the belief that 'a chill makes you ill' was (and to a greater or lesser extent probably still is) deeply ingrained in our national consciousness. This concept has been fully discarded by scientific medicine – but does science really hold all the answer cards – or is it once more failing to see the wood for the trees?

There is good evidence that Hardy's apparent obsessive interest in, and recording of, minor illness was not unusual for its time. This can be partly understood by the fear in the 'pre-antibiotic era' that any seemingly trivial illness might rapidly prove fatal and therefore could never be ignored. Also, the emergent germ theory of disease promoted the concept that illness was due to a single transmissible and identifiable infective agent – as dramatically demonstrated in the Cholera epidemics of 1848/9, 1853/4 and 1866, the second of which decimated the population of the 'Mixen Lane' area of Fordington.

The inevitable sequela of this idea was to seek to identify the infective source and the route of transmission of any illness, although Hardy had a deeply ingrained tendency to associate illness with environmental (and psychological) factors other than those revealed by the bacteriologist. Hardy's record of colds and influenza is part of an enduring literary tradition. In this context, Roy Porter writes that Disraeli:

> never enjoyed solid good health, according to his letters or his biographers. His correspondence, like Pope's or Walpole's in the previous century, is littered with doubts about his health and ejaculations about his lifelong fear of the east wind. His male figures, like himself, are racked with minor illness ...
>
> (Porter 1998: 146)

I suspect that Pope set the precedent with his literal statement 'this long disease, my life' (Pope 1966: 331) – a concept which subsequently flourished in rich Romantic soil but remains today a valid reminder that there are no agreed definitions as to what constitutes disease as opposed to the effects of natural processes – aging, aberrant behaviour, substance abuse and so on. In Hardy not only does a chill make you ill, it is frequently enough to kill – particularly if you are an inhabitant of his earlier fiction.

Thus Mr Brown, a vital witness in *Desperate Remedies* made the fatal mistake of going to live in Cornwall, where he rapidly succumbed to 'the rainy west winds they get there' (*DR* 313). Mr Knight is terrified that the same will happen to Elfride, after having devotionally removed her (substantial) undergarments to save his life, declaring that 'the rain and wind will pierce you through; the chill will kill you' (*BE* 221). Fanny Robin's death is initially incorrectly assumed to 'have been brought on by biding in the night wind' (*FM* 285). Liddy similarly fears that Bathsheba 'will die of a chill' (*FM* 311) after her nocturnal retreat to the malignant swamp. Poor Ethelberta's first husband, 'a minor like herself, died from a chill caught during the wedding tour' (*HE* 33).

In Chapter 4 of *A Laodicean*, written as Hardy was himself just falling seriously ill, Mr Power 'died from a chill caught after a warm bath' (*AL* 27). This pattern continues consistently throughout Hardy's fiction with Swithin St Cleeve attempting suicide by flinging himself down on a patch of heather in the pelting March rain; he survives as does Lady Constantine who runs in the rain to the tower 'at the risk of a severe cold' (*TT* 61). Swithin's attempt is subsequently repeated successfully by both Giles and Jude who achieve Hardy's aim of premature passage through 'the all-delivering door!' (*CP* 152) by exposure to unremitting rain and wind, when already weakened by pre-existing illness (Typhoid Fever and Consumption respectively). Pierston tries the same thing 'in the bleakest churchyard in Wessex' (*WB* 329) but manages merely to murder his own artistic sensibility. In Brazil, 'drenched in a thunder-storm', Angel survives but his companion dies of the fever (*TD* 358).

Hardy notes that the topography of the damp north-eastern side of Casterbridge keeps the local doctors in business. Henchard catches cold from standing in wet meads, Marty from having her hair cut and young Steve becomes seriously ill from immersion in cold water at West Poley. There is a consistent culture throughout Hardy's fiction that exposure to cold or damp will make you ill, often with fatal conse-quences. Has scientific medicine completed debunked the chill? Or is it rather that in this age of greatly improved housing, heating, sanitation, nutrition and anti-microbial therapy, doctors can conveniently ignore long-established cultural beliefs about health and well-being?

The Family Physician describes itself as 'a manual of domestic medi-cine by leading physicians and surgeons of the principal London Hospitals' – it was published in 1884 and gives a detailed explanation of 'the somewhat complex process which is known as "catching cold"':

Catching cold is one of the most general and most prolific causes of disease. Insufficient clothing is undoubtedly a very frequent cause … the exposure of the thighs and legs of children … evening dress affords very light protection against cold and draught. There can be no doubt that many cases of consumption have their origin in wearing insufficient clothes at evening entertainments. Neglect-ing to wear flannels in the winter is a prolific source of cold. The origin of a cold may in many instances be traced to getting wet through. Damp often gives rise to cold. A damp house or room, or a house with a damp cellar is an abomination. Nothing can be more prejudicial to a person's bodily welfare than sleeping in a damp bed. Prolonged bathing often gives rise to cold.

(Physicians 1883/4:180–1).

Doctors, as I have suggested, may just be reflecting back the prejudices of the society that pays their fees. This whole vast empire of 'catching cold' was completely demolished over the ensuing century by scientific 'evidence-based' medicine, but is medical pseudo-science really no more than a continuing effort to 'keep the customer satisfied'? Thus to feed the consumer the message which they want to hear rather than this list of admonitions which closely resemble the diatribe of some ancient maiden aunt? In the 46 years between March 1879 and October 1925, Thomas Hardy suffered more than 57 episodes of Acute Upper Respiratory Tract Infection, which he deemed to be of sufficient severity or importance to be worth either recording for posterity in his ghosted autobiography or referring to in his correspondence. By the time most of these letters were written, he was part of the literary establishment and well aware that his outgoing correspondence was likely to be preserved for the benefit of future generations. Some of these individual episodes of what is technically minor illness are referred to in ten or more letters to the same or different correspondents. As he wrote in 1905: 'I'm a martyr to influenza myself' (*CL* 3: 161). He frequently identified the source of his illness, which was very seldom another infected person but rather almost invariably the result of 'catching cold'. The other common identifiable aetiological factor was the impure atmosphere of the great cities – mainly London but also Paris and Rome. As the London season ran from April to August, the inevitable 'London influenza and throat trouble' (*CL* 3: 312) might well be seasonal allergic rhinitis.

This remains a possibility for The Common Cold Information Centre at the University of Cardiff, who provide impartial evidence-based advice, state that 75 per cent of colds occur in the winter months whilst Hardy suffered most of his infections in the period April to July, which is the main hay-fever season. If 75 per cent of colds occur in the winter months, then surely a chill must make you ill? Their reply: 'There is no evidence that chilling the body causes an increased susceptibility to infection or an increase in the severity of symptoms.'

More colds occur in the winter because:

We spend more time indoors in poorly ventilated homes and offices
There is less ultraviolet (sunlight) to kill the viruses

The cold virus replicates more rapidly in a cool nose
We are more stressed in the winter with consequent reduction in immune response
Christmas encourages colds – stress, visitors & parties
Schools & Colleges spread colds – term-times are mainly in winter
                    (http://www.cf.ac.uk.biosi/associates/cold/info.html 2–3)

This twenty-first-century evidence-based mythology has turned much traditional belief on its head – we are now falling ill because houses are not draughty enough and because we don't go outside in the cold and damp! In another 120 years time will these facts appear as fallible as those of *The Family Physician* do now? The change has been a gradual evolution for *A Short Textbook of Medicine* published in 1975 states that for Coryza 'chills and dampness seem to be predisposing factors' (Houston, Joiner and Trounce 1975: 190).

The Common Cold Information Unit also state 'that adults suffer 2 to 5 colds per year' and that 'as we get older we get fewer colds', because each cold is due to a separate distinct rhinovirus to which the body generates antibodies. They admit that colds can be fatal but in this century only in 'babies and the very elderly'. They also state that 'the densely populated cities of the modern world provide ideal breeding grounds for the common cold virus.' This fits nicely with Hardy's view that visiting London always made him physically unwell although a further factor with which he would undoubtedly be in full agreement is their discovery that: 'psychological stress affects the immune system, suppressing the person's general resistance to infection' (http://www.cf.ac.uk.biosi/associates/cold/info.html 1,4 and 5).

The facts which the Common Cold Unit have proved by 'experimental studies', Hardy had long since understood through intuitive observation of his 'fellow-wights' – including the belief that the safest way to remain well was to shut himself away in the countryside and refuse to see visitors, much to Florence's chagrin.

From the statistics given, the incidence of Hardy's upper respiratory tract infections does not appear excessive although their frequency does not decline with age, which is certainly contrary to modern medical experience. In fact, his rate of catching colds more than doubles from the time he first met Florence Dugdale during the summer of 1907 – prior to this event he is recorded as having suffered 0.78 episodes of cold or influenza on average per annum; from meeting Florence until his death just over 20 years later he suffered on average two recorded episodes of cold or influenza per annum. There are a number of possible explanations for this change – Florence was a younger and more sickly person who when first encountered was still dabbling in school teaching and hence tapping into a ready source of infection.

By describing her as being a 'more sickly person', I mean both that she did in reality suffer more illnesses than the average woman of her age but that also she was a person more conscious of illness. As such she is likely to have raised Hardy's level of consciousness of illness and made him worry about and report symptoms which he previously would have not noticed or would have completely ignored. Furthermore, encountering Florence almost certainly increased Tom's levels of stress which would also have lowered his resistance to infection. The evidence is quite clear that he travelled less frequently to London in the last two decades of his life so that was not a factor in his frequent colds in old age. Under Florence's regime, however, many more frequent and younger visitors were received at Max Gate, which would have increased Hardy's exposure to rhinoviruses.

So where does this research leave the ancient danger of 'catching cold' and all Hardy's characters who die or nearly catch their deaths through this process? Little changed is the answer because Mr Brown, Mr Power, Swithin, Giles, Jude and Pierston all died or nearly died because of their psychological circumstances. The immune suppression caused by their distress acted as the catalyst, which allowed the cold, the damp and the bacteria to do their worst. As always in Hardyan medicine, this represents a triumph of the psyche over the soma – and whatever slant contemporary clinical science chooses to place on the outcome, the outcome remains unchanged – and vigorously resilient to evidence-based analysis.

'Common Sense' makes it hard to accept that exposure to freezing rain and driving wind is not going to have a deleterious effect on health. But at least Hardy's characters did not suffer the indignity of falling ill because their houses were too well insulated and they did not expose themselves to the fresh air frequently enough! I am pleased to report that belief in 'catching cold' lives on in the thriving world of alternative medicine. 'Pathogenic dampness' is the root cause of much illness, according to traditional Chinese medicine. The 'exopathic' as opposed to the 'endogenous' form of pathogenic dampness is caused by 'damp climate, wading in water or being caught in a rain, as well as living in a damp environment' (http://www.rchm.co.uk/articles).

This belief also survives in the world of veterinary medicine, which seems wholly appropriate because that great equine heroine of Victorian children's literature Black Beauty, whose eponymous tale was published in the same year as *The Return of The Native*, all but dies from a chill because her young and inexperienced groom gives her a bucket of cold water but fails to dry her off and cover her with a rug after a rapid canter on a cold night to fetch the doctor. The current veterinary advice remains that:

> A wet sweaty horse should never be turned out if the weather is cold or wet; he should be kept in a stable until he is dry or he will be at risk from cold and chills.
>
> (http://www.ihsgb.freeserve.co.uk)

Purblind vision (*CP* 780)

After colds and influenza (57 recorded episodes), Hardy most frequently complains of depression, listlessness and lack of energy (37 recorded episodes from the age of 30 onwards). Numerically, the next most frequent health problem is sore painful eyes, discharging 'rheum' – an illness which started during the London Season of 1889:

> Hardy had suffered from rather bad influenza this summer in town, and it left an affection of the eye behind it which he had never known before; and although he hoped it might leave him on his return to Dorchester it followed him there. He was, indeed, seldom absolutely free from it afterwards.
>
> (*LY* 83)

This chronic eye disease would currently be labelled keratoconjunctivitis sicca, which in its mildest form can be understood as a senile desiccation of the tear ducts. It is, however, more properly classified as an auto-immune disease, sharing a common aetiology with Hardy's recurrent episodes of arthritis and his suspected acute nephritis (Kumar 2002: 564). His mother, who was a voracious reader, had as a young woman suffered a terrifying attack of loss of vision, which was diagnosed at the time as Acute Opthalmia, and she was advised to cease reading forthwith. In retrospect, this episode may well have been no more than migraine. Hardy, retreating back to Dorset from London on the grounds of ill-health in 1867 cites two problems – the stench from the River Thames at Adelphi Terrace and the effects of confining himself in his rooms 'every evening from six to twelve reading incessantly' (*EL* 70).

Five years later, Hardy, having received the meagre sum of £30 for the copyright of *Under the Greenwood Tree*, was contemplating abandoning literature for architecture but Horace Moule urged him not to in case 'anything were to happen to his eyes' – it being possible to dictate a novel or poem but not an architectural drawing (*EL* 90). Shortly after this discussion, Hardy did indeed notice a problem with his eyes ('floating specks on the white paper in front of him') and, on Moule's advice, sought the opinion of William Bowman who was Surgeon Royal at Moorfield's Hospital. There is no record of the outcome of this consultation and Hardy's eyes seem to have suffered no lasting damage from this possible 'opthalmia'. Gittings thus suggests that there is an 'autobiographical element in Clym's blindness' (Gittings 1978: 151).

The text of *The Return of the Native* is suffused with images of sensory deprivation. On the opening page, the reader is informed that the heath 'could best be felt when it could not clearly be seen' (*RN* 9). Clym's re-emergence on Egdon makes Hardy draw reference to 'the deaf Dr Kitto' (*RN* 115) and then 'Blacklock, a poet blind from his birth' plus the blind Professor Sanderson who gave 'excellent lectures on colour' (*RN* 190). Mrs Yeobright directly reinforces this theme as she berates her infatuated son: '"You are blinded, Clym," she said warmly. "It was a bad day for you when you first set eyes on her"' (*RN* 194).

Once Clym is married and living at Alderworth with Eustacia, Mrs Yeobright dismisses him in conversation with Thomasin: 'Sons must be blind if they will. Why is it that a woman can see from a distance what a man cannot see close?' (*RN* 214).

Unfortunately for her love-led son, this rather laboured metaphor was meanwhile becoming a painful reality. In their hot July days of delightful rustic seclusion, Clym and Eustacia 'enclosed in a sort of luminous mist' appear to have become one (*RN* 241). By August, after five or six weeks in 'Eden', Clym 'resumed his reading in earnest', studying indefatigably ... 'into the small hours during many nights' (*RN* 242, 250). One morning:

> he awoke with a strange sensation in his eyes. The sun was shining directly upon the window-blind, and at his first glance thitherward a sharp pain obliged him to quickly close his eyelids. At every new attempt to look about him the same morbid sensibility to light was manifested, and excoriating tears ran down his cheeks ...
>
> (*RN* 250)

Clym covers his eyes with a bandage, but is no better by the next morning. The surgeon who arrives towards evening 'pronounced the disease to be acute inflammation induced by Clym's night studies' and exacerbated by 'a cold previously caught' (*RN* 251). Clym has had the misfortune to develop 'Acute Opthalmia', a condition currently known as 'anterior uveitis' or 'acute iritis'. Graham recommends, 'The patient should be kept quiet and in a chamber where ... the light ought to be wholly excluded' (Graham 1864: 563). Thomas Hardy records how 'Clym was transformed into an invalid'. He was shut up in a room from which 'all the light was excluded' (*RN* 251); for in anterior uveitis, 'light seems positively hurtful to the eye' (Trevor-Roper 1974: 39). Clym's condition unfortunately merges into what Graham refers to as 'Chronic Opthalmia', a state in which goggles and suppressed light are an ongoing necessity and where his vision, 'like the wings in *Rasselas*, though useless for his grand purpose' (*RN* 252), sufficed for furze-cutting or itinerant preaching. The surgeon cautioned him that any further eye-strain would incur the risk 'of reproducing opthalmia in its acute form' (*RN* 251). For as a modern textbook confirms:

> Acute iritis tends to last for weeks or even months, relapses being common, and leaving a proportionate amount of permanent visual damage. If the iritis becomes chronic, the sight is insidiously reduced by exudate ...
>
> (Trevor-Roper 1974: 39)

Late nineteenth-century medical texts give detailed lists of the causes of Acute Opthalmia, amongst which are occupations which entail 'great exertion of the eye', followed by:

> (m) Inordinate indulgence of the sexual propensities has often a powerful influence, especially in connection with any of the preceding causes; the eyes sympathising remarkably with the generative organs.
>
> (Copland 1866: 1, 848)

It is not coincidence that causes Hardy to inform us at the start of this episode that Clym and Eustacia had been 'consuming their mutual affections at a fearfully prodigal rate' (*RN* 241), for Copland's catalogue of causes of 'opthalmia in its acute form' continues into 'Gonorrheal Opthalmia' and Opthalmia occurring in 'patients tainted by the syphilitic poison' (Copland 1: 861, 874). In modern medical terms, anterior uveitis occurring in isolation in a man in his twenties could very likely be due to Reiter's Syndrome, a sexually transmitted disease causing urethritis and at times arthritis, the ophthalmic symptoms of which usually develop within two months of the initial sexual contact.

Poor Clym was thus blinded both literally and metaphorically through his encounters with Eustacia. Hardy sought advice on this subject from his Hertfordshire aunt's brother-in-law Dr Sharpe, who confirmed Hardy's belief that a young man might go temporarily blind 'from continued study late at night of small print or Greek characters' (letter in *DCL*). It is, however, most probable that Hardy was aware of the venereal associations of Acute Opthalmia, whichever micro-organism was responsible for the pathological process. Urethritis is most frequently asymptomatic in the female. Reiter's Syndrome affects men only; the implication being that Eustacia brought infection to the marital bed from previous contacts in her favourite port and garrison-town of Budmouth where venereal disease was rife. Alternatively, she may have passed the infection on to Clym from her immediate past partner 'The Rousseau of Egdon', Damon Wildeve (*RN* 215).

'A gammy leg' (Patten 1962: 29)

You did not walk with me
Of late to the hill-top tree
   By the gated ways,
   As in earlier days;
   You were weak and lame,
   So you never came,
And I went alone, and I did not mind,
Not thinking of you as left behind.
          (*CP* 340)

Emma's lameness is another rather nebulous area, where the extant evidence is insufficient to lead to any definite conclusion. In *Some Recollections*, she makes several references to 'my occasional lameness suffered from childhood' (*ER* 48); also admitting that at St Juliot 'riding about on my Fanny I enjoyed the place immensely' (*ER* 47), the implication being that on horseback she enjoyed a freedom and a mobility which was lacking when she stood on her own two feet. The young architect from Weymouth with 'a beard and a rather shabby great coat', out of the pocket of which protruded the 'blue paper' of a poem (*ER* 55), no horseman himself, was very much taken with the ways of: the woman riding high above with bright hair flapping free – The woman whom I loved so, and who loyally loved me (*CP* 350).

To Hardy's eyes Emma, like Bathsheba, 'appeared to be quite at home anywhere between a horse's head and its tail' (*FM* 15), although there is no surviving confirmation as to whether Emma, like Bathsheba, disposed of the obligatory lady's side-saddle and preferred to ride astride her mount. All Hardy's recent biographers and Emma's biographer, Denys Kay-Robinson, have drawn attention to the intermittent nature of Emma's lameness. For example, she appeared to clamber freely over the cliffs at Swanage in the summer of 1875, but became lame the following summer when Hardy had walked her too far in the Black Forest. On this occasion, Hardy successfully treated Emma with 'a thick brown mysterious fluid' purchased from an Italian Apothecary (Millgate 1984: 114). Millgate and other biographers speculate that Emma was unable to dance due to her lameness and that as a consequence of this, Hardy became enamoured with more nimble-footed partners. This appears a laborious and unnecessary attempt to justify Hardy's natural susceptibility to 'those beauties bright as tulips blown' (*CP* 399).

On holiday in 1887 Emma again had to rest, 'my knee being jointless' (*ED* 173) and there was subsequent correspondence concerning referral to a London orthopaedic surgeon (*CL* 1: 224) but this appears to have not been followed through, most likely because of Emma's innate objection to any form of medical intervention. In the last decade of the nineteenth century, Emma swapped the horse's saddle for the bicycle saddle. Her consummate mastery of the former was matched by a profound inability to control the latter. Her life became a series of bicycle accidents leading to recurrent foot and hand injuries and 'ancle sprains', assiduously documented by her husband in his correspondence (*CL* 2: 174, 176, 181, 256; 3: 23). These injuries may well have caused the lameness, which prevented the older Emma from accompanying Hardy on his daily walks. The weakness referred to in the poem 'The Walk' was most probably due to her incipient cardiac failure.

Gout

At the age of 57 Emma also complained of ongoing 'gout in her wrist' (*LH* 10). By this stage of her life, medical practitioners had generally accepted the scientific explanation of gout being the result of hyperuricaemia, following Alfred Garrod's pioneering *Treatise on Gout and Rheumatism*, first published in 1859. Gout was beginning to lose its status as 'an exclusive socio-biological club', 'the crest and credo of the upper class' male (Porter 1998: 141, 143). Both Hardy and Emma's diary accounts confirm that on 7 March 1870, the Reverend Caddell Holder, Emma's brother-in-law, was confined to bed with gout, as it would clinically be understood today. Hardy already had direct experience of this disease, for it was gout that prevented Hicks from working in 1867, causing Hardy to return to Dorchester to give him assistance. When Hicks died two years later, this appears to have been attributed to gout – a cause of death that was soon to become untenable in the age of scientific medicine. Caddell Holder's illness is directly matched by that of his fictional counterpart Parson Swancourt, a 'fine red-faced handsome man of forty', who unable to come downstairs to greet the architect Stephen Smith, because 'I can't even bear a handkerchief upon this deuced toe of mine, much less a stocking or a slipper' (*BE* 9).

The ever-attentive Elfride offends her father greatly by trying to gently place a blanket on his inflamed great toe. This episode of gout is a very clear example of the free interchange of fantasy and reality in Hardy's fiction. His Wessex is indeed a 'partly real, partly dream country' (*FM* xvii). Swancourt/Holder is used to coping with his own gout with the aid of a 'gout-specific' and well understands that 'it generally goes off the second night' (*BE* 25).

Porter observes that in art 'swollen, inflated' gouty men are 'almost phallic grotesque objects' and that 'the gouty male is ever ready for erotic play that is less than direct'; if not physically capable of it himself, 'he is at least an observer of and an ancillary participant in the action' (Porter 1998: 248). There is more than a tint of this shade in Parson Swancourt, but what this tells us about Caddell Holder is best left as speculation. Similarly, no record survives of the Rector of St Juliot's reaction to this clear portrait of himself in a novel published by his sister-in-law's fiancé.

In his third *Literary Notebook*, Hardy juxtaposes an observation that 'very few men are in perfect health after the age of 35 – they have gout ...' against a note that 'the modern tendency to defer the age of marriage was physiologically undesirable' (*LN* 3: 382). He concludes that 'people should get over their love-making early in their history', and that 'premeditated planned marriage' after the age of 35 was 'an abhorrence'. It seems likely that he excluded himself from this generalisation on the grounds that he was 'a young man till he was nearly fifty' (*EL* 42). Unlike Emma, Hardy astutely never claimed to be afflicted by gout. For a start, he came from too humble a background to aspire to such a malady. Also, unlike Emma, he appears hardly to have ever touched alcohol, excepting the odd glass of Champagne for medicinal purposes to treat influenza as an old man (*LH* 220), however much the poet in him proclaimed, 'Sweet Cyder is a great thing' (*CP* 474). Many of Hardy's peers embraced gout – Wilkie Collins, Conrad and Coleridge, to name but a few. Tennyson claimed to have gout which caused brief attacks of inattentiveness (Porter 1998: 160) – these almost certainly were due to inherited Temporal Lobe Epilepsy, for his father was an overt epileptic. At the end of *Middlemarch*, Lydgate retires from practice to compose a treatise on gout but then succumbs himself to 'suppressed gout', which appears really to be a quite severe reactive depression. Gout in the nineteenth century was, therefore, a diagnostic label of convenience, sported by doctors and patients alike, to cover a wide variety of illness, real and imagined, especially in males in the upper echelons of society.

The coming of scientific gout, measurable and recordable through a simple blood test or the microscopic inspection of a tophus, meant that much of this illness had to subsequently find shelter under new diagnostic labels. Hardy's one description of conventional full-bloodied gout is the case of Squire Dornell, in the short story, 'The First Countess of Wessex'. Dornell is a 'hot-tempered gouty' and 'impulsive' man, a larger-than-life eighteenth-century character who bears more than a passing resemblance to Fielding's Squire Weston. Hardy describes Dornell's gout as being 'so violent as to be serious'. Dornell ultimately kills himself by repeatedly overdosing on his 'gout-specific', 'against whose use he had been repeatedly warned by his regular physician' (*ND* 21–4). Gout as a cause of death never seems to have received an explanation in contemporary medical textbooks, although it is frequent in nineteenth-century fiction and appeared in reality on death certificates. As to Emma's gout, it appears to have settled spontaneously – at least no further mention was made of it after 1900, when more pressing problems perhaps began to absorb her attention.

Emma's further medical claim to fame is the attack of malaria from which she allegedly suffered after lingering 'for rather a long time in the underground dens of the Coliseum' (Millgate 1984: 197) in the spring of 1887. Denys Kay-Robinson confirms that the Colosseum was at this time 'plagued with anopheles mosquitoes' (Kay-Robinson 1979: 130), which accords with *The Family Physician*'s description of the Pontine Marshes as enjoying 'an unenviable reputation for the production of malaria' or 'ague' (Physicians 1883/4: 81), which was thought to be caused by a wind-borne miasma. Hardy's description of a febrile illness that recurred: 'At the same date in the spring for three or four years afterwards ... in decreasing strength, till it finally left off appearing' (Millgate 1984: 197) does not fit any currently understood variety of malaria, although it goes well with the nineteenth-century name of 'Remittent Fever'. This episode of illness was one of the many references to Emma which Florence excluded from *The Early Life*, but which were subsequently reinstated by Millgate.

Cholera

Hardy repeated the pattern of close interweaving of fiction and reality, demonstrated by the illnesses of Parson Swancourt and the Reverend Caddell Holder, in his description of the Dorchester Cholera epidemic of 1854. Here the real life experiences of the Reverend Henry Moule, Vicar of Fordington form the basis of the experiences of the Reverend John Maumbury in the short story 'A Changed Man'. Moule was a courageous man who laid the responsibility for this devastating epidemic firmly at the feet of Prince Albert who, as guardian of the Duchy of Cornwall for his young son, the Prince of Wales, owned the area at the east end of Dorchester, subsequently fictionalised by Hardy as 'Durnover'. In a series of published open letters to the Prince, Moule described how: 'about 1,100 persons are congregated in a set of dwellings, many of which are of the most wretched description, and utterly destitute of the ordinary conveniences of life' (Moule 1968: 4).

Moule explains to Prince Albert how 'vice, in its worst forms abounds amongst the people' (ibid.: 5) – a sentence subsequently echoed by Hardy as 'vice ran freely in and out of certain doors of the neighbour-hood' (*MC* 328). Moule also describes how the excrement from these houses 'is cast either into an open or wretched drain in the street, or into the mill pond'; a pond which formed the chief water supply for the population. In the autumn of 1849, Dr John Snow in London and Dr William Budd in Bristol had simultaneously published evidence that Cholera: 'was not breathed in through the lungs, as the miasma-tists believed, but swallowed in drinking water, and that it was spread by the excretions of the sick infecting the water drunk by the healthy' (Longmate 1966: 183).

Dr Snow proved his theory when, on 7 September 1853, he per-suaded the authorities to remove the handle of the Broad Street pump, and within days dramatically ended the Soho Cholera outbreak. When Cholera spread to Millgate Prison during this same epidemic, the Home Secretary made the unwise decision to evacuate the prison to the Dorchester Cavalry Barracks, empty because their troops were in the Crimea. Henry Moule, completely conversant with Dr Snow's findings, immediately realised the grave risk that this evacuation posed to the population of Dorchester.

Within a few days of the prisoners' arrival, Moule discovered that 'two women residing in Holloway-row had contracted to wash for the convicts' (Moule 1968: 5). Fearing an outbreak of Cholera, he unsuccessfully petitioned the mayor to put a stop to this procedure. Within a few days a child fell ill and died from Cholera, and the disease spread rapidly amongst the impoverished population of Fordington. Moule worked tirelessly to ease the suffering of those stricken by Cholera and to do all he could to prevent the further spread of infection. Like Mr Maumbury, his house: 'was close to the most infected street, and he himself was occupied morn, noon, and night in endeavours to stamp out the plague and in alleviating the suffering of the victims' (*CM* 16).

Hardy's use of the term 'the plague' is a reflection back to his favourite childhood book, Harrison Ainsworth's *Old Saint Paul's*, which is a detailed account of the population of London's response to – and ultimate decimation by – the outbreak of Bubonic Plague in 1665/6. Both Maumbury and Moule supervised the large bonfires which were established at Durnover Cross, and on Fordington Fields, both to 'purify the air' and destroy contaminated 'bedding and clothing' (*CM* 20). The infected excrement-soaked clothing was carted on to the moor on wheelbarrows to be thrown into the fires, closely paralleling events described on Finsbury Fields in *Old Saint Paul's*. As a child, Hardy witnessed from the safe distance of Higher Bockhampton, the sky being illuminated nightly by the conflagrations on Fordington Fields.

Moule was a hero in a distinctly non-Hardyan mode – steadfast, energetic, sincere, a dedicated Christian, an evangelical who firmly believed in practising what he preached – a man of science, a man of God and a man of action. He was a man unassailed by the self-doubt and introspection that haunts Hardy's main protagonists. The true story of Henry Moule so overshadows and eclipses that of John Maumbury and his wife that it makes *A Changed Man* seem an insignificant tale. Hardy admittedly appears not to have been overpleased with it himself, remarking that it seemed 'on the whole, to be the best of a poor bunch' (Millgate 1982: 493). Not for the first time, reality proved more powerful than fiction.

Typhoid

The nineteenth-century tendency to allow sewage to contaminate water supplies was responsible for the demise of a more typically Hardyan hero, Giles Winterbourne, the man 'whose fingers were endowed with a gentle conjuror's touch in spreading the roots of each little tree' (*TW* 64). Dr Fitzpiers pronouncement over the dying Giles that 'this seems like what we call a sequel, which has followed some previous disorder – possibly typhoid' (*TW* 320) appears to fully justify Grace's belief that her estranged husband was 'the only one man' capable of saving her beloved's life. Hardy, whose notes on Koch's Postulates and the Germ Theory of Disease still survive, has given in Giles's illness a very clear portrait of the course of Enteric Fever or Typhoid. To find an equally clear account one has to look into twentieth-century textbooks; late nineteenth-century medical tomes are still struggling to differentiate between Typhus and Typhoid and lack the clarity of Hardy's account.

There is no evidence as to where Hardy obtained his medical advice at this stage in his career – it is unlikely to have been Dr Sharpe who was already retired from practice when Hardy consulted him about *The Poor Man and The Lady* in 1867/8. As the information was almost ahead of its time, it is most probable that he sought the advice of one of the eminent London physicians with whom he was well acquainted; most probably Sir Clifford Allbutt. It is also possible that this accurate account of Typhoid is based on Hardy's own observations or experience for the disease was endemic in Victorian England. Somewhat ironically, it was the cause of the premature death of Prince Albert only seven years after Henry Moule's correspondence with him concerning the unsanitary state of the Prince's properties in Fordington.

Giles 'had had a serious illness' during the previous winter (*TW* 224); on the surface he had made a full recovery, but the severe blow to his psyche caused by Grace's flirtatious reappearance, and then disappearance, from the scene was more than his soma could tolerate, 'A feverish indisposition, which had been hanging about him for some time' 'seemed to acquire virulence with the prostration of his hopes'. 'He did not think the case serious enough to send for a medical man' (*TW* 295) and was slowly convalescent from this relapse until forced by propriety or Grace, or both, to sleep under 'hurdles thatched with brake-fern' on a stormy autumnal night of continuous rain. His knees tremble, his pulse throbs, his palm is hot and shaky, his gait stiff and weary, his cough continuous. Enteric fever is now known to be a disease in which relapse can occur during convalescence, in which patients can go through 'the whole course of typhoid three times'. The initial symptoms of typhoid are: 'headache, aching in the limbs, tiredness and fever ... cough and broncho-pneumonia are also common in the first few days and may dominate the clinical picture' (Houston, Joiner and Trounce 1975: 507).

Grace, seemingly abandoned in One-Chimney Hut, not having seen
Giles for over 24 hours, becomes conscious of sounds other than the
repeated cough:

> They were low mutterings; at first like a person in conversation, but
> gradually resolving themselves into varieties of one voice. It was an
> endless monologue, like that we sometimes hear from inanimate
> nature in deep secret places where water flows, or where ivy leaves
> flap against stones; but by degrees she was convinced that the voice
> was Winterbourne's. Yet who could be the listener so mute and so
> patient? For though he argued rapidly and persistently nobody
> replied.
>
> (*TW* 312)

Grace at last manages to free herself from the shackles of Victorian propriety and discover Giles in his hovel 'his hat off, his hair wild and
matted'. 'His arms were flung over his head; his face was flushed to an
unnatural crimson' (*TW* 313). His eyes had a burning brightness but
were unseeing, for in his comatose condition he did not recognise her.
The patient is severely ill and has passed into the 'typhoid state':
'in which he remains throughout the 24 hours in what has been called
a "coma-vigil", drowsy and confused but continually muttering to
himself, plucking at the bedclothes, and groping for non-existent
objects' (Houston, Joiner and Trounce 1975: 508).

Grace sets up her own vigil by his bedside, doing 'all that a tender
nurse could do' (*TW* 314) in true Florence Nightingale fashion but
no avail. She summons Dr Fitzpiers by the time-honoured method of
throwing gravel at his bedroom window. A cursory medical examination reveals that Giles's feet and hands are blue and cold, and the
doctor gives his professional judgement that:

> nothing can be done, by me or any other man. It will soon be all
> over. The extremities are dead already.
>
> (*TW* 320)

In less than an hour, after 'an interval of somnolent painlessness and
soft breathing' (*TW* 321), Giles slips quietly away. Grace, in her
bereavement, is plagued by guilt. Her husband ultimately reassures her
that 'Winterbourne's apparent strength during the last months of his
life must have been delusive'; that a person's apparent recovery from a
first attack of that 'insidious disease' was a 'physiological mendacity'

(*TW* 339). Typhoid is a killer; no more could have been done about it. That is the message of the man of science well-versed in germ theory. The reader knows that Giles was not killed by a bacterium; he died from a broken heart. Marty will not forget this until she forgets 'home and heaven', 'for you was a *good* man, and did good things!' (*TW* 367).

3
Endgames

Atherosclerosis

> When told that some too mighty strain
> For one so-many yeared
> Had burst her bosom's master-vein,
> His doubts remained unstirred.
>
> *(CP 47)*

Ischaemic heart disease is a rare cause of death in Hardy's fiction, far less common than the dreaded 'chill'. It was, however, to be the ultimate cause of death of both Emma and Thomas Hardy, and of Hardy's 'rare fair woman', Florence Henniker (*CP* 320; *LY* 230). Florence Hardy was carried off by that other twentieth-century epidemic, carcinomatosis. Jemima Hardy's death appears to have been attributed to old age, even today quite acceptable at the age of 91. Thomas Hardy's father was certified by Dr Fred Fisher as having died from 'Atrophy of the Liver & Exhaustion' (Millgate 1982: 325) – a solid nineteenth-century diagnosis. Hardy's own death certificate also states a mode of dying in 'Cardiac Syncope' rather than a cause of death. There was no other identifiable family history of vascular disease, apart from his brother Henry suffering a minor stroke in March 1914.

This sudden emergence of an epidemic of cardiac disease was a reflection of the scientific route down which medicine was being propelled by the widespread uptake of such useful measuring devices as the sphygmomanometer and the clinical thermometer and such enhancers of perception as the stethoscope and the ophthalmoscope. Hardy's friend, Clifford Allbutt, was an outstanding contributor to this process, culminating in the publication of *Diseases of the Arteries and Angina Pectoris* in 1915. These discoveries are a far cry from Hardy's solid Max Gate reference book *Modern Domestic Medicine*. In common with many other Victorian textbooks, a clear and detailed clinical description is given of the suffocative 'Breast-Pang – called by medical men angina pectoris', which was first described by 'the celebrated Dr Heberden' in 1768.

The progressive nature of the condition 'seizing the subject suddenly whilst walking, and especially uphill and postprandially' is well understood, as is its relationship to age, male sex, obesity, sedentary occupation and anxiety; and not surprisingly, the potential exacerbating effects of cold or windy weather are also understood (Graham 1864: 318–19), but then:

> So little is positively known about the real cause or nature of angina pectoris, that it is not worth while discussing this subject. We may mention, however, that in many cases where death has occurred suddenly during an attack, the heart has been found to be perfectly healthy. Angina pectoris is much more common in the upper classes of society than in the middle or lower. It is said by some writers never to occur among the poor ...
>
> (Physicians 1883/4: 101)

So even if Hardy's father had had ischaemic heart disease, this diagnosis would have been excluded on social grounds from his death certificate.

The Physicians' account recommends the prescription of a solution of nitro-glycerine taken by mouth every four hours, with an extra prophylactic dose 'immediately an attack is felt coming on'. This may produce 'a little headache' (Physicians 1883/4: 103) – so suddenly we are back on very familiar territory. Graham, however, is more positive about the pathology of the condition, averring that:

1. It is a neuralgia of the nerves of the lungs and heart
2. Organic lesions found in fatal cases are coincidence.

This was a widespread medical belief at the end of the nineteenth century for, as Copland states: 'the most accurate post-mortem examination has not been able to detect the slightest indication of structural derangement' (Copland 1866: 1, 64). There is a strong implication in each of these accounts that breast-pang is a form of hypochondriasis, a disease for wimps. In fact, Graham, whilst admitting that Heart Disease is much more common in men than in women, relegates his main account of the disease to a supplement at the end of his volume *On the Diseases of Females*, where the author 'thought it advisable' to 'introduce the subject'. Having put this disease securely in its place, he then gives the most helpful advice that for heart disease 'exercise and quietness are the grand remedies'! (Graham 1861: 782).

From amongst this foggy mire of misinformation, one other concept emerges – namely that ischaemic heart disease is due to 'a collection of fat about the heart' (Copland 1866: 1, 65). The condition of a 'fatty heart' 'is essentially an appanage of middle to advanced life', less common 'among those who earn their daily bread by manual toil' but a favoured condition of 'gross beer-drinkers, and ... spirit-drinkers' (Physicians 1883/4: 330–1). The doctor in Shaston, clearly well read in this condition, recognised in John Durbeyfield one who indulged in beer rather than manual toil. For as Joan Durbeyfield confidently explains to Tess:

> 'It is not consumption at all ... it is fat round his heart.'
> 'At the present moment,' he says to your father, 'your heart is enclosed all round there, and all round there; this space is still open. As soon as it do meet so ... off you will go like a shadder. You mid last ten years; you mid go off in ten months, or ten days ...'
>
> (*TD* 16–17)

This fatty strangulation theory presumably arose from misinterpretation of post-mortem findings – the fat presumably overlying scar tissue at the site of previous myocardial infarction. To have a 'poor weak father with his heart clogged like a dripping pan' (*TD* 84) was one of the many burdens Tess had to carry in her young life – and with which the manipulative Joan could successfully chastise her. Ultimately and unexpectedly, whilst Joan is seriously ill, Sir John drops down dead 'and the doctor who was there for mother said there was no chance for him, because his heart was growed in' (*TD* 368). Poor forlorn Tess – how much was her heart 'growed in' also!

In the fiction and poetry, stress not infrequently touches 'an overstrained heart too smartly' (*TT* 262) – this is the fate of Lady Constantine on being reunited with Swithin, of Clark the hero of 'Enter a Dragoon', who is another young victim of fatty degeneration (*CM* 163–4), and of young-at-heart Jenny, already alluded to in 'The Dance at The Phoenix' (*CP* 47). Lady Caroline's sweet young secret husband dies abruptly, whilst 'excited and angered', of what almost certainly was congenital aortic stenosis in 'The Marchioness of Stonehenge' (*ND* 79–80); less surprisingly perhaps, a post-mortem examination confirms that stress has caused Uncle Benjy's 'poor withered heart' to crack (*TM* 310); and the surgeon examining Mrs Yeobright in the hovel on the heath confirms that 'physical exhaustion has dealt the finishing blow' to a previously affected heart (*RN* 306).

The only direct reference to Angina Pectoris in Hardy's fiction occurs in his last finished novel *The Well-Beloved*. It seems appropriate that Avice II, belonging to a younger generation than Hardy or Pierston, should fall prey to that younger generation's up and coming disease; however unlikely it might be that a non-smoking woman in her forties would die from ischaemic heart disease, but fitting perhaps in a book which is a tale of the triumph of passion over reality. The widow's illness was 'said to be due to angina pectoris' – Hardy's careful phraseology betrays his ever-sceptical attitude towards medical opinion. Avice had 'been visited by sudden attacks of this sort not infrequently in late years' (*WB* 303) – a phrase which neatly parallels that of the upwardly mobile status of the diagnostic term! She dies in bed 'in the position in which the nurse had left her', her facial expression precisely that which had characterised her 'when Pierston had her as a girl in his studio' (*WB* 321). Although Hardy in his last novel has adopted the contemporary medical terminology of physical illness, the doctor still confirms that Avice's death:

> had undoubtedly been hastened by the shock of ill news upon a feeble heart, following a long strain of anxiety ... he did not consider that an inquest was necessary.
>
> (*WB* 321)

The psychological remains to the fore. This is not only as the principle aetiological factor in illness, but in the deeper propensity for Hardy's life to imitate his fiction. The death of Avice I caused in Pierston an outpouring of emotion towards her of an intensity which far exceeded anything he had felt for her whilst she was alive: 'He loved the woman dead and inaccessible as he had never loved her in life' (*WB* 58). This proved to be the *Veteris vestigia flammae* (*CP* 338), which were to enkindle Hardy's most intense and passionate outpouring of love poetry. Just as Hardy had predicted in his fiction these passionate feelings more than 20 years before they were to happen for him in reality, so in the death of Pierston's once-beloved Avice II he predicted the death of his own once-beloved Emma. Like Avice II, Emma was found by the maid unexpectedly dying alone in bed in the morning. In each case the doctor was summoned, but the patient was past all medical attention by the time help arrived.

The details of Emma Hardy's final illness are, at first sight, as muddied as Hardy's illness of 1880/1. Dr Benjamin Gowring had set up in practice at 49 High Street West, Dorchester, in succession to the Hardy family's long-established Fred Fisher. He certified Emma's death as due to 'impacted gallstones and heart failure', and privately told Hardy that the heart failure was 'from some internal perforation' (Millgate 1982: 485). This is not terribly helpful. Both gallstones and heart disease can cause chest pains; the two conditions can at times be difficult to differentiate. If Dr Gowring did suspect that Emma's death was due to a perforation, then the most likely explanation would be perforation of the gall bladder – an extremely painful and rapidly fatal condition in which bile leaks into the peritoneal cavity – against a background of Chronic Cholecystitis. This would fit the immediate facts of her death. Dr Gowring was obviously unsure which pathology was to blame so he named both and, like the 'local practitioner' who attended Avice II, did not want the inconvenience of a post-mortem.

Dr Gowring had visited Emma on the day before she died and said that she was not seriously ill, but suffering from dyspepsia and 'want of nourishment' (Kay-Robinson 1979: 227). Hardy rapidly descended into pathological guilt about the sudden and unexpected death of his 'West-of-Wessex girl' (*CP* 572) and was too bent on blaming himself to consider the doctor's role. But to be fair to Gowring, Emma, after refusing to see him at all during the previous week, allegedly would not allow him to examine her on the eve of her death. The term 'impacted gallstones' is not helpful as a cause of death. In current parlance, if this term is used, it refers to stones obstructing the cystic duct and thus not allowing bile egress from the gall bladder – a circumstance that would be more commonly labelled 'Acute Cholecystitis'. Alternatively, if Dr Gowring envisaged the stones as impacted in the Common Bile Duct, then this would be a much more serious scenario causing obstructive jaundice and death through hepatic failure. Unlike the circumstances described in Gosse's letter to Hardy, there is absolutely no evidence that Emma was jaundiced – had she been so, then her death would have been more expected by those around her. Probably for 'impacted gallstones', it is safer to read 'chronic cholecystitis'.

Benjamin Gowring does, however, appear to have specialised in rather imprecise diagnoses. When Mary Hardy fell ill in January 1914, he visited her and informed the family that she was suffering from 'extreme weakness of her stomach' (*CL* 5: 8)! At the beginning of

November 1915, Mary became acutely dyspnoeic and unwell. When she died three weeks later, Dr Gowring certified that her death was due to 'emphysema', although she was a life-long non-smoker, who had always lived and worked in a rural environment. It would seem more probable that her death was due to Congestive Cardiac Failure.

Florence Hardy, quite an expert on the sick role, had a very low opinion of Dr Gowring, which, in part at least, probably originated from Hardy himself. Writing to Sydney Cockerell seven years after this event, Florence, tactful as always, states that:

> I distrust Dr Gowring, whom I have invariably found wrong in his diagnoses. You remember his saying my husband had cancer, and then some other horrible complaint, when it was probably merely influenza. I think my sister Eva can form a more correct opinion of a case than Gowring. Every specialist I have consulted after him has declared him to be utterly wrong.
>
> (*LH* 190)

At the time when she finally fell ill and died, Emma had a six-year history of suspected heart disease. The first episode on 30 May 1906 – which comprised a 'strange fainting-fit' whilst gardening, during the course of which Emma's heart 'seemed to stop' – is recorded in *The Later Years*, followed by an explanatory note in parenthesis to the effect that 'Mrs Hardy died of Heart Failure six years after' (*LL* 119). The fairly meagre extant evidence concerning Emma's health between this date and her death at the end of November 1912 has been picked over, inflated, reshuffled, filled out and recast by serial biographers without advancing our understanding one iota. Millgate's marshalling of the facts in his biography of Hardy (1982) is probably as close as anyone is going to get to an objective presentation of the available information.

There seems to be little doubt that Emma was at times suffering from anterior chest pains on exertion, which almost certainly were due to Ischaemic Heart Disease. She had a positive family history of this condition, her brother Richard Gifford having been 'disabled from an early age by Angina Pectoris' (*ER* 28). When Emma employed Dolly Gale as a personal maid in 1911, it was on the basis that 'her health was poor and she was getting weak'. Dolly also states 'Mrs Hardy permanently suffered a pain in her back and constantly asked me to pat her back to give her relief' (Gale 3). Millgate suggests that these back pains were due to Gall Bladder disease (Millgate 1982: 484). This is an unlikely scenario because Cholecystitis tends to cause acute pain – usually felt in the right upper abdomen.

Chronic back pain is more likely to be due to degenerative osteo-arthritis in the spine causing nerve-root pressure. When Dr Gowring took over from Dr Fisher, he was presumably given the benefit of retaining Dr Fisher's records. It is likely that at some time between 1906 and Dr Fisher's retirement in 1910, he saw (and possibly examined) Emma and recorded a putative diagnosis of gallstones – a common condition in a plump lady of Emma's age. It does not appear that Emma had ever seen very much of Dr Gowring. Dolly Gale, who records much fine detail, does not remember him visiting at all until he came to certify Emma's death.

There can be no doubt that some acute event did occur to Emma on the morning of 27 November 1912. Dolly remembers that: 'She was moaning and terribly ill. A great change had come over her since the previous evening' (Gale 5). Emma with her known ischaemic heart disease may well have suffered a myocardial infarction on waking that morning. It is also certainly possible that she may have perforated her gallbladder. Alternatively, her gradual deterioration that autumn – her weakness, her weight loss, her anorexia, her persisting back pain could have been due to some other undetected pathology such as a gastro-intestinal or breast malignancy with spinal secondaries.

We will never know because she was never properly assessed or examined. At least, hopefully, her self-administered Liquor opii sedativus gave her some relief of pain. I see no particular reason to castigate either her husband or her medical attendants – she did not seek the help of either. Dr Gowring's death certificate was the result of the kind of reasonable guesswork, which (pre-Shipman) was considered acceptable in these circumstances.

By the kind of coincidence which Hardy intuitively understood but which has often baffled even his more perceptive critics, Tom experienced his first definite symptoms of heart disease six and a half years before the illness was to kill him – just as Emma had done 16 years previously. Towards the end of July 1921, Hardy became conscious of anterior chest pain on exertion. Dr Gowring visited him at home and in Millgate's words 'reassuringly, if unromantically, diagnosed indigestion' (Millgate 1982: 536). This diagnosis must have been based on history alone because ischaemic heart disease in the absence of hypertension or cardiac failure would reveal no abnormal signs to the stethoscope and sphygmo-manometer. Hardy at the time was aged 81 and had a positive family history in that his brother Henry, 11 years Tom's junior, had had a slight stroke in March 1914 and significant heart trouble in December 1915.

The truth is that Dr Gowring gave Hardy, and more particularly Florence, the assurance which they wanted to hear, without any evidence to back up his reassurance. The likelihood is that Hardy was experiencing symptoms of ischaemic heart disease and that Gowring, even if he suspected this, took the view that in an 81-year-old man it was best to let nature take its course rather than raise unnecessary anxieties and unfulfillable treatment expectations by taking the problem any further. Hardy probably was best left to cope with his angina unmolested by medicine. The world could well have been deprived of Hardy's last two volumes of poetry had Dr Gowring taken a more interventionalist stance. Apart from the inevitable recurrent colds, occasional influenza (nineteenth-century definition), sore, weak rheumy eyes, and a number of episodes of anxiety over Florence's health (most acute when she was away in London, submitting to surgery), Hardy's health rumbled on much the same over the next six years.

The sickly infant who had been cast aside as dead at birth and had never been expected to survive until adolescence had proved a tough old bird – in fact, most descriptions of Hardy in old age resort to avian imagery, as in Mrs Winifred Fortescue's unflattering 1910 portrait of him as 'an ancient moulting eagle' (Gittings 1978: 179). In *The Later Years* he admits to the brooding sadness of an Involutional Melancholia (*LY* 257) but this was hardly news for the boy who, at the age of six, had upset his mother by informing her quite solemnly that he would have preferred never to have been born (*EL* 19–20).

Hardy's final illness is well-documented, although inevitably the more versions on offer, the more contradictions arise. In the autumn of 1927 he had been weaker and more tired than usual. On 11 December he felt too weak to work – he sat at his desk and did nothing. Shortly after this he took to his bed, not getting up at all apart from toilet needs after Christmas Day. Florence summoned Dr Mann at the first opportunity. Edward Mann, who was the junior partner to Dr Gowring's successor, Dr Nash Wortham, made a diagnosis of heart failure secondary to old age and advised rest. His management quite correctly comprised masterly inactivity.

He appears, however, to have been thoroughly attentive to Hardy, who seems to have been a stoical and uncomplaining patient. Before Christmas, Florence sought the second opinion of Sir Henry Head FRS, whom the Hardys knew socially. He was a former Consultant Physician and Neurologist from The London Hospital, now retired to Forston House near Dorchester. According to Florence's correspondence, he initially concurred entirely with Dr Mann's management, but was less happy when Dr Mann prescribed Digitalis after Christmas in an attempt to improve Hardy's cardiac output (*LH* 257–8). In order to settle any contention, Dr Mann arranged on Monday 2 January for a domiciliary visit by Dr Edward How White, who was Consultant Physician at the Royal Victoria Hospital, Bournemouth, with a special interest in Cardiology. According to Florence, Dr White confirmed Hardy's own long-held views that he was a young man for his age: 'his organs all sound and his arteries like those of a man of 60' (*LH* 259). As the week progressed, Hardy seemed to be holding his own and on Friday 6 January Dr Mann stopped the Digitalis, telling Florence 'he thought it would otherwise lose effect' (*LH* 260). Dr Mann may have been worried about Digitalis toxicity (he would have been using Digitalis Prep Tablets) or thinking that it might be wiser to stop this drug, of which one physician disapproved and to which the other appeared to be indifferent.

Unfortunately, within 48 hours of stopping the Digitalis, Hardy's condition had deteriorated dramatically. Dr Mann detected signs of hypostatic pneumonia – attributed to spending so long reclining in bed – in addition to the congestive cardiac failure. Hardy rallied on the evening of Wednesday 11th – enough to engage in a conversation about 'Haldane's recently published *Possible Worlds*' (Millgate 1982: 571) with Dr Mann when he called in after his evening surgery. As Mann was in the process of leaving the house, Hardy suddenly gave 'a short sharp cry' and 'complained of acute pain in his chest' (Gibson, J. 1999: 240). He became increasingly dyspnoeic and died 'in a very few moments' despite Mann's application of 'all stimulants' (Letter in *DCM*). To rephrase Mann's death certificate in contemporary terminology, Hardy died from Congestive Cardiac Failure secondary to Ischaemic Heart Disease. There may well have been an element of rheumatic heart disease in Hardy's cardiac failure – dating from his 'Wasted Illness' of 1880/1.

Dr Mann was ever the caring family doctor; his duties included travelling up to the Westminster Abbey interment of Hardy's ashes with Florence, seeing her safely through the service and safely back home again. Here was a doctor of whom Hardy might well have approved – except for the fact that he had wanted to be buried at Stinsford in the first place!

'This long disease, my life' (Pope 1966: 331)

As already implied, Florence's life appears to be have been one long tale of sickness, medical intervention and then yet more sickness. On the whole, Hardy treated his wife's major preoccupation with sympathy and solicitude but as Florence indulged in one more expensive and obscure London treatment after another, there were inevitably times when his irritation broke through. Writing to Sydney Cockerell in April 1916 he regrets that: 'my wife is not as strong as she ought to be in this good air, & I can't think why' (*CL* 5: 155) and curtly to Florence herself after a further operation in April 1921, 'I don't quite see how the removal of a symptom cures the disease' (*CL* 6: 81).

Florence appears to have suffered from an impaired immune response. As a child, she was frequently absent from school due to 'colds, influenza and sore-throats' (Gittings 1979: 14). As an adult this tendency continued unabated making her teaching career a disaster because she was never well enough to properly fulfil her duties. It was not until the age of 27 that she finally abandoned school on the advice of a London ENT surgeon. She continued to be ill, however, mainly with endless upper respiratory tract infections. It is small wonder, therefore, that Hardy developed an increasing propensity to complain of colds after befriending Florence, or that: 'both her local doctor and her London Specialists were kept busy with her' (Gittings 1979: 99).

She tried a number of obscure treatments for her chronic catarrh, including a protracted course of inoculations in London from her Harley Street bacteriologist, Dr Harry Butterfield (*LH* 137), who was recommended to her after the surgical attentions of Mr Macleod Yearsley failed to benefit her. She was one of those depressed, but somewhat irrepressible patients, who always believe that the next 'cure' (usually surgical) will be the definitive one. The whole cycle of symptom – consultation – expert opinion – operation – convalescence – further symptom has its psychological high points as well as its inevitable tendency to generate depression. Seven days after such 'curative' surgery at her favourite clinic, The Fitzroy House Nursing Home, which had originally been established by Sir Frederick Treves, the Dorchester-born surgeon, Florence wrote to Siegfried Sassoon that: 'As it is I feel better – & happier – than I have felt for years & I depart joyfully – tomorrow – by car for Max Gate' (*LH* 212).

This state of post-operative euphoria was to be followed by a reactive depression with multiple symptoms of anxiety, out of which arose Florence's pathological jealousy of Gertrude Bugler. It is likely that her relative immune deficiency gave her an increased susceptibility to malignant disease. Her first brush with cancer came in September 1924 when Sir James Sherren removed a suspected malignant swelling from her neck. The details of the histology do not appear to have survived but it seems likely that it was, in fact, a mixed parotid tumour (*CL* 6: 272–80).

In April 1937, she was referred with abdominal symptoms to Mr Ernest Lindsay, Consultant Surgeon at the London Hospital. He performed a laparotomy at Fitzroy House. The case was 'an open and shut' for the rectal carcinoma was too advanced for surgical intervention (*LH* 347). Florence was nursed in the drawing room at Max Gate in a hospital bed, which could be wheeled through the conservatory into the garden (*LH* 349). This exemplary terminal care continued until 17 October, when death at last caught up with a woman who had spent so much of her life being ill and the rest of it caring for the elderly, most especially her renowned but difficult husband.

The (mad) woman in the attic

Emma's mental health is an issue which has received much – often quite polarised – critical comment, but about which there are no generally accepted conclusions. The subject had, until very recently, received scant attention from medical historians. I begin with a letter written by Emma in February 1896 to her sister-in-law Mary Hardy, then Headmistress of Bell Street Girls' Junior School in Dorchester. At the time, Emma was recuperating in Sussex from a severe attack of eczema. Tom was in London. It was the year of 'Wessex Heights'.

> Worthing Sussex
> Feb. 22 [1896]

Miss Hardy

I dare you, or any one to spread evil reports of me – such that I have been unkind to your brother, (which you actually said to my face) or that I have 'errors' in my mind (which you have also said to me) and I hear that you repeat to others.

Your brother has been outrageously unkind to me – which is *entirely your* fault: ever since I have been his wife you have done all you can to make division between us; also, you have set your family against me, though neither you nor they can truly say that I have ever been anything but just, considerate & kind to you all, notwithstanding frequent <u>low</u> insults.

As you are in the habit of saying of people whom you dislike that they are 'mad' you should, & may well fear, least the same be said of you; what you mete out to others shall be meted to you again; & I have, heard you say it myself, of people. I defy you ever again to say such a thing of me, or for you or any one, to say that I have done anything that can be called unreasonable, or wrong, or mad, or *even unkind*! And it is a wicked, spiteful & most malicious habit of yours.

Now – what right have you to assert that I have been no 'help' to my husband? That statement, false & injurious, as it is, you have constantly repeated without warrant or knowledge of the matter.

How would you like to have your life made difficult for you by anyone saying, for instance, that you are a very unsuitable person to have the instruction of young people?

You have ever been my causeless enemy – causeless, except that I stand in the way of your evil ambition to be on the same level with your brother by trampling upon me. If you did not know, & pander to his many weaknesses, & have secured him on your side by your crafty ways, you could not have done me the irreparable mischief you have.

And doubtless you are elated that you have spoilt my life as you love power of any kind, but you have spoilt your brother's & your own punishment must inevitably follow – for God's promises are true for ever.

You are a witch-like creature & quite equal to any amount of evil-wishing & speaking – I can imagine you, & your mother & your sister on your native heath raising a storm on a Walpurgis night.

You have done irreparable harm but now your power is at an end.

E

If you will acknowledge your evil pride & spite & change your ways I am capable of forgiving you though I cannot forget or trust your nature but I can understand your desire to be considered cleverer than I – which you may be, I allow.

Doubtles (sic) you will send this on to your brother but it will not affect me, if you do – as he will know from me that I have written thus to you – which I consider a duty to myself.

(*LH* 7/8)

The spelling mistake and the tortuous obscure construction in the final paragraph betray her emotion at this point – a mixture of guilt, anger and fear towards Hardy. There is much transference going on in this sad – and in places overtly paranoid – epistle written 20 years into the Hardy's marriage when Emma was 55 years old; Emma's own failings in the marriage become here the very crimes of which she accuses Mary. By this stage in her life, Emma had converted from the agnosticism, which she professed at the time of her first meeting Hardy, to Evangelical Christianity. The letter is structured like an evangelical sermon, casting damnation on the wicked before rising to a mystic conclusion, in which Satan (here Mary) is defeated – then offering the chance of forgiveness in a brief postscript. Emma's God appears to be an Old Testament Jehovah – for there is no attempt at conciliation or understanding in the letter; the impression being given that a plague of locusts will shortly descend on Higher Bockhampton. Emma accuses the Hardy family of calling her 'mad' and of having 'errors in her mind' – so this was obviously not a new issue in 1896, nearly 17 years before Emma's death. This somewhat refutes the arguments of Seymour-Smith and others, who claim that her problems only occurred as a form of terminal senile decay in the closing months of her life. Even allowing for the fact that marriages and families tend to bring out the worst in people, this letter, which includes a threat to try to lose Mary her job, can hardly be described as the product of a wholly stable and mentally healthy person.

Around the time that the letter was written, Hardy had workmen in at Max Gate, constructing two new attic rooms in the roof space above his study. These would be accessed from a new staircase, making them completely separate and independent from the servants' bedrooms at the front of the house. The bedrooms were being constructed at Emma's request because she wished to have 'an eyrie' of her own. This was not such a strange request as it might appear, for there is plentiful evidence that at that time many middle-class women wished to banish themselves like voluntary Bertha Masons to the attics of their homes. This was an early expression of the Women's Suffrage movement – the same process that lead Virginia Woolf 30 years later to write *A Room of One's Own* (1928).

Bertha Mason was seen as a proto-feminist, the victim of a male-dominated oppressive society. She became a self-made woman rather than a mad woman. This concept would have appealed particularly to Emma who saw herself as a writer of equal status with her husband. It also would have appealed because she had a significant family history of mental illness. To be a madwoman in your own attic was also to acknowledge that female mental illness was an arbitrary construct of a male-dominated society and medical profession. In addition, as Gittings observed, Emma:

> determined to rival the aristocratic 'women in London' of whom she was so jealously contemptuous, by having a set of boudoir apartments of her own, copying the fashion of these emancipated ladies

who had often entertained her husband *tête a tête* in such intimate surroundings.

(Gittings 1978: 189–90)

By 1898 she had definitely moved into this pair of rooms and here she appears to have slept for the remaining 14 years of her life. Gittings's description of 'boudoir apartments'is far from the truth. Both rooms are small and irregular with maximum floor dimensions of 14 feet by 10 feet; in both rooms the roof encroaches on three sides so the available space is much less than these dimensions suggest. There is basically room for a bed and one other piece of furniture in each room. They are approached by a steep narrow staircase with a bend in it. The servants'quarters at the front of the house are luxurious by comparison. Emma was a heavy woman who had been lame from childhood; getting up and down the stairs would have been difficult even when she first retired there at the age of 58.

The accommodation offered was spartan compared with the large airy Victorian drawing room where visitors were received on the ground floor and the substantial bedroom above it where Hardy slept or the large room on the first floor, with extensive views, which he used as his study. Predictably, temperature control in the attic was a major problem, as confirmed by Dolly Gale, who was Emma's personal maid for the final year or so of her life:

> There was always a fire burning in Mrs Hardy's bedroom on the attic floor where she habitually lived … She or I were always building up or reducing the fire. It was either too hot or too cold in the room. It was difficult, if not impossible to get just the right temperature …
>
> (*THYB* 1973/4: 4)

The point I am labouring is that whilst on the surface, retreating to the attic to assert your independence from your husband might seem a smart thing to do, Emma carried the associated deprivation to such extremes that it must lead one to question her mental health. There are a number of contemporary witnesses to Emma's well-being at this time. George Gissing stayed with the Hardys at Max Gate in September 1895. He subsequently, in correspondence, described Hardy himself as 'good, gentle and poetically minded' although 'born a peasant' and retaining 'much of the peasant's view of life'. But:

> Most unfortunately he has a very foolish wife – a woman of higher birth than his own, who looks down upon him and is utterly

discontented ... A strange unsettlement appears in him; probably the result of his long association with such a paltry woman.

(Gibson 1999: 50)

Witnesses from the first decade of the twentieth century, questioned by Denys Kay-Robinson nearly 70 years later gave the collective opinion that in Dorchester:

Many considered Hardy slightly potty and most were sure Emma was potty without qualification. The knowledge that she had disseminated religious tracts, the rumour that she had begun to compose poetry and the sight of her careering down High Street in her green velvet dress on a green bicycle was enough to convince the average towns-person that here was a lunatic, if a harmless one ...

(Kay-Robinson 1979: 188)

Bicycling was indeed one of the 'boyish excesses of the so-called "new woman"' (Sturgis 1995: 116). A handful of Emma's poems had been published – mainly in the local press – not on merit, but solely on the strength of her husband's name. In 1911 she paid for the publication of a slim volume of her verse entitled *Alleys*, followed in April 1912 by a volume of religious tracts entitled *Spaces*. Both items were reissued in 1966 by J. Stevens Cox's with a forward by an eminent Hardy scholar, Professor J. O. Bailey. His assessment was that these effusions revealed that Emma had 'a tendency to confuse fantasy with fact' (Bailey 1966). Michael Millgate was more forthright stating that *Spaces* shows evidence of 'obvious mental disturbance' (Millgate 1982: 479).

In 1961, Leonie Gifford, the daughter of Charles Gifford, Emma's first cousin, and a favourite of the aging Emma, wrote down her memories of life at Max Gate, when she stayed there as a 14-year-old girl. She described Emma as 'most eccentric', with a number of obsessions, amongst them a belief that the Pope was about to invade England; keeping a basket of food packed in preparation for flight from the advancing Catholic horde. She also described Emma as 'the most incompetent housekeeper', with 'never so much as a single flower in the house or garden' – consistent, at least, with Hardy's poem 'The Spell of The Rose'.

Much critical attention has been paid to an incident in 1910 when Emma told Florence Dugdale that she believed Hardy resembled Dr Crippen and that she was afraid that he was about to poison her. Florence wrote to Clodd at this time, stating that 'Mrs Hardy seems queerer than ever' (Kay-Robinson 1979: 214). Seymour-Smith suggests that this delusion was a sign of developing senile dementia; but complex delusions of this sort are not an accompaniment of Alzheimer's Disease and there is certainly inadequate evidence to support this contention. Emma was obviously having a difficult time because Florence and Thomas were basically carrying on an illicit relationship under her very nose in her own house – even if she was in self-imposed exile in her 'eyrie' most of the time. Kay-Robinson's explanation that the Dr Crippen episode was a joke intended to disconcert the nervous, neurotic and guilty Florence would be plausible, in the absence of confirmatory evidence that Emma suffered from paranoid delusions.

When Henry Newbolt and W B Yeats came to dinner at Max Gate on 2 June 1912, to present Hardy with a gold medal on behalf of the Royal Society of Literature, Emma gave Yeats: 'much curious information about two very fine cats, who sat to the right and left of her plate on the table itself ...' (Gibson 1999: 99). Three months later, when Edmund Gosse and Arthur Benson were also the Hardys'dinner guests, the latter described Emma, in his diary, as: 'a crazy and fantastic wife ... an absurd, inconsequent, huffy, rambling old lady ... so queer yet treated as rational ... must be half-insane ... absurdly dressed' (ibid.: 106).

A number of other similar accounts have survived. Christine Wood Homer, of Athelhampton Hall, who described herself as 'a friend of the Hardy family' confirmed Emma's 'very strange behaviour' and her fixed irrational belief that her own literary talents were equal – if not superior to – her husband's: 'She was a peculiar woman ... an increasing embarrassment to her husband. At first she had only been childish but she got steadily worse with advancing age and became very queer and talked curiously' (Wood-Homer 1964: 10, 12).

This view is confirmed by other witnesses including the daughter of the Hardy's then General Practitioner, Dr Fred Fisher, who said that 'Emma's mental condition progressively deteriorated' (Kay-Robinson 1979: 234). Unfortunately, no record survives of Fisher's own opinion; his only extant comment being in a letter written to Lady Hoare in 1928, concerning his visits to Max Gate 40 years previously. Here he identifies Emma as the cause of 'much of the great man's pessimism and depression' (Millgate 2004: 286). Emma died suddenly on 27 November 1912, having refused to allow Dr Gowring to examine her when he had called on the previous day. During the latter months of her life, she had been in continuing pain, probably due to a combination of gallstones and spinal osteoarthritis. It appears that she had been self-medicating for months with Liquor opii sedativus, which contains a mixture of Sherry, pure alcohol and opium. This medication was freely available over the counter at that time. Regular usage of this powerful and addictive product could certainly have been enough to cause Emma to behave in a peculiar way in the last months of her life.

At this stage in the procedure, there is insufficient evidence to make any kind of psychiatric diagnosis. What one can say is that Emma was definitely eccentric and probably had been so most of her life; she held some extreme views – both in terms of her religious beliefs and her refusal to acknowledge that her husband was a major world literary figure. She had a poor marital relationship, was probably lonely (the maid Dolly Gale claims that she never 'saw or heard the Hardys speak to each other' (Gale 6)) and was probably addicted to a powerfully sedative medication containing a combination of alcohol and opium. In addition, she had a definite family history of atherosclerosis (arterial narrowing) and probably died from a myocardial infarction (heart attack) so it is likely that cerebral atheroma (clogged arteries) was contributing to her apparent cognitive impairment.

Post-mortem changes

The Interloper
'And I saw the figure and visage of Madness seeking for a home'

There are three folk driving in a quaint old chaise,
And the cliff-side track looks green and fair;
I view them talking in quiet glee
As they drop down towards the puffins' lair
By the roughest of ways;
But another with the three rides on, I see,
Whom I like not to be there!

No: it's not anybody you think of. Next
A dwelling appears by a slow sweet stream
Where two sit happy and half in the dark:
They read, helped out by a frail-wick'd gleam,
Some rhythmic text;
But one sits with them whom they don't mark,
One I'm wishing could not be there.

No: not whom you knew and name. And now
I discern gay diners in a mansion-place,

And the guests dropping wit – pert, prim, or choice,
And the hostess's tender and laughing face,
And the host's bland brow;
But I cannot help hearing a hollow voice,
And I'd fain not hear it there.

No: its not from the stranger you met once. Ah,
Yet a goodlier scene than that succeeds;
People on a lawn – quite a crowd of them. Yes,
And they chatter and ramble as fancy leads;
And they say, 'Hurrah!'
To a blithe speech made; save one, mirthless,
Who ought not to be there.

Nay: it's not the pale Form your imagings raise,
That waits on us all at a destined time,
It is not the Fourth Figure the Furnace showed;
O that it were such a shape sublime
In these latter days!
It is that under which best lives corrode;
Would, would it could not be there!

(*CP* 488)

This poem, which first appeared in *Moments of Vision* in 1917, is generally taken as confirmation that Hardy considered Emma to be afflicted
by 'The Interloper' – the hereditary tendency to mental instability
which ran in her family. In manuscript the poem is entitled 'One Who
Ought Not To Be There'. Hardy added the epithet 'And I saw the figure
and visage of Madness seeking for a home' for the 1923 edition of
Collected Poems. This motto appears to be a quotation, but despite
widespread enquiries, I have been unable to identify a source for it and
suspect, therefore, that Hardy made it up. A lot of the evidence about
the poem comes from Vere Collins's *Talks with Thomas Hardy*. Now,
Collins is not the most reliable of witnesses; however, in the absence of
any other explanation, it is reasonable to accept that Hardy acknowledged that the poem was about madness and that all of the 'three folk'
in the poem were thus afflicted. Hardy rather wryly admitted to Collins:
'Yes, I knew the family' (Collins 1928: 25). Florence subsequently filled
in all the details about the Giffords.
  This brings us to the nub of the argument about Hardy's opinion
on Emma's mental well-being. No statements from Hardy on this subject

appear to have survived from the time when Emma was still alive. There is no doubt that he made a number of such statements after she was dead. The dismissive argument takes the line that Hardy only did this under duress from Florence, who was determined to discredit her predecessor by fair means or foul. This argument also discounts any history of mental illness in the Gifford family as only a few minor aberrations of the kind that might be expected in any family, but which Florence latched on to and inflated out of all proportion. The third part of the argument is that Florence's views gained general acceptance down the acknowledged Florence–Purdy–Millgate route. It is interesting here to note that in Millgate's revised biography of Hardy, he has deleted one or two of the less well supported allegations against Emma (Millgate 2004: 490).

After careful consideration, I do not subscribe to this argument. Putting Florence's interventions completely to one side, there remains convincing evidence that Hardy did believe that Emma was mentally unstable, but forbore from discussing it until after her death. A number of his letters on the subject were written shortly after Emma died at the time of his most intense feelings of remorse over her death. This was contemporaneous with the composition of the poems of 1912/13.

Any opinions he gave about Emma at the time were straight from the heart, not the result of undue influence by Florence, with whom he was only in intermittent contact. If Florence had such influence over him at that time, surely she would have stopped him composing these intensely beautiful lyrics about Emma? She did not and could not possibly have had such influence. Likewise, his views about Emma were his own and nothing to do with Florence's machinations. With regard to the evidence about the Gifford family, this has been first overstated and then too hastily dismissed by opposing critical camps, without a medical opinion being obtained to evaluate such information as is available.

With regard to Emma, a letter survives addressed to Hardy from Kate Gifford dated 25 November 1914 in which her cousin states: 'Emma and I met at my brothers at Blackheath not long before her death & I was glad to see her again … It must be very sad for you that her mind became so unbalanced latterly' (Bailey 1970: 387).

This is an affectionate member of Emma's own family referring to her as 'unbalanced'. Hardy himself recurrently makes reference to Emma's mental ill-health in letters written shortly after her death; for example, noting 'certain painful delusions she suffered from' (17/12/12, Seymour-Smith 1994: 771), 'sheer hallucination in her, poor thing' (29/1/13, CL 4: 255), and to Florence, 'suppose something should happen to you physically, as it did to her mentally' (9/3/13, *CL* 4: 260), also Emma's 'slight mental aberration' (16/2/14, *CL* 5: 16), and 'her mind was a little unhinged' (6/3/14, *CL* 5: 19). He wrote to Kate Gifford at greater length: 'In later years an unfortunate mental aberration for which she was not responsible altered her much, and made her cold in her correspondence with friends and relatives, but this was contrary to her real nature ...' (*CL* 5: 64).

All these references date from the two years immediately following Emma's death, during the time when Hardy was grieving most intensely. I think that they must be taken as genuine statements and treated completely separately from Florence's subsequent amplifications and distortions, which I shall wholly ignore. I need to dismiss one other piece of evidence. Miss Irene Cooper Willis, one of Florence's executors, after Florence's death painstakingly read through all the correspondence to and from Emma Hardy, held by the Dorset County Museum. She concluded that: 'These letters appear to me to dispose of the idea that Mrs Hardy No. 1 was "mad" – as Mrs Hardy No. 2 so often declared' (Bailey 1970: 387).

The fatal flaw in this argument is that the letters, which she inspected, were those which survived Hardy's destruction of all controversial material left behind by Emma. In other words, her conclusion is of no value at all.

The Gifford family

The evidence is hazy because there is much critico-biographical speculation arising from a minimum of fact. Out of this cloudiness, emerge the following facts:

1. John Gifford, Emma's father, was an alcoholic who, although trained as a solicitor, was not in regular employment.
2. Philip Gifford, his brother and therefore Emma's uncle, died before Emma was born – 'non compos mentis' after 'a deep decline'. On the basis of the fact that the eldest of these Gifford brothers, William, died from Tuberculosis, Gittings attributes Philip's death to tubercular meningitis, but there is absolutely no evidence to support this suggestion.
3. Emma's eldest brother, Richard, was admitted to the County Asylum at Bodmin in January 1888 having attempted suicide and suffering from self-neglect and severe delusions. He was subsequently transferred to Bethlem and then to the Warneford Asylum at Oxford,

where he eventually died in 1904 aged 69. The cause of death was given as Dementia. Both Gittings and Seymour-Smith wish to attribute his mental illness to Chronic Renal Disease from which he was also suffering. His renal insufficiency could not cause such symptoms and would certainly not be responsible for the psychiatric illness which kept him an inpatient for 16 years.

4. Lillian Gifford, Emma's niece, suffered a nervous breakdown in 1919, for which she was committed in a paranoid state to the London County Council asylum at Claybury in Essex. Hardy was fond of Lillian because 'her childlike speech and behaviour reminded him of Emma' (Millgate 2004: 453). Encouraged by Emma to regard herself as a lady, Lillian never married and was never gainfully employed, eking out a shabby existence in lodging houses on an annuity provided by Hardy.

5. Leonie Gifford, 'Emma's much loved second cousin' (Gittings 1975: 188) suffered a series of 'nervous breakdowns' from her forties onwards.

That is the family history as best as I can work it out. Doing so gave me some sympathy for Florence. I found it really quite difficult to work out which Gifford was which. It may well be that some of Florence's so-called 'false accusations' against the Gifford family were just the understandable result of not getting the family tree completely straight!

This history does not immediately suggest an inherited madness, a poetic 'interloper' passing through the generations. It does, however, show that Emma had two first-degree relatives with significant mental health problems – an alcoholic father and a brother who most likely had 'dementia praecox'or Schizophrenia, in current terminology. It is also possible, if not probable, that the uncle who died 'non compos mentis' after a protracted decline was suffering from Catatonic Schizophrenia. Interestingly, Lillian, Leonie and Emma herself, all deteriorated mentally in middle life; the two cousins spending a spell in mental institutions. In the summer of 1912, Sir Clifford Allbutt, Regius Professor of Physic at Cambridge, is alleged to have told Hardy that he considered Emma certifiable. However much Tom may be blamed for his lack of marital support to Emma, he did provide her with a secure protected environment, in which all her foibles were tolerated. It is very likely that with a less supportive and understanding home environment, Emma too could have ended her days in an asylum.

We do not have a definite diagnosis. Ignoring the alcoholic, we have one probable and one possible schizophrenic and three women who deteriorated mentally in their forties. Schizophrenia is a disease with a definite inherited tendency; it is also common and carries an association with extreme religious views or experiences. Relatives of schizophrenics often have Schizoid Personalities without developing the full-blown disease. Emma certainly suffered from paranoid delusions and irrational beliefs; Professor Bailey considers that her writings reveal a difficulty in distinguishing fantasy from reality. Emma also developed in later life a habit of wandering off to stay in seaside hotels out of touch 'with home and with reality' (Millgate 2004: 394). This tendency to drift away from home, particularly abroad – as Emma did unannounced in the autumn of 1903 – is a recognised schizophrenic trait.

I think that this is as near as anyone can get to a definite diagnosis. It is quite fascinating that this fits with Hardy's concept of 'The Interloper'. Also, one must not forget that in the nineteenth century, even more than today, mental ill-health carried a significant social stigma and families would always be reluctant to reveal evidence of such illness. In other words, it is quite probable that there were more mental health problems in the Gifford family than ever came to light. Florence's tendency to overstate the case has probably proved counterproductive in tending to throw people completely off the scent.

The standard international classification of psychiatric diseases, DSMV–IV includes the condition currently known as Schizoid Personality Disorder. Affected individuals tend to be introverted and are often 'seen by others as eccentric, isolated or lonely'. They are usually 'sweet children' who maintain a child-like demeanour throughout adult life. As adults they remain emotionally immature, 'with little, if any, interest in having sexual experiences with another person', but often become strongly emotionally attached to animals. They tend to choose solitary activities and often 'appear to be self-absorbed and engage in excessive day-dreaming' (Gelder 2000: 928–9). Such personality traits fit quite comfortably with the majority of outstanding descriptions of Emma. The inherent lack of libido may well have been a factor in the Hardys' subfertility.

Conclusions

After a careful assessment of all the available evidence, concerning Emma's mental health, I consider that she was psychiatrically unwell in the later years of her life. On the issue of hereditary mental illness in the Gifford family, my review of the family history implies a tendency to Schizophrenia.

My opinion. It is likely that Emma suffered from a schizoid personality disorder, the effects of which were compounded in her last years by a probable early vascular dementia and the overuse of a medication containing alcohol and opium.

4
General Practice

General Practitioners

A physician cannot cure a disease, but he can change its mode of expression.

(EL 295)

This quotation occurs in isolation as a separate paragraph in an entry in *The Early Life* dated 9 May 1890, three weeks before Hardy's fiftieth birthday; it does not apparently relate to any of the material around it and Hardy offers no explanation. The only clue may lie in the final sentence of the preceding paragraph: 'Yes, man has done more with his materials than God has done with his.' Hardy is, I believe, seeing his role as a writer as analogous to that of a doctor: the poet cannot find an answer for life (that role belongs to God who is disinterested or dead), but he may be able to alter man's understanding of it and thus ameliorate his suffering a little. It is pertinent that Hardy saw himself as a kind of spiritual or psychological physician because doctors in general do not fare well in his fiction. Hardy would indeed have felt some empathy with them because in his own craft, he was very much a General Practitioner – a poet, a novelist, a dramatist, a musician, an historian, an artist, an architect and a naturalist.

The General Practitioners in Hardy's fiction span the final three decades of the nineteenth century. They are, however, almost without exception portrayed as unprofessional, incompetent and unscientific; not only that, but they generally overcharge their patients, whilst remaining themselves impecunious. From *Desperate Remedies* (1871) to *Jude the Obscure* (1896), both of which have a contemporary setting, the capabilities of Hardy's fictional doctors do not appear to improve, despite the rapid advance of scientific medicine during that period. By the time of *Jude*, in fact, medical practice seems to have reverted almost entirely back into the hands of the quack doctor – Vilbert, whose business is flourishing despite 80 years of medical licensing and nearly 40 years of compulsory registration. The only registered practitioner to appear in *Jude* is 'an advanced man', who understands 'new views of life ... the coming universal wish not to live'. This premature postmodernist, like Vladimir, 'can give no consolation' (*JO* 333). In 60 years, medical idealism has come full circle from that advanced man Dr Lydgate, who saw his highest duty as to 'take care of life and to do the best I can think of for it' (Eliot 1987: 703).

Hardy's inclination towards 'alternative medicine' may have been in part inherited, for his maternal grandmother, Betty Swetman, 'doctored half the village' of Melbury Osmond, the original model for Great Hintock where Fitzpiers was subsequently to practise, 'her anchor sheet being Culpeper's *Herbal* and *Dispensary*' (*EL* 8). Informed opinion was also on Hardy's side in this debate: 'The President of the Royal College of Physicians is so nearly on a par with the meanest herbalist. The result of the longest, most profound medical experience is so often a discussion on the worthlessness of medicine' (*Times* Editorial 1856).

Physician Vilbert, that 'skilful practitioner' (*JO* 396), on the other hand, offered 'celebrated pills that infallibly cure all disorders of the alimentary system' as well as 'asthma and breathlessness'. His tablets were 'two and three-pence a box – specially licensed by the government stamp' which of course they were not, because he was completely unlicensed and unregistered. Selling these along with his 'golden ointment, life-drops and female pills' (*JO* 21) gave him a far more secure income than the average General Practitioner.

Vilbert's love philtres, at five shillings a phial, take therapeutics back to the world of Greek mythology or medieval fairy-tale, where such substances most likely evolved as an explanation for the human tendency to 'love-at-first-sight'. The efficacy of Vilbert's love potion, like that of all his remedies, was probably dependent upon suggestion but that could be seen as its major benefit, because – unlike the conventional medicines of the time, which generally contained either opium or laudanum or were violent purgatives or laxatives – it would do the patient no harm. Vilbert's medications therefore stood in much the same relation to the official nineteenth-century pharmacopoeia as twenty-first century homoeopathic remedies stand to prescription-only medicines. In both cases, the former are safe and may be effective; the latter may be effective but have the potential to be extremely dangerous.

There is strong evidence to suggest that in his portrait of Physician Vilbert, Hardy was describing a real itinerant quack, Dr William Gilbert. When Arabella re-encounters Vilbert after an absence of many years, she exclaims 'you don't look a day older than when you knew me as a girl' (*JO* 289). Vilbert attributes this 'immunity from the ravages of Time' to regularly taking his own pills (*JO* 290). An article in *The Bridport News*, dated 21 February 1896, describes the then 103-year-old Gilbert as:

> the last of the old school of travelling pill doctors. Old men can remember him as a man when they were boys; he has been coming and going periodically with his pills for considerably over eighty years. He was a great walker ... the distances he traversed were often marvellous, and often 'negotiated' six miles an hour ... by his wife he had no less than 12 children ...
>
> (*THSR* 1978: 118–19)

Whilst Gilbert's longevity may, like Vilbert's protracted middle-age, be attributable to taking his own 'celebrated pills', he clearly did not wish to waste his valuable stock of 'female pills' on his own wife!

Jude called the last registered medical practitioner in a Hardy novel for the same reason that Miss Aldclyffe summoned the first one – to perform a statutory function, that is, to confirm death. Here the doctor has limited room for error – even in the extraordinary circumstances of triple paediatric fratricide/suicide. The doctor in *Desperate Remedies* not only confirms death but also states the time it occurred – his medical knowledge is on fairly safe ground here, for there is no one to dispute this assertion. The circumstances of Mr Aldclyffe's death also are far from ordinary, for he died alone in a room immediately below the one in which his daughter was locked in a lesbian embrace with her newly employed maidservant, who just happens to be the child of her former lover. It is no coincidence that both women are called Cytherea, an alternative name for Aphrodite, and also the name of the heroine of Hardy's favourite childhood book, Ainsworth's novel of 1841, *Old Saint Paul's*.

From here on, the medical practitioners in *Desperate Remedies*, which was published in the same year as *Middlemarch*, where 'medical knowledge' is recognised to be 'at a low ebb' (Eliot 1987: 91), fail at every turn. Farmer Springrove's ancient Three Tranters Inn and adjoining row of thatched cottages are incinerated. Next morning:

> They sifted the dust of his perished roof-tree,
> And all they could find was a bone.
>
> (*CP* 74)

At the subsequent inquest the surgeon, who presumably is the same doctor who attended Mr Aldclyffe – he is certainly just as dogmatic – testifies to the coroner that the small fragments found, namely 'a portion of one of the lumbar vertebrae' and 'the extreme end of the os femoris' are both human and that 'there was no moral doubt that they were a woman's'. From these fragmentary remains, he is able to give the cause of death as being 'crushed by the fall of the west gable'. On the basis of this highly dubious evidence, the jury finds that 'Mrs Manston came by her death accidentally' (*DR* 201). As the story unfolds, the doctor's opinion is shown to be worse than useless – the two pieces of bone being ancient fragments discarded in the churchyard when a new grave was dug and tossed by Manston into the embers of the fire. Could a trained medical scientist really have been so gullible? The answer is in the affirmative because Hardy, like Bernard Shaw 40 years later, believes that medical science:

> is as yet very imperfectly differentiated from common cure-mongering witchcraft; that diagnosis is only a choice among terms so loose that they would not be accepted as definitions in any real exact science.
>
> (Shaw 1946: 13)

Subsequent events in the novel confirm this opinion. Cytherea notices that her brother Owen has developed a limp. Owen makes light of his symptoms, but the pain in his lower leg worsens to the point where he can hardly walk. Reluctantly, he consults Dr Chestman who skilfully diagnoses 'some sort of rheumatism', prescribes hot bran, liniments and 'severe friction with a pad', and reassures his patient that he will 'be as right as ever in a very short time' (*DR* 223). Owen deteriorates so the good GP tries 'pricking the place with a long needle several times'. When this magic does not work either, Owen shrewdly notes that 'Dr Chestman was in doubt about something' and demands a second opinion. The combined revised medical opinion is that the problem is no longer rheumatism but erysipelas so: 'they began treating it differently as became a different matter. Blisters, flour, and starch seem to be the order of the day now – medicine, of course, besides' (*DR* 224).

As his condition continues to deteriorate, Owen manages to maintain the same detached ironic tone towards both his illness and his incompetent medical attendants, admitting that the 'suspense is wearing me out'! Ultimately, 'notwithstanding the drain upon their slender resources', the brother and sister decide that a third doctor should be consulted. This doubtful medical triad at last 'hit the nail on the head' or so he hopes – they operate under chloroform having 'discovered that the secret lay in the bone' (*DR* 225). What the secret was, they fail to tell him and cannot between them give him any idea when he may be fit to return to work – 'they would not, or could not tell' (*DR* 226). The problem here is either that the doctors are applying wholly spurious and unjustifiable 'professional' secrecy – on the basis that the patient is not capable of understanding his illness – or that we have doctors who are such incompetent bunglers that they cannot give any information to the patient because their treatment is entirely 'empirical', which is a euphemistic way of saying they don't have a clue what they are doing. Either way, the effect on the patient is completely demoralising, totally disabling and ultimately degrading. Hardy paints a most accurate picture of Owen's accumulating frustration and progressive despair.

Almost certainly, Owen was suffering from Osteomyelitis of the Tibia, probably tubercular in origin. Although this was a not uncommon condition, my searches of the literature, both medical and orthopaedic, have surprisingly failed to yield an adequate contemporary account. The treatment of choice, undoubtedly, would have been 'early drainage' (Aston 1967: 211) – the 'operation for its removal' 'under chloroform', to which Owen submits (*DR* 225).

There is no information extant, which permits us to speculate even on Hardy's medical sources in this case – but the description is too realistic not to have been based on an actual experience. Predictably, the surgery is of no lasting benefit to Owen and he is faced with a choice of a further operation, which he cannot afford, or being sent to the County Hospital. Miss Aldclyffe helpfully defines this as 'only another name for Slaughter House' (*DR* 228), a place where amputation is preferred to more conservative treatments because it promotes a more rapid 'through-put' of patients – an issue well understood by twenty-first century NHS managers. Objective evidence from that time supports Miss Aldclyffe's opinion for:

> Hospitals were dark, over-crowded, ill-run and insanitary ... patients admitted with one complaint soon contracted another, with possible fatal consequences ...'
>
> (Youngson 1979: 24).

And when Dr Lydgate first arrives in Middlemarch, Lawyer Standish assures Mr Bulstrode, Chairman of the Hospital Management Committee that:

> if you like him to try experiments on your hospital patients, and kill a few people for charity, I have no objection.
>
> (Eliot 1987: 91)

In order to finance further surgery to Owen's leg, Cytherea, against all her natural inclinations, marries Manston. By the time she has forced herself to do this, and 'contrary to the opinion of the doctors' (*DR* 243), Owen's leg had gradually healed, so Cytherea has sacrificed her future in vain and the doctors are, as usual, wrong. Thenceforth the novel proceeds smoothly without medical intervention; until, on being informed without any warning that Manston had committed suicide in gaol, Cytherea Aldclyffe 'shrieked – broke a blood-vessel – and fell upon the floor'. We are told that 'severe internal haemorrhage continued for some time and then stopped'; she had suffered from this before (*DR* 395). Both a physician and a surgeon attend Miss Aldclyffe, for she is a Lady; they engage in a whis-pered conversation and then collectively announce that the patient is 'out of danger' (*DR* 396). Miss Aldclyffe is wise enough to know better than either of them – she rejects their opinion and confirms her own assess-ment, by promptly dying. So Owen recovers and Miss Aldclyffe dies – both in direct contradiction to their doctors' expectations. Conventional medical care in Wessex has very little to commend it.

Miss Aldclyffe's death represents one of only two instances of illness in Hardy's fiction where the source of medical information is clearly iden-tified. In 1867, writing his first novel, *The Poor Man and The Lady*, Hardy sought an illness, which would cause his heroine to collapse but to remain conscious and communicative to the end. He wrote to his Aunt Martha's brother-in-law, Dr George Brereton Sharpe, who suggested pul-monary haemorrhage due to consumption. Unable to find a publisher for *The Poor Man and The Lady*, Hardy recycled much of the material from it into his subsequent fiction, especially *Desperate Remedies* where the heroine dies in the manner proposed by Dr Sharpe:

> For the young lady I think haemorrage (*sic*) on the lungs, begin-ning with a slight spitting of blood would be most suitable – it is less prosaically common than inflammation would be for your purpose. Haemorrage would very naturally follow the hurry and exertion – and if you like – external chill that the enterprise you name would entail. It also admits your object of perfect self-possession & consciousness till a last sudden flow of blood stops utterance and produces suffocation with the mind perfectly clear.
>
> (Sharpe 21/1/68, *DCM*)

Hardy's original letter to Sharpe, who had by this time abandoned medi-cine for the Church, does not survive. Although willing to seek medical advice on how best to dispose of his fictional characters, Hardy appears in general to have held the medical profession in low esteem. This repre-sents a conventional rather than exceptional view for his time as:

> Victorian society had limited confidence in the power of medical 'science' and serious reservations about medical men's social author-

ity and prestige. The newly qualified doctor might view his licence with pride ... but he was confronted by a public whose recognition of the value of qualified practice was less than whole-hearted.

(Peterson 1978: 38, 90)

This also begs the question – has society or human nature changed so very much in the 140 years since then? The answer again must be in the negative, for in the twenty-first century, 'Alternative Medicine' is a multi-billion pound business. The nineteenth-century was, however, a time of major change for clinical medicine, which was striving for acknowledgment as a liberal profession. This was a consequence of the rapid emergence of the middle classes, which had pushed professional values and aspirations to the forefront of European culture.

Medicine as a profession

Henry VIII had established the Royal College of Physicians in London in 1518; the Royal College of Surgeons followed nearly 300 years later in 1797. Members of these two Colleges were a small medical elite who generally treated only the upper echelons of society. At the start of the nineteenth century, there was a free market in health care for 'every one had the liberty to practise who could procure patients' (Merrimum 1833: 11). Some of these practitioners were members of the Society of Apothecaries, which had broken away from the Grocer's Company back in 1617, but the majority of practitioners up to 1815 had, like Dr Vilbert, no formal qualification or training. A study in that year in four districts in the North of England 'revealed 266 General Practitioners of whom only 68 had received any sort of medical education' (ibid.: 11, 12). In 1815 an Act of Parliament gave power to the Society of Apothecaries to licence all apothecaries (General Practitioners) in England and Wales.

Although the Society of Apothecaries, whose prime interest was in the production and sale of medicaments, took on this work somewhat reluctantly, they had by 1840 'examined 11,564 and passed 10,033 General Practitioners' (Kidd 1842: 16). These reforms, however, represented quite limited progress with which neither the general public nor the General Practitioners were satisfied. Early in the tale of Middlemarch, set about 15 years after these reforms had occurred, Mr Bulstrode remarks that: 'The standard of the medical profession is low in Middlemarch. I mean in knowledge and skill; not in social status ...' (Eliot 1987: 121). To which Dr Lydgate replies:

Yes; – with our present medical rules and education, one must be satisfied now and then to meet with a fair practitioner. As to all the

higher questions which determine the starting point of a diagnosis –
any glimmering of these can only come from a scientific culture of
which country practitioners have usually no more notion than the
man in the moon.

(Eliot 1987: 121)

The young idealist Lydgate, fresh from the two European centres of
excellence – Paris and Edinburgh – believes vehemently in medical
reform, which was not to come in his lifetime. Long before Parliament
can resolve this issue, the combined realities of marriage and General
Practice have sapped his zeal and turned him into an effective wage-
earner. George Eliot, with the help no doubt of George Henry Lewes,
produced in *Middlemarch* a thorough and well-researched portrait of
the mid-nineteenth-century medical profession:

> General Practice was slowly transformed by a professionalism
> based upon diagnostic skills; a product of the new medical schools
> with their (Parisian) stress upon rigorous diagnosis and (German)
> emphasis upon laboratory investigation. The prime purpose was
> diagnostic ...

(Porter 1997: 677)

Although the first attempts at further legislative reform were made
in 1830, it was to be over 25 years before a medical reform bill – the
tenth or eleventh such Act to be drafted – finally made it through
Parliament. The long delay was due to the blocking power of vested
interests – principally the Royal College of Physicians who had no wish
to see their exclusive status diminished by having to share a common medical register with humble surgeons and even more lowly
General Practitioners. The National Institute of General Practitioners in
Medicine, Surgery and Midwifery was founded in the 1830s to try
to promote reform. In August 1848, this body published a report
recommending:-

1. The establishment of a Royal College of General Practitioners
2. The establishment of a General Medical Council
3. The construction of a Medical Register

(*NIGP* 25–6)

The report contained a draft charter for the proposed RCGP – it was to
take another 104 years for such an organisation to be established in

England – and even then only after considerable public concern about poor care in the new NHS:

> There are no real standards for general practice ... the conduct of general practice and the individual practitioner is inextricably inter-woven with commercial and emotional considerations, which too often negate the code of medical ethics by which the public are supposedly safeguarded ... hence material and moral issues have become inseparable ...
>
> (*Lancet* 25/3/1950: 555)

How little the world had changed over the 120 years from Dr Lydgate's time in Middlemarch to the sombre post-war Britain in which my parents first started practice.

Back in 1848, Parliament continued to procrastinate. The Worshipful Company of Apothecaries, who had always been a reluctant participant in medical registration, sent a pleading letter to Lord Palmerston, in which they observed that most prescribing was being carried out by:

> chemists, without the slightest knowledge of anatomy or pathology; whilst ignorant and mendacious quacks reap from the credulous with impunity by their nostrums, a gold harvest; thus endangering human life to a great extent ... the public must be protected and the regularly educated Medical Practitioner be placed in the position that he is entitled to hold ...
>
> (Various 1833–54: 6)

The central phrase in this impassioned address, unfortunately, appears to be 'gold harvest': it was, and still is, ultimately, all about money. Medicine, however, needed its professional status to be legally enshrined and in what better way than to establish a General Medical Council as a sub-committee of The Privy Council? If Dr William Gilbert read this pub-licly printed letter, he would have been laughing to the bottom of his boots, the gold coins rattling in his pockets! After ten years of further debate, the profession was finally unified by the Medical Act of 1858, which set up The General Medical Council of Education and Registration – thus enacting two out of the three reforms sought by the NIGP. At the time that the GCMER was established it was considered that 'one in three (doctors) were practising without qualification' (Smith 1994: 1). An addendum to the NIGP's 1848 report contained a petition from members in Shropshire, proposing a joint board of examiners from the RCP and the RCS for General Practitioners. It took 25 years further debate for this single portal of entry to General Practice to be established as the Conjoint Board; in 1886 this qualification became mandatory.

Dr Lydgate and Dr Fitzpiers

Dr Lydgate/Dr Fitzpiers, an orphan of aristocratic extraction, came fresh to country practice, a young newly qualified idealist who saw himself as a scientist, a keen dissector and anatomist, who believed both in new medical methods and in naturalist therapy. Lydgate/Fitzpiers was a love-led man, who yet had no intention to marry, but within a short time in practice found himself married, disastrously and unhappily, to a woman who had been educated to a pitch far above her parental origins. His first pregnancy ends in a late miscarriage, precipitated by an accident. Lydgate/Fitzpiers does not see medical practice as a business, but rather as an outlet for his reforming and philosophical ideals. As his practice fails, he is described as an obscure country practitioner, doomed both to perpetual unhappiness and to having to live with tradespeople. Not only does he fail financially, but his behaviour causes him to lose his reputation locally so that he is blackballed by his patients, who desert him for more staid rival practitioners. Ultimately, Lydgate/Fitzpiers has no choice but to leave the area with his wife and set up in practice elsewhere, a much-chastened man.

A reader first taking up a copy of *The Woodlanders* in 1887 could not be blamed for experiencing a strong sense of *déjà vu* if they had happened to have read *Middlemarch*, published 15 years previously. Maybe the similarity is just one of those coincidences which occur, for scientifically explicable reasons, so frequently in Hardy's fiction. More likely, there must have been a considerable subconscious, if not overtly conscious, influence of Eliot's Dr Lydgate on Hardy as he penned the story of Dr Fitzpiers – a story, which was initially, entitled 'Fitzpiers at Hintock'. It could be argued that the life history and medical practice of Dr Fitzpiers were very much peripheral concerns to Hardy when he wrote *The Woodlanders* and that therefore a little bit of unintentional plagiarism from Eliot was of no significance. Indeed, when Hardy first wrote a preface to *The Woodlanders* – for the 1896 Edition – he stated unequivocally what the novel was about: 'the question of marital divergence, the immortal puzzle – given the man and woman, how to find a basis for their sexual relation ...' (*TW* 368).

Current criticism, however, emphasises the Darwinian aspects of the text, continuing to relegate Fitzpiers's medical practice to the role of plot accessory. Hardy added an 'Additional Postscript' to the revised 1912 edition on the topic of the 'exact locality of Little Hintock' (*TW* 369), which had gradually relocated eastwards to the Wessex village of Marshwood, which is known on the ground as Middlemarsh. Thus Dr Lydgate of Middlemarch was cloned 'into Dr Fitzpiers of Middlemarsh.

Eliot and Hardy

Hardy, however, appears to have been somewhat diffident about any possible influence which George Eliot may have had on him. There are only three references to her in *The Life*, two of which refer to her death. In each reference, he appears to regard Eliot as being renowned as a promoter of Comtean positivism rather than as a novelist. The *Spectator* in its favourable review of the first instalment of *Far from the Madding Crowd* in January 1874 had noticed a distinct similarity of style and speculated that the novel might indeed be written by Mary Ann Evans, using 'Thomas Hardy' as an alternative pseudonym to the usual George Eliot. In *The Early Life* Hardy is understandably contemptuous of this suggestion:

> a guess hazarded that it might be from the pen of George Eliot – why, the author could never understand, since *so far as he had read the great thinker* – one of the greatest living, he thought, though not a born storyteller by any means ...
>
> (*EL* 1: 74)

It is not his most lucid piece of prose – the italics are mine – for how far had he read the novelist whom he prefers to label a great thinker? The clues are few or have been deliberately obscured. In Millgate's recently reconstructed list of the contents of Hardy's Max Gate library, as at the time of his death, most Victorian novelists are well represented, but surprisingly he does not have a copy of a single George Eliot novel. Her presence is confined merely to *A George Eliot Reader*, published in 1916, long after Hardy's fiction was safely behind him. On the shelves at Max Gate, however, Hardy held five Brontë volumes, some Wilkie Collins, 'all 34 volumes of Lloyd's sixpenny Dickens' (Millgate 2001: 317), no less than three copies of *Madame Bovary*, one of which is inscribed with the name 'Emma Hardy', three Gissing novels, seven books by George Moore and three novels apiece by Trollope and Mrs Humphry Ward. Can this discrepancy merely be attributed to the fact that 'so far as he had read the great thinker' he had no wish to retain a single volume of her fiction, or was Hardy attempting to cover his tracks? He certainly appears to have been somewhat coy about Eliot in general, although occasionally the mask slips and he displays a detailed knowledge of her works, as revealed in his letter to Gosse of 8 August 1898 concerning *Adam Bede* (*CL* 2: 200).

In the autumn of 1901, Hardy declined two successive offers to write about Eliot – the first from publisher William Blackwood, who was seeking an author for a 'volume dealing with George Eliot' (*CL* 2/299), and the second a more humble request from Mrs F B Fisher, wife of Hardy's general practitioner. In refusing both these solicitations, Hardy did not use the excuse of an incomplete knowledge of Eliot. Millgate has added to *A Biography Revisited* the fascinating information that in the 1920s on Hardy's study wall alongside family photographs hung not only a portrait of his beloved Shelley but also one of George Eliot – that writer towards whom Hardy claimed to be wholly indifferent.

Evidence of Eliot's probable influence on Hardy – other than this link between Lydgate and Fitzpiers – has been noted by several eminent, and sympathetic, Hardy scholars, particularly Pinion, Millgate and Gibson; and Rosemary Ashton, from the Eliot perspective, is convinced that Hardy 'was influenced by *Felix Holt* when writing … *Tess*' (Ashton 1996: 286). Contemporary critics were less kind than subsequent scholars complaining, for instance, that *Far from the Madding Crowd* was a re-writing of *Adam Bede* and that *The Hand of Ethelberta* was copied from *Daniel Deronda* – both published in 1876, though fortunately for Hardy *Ethelberta* appeared first (Millgate 1982: 173, 181). There has been ongoing critical doubt as to which novelist was first to use the name 'Wessex'. Eliot certainly refers to Wessex in *Daniel Deronda*, but Hardy twice uses this resurrected geographical term in the first two pages of Chapter XLIX of the serial version of *Far from the Madding Crowd*, which appeared more than a year before Eliot's last novel. My own research, however, has shown this debate to be somewhat irrelevant for the term was already in popular usage 16 years before Hardy adopted it: 'Curiously impassive people, we Wessex worthies, when we are a little ground down with trouble' (Kingsley 1866: 411).

This citation is from Charles Kingsley's *Two Years Ago*, first published in 1855; a novel set in the fictional north Devon village of Aberalva, based on Clovelly where Kingsley was Rector. It is the story of a young doctor, Dr Tom Thurnall, fresh from the Universities of Paris and Glasgow, who heroically attempts to fight the Cholera epidemic of 1853, doing battle especially with a reluctant and recalcitrant board of guardians. The novel bears more than a passing resemblance to *Middlemarch*, such is the long and winding thread of influence! With regard to Wessex, I suspect that the term was in more general use in the mid-nineteenth century than has subsequently been acknowledged. It was left to Hardy to adopt it as a most successful brand name.

The constant critical harking on similarities with Eliot is thought by Millgate to have caused Hardy to take deliberate evasive action (Millgate 1982: 249) but as Pinion concludes 'how much he was influenced by her novels (remains) conjectural' (Pinion 1968: 206). This does not detract, however, from the striking similarities between Lydgate and Fitzpiers. In my analysis, I looked at 25 criteria concerning the two doctors' backgrounds, personal life and professional practice; on 19 out of the 25 criteria their experiences were either identical or very similar; on four criteria there was information about Lydgate and not Fitzpiers; and only on two criteria were their marked differences – namely on their choice of place to practise and on their attitude towards General Practitioner dispensing. I will deal with these two major differences first and then look in some detail at the similarities between the two doctors.

But even these two differences have their origin in a common characteristic shared by both doctors – that they are both idealists, naïve to the humble realities of everyday general practice. Lydgate's fashionable training has filled him with a reforming vigour but has given him neither the tact nor the business acumen, essential for survival in the hostile world of small-town medicine. His campaign against dispensing is due to a misplaced idealism, which equals Fitzpiers's belief that he can set up his plate on a cottage in a wood and find a viable practice forming around his door. Although published 15 years apart, the setting of the novels is over 50 years apart. The action of *Middlemarch* takes place in approximately 1829–32, although some of George Eliot's medical detail appears to be a decade or so premature. The action of *The Woodlanders* spans the years 1876–9.

Hardy goes to considerable pains in *The Woodlanders* to explain why Fitzpiers chooses to set up practice in an isolated village, surrounded by woodland. Indeed, the first mention of the doctor – on the fourth page of the novel – is a description of him living in Little Hintock 'not because there's anybody for'n to cure there but because 'tis the middle of his district' (*TW* 8). Later we are given details of how the scientist in Fitzpiers used a compass to locate the right place to practise; this is spurious science driven by wholly romantic notions. A practice depends on patients and there can be no logical reason for setting up in practice in a place that is both sparsely populated and already covered by at least four

Practitioners. Hardy needs Fitzpiers to be in the wood for the story to progress and consciously works hard to cover up his doctor's unlikely choice of area in which to practice. Not surprisingly, after three months in practice, Fitzpiers admits 'I don't seem to get many patients' (*TW* 49). Lydgate starts at least with what had been a viable practice for his predecessor, Dr Peacock.

GP Dispensing

Both Lydgate and Fitzpiers are from aristocratic backgrounds and both perhaps suffer from an associated inability to be humble, to accept the humdrum and the everyday and to listen to advice – especially when it is offered by those who are older and wiser, but socially inferior to themselves. Early in his time at Middlemarch, Lydgate fails to heed Mr Farebrother's instructions that 'a young doctor has to please his patients' and has to 'learn to be bored' (Eliot 1987: 168, 169). At the time that Lydgate arrived in Middlemarch only physicians – that is Members of the Royal Colleges of Physicians of London, Edinburgh and Glasgow – could charge for consultations; surgeons (FRCS) could charge for operations, but humble apothecaries (General Practitioners) could legally only charge for medications. Lydgate believes that:

> it must lower the character of practitioners if their only mode of getting paid for their work was by their making out long bills for draughts, boluses and mixtures.
>
> (Eliot 1987: 424)

Typically and ironically, Lydgate makes this remark to Mawmsey, the grocer whose own living does depend on exactly that kind of activity; and whose Worshipful Company of Grocers was the original parent of the Society of Apothecaries. The patients themselves can see no point in a consultation without a prescription and do not expect to pay for that illusionary drug 'the doctor'. Mrs Mawmsey: 'Does *he* suppose that people will pay him only to come and sit with them and go away again?' (ibid.: 426).

In 1834, an apothecary who identified himself only as 'a Junior Practitioner' published an open letter addressed to Henry Warburton Esq. MP, Chairman of the Committee of Enquiry into the state of the Medical Profession. This real life Lydgate complained that:

> In the present state of the law, an apothecary can only charge for the value of medicines delivered – this has given rise to a system of

drenching the sick with medicine in a variety of useless forms, for the purposes of increasing the amount of remuneration.

(Junior Practitioner 1834: 19)

This remained the legal position in 1834, despite a test case being taken through the courts which had ended that year in a judgement given on appeal by Lord Tenterden that an apothecary could charge for home visits. Lydgate's reforming and revolutionary course of action was therefore actually illegal at the time when he was practising in Middlemarch. It appears that this situation remained the norm for most of the nineteenth century for Conan-Doyle, writing from his experiences of General Practice in the 1880s, explains that:

the consultations were gratis – but they have to pay for the medicine. And if a patient wishes to come out of turn he has to pay half a guinea for the privilege. There are generally twenty a day who would rather pay than wait several hours.

(Conan-Doyle 1912: 138)

Lydgate's more experienced professional colleagues wisely scoffed at the young zealot. Mr Wrench objected to 'medical men fouling their own nest' on the grounds that 'a general practitioner who dispenses drugs couldn't be a gentleman' (Eliot 1987: 428), whilst Mr Toller took the pragmatic view that it will benefit his friend little Dibbits, the chemist, who 'will get rid of his stale drugs then' (ibid.: 427).

A hundred and seventy years after Lord Tenterden's judgement, General Practitioner Dispensing remains a contentious issue with rural GPs (essential service) in dispute with both their urban colleagues (green eye for the income) and the Pharmaceutical Association (only a chemist is qualified) for over the intervening years the Lydgates got their way and urban GP Dispensing was prohibited. In the new millennium, New Labour, with its New Contract for General Practice, pledged to totally abolish GP Dispensing once but this was just another politician's promise – 'an insubstantial pageant faded' (Shakespeare 1611 IV.i.155).

Lydgate's real problem was that he came from an aristocratic background and instinctively wished to behave like a practitioner with a university degree, in other words a physician. Presumably, his being orphaned meant that he lacked the requisite finances for graduation, despite having studied in Edinburgh.

Fitzpiers adopts a much more pragmatic approach than the high-minded Lydgate, giving 'a bottle of bitter stiff stuff for this and that old woman' and acknowledging 'the bitterer the better' (*TW* 115), unlike his colleague old Jones, who disappointed Cawtree with a medicine that 'had no taste in it at all' (*TW* 30). Fitzpiers is contented to dispense 'a few simple stereotyped prescriptions' (*TW* 115) for the workfolk but for Grace, who is a lady, he conjures up a small vial containing an opaline liquid and bearing 'an inscription in Italian' (*TW* 329) – this proves an effective remedy against incipient Typhoid Fever. It takes an embittered wife to point out to Lydgate the error of his ways:

> Why should you not have a good practice, Tertius? Mr Peacock had. You should be more careful not to offend people and you should send out medicines as others do ... It cannot answer to be eccentric; you should think what will be generally liked.
>
> (Eliot 1987: 618)

The 27-year-old Dr Lydgate and the 27-year-old Dr Fitzpiers both fail in their first practices for the same two reasons. Firstly, an inability to understand that they are tradesmen and have to ensure both that the money keeps coming in (dispensing) and that they generate further business by keeping the customer satisfied. Both doctors are described as finely formed, handsome men, which gives them an innate advantage – for most of a General Practitioner's customers are women and reputation is made or destroyed by women's gossip. Charles Bovary, inadequate in so many other ways, had this knack, but the requisite commitment to practice destroyed his marriage, his wife and ultimately himself. Both Lydgate and Fitzpiers failed to follow up their paying practice 'with the assiduity that would have been necessary for developing it' (*TW* 135). The second major failing common to both doctors was to marry both inappropriately and too soon.

Love-led men

Scientist or not, Lydgate's character is driven by a deep-seated romanticism. Studying Galvanism in Paris, he falls profoundly in love with Laure, an actress – in true Hardyan fashion – 'as a man is in love with a woman he never expects to speak to' (Eliot 1987: 146). She stabs her husband to death on stage, giving the fledging doctor the perfect opportunity to dash to her aid. He then pursues her across France with a desperate proposal of marriage; in response, she informs him coldly that her husband's death was no accident and that although 'You are a good young man', 'I do not like husbands.' (ibid.: 149). This proves a sufficient disincentive to cool his ardour and send him back to his galvanism. Before parting, Laure innocently asks him: 'Are all Englishmen like that?' (ibid.: 148).

This question is matched by Giles Winterbourne's innocent enquiry to Fitzpiers who has just 'rhapsodised to the night' (*TW* 114) about the electric charge produced in him by Grace Melbury, to whom he has never even spoken: 'Is it part of a country doctor's duties to learn that view of things?' (*TW* 115).

Hardy was writing about both these practitioners when he confirmed that 'the doctor was not a practical man, except by fits, and much preferred the ideal world to the real' (*TW* 112). Both young practitioners, however, set up in practice with the clear intention that they must become fully established and financially secure before considering the possibility of marriage. Although Rosamond/Grace has many attractions: 'Anything, like matrimonial intentions towards her, charming as she is, would be absurd. They would spoil the recreative character of such acquaintance' (*TW* 134).

Lydgate tries to concentrate on 'Louis' new book on fever' (Eliot 1987: 159) but despite 'medicine and biology and scientific enquiry' becomes wholly entangled in the 'gossamer web' (ibid.: 333) spun by that 'raw country girl' (ibid.: 154; *CP* 159). Fitzpiers, following in Lydgate's footsteps, hopes 'to do better things than marry and settle in Hintock' (*TW* 116), whilst Lydgate becomes wholly ensnared by the machinations of the spoilt and materialistic Rosamond, whose aim is to trap a handsome aristocrat from outside Middlemarch – in direct opposition to her parents' best endeavours.

Hardy does not really describe any courtship between Grace and Fitzpiers. This is quite typical of a world in which voyeuristic fantasy forms a more solid basis for enduring affection than actual contact between the lover and the beloved. Hardy makes it clear that Grace does not love Fitzpiers – this most insipid of Hardyan heroines, if capable of love, only ever loves Giles Winterbourne. With Fitzpiers, Grace is somehow mesmerised by his 'strange influence' (*TW* 162), 'an intoxication' in her brain, which 'passed off somewhat with his withdrawal' (*TW* 164). If anybody courts Fitzpiers, it is George Melbury who is infatuated with this man of science, 'whose family were lords of the manor for I don't know how many hundreds of years' (*TW* 160).

George assiduously prepares each evening for his courtship of the young doctor by studying 'Galen, Hippocrates, and Herophilus' (*TW* 162). To Mr Melbury, like Mr Vincy, a daughter is really just another business enterprise and he must work hard to secure the best return on his investment. This treatment of women as mere chattels is further borne out by

Melbury's degrading scheme for donating his expensively reared daughter to Winterbourne in reparation for the theft from Winterbourne's father of the woman who became Melbury's first wife. Melbury's contention that his resolution held good until 'the devil tempted him in the person of Fitzpiers's (*TW* 226) confirms the strong biblical undertones of this passage for: 'thou shalt not covet thy neighbour's wife, nor his manservant, nor his maidservant, nor his ox, nor his ass ...' (Bible 61).

It does not work to the benefit of either doctor that they find themselves married to women from relatively humble backgrounds who have 'been educated to a ridiculous pitch' (Eliot 1987: 162). Hardy follows Eliot's line exactly here, for as Cawtree observes: 'to keep a maid at school till she is taller out of pattens than her mother was in 'em – 'tis tempting Providence' (*TW* 27).

In both cases, the father's thoughtful investment proved to be an imprudent and overwhelming burden for the son-in-law struggling in the harsh world of nineteenth-century general practice. In his 'facts' notebook Hardy copied from the Dorset County Chronicle dated 14 January 1830:

Distress in the Medical Profession, particularly country practitioners, in an unparalleled degree. Long journeys – improbability of being paid – great numbers have embarked for America ...

(*FN* 192)

Eliot's researches paint the same picture for Lydgate, with the year's bills coming in, had 'nothing to depend on but slow dribbling payments from patients who must not be offended' (Eliot 1987: 616). Royston Pike revealed the other side of this coin in 'The Life of a Farm Labourer', which records that 'the doctor's bill proves a heavy item, but the doctor is kind, and will wait till they can pay him' (Pike 1967: 103). Whilst Lydgate's father-in-law is unwilling to throw good money after bad, once his daughter has secured a worthless match, Fitzpiers does have the advantage of a father-in-law who appears to be willing to bail him out on an ongoing basis: 'the few golden hundreds of the timber-dealer, ready to hand' forming 'a warm background to Grace's lovely face' (*TW* 171). However, it is indiscretions, other than financial, that ultimately destroy both practitioners – Lydgate for associating too closely and openly with the criminal Bulstrode and Fitzpiers for publicly flaunting his penis in the wrong places. Before exploring that issue further, I would like to consider 'What Sort of Doctor' (RCGP Study 1985) Eliot and Hardy have presented us with.

'What Sort of Doctor?'

By coincidence, in each of the novels we are given details of ten cases treated by the general practitioner. Lydgate's first case and Fitzpiers's last are both Typhoid Fever. Lydgate cures Fred Vincy, but Fitzpiers does not stand a chance with Giles, who is moribund by the time Grace decides to seek medical attention. It would seem probable that country-girl Grace has been refined away from the physical at her Lady's College – her sexual relationship with her young full-blooded husband apparently does nothing for her and it certainly does nothing for him as he returns from their honeymoon overcome by 'an indescribable oppressiveness' (*TW* 179) and seeks physical relief elsewhere as soon as the opportunity presents itself. Similarly, she fails to cope with the physical in her relationship with Giles, to the extent that she cannot even notice when he is mortally ill. Undoubtedly, the Melburys set her a poor example at home in their barren marriage of convenience.

Lydgate, whose practice is far more extensive than Fitzpiers's, treats three cases of ischaemic heart disease – Mr Featherstone, Mr Casaubon and Mrs Gobby – all of whom ultimately die but since he has no effective remedies available to him except opium for analgesia, he can hardly be blamed for that. In Paris he has studied the methods of Professor Laennec and therefore comes to Middlemarch not only equipped with a wooden stethoscope (see Plate 1) but also understanding fully how to use it. Laennec rejected the then commonly accepted theory of 'fatty degeneration of the heart' (Laennec 682/3) because it did not concur with post-mortem findings. He believed that the causative pathology for cardiac ischaemia was 'ossification of the coronary vessels' (Laennec 739) – these lesions, first described by Heberden and Parry, were what is now known as atheroma. This is one of several areas where the outcome of my researches differs from Eliot's, for Lydgate tells Casaubon that he is: 'suffering from what is called fatty degeneration of the heart, a disease which was first divined and explored by Laennec ...' (Eliot 1987: 407).

In the preceding paragraph, I have cited the 1838 English translation of the third French edition of Laennec's *A Treatise on the Diseases of the Chest and on Mediate Auscultation*, which was his standard work. Here he clearly rejects the then popular theory of 'fatty degeneration of the heart'. It must have remained in medical vogue, however, for it was the cause of death that Hardy used for John Durbeyfield in *Tess* (1891). As already suggested, it seems quite plausible that *Middlemarch* was a significant source of Hardy's own information and thus the error was perpetuated. It is possible that Eliot used an earlier edition of Laennec's work for *Middlemarch*, but this would be inconsistent with her other errors, where generally she is ahead of herself, rather than behind the times. Alternatively, the problem may be one of translation – it could well be that Eliot read the work in French – in the English translation Laennec does discuss fatty degeneration quite extensively, but ultimately rejects the theory. But the medical wheel is forever turning full circle – the latest discovery from US researchers is that 'the fat which surrounds the coronary arteries might play a key role in the development of cardiovascular disease' (*General Practitioner* 21/4/2006).

In examining Casaubon 'Lydgate not only used his stethoscope ... but sat quietly by his patient and watched him' (Eliot 1987: 277). The advice, which he gives to Mr and Mrs Casaubon on immediate management and ultimate prognosis, could not be faulted to this day. Lydgate also successfully treats Lady Chetham, Bulstrode's hypochondriasis and Nancy, the charwoman, whom he saves from unnecessary surgery recommended for a non-existent tumour by Dr Mitchin, one of the town's two physicians.

Lydgate steers Trumbull, the auctioneer, successfully through pneumonia by the expectant method. No drugs were prescribed, the thermometer was used diligently, and in twenty-first-century fashion Lydgate took the patient into his confidence 'as a partner in his own cure'. The thermometer used would have been Fahrenheit's cumbersome device since the 'short' clinical thermometer, which greatly facilitated the routine taking of temperatures, was not to be invented by Clifford Allbutt until 1866. Mr Trumbull claims to be not 'altogether ignorant of the *vis medicatrix*' (Eliot 1987: 431) – the type of management Lydgate is pursuing was known as the *vis medicatrix naturae* – the healing force inherent in nature. This sceptical approach to therapeutics was initially an off-shoot of Romanticism but gained increasing respectability as the century advanced for:

> statistical studies in public hospitals showed that many common remedies had little or no influence on the outcome of diseases ...
>
> (Worboys 2000: 29)

And

> prescriptions killed patients more readily than the diseases for which they were prescribed.
>
> (Youngson 1979: 18)

With scientific approval, this therapeutic nihilism acquired the more positive title of Naturalism. *Modern Domestic Medicine*, which Hardy

1 Laennec's wooden stethoscope – as used by Tertius Lydgate

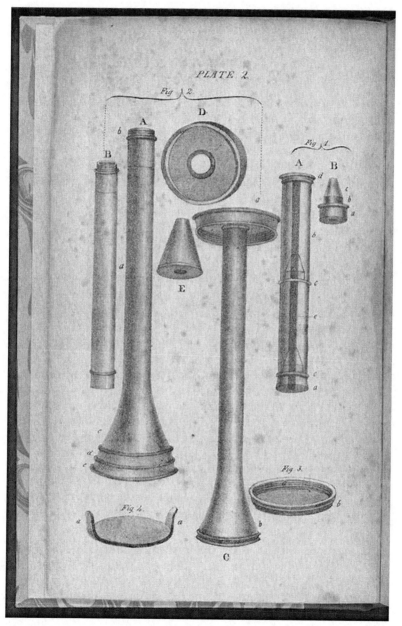

Source: From *A Treatise on the Diseases of the Chest and on Mediate Auscultation*, courtesy of The Wellcome Trust.

appears to have purchased in the 1860s, strongly promotes 'the restorative powers of nature' (Graham 1864: 279). Predictably, Fitzpiers followed Lydgate's example in trying to practise Naturalism but this often fell on deaf ears in Little Hintock, a village which appears mainly to be modelled on Higher Bockhampton: 'where people could not believe that Nature herself effected cures, and that the doctor's business was only to smooth the way' (*TW* 316).

Both Lydgate and Fitzpiers aimed to: 'assist rather than hinder the healing process ... to avoid poisoning patients with drugs or weakening them through ritualistic venesection' (Logan 1997: 174).

Lydgate also tried the latest non-interventional methods in treating Raffles for *Delirium Tremens* and might have succeeded here also if it were not for the non-compliance of Raffles' carers with the treatment regime – overdosing him with opium and not withholding further alcohol. Ultimately, Lydgate's Naturalism was probably responsible for his own death from Diphtheria; although by this time he was a chastened man who 'regarded himself as a failure' (Eliot 1987: 791), despite the fact that his successful practice had kept Rosamond and her children in the style to which she was accustomed for many years. Of the ten cases described in any detail, five die but through no fault of the doctor's.

The statistics for Fitzpiers are much the same – a 50 per cent mortality rate, having discounted his two spurious cases, namely Suke Damson and Felice Charmond; the latter of course does die, but not as a result of Fitzpiers's *medical* attentions. Fitzpiers's first detailed case is John South, a woodman, who is haunted by the elm tree, which grows opposite his house. He claims: 'that it is exactly his own age and that it has got human sense, and sprouted up when he was born on purpose to rule him and keep him as its slave' (*TW* 101).

This information is given to the doctor by Marty, the patient's daughter, who adds the helpful comment that 'others have been like it afore in Hintock'. Fitzpiers, trained at one of the London teaching hospitals and qualified LSA and MRCS, would not have experienced anything like this in his undergraduate teaching, which included general medicine, surgery, obstetrics and the new science of pathology. South is apparently afflicted by severe paranoid delusions – there does appear to be a higher than average incidence of this type of problem in men, such as woodmen or gamekeepers, who work largely on their own. It is debatable whether this is the result of their solitary occupation or whether this kind of work attracts those with paranoid tendencies in the first place.

South is suffering from a 'Monomania', also termed a 'Mono-Psychosis', the principal symptom of which is an 'insane delusion', defined in 1887 by Sir Thomas Clouston, Physician Superintendent of The Royal Edinburgh Asylum for the Insane, as:

> A belief in something that would be incredible to sane people, of the same class, education or race as the person who expresses it, this resulting from diseased working of the brain convolutions.
>
> (Clouston 1887: 244)

The 'diseased working of the brain convolutions' is, of course, a wonderful piece of pseudo-science, readily visible under the microscope to the suggestive eye. As far as treatment is concerned, Graham recommends that:

> The patient should rarely be opposed in the expression of his sentiments ... A very grand object is to gain the patient's confidence, and in order to effect this, we must humour his foibles and seem to fall in with his views ...
>
> (Graham 1864: 529)

Fitzpiers, however, considers that the best way to treat South's psychosis is to confront the problem head on, by removing the apparent cause of the illness. Fitzpiers does not listen to his patient nor does he try to establish any form of empathy with him. Instead, he makes the decision to fell the tree, despite the fact that South has told him, firstly, that the tree's life and his own are bound together in some magic inexplicable way – that it is a form of doppelgänger; and, secondly, that the tree will be the death of him. He has failed to note the significance of the fact that South is completely obsessed with the tree and that his entire life at present consists of sitting at his window: 'watching its every sway, and listening to the melancholy Gregorian melodies which the air rung from it. (*TW* 91).

In short, Fitzpiers does not treat South or his serious illness with anything like the respect they deserve. He does not have either the patience or the psychological insight to begin to deal with the problem properly. Completely abandoning Naturalism, one of the basic precepts of which was to live and let live, he opts for the quick fix – the melodramatic solution. He kills the tree and kills his patient. Appropriately, South collapses with the felling of the tree, but lingers on to die with the setting of the sun. 'Damned if my remedy hasn't killed him!', murmured the doctor (*TW* 102). Next please!

This unusual case spawns an offspring:

> You interest me very much ... I had hardly expected so dolio-cephalic a skull or such well-marked supra-orbital development. Would you have any objection to my running my finger around your parietal fissure? A cast of your skull ... until the original is available, would be an ornament to any anthropological museum. It is not my intention to be fulsome, but I confess that I covet your skull.
>
> (Conan Doyle 1976: 6)

This is Dr James Mortimer, 'humble MRCS', rural practitioner from Dartmoor addressing Sherlock Holmes in *The Hound of the Baskervilles*, but it would do nicely for Fitzpiers addressing Grammer Oliver. Phrenology or the study of the shape and size of the cranium as an indicator of character and mental faculties was a serious pseudo-science throughout the nineteenth century. Hardy studied phrenology and its offshoot physiognomy 'as a window to character with the considered intentness of a scientist' (Thurley 1976: 31). In the initial description of Lydgate in Middlemarch, his 'fine brow' (Eliot 1987: 90) is taken to confirm his superior intelligence. Fitzpiers, on his first appearance at Little Hintock, is similarly noted to be 'finely formed' (*TW* 100). It is easy to understand why Fitzpiers, whose science owed more to Shelley than to Hunter or Harvey, would be drawn to phrenology for he was not 'a merciless, unwavering irresistible scientist' (*TW* 124), but rather a dilettante; a man who was happy igniting chemicals to illuminate the woodland darkness with artificial rainbows.

Fitzpiers was fascinated by Grammer's 'very large organ of brain' (*TW* 49). He correctly quotes a scientific talking point of the time – that anatomists had found women's brains to be generally smaller than their male counterparts – a fact that was being used by some authorities to counter both nascent feminism and Darwinism and reassert male superiority as ordained by God in the book of Genesis. Grammer Oliver, here, is in eminent company, for when the phrenologist George Coombe examined George Eliot in 1851, he was struck by 'her very large brain' (Ashton 1996: 89).

The action of *Middlemarch* opens in 1829, in January of which year William Burke had been hanged in Edinburgh for the murder of at least

15 victims whose bodies he had then sold to Dr Robert Knox, a leading local anatomist. This inevitably generated considerable popular anxiety about body-snatching and general misunderstanding and confusion about anatomical study and post-mortem examinations. Mrs Dollop, the landlady of the Tankard, in the appropriately named Slaughter Lane, stirs up ill-feeling against poor Lydgate for wanting 'to cut up Mrs Goby' (Eliot 1987: 422) who had died 'apparently of a heart-disease not very clearly expressed in the symptoms' (ibid.: 434). Once Lydgate falls totally from favour through his association with Bulstrode, Mrs Dollop can confirm that he has been 'cutting up everybody before the breath is out o' their body' and that he knows 'drugs as you can neither smell nor see, neither before they're swallowed nor after' (ibid.: 690).

Hardy copied into his 'facts' notebook two extracts from the *Dorset County Chronicle* of 1827, the first concerning 'Resurrection-men', as they were commonly called, and the second entitled 'Body-snatching on large scale', concerning a man who bought a house adjoining a large churchyard in Bath, from which he exhumed bodies at night to sell to anatomists at £12 per head (*FN* 86, 94). It is small wonder then that this issue also spilled over from *Middlemarch* into *The Woodlanders*; despite the passage of the Anatomy Act in 1832, designed to forestall such criminal activity.

Grammer Oliver having sold her body to Fitzpiers for posthumous use, having spent some of the money, and then having witnessed the death of South from apparent morbid anxiety about a tree, develops an increasingly severe anxiety state about her own predicament. Eventually she becomes paralysed by fear, falls to the floor and is put to bed. Although superficially the case resembles that of South, it is really quite different – this woman is not in any way psychotic – her illness is a hysterical reaction to the circumstances outlined above. She remains shrewd and calculating and the one thing that she is certain of is that she would not consult 'a doctor; in other words, Fitzpiers' (*TW* 121). Fitzpiers does not get the chance to treat this patient, other than by removing the cause of her anxiety by proxy. Fortunately, unlike the case of South, the patient recovers – because of herself, rather than the doctor.

When Grace visits Fitzpiers to recover the 'fiendish compact' which Grammer has signed, the doctor invites her to peer into his microscope. She sees 'a cellular tissue of some indescribable sort'. Fitzpiers explains that it's just 'a fragment of old John South's brain, which I am investigating' (*TW* 133), looking presumably for 'the diseased working of the brain convolutions' (Clouston 1887: 244). How did he come by this? We know that South's body lay in an open coffin in Marty's own chamber prior to burial, for the moon-beams stream across his still profile 'sublimed by the presence of death' (*TW* 105). Did Fitzpiers perform his own post-mortem examination on South or did he just sneak a piece of brain out through a burr hole? Either way, Fitzpiers shares Lydgate's appetite for pathological tissue to sneak home for quiet perusal. Fitzpiers explains to Grace that he is carrying on:

> simultaneously the study of physiology and transcendental philosophy, the material world and the ideal, so as to discover if possible a point of contact between them ...
>
> (*TW* 133)

These aspirations closely parallel Lydgate's scientific endeavours. Lydgate links his investigation of 'the philosophy of medical evidence' (Eliot 1987: 212) with a search for the 'primitive tissue' (ibid.: 144) from which all living organisms evolved. Under the influence of Bichat, the French physiologist:

> he longed to demonstrate the more intimate relations of living structure and help to define men's thought more accurately after the true order.
>
> (Eliot 1987: 144)

Neither of these scientific hypotheses is easy to understand in modern terms but there can no doubt that both Hardy's Fitzpiers and Eliot's Lydgate are trying to use microscopic anatomical studies to investigate the links between cellular structure and physiological function, which they then extrapolate into links between the real and the ideal, the physical and the psychological. They are a pair of young idealists with microscopes. As Eliot points out, 'the dark territories of Pathology' were at that time 'a fine America for a spirited young adventurer' (ibid.: 143). Unfortunately for, and unbeknown to, Grammer Oliver, the fact that Fitzpiers had obtained part of South's brain without ante-mortem permission suggests that he would probably do the same with her corpse, written compact or no.

Fitzpiers's recorded medical successes seem to be quite limited, but we are told of a cottage patient and a woman in White Hart Vale who recover well under his Naturalist guidance. Fitzpiers's major medical achievement is his self-management of the severe injuries he sustains when Melbury pushes him from his horse. 'People do not fall headlong on stumps of underwood with impunity' – Fitzpiers stumbles along for 50 yards then reels and falls to the ground, dripping blood from his head (*TW* 264). He eventually crawls for more than a mile to the sanctuary of Hintock House, where he informs Felice that he is half dead from loss of blood. He admits to having initially saved himself by making 'a tourniquet of some halfpence and my handkerchief' (*TW* 267).

Rather than seek help from any other practitioner, Fitzpiers realises that his best hope of recovery is to rest and leave healing to Nature. This was a wise move because had he called upon one of his (older) neighbouring colleagues or been transported to the nearest hospital, the 'active treatments' prescribed would most likely have killed him. This was the unfortunate experience of Sir Robert Peel, who fell from his horse in 1850, sustaining multiple injuries; he was treated by the standard:

> antiphlogistic system – copious bleeding (including the application of leeches), violent purgatives and a restricted liquid diet ... until he died.
>
> (Youngson 1979: 18)

Transgressions

During his courtship of Rosamond Vincy, Lydgate often entertains her in the evening by discussing details of interesting cases he has dealt with during the day. Confidentiality did not yet appear to be an important issue for the emergent medical profession. One evening they are talking of Mrs Casaubon, who is likely soon to be widowed because of her husband's heart disease. Rosamond teases Tertius by asking:

> 'Do you think her very handsome?'
> 'She is certainly handsome, but I have not thought about it,' said Lydgate.
> 'I suppose it would be unprofessional,' said Rosamond, dimpling.
>
> (Eliot 1987: 284)

The blurring and crossing of boundaries in the doctor–patient relationship is an emergent issue in *Middlemarch*, which Hardy takes to full bloom in *The Woodlanders*. Lydgate's reforming zeal mutates into Fitzpiers's repeated infringement of commonly accepted taboos. As Rosemary Ashton has observed: 'It is Lydgate's tragedy that he, the medical man who is so scrupulous about making the right connections in his pursuit of scientific researches, does not 'get his mind clear' in his emotional and social life' (Ashton 1983: 74).

The doctor–patient relationship between Lydgate and Rosamond becomes a husband and wife bond – and why should it not? The marriage goes disastrously wrong, but that is because both parties to it are impractical and quite detached from domestic or financial reality: Lydgate because of his idealism and Rosamond because of the deeply ingrained consumerism of a spoilt childhood. It would have been better for both if this particular doctor had not married this particular patient, but that hardly constitutes 'infamous conduct in a professional respect' (Smith 1994: 36), even though, in this relationship, the licence 'to touch is ultimately self-sacrificing, if not self-destructive' (Rothfield 1992: 113).

Eliot, as a social meliorist, is gently teasing at the boundaries, which Hardy is to rip asunder in *The Woodlanders*. Influenced, no doubt, by her personal experience of the social stigmata attached to forbidden relationships, Eliot remains conscious of both sides of the coin. Why should a doctor and patient not be free to love each other if they so choose? But how does one protect a woman from a man who has intimate access to her mind and body for professional purposes? This latter question had been topical ever since the advent of the accoucheur or man-midwife in the eighteenth century for:

> the accoucheur insinuated himself into the home of the pregnant woman; by sight and by touch – a term which was used technically to describe the gynaecological examination, but which was also slang for sexual intercourse – he became acquainted with every charm a woman possessed ... it was not difficult for the accoucheur to seduce his patient into an illicit sexual relationship.
>
> (Moscucci 1900: 118)

Mrs Dollop would whole-heartedly agree: 'I know what those doctors are. They're a deal too cunning to be found out' (Eliot 1987: 690). Both Eliot and Hardy appreciate that the issue is more complex than this and would concur with the views of Cecil Helman, a twenty-first century anthropologist that: 'The boundaries between doctor and patient are more permeable than they appear. Sometimes it is patients who heal doctors and not the other way round ... satisfying the doctor's deep 'need to be needed' (Helman 2003: 11).

The doctor–patient relationship is very much a two-way process both in the consultation and beyond it. This quotation, an example of twenty-first-century medical theorising, expresses an understanding, which was already evident to both Hardy and Eliot in the nineteenth century. Dr Fitzpiers, however, who might well be described as the Rousseau of Little Hintock, a fictional incarnation of Hardy the 'Rousseau of Egdon' Heath (*RN* 216), goes in for serial sexual relationships with his patients. He moves in quick succession from Suke Damson to Grace Melbury, whom he has no choice but to marry, and thence to Felice Charmond, with whom he elopes when the pressure is getting too much in the woodlands.

Fitzpiers, on obtaining his medical qualifications (LSA MRCS), would have had to pay a one-off registration fee to the GCMER, and was expected to be bound by their gentlemanly rules of conduct. However, as has been noted, he 'was not a practical man' (*TW* 112) and such thoughts probably never entered his head. He cannot altogether be blamed for this because the GCMER (shortened to GMC in 1951), although it has a responsibility for medical education, has never seen one of its roles as being to educate medical students and doctors into the full details of its disciplinary rules. The unfortunate are left to discover these by mischance. As recently as 1986, a practitioner appearing before the Professional Conduct Committee repeatedly asked them 'for an indication as to what she should do' to avoid appearing before them in the future and was told that providing such information was 'not their role' (Smith 1994: 156).

After nearly 30 years of intense debate – as portrayed in *Middlemarch* – a successful Medical Reform Bill was passed through Parliament in 1858. This established the General Council for Medical Education and Registration. One of the principal duties of this new organisation was to establish and maintain a register of all properly qualified medical practitioners. As well as setting educational standards to determine which practitioners were fit to be placed on the register, Parliament agreed that 'they must have some authority to supervise and control'. Section XXIX of the Medical Act 1858, therefore, reads as follows:

> If any registered practitioner shall be convicted in England or Ireland of any felony or misdemeanour, or in Scotland of any crime or offence, or shall after due inquiry be judged by the General Council to have been guilty of infamous conduct in a professional respect, the General Council may, if they see fit, direct the registrar to erase the name of such medical practitioner from the register.
>
> (Smith 1994: 1)

This disciplinary office, or 'penal duties', as they were then described, appears to have been a function which the Council was originally most reluctant to undertake; for at every available opportunity cases were passed to other authorities or bodies, indicating 'a general distaste for examining the failings of their colleagues' (ibid.: 63). However, the full Council heard the first such case in March 1859 – and a steady trickle continued annually thereafter; although, in some early years there were no disciplinary cases at all. Not until the Medical Act 1950 was a separate disciplinary committee of the council established. It is not easy to obtain details of the early cases – if records do exist. Researchers are only allowed access to minutes of public meetings of the council and its committees. As hearings involving what the council describes as 'improper sexual or emotional relationships with patients or their families' (ibid.: 101) were, and are, almost invariably held *in camera*, information is seldom available beyond the charge against the practitioner and the verdict.

It was not until 1872 that the first two doctors appeared – one before the English Branch Council and the other before the Scottish Branch Council – on charges respectively of 'sexual intercourse with patient' and 'adultery with patient'. The GCMER was not in a rush to wash its dirty linen in public, particularly in the high Victorian period, and there is no mention at all of these cases anywhere in the Council minutes. Following these first two such cases, a standard formula for the charge was developed: 'Adultery with Mrs 'A' – named in divorce' – the first such case being heard in June 1882 and a further case in July 1887 – by which time the GCMER had heard 140 cases, only four of which involved 'improper relationships'.

This analysis is slightly hampered by the fact that the Council, early on, had a habit of disciplining doctors for 'unstated' allegations, which might well or might not have involved personal relationships. Suddenly and inexplicably in the early Edwardian period, there was a rush of cases – between June 1901 and November 1905, no less than 11 doctors appeared on a variety of sexual charges. Russell Smith in his well-researched book *Medical Discipline* suggests, by way of explanation: 'that, where cases receive wide publicity in the press ... there may be some tendency to alert other potential claimants to the GMC's existence or function' (Smith 1994: 100).

Alternatively, we may well be witnessing here a delayed effect of the moral backlash which followed the Oscar Wilde trial. How many of these doctors had read *The Woodlanders* and thought, consciously or unconsciously, that they might turn fiction into reality? If Fitzpiers can get away with it, why shouldn't they? The fact that in the first 43 years of the GCMER only four doctors had been charged with having sex with a patient, and that only one of them had been permanently erased, suggests that the Council's 'penal duties' cannot have been much of a deterrent.

Putting Hardy to one side, sex between doctors and their patients was also part of the staple diet of Victorian pornographic fiction: 'All my patients who showed the least susceptibility were overcome by my potent argument and vigorously fucked' (Marcus 1964: 237). This particular narrator-physician's 'argument' was that 'vigorous fucking', preferably by the physician, could cure most diseases – especially in those patients whom he described as 'unripe beauties'.

However, with the death of Queen Victoria, circumstances suddenly changed at the GCMER. With these cases also, at last, the Council recorded brief details in their minutes, although to a standard formula giving the name of the doctor and his qualifications and stating that he had:

> been summoned to appear before the COUNCIL in consequence of a judgment given in the High Court of Justice, Probate, Divorce and Admiralty Division, on December 21, 1900, in the case of Harvest v. Harvest and Knightley.
>
> (GCMER 1902: 47)

There then follow details of whether or not the accused doctor or complainant appear in person and the names of Counsel and Solicitors – several of the GPs had shrewdly sent apologies on such grounds as 'Mr Park, under contract with a steamship company, had been obliged to go abroad' (GMC 1902: 60) or the 'doctor apologises to the Council but he is absent in India'. These absentees were wise men, for following a hearing *in camera*:

> The PRESIDENT announced the decision of the Council as follows:- 'That the Council do now judge Mr. Edred Fitzpiers to have been guilty of infamous conduct in a professional respect, and do direct the REGISTRAR to erase from the *Medical Register* the name of Mr. Edred Fitzpiers.
>
> (adapted from GCMER 1901 47)

This became the standard formula – the citing of a doctor in a divorce case was in itself grounds for erasure, whether or not the doctor had stood in a professional relationship to the wife. It was easy work – rubber-stamping for the GCMER – and safer and simpler than looking into what had actually happened in these relationships. This approach was justified by the Council as recently as 1955 on the grounds that it had 'to maintain the highest professional and ethical standard of an honourable calling' (Smith 1994: 55–6), which takes one right back to Lydgate and the reformers of the 1830s who were working hard to establish medicine as 'an honourable profession'.

It is also interesting to note that most of the doctors in these early cases were young men – around the age of 30 – mostly qualified for less than a decade – the records do not reveal the ages of their lovers, who all by definition were married women – one wonders who really was the guilty party? But once the case was proven, that is, once the divorce petition was successful, the doctor would automatically be found guilty of 'infamous conduct' and the only sentence that the GCMER could hand out was erasure. Once erased for a sexual offence, it was a major struggle to become reinstated on the register, beyond the capabilities of most such doctors and their legal advisors. A doctor who had been automatically erased in 1876 after being found guilty by a criminal court of the dubious offence of 'attempted sodomy' (not with a patient), pleaded with the Council in 1882 for re-instatement, arguing that they had turned his legal punishment:

> into a life-long infliction for my wife and child who are innocent, not to mention myself ...
>
> (Smith 1994: 58)

but to no avail. He obviously had attended a public school, but not the same one as the buggers on the Council! Alternative practitioners have the advantage of being unregistered and hence safe from such disciplinary worries. Once Arabella has secretly dosed Vilbert with his own love-philtre, he feels free to place 'his arm round her shoulders' and 'kiss her there and then' (*JO* 396). The same applies, perhaps unwisely, to certain forms of psychotherapy. Freud rapidly disowned his Hungarian disciple Ferenczi, when he introduced a 'therapeutic practice', which 'involved kissing his patients ... and allowing them to kiss him' (Webster 1995: 396).

So what were Hardy's intentions in his portrayal of Dr Fitzpiers? There are a number of possible explanations, in each of which there may be an element of truth. One could take the line that he was unaware of professional ethics and that Fitzpiers, whose approach to love resurfaces in the character of Jocelyn Pierston, was simply a typical Hardyan love-led man following his irresistible inclinations and finding the true path to unhappiness. It can be more strongly argued that *The Woodlanders* extends and expands on Eliot's tentative exploration in *Middlemarch* of the effects of transgressing established boundaries in the doctor–patient relationship.

Hardy can also be seen to be making a poet's point to the GCMER and all other such adjudicators and legislators – that human relationships do not translate into the black and white legal language of guilt and innocence. In his 1896 preface, Hardy confirms that he was here – as subsequently in Jude – making this point with regard to marriage (and un-marriage) legislation. Hardy was himself aware of local doctors who had had sexual relationships with their patients. In *The Early Life* on Christmas Day 1890, he records 'another curious story':

> Mil [Amelia] C— had an illegitimate child by the parish doctor. She christened him all the doctor's names, which happened to be a mouthful – Frederick Washington Ingen – and always called him by the three names complete. Moreover the doctor had a squint, and to identify him still more fully as the father she hung a bobbin from the baby's cap between his eyes, and so trained him to squint likewise.
>
> (*EL* 302)

Herewith, an aggrieved young woman who obviously felt badly let down by the village doctor but found that she could do no more about it than tarnish the doctor's reputation locally by ensuring that everyone knew whose child she was raising. Hopefully, it would be a warning to other girls in the village. To make a formal complaint to the GCMER would have been beyond Mil's capabilities, even though she sounds a spirited and enterprising girl. The GCMER/GMC can only take evidence in the form of a Statutory Declaration or a Court Judgement and no rural solicitor would have taken up Mil's complaint against a local professional man. In any case, in its first 40 years or so, the GCMER appeared to play the role of a Gentleman's club – supportive to its own and not wanting to pry too much into its member's misdemeanours, which is why sexual misconduct cases only proceeded if a doctor was cited as co-respondent in successful divorce proceedings. Among the charges levelled against doctors in that early Edwardian glut of misconduct were several which would have exactly fitted Dr Fitzpiers's behaviour; namely, 'Abuse of position to ruin a married lady patient', 'Seducing and eloping with a female patient' and 'Eloping with a married patient, Mrs C' (Smith 1994: 250–1).

Infamous conduct

Fitzpiers lurks on the edge of the wood as the village girls join in woodland courtship magic on Old Midsummer Eve – he captures the fleeing

Grace in his arms and promises to 'keep (her) there all our two lives!' (*TW* 148). Grace quite coldly asks to be released. Freeing her, he stands still in a Midsummer Night's Dream, voyeuristically listening to 'subdued screams and struggles, audible from neighbouring brakes' (*TW* 148). Then 'on a sudden another girl came bounding down' – 'a fine-framed young woman with bare arms' – seeing the doctor she playful invites him to 'kiss me if 'canst catch me, Tim!' (*TW* 149). A protracted moonlight chase ensues, Fitzpiers unconcerned about the problem of mistaken identity. If, indeed, there was any mistake – because it was Suke, in the first place, who invited Grace to attend the midnight frivolities. Grace was thus inadvertently acting as a decoy to draw the handsome, irresistible Doctor into the wood for Suke's consumption.

Suke, who appears to be 'practised at the art of seduction', eventually beds down in a half-made hay meadow where she woos the 'now <u>thoroughly excited</u>' (*TW* 149) doctor with snatches of a folk song 'in which the lover invites his sweetheart into bed and she becomes pregnant' (*TW* 396). Fitzpiers imprints the purposed kiss, then sinks down on a hay-<u>cock</u>, 'panting with his race' (*TW* 150). 'It was daybreak before Fitzpiers and Suke Damson <u>re-entered</u> Little Hintock' (*TW* 150). Hardy is here, as always, playing a game with his Grundyian editors – innocently pushing the language as far as he can, without incurring their wrath – as the words, which I have underlined imply.

The doctor and the patient are having a good time together and fortunately, unlike the folk song, no pregnancy ensues. Suke probably has a supply of Vilbert's female pills because Fitzpiers, as a doctor, would not be able to provide contraceptives. The relationship continues – Grace happens to witness Suke's departure from Fitzpiers's house early one morning – this sends her into a reverie but she is a weak character [suppressed/depressed?] and too readily accepts Fitzpiers's just plausible excuse. By the time that the truth is revealed, she has married him and no longer cares anyway.

Suke's affianced Timothy Tangs similarly does not obtain definite confirmation of the relationship until they are married. A true countryman, he does not give a moment's consideration to a statutory declaration and the GCMER, but instead sets a man-trap for the errant doctor, knowing that rough justice works. Fitzpiers, characteristically, has a lucky escape, whilst young Tim removes Suke to New Zealand and seductions new. This case would undoubtedly be classified as 'infamous conduct in a professional respect' at the GMC. Hardy's angle is much more subtle and well ahead of general opinion at that time – their coition satisfied a biological need in both of them, did no one any harm, did not bring unwanted children into the world so what has blame got to do with it? That is perhaps too kind on Fitzpiers, the serial philanderer, preying on his patients. Tears after all, overcame Suke on her wedding day:

> At last one pays the penalty –
> The woman – women always do.
>   (CP 139)

Grace Melbury: Serious Professional Misconduct Case No. 2. Hardy makes it extremely difficult for the reader to get excited about Grace – she engenders the kind of enthusiasm with which most men would approach a blow-up doll. This is her problem – as to a somewhat lesser extent it was Rosamond's – that she is manufactured goods, all artifice, no soul. Melbury's workfolk, indeed, describe Grace as 'a halfpenny doll' (TW 157), a description, which in the 1896 edition, is amended to 'a waxen figure'. Even her love for Giles is unconvincing. Jacobus suggests that this reflects Hardy's growing disillusionment with the trade of novel-writing which caused him to go 'about the business mechanically' (Kramer 1979: 122).

If Fitzpiers, at the time of Giles's death, had not been trying to wheedle his way back into Grace's bed and if he had not become sexually aroused by Grace's (false) confession of their lovemaking, he might have acted as a more responsible doctor. In which case he would not have issued a death certificate – for Giles was already moribund when he first examined him – but would more properly have reported the death to the coroner. At the subsequent inquest, Grace would have not appeared in a good light. The jury would have been most interested to know why she did not call for medical attention sooner and why she left a sick man unattended, lying on the ground in a wood with virtually no shelter during a protracted rain-storm whilst she herself was snugly ensconced in his cottage? It is doubtful whether George Melbury's money could have bought her out of the criminal charges, which would have most probably ensued.

Grace, however, has the capacity not only to fascinate (TW 147), but also to be fascinated by, the alchemist surgeon who enkindles the woodland darkness with strange aurora; indeed, at their very first meeting we learn that 'an indescribable thrill passed through her' (TW 128). Fitzpiers uses both this mesmeric power and his professional influence over the family to entice Grace, who is his patient, into marriage. Rather than pursuing the impossible and unworkable divorce laws, Melbury would have done better to file a Statutory Declaration with the GCMER – Fitzpiers's desertion of his wife to elope with a widowed lady patient who then dies abroad from a mid-trimester miscarriage of Fitzpiers's baby, after having been shot by a former lover would have stirred the Council into action. After his erasure on these grounds, I suspect that the lawyers would have found a more effective way of applying the divorce laws (as Jude and Arabella did) and Grace ultimately would have been free to marry Giles. The newspaper publicity might have brought forward the timing of that Edwardian bulge in sexual cases.

Felice Charmond is every young doctor's nightmare: a wealthy but thoroughly bored, sexually frustrated former actress living alone in a mansion, desperate for male company. Newly married and overtaken by 'an indescribable oppressiveness' (*TW* 179) 'at being doomed to live with tradespeople' in a miserable woodland hamlet (*TW* 255), Fitzpiers is summoned in the darkness to the big house because the mistress has overturned her carriage. He arrives, anxious and over-equipped, as doctors tend to be in such circumstances. Instead of an injured patient, he is confronted by:

> a woman of full round figure reclining upon a couch ... a deep purple dressing gown formed an admirable foil to the peculiar rich brown of her hair-plaits; her left arm ... was nearly naked up to the shoulder ... between the fingers of her right hand she held a cigarette ...
>
> (*TW* 187)

Fitzpiers's quite natural question about 'where she was hurt' provokes the seductive and highly unnatural response: 'That's what I want you to tell me.' In his autobiography, *Adventures in Two Worlds*, A. J. Cronin describes a very similar real-life scenario:

> Miss Malcolm lay back and entwined her arms tenderly around my neck. 'Good Heavens!' I stammered. 'You mustn't do that.' Everything in my training revolted at the idea. Conduct unbecoming in a professional respect! A man might lose his diploma, be struck off the register for less. Panic seized me.
>
> (Cronin 1977: 98)

Fitzpiers, being a doctor in the Hardyan mould, sees the world through rather different eyes; he carefully and tenderly examines Felice's full, round exposed arms and promises to come back on the next day for more. Mrs Charmond is 'a patient ... in no great hurry to lose that title' (*TW* 192), but the doctor is equally or even more keen to fix up ongoing appointments to review her non-existent injuries. He becomes thoroughly and utterly infatuated with this woman – who is enjoying 'an indefinite idle impossible passion' (*TW* 200) – to the neglect of his wife, his practice and his professional reputation – nothing else matters to him at all. Everybody knows what he is up to and nobody can stop him. This is true infamous conduct in a professional respect.

It is unlikely that the GCMER would have made much of Fitzpiers's twin-pronged defence entreaties; firstly, to 'see how powerless is the human will against predestination' (*TW* 189), and, secondly, to acknowledge that he feels as if he 'belonged to a different species' from the majority of his patients (*TW* 179).

Lost in the woods on a cold March night, Grace and Felice bed down together in a night-long embrace, strongly reminiscent of the two Cythereas's experience. In the course of this encounter, which is really a kind of 'kiss and tell', Felice confirms that her relationship with Edred is sexual. Grace immediately warms to her – Hardy's psychology is subtle, superb and confusing, but eminently more plausible than Freud's.

The simple explanation is that Grace's sexual feelings are mainly lesbian – the only occasions on which the reader feels positive towards her are when she in the company of other women – here in the wood with Felice, in the extraordinary scene where Suke and Felice invade her bedroom in the night, and towards the end of the story where she tends Giles's grave in simple companionship with the admirable and much neglected Marty. The night-time invasion of her bedroom by Fitzpiers's desperate lovers is precipitated by Melbury who, like Timothy Tangs, uses violence against Fitzpiers rather than pursuing appropriate professional and legal restitution. Then Grace exclaims, 'Wives all, let's enter together!' (*TW* 405), she might well have added: 'Sign up here for the GCMER!'

Felice's subsequent elopement with Fitzpiers leads only to her untimely death. If Grace had been granted the opportunity to help Felice 'unlock her inner self', the pair might have lived happily together at Hintock House. But that is assuming too much of Grace. The reader is left to fantasise in this way because Hardy, that expert on a woman's soul, has, on this occasion, carefully created a vacuum around his leading female character. She appears to have no driving force – is passive, submissive and 'possessed by none of the feline wildness which it was her moral duty to experience' (*TW* 209).

Although Hardy may have seen Grace's inner insubstantiality, which causes her to question 'but life, what was it, and who was she?' (TW 261), as consistent with nihilist philosophy, she is thoroughly unconvincing as a true Hardyan heroine in the Tess mould, wishing to 'have my life unbe' (*CP* 177). Ninety percent mouse, and with Giles dead, she studies the marriage service in her prayer-book before being seduced (or mesmerised) back into the clutches of her temporarily repentant husband. Fitzpiers, being a consummate actor, loves a change of role – which in theory should make him good at the game of General Practice consultation. And by now. Melbury has learnt what the reader long suspected:

> that the woman walks and laughs somewhere at this very moment whose neck he'll be coling next year as he does hers tonight; and as he did Felice Charmond's last year; and Suke Damson's the year afore!
>
> (*TW* 414)

But as Old Timothy observed early in the novel:

> 'tis a strange thing about doctors that the worse they be the better they be. I mean if you hear anything of this sort about 'em, ten to one they can cure ye as nobody else can.
>
> (*TW* 30)

Afterwards

In the final analysis Fitzpiers and Lydgate could both be described as more 'sinned against as sinning' and if we accept Old Timothy's assessment – which has its appeal as solid folk wisdom – then the outlook for Fitzpiers may not be all bad. Remembering that it was mainly young men who appeared before the GCMER on sexual charges, there is a chance that Edred did not form part of that Edwardian bulge but settled into prosperous practice as a married man, thus emulating Lydgate – for Eliot does not leave her doctor's future open to speculation but tells us that although 'he had gained an excellent practice ... he always regarded himself as a failure' (Eliot 1987: 791). Hardy gives us three partial alternative endings in the last chapter of *The Woodlanders*, out of which Melbury's unhappy prediction appears the most probable. However, there is evidence outside this novel of Fitzpiers's ultimate fate.

Firstly, in the fate of Dr Grove, the father of Phyllis in 'The Melancholy Hussar of the German Legion'. Grove was a professional man:

> whose taste for lonely meditation over metaphysical questions had diminished his practice till it no longer paid him to keep it

going ... he had relinquished it ... and now ... he stayed in his garden the greater part of the day, growing more and more irritable with the lapse of time, and the increasing perception that he had wasted his life in the pursuit of illusions.

(WT 30)

Grove, undoubtedly, shares many characteristics with Fitzpiers. This story was published the year after *The Woodlanders* in *Wessex Tales*, so this could well be seen as an epitaph on Fitzpiers.

An alternative option is Dr Charlson in 'Fellow-Townsmen', who is always borrowing money, and can never make ends meet. His course is steadily downhill and by the end of the story, he has deteriorated into 'a shambling, stooping, unshaven man, who at first sight appeared like a professional tramp' (*WT* 109). Like both Lydgate and Fitzpiers, Charlson had started life as 'a man not without ability', yet one who could not prosper. He did not suffer fools gladly, 'he was not a coddle' and worse still, Hardy states that 'his look was quite erroneous' for 'he had a full-curved mouth and a bold black eye that made timid people nervous'; very different from 'the only proper features in a family doctor', namely 'the quiet eye, and the thin passionless lips' (*WT* 80).

Compare this view with Harold Massingham's description of Hardy in 1918 as looking like 'a country doctor, old style, with humour in the mouth and tragedy in the eyes' (Gibson, J. 1999: 122). Dr Charlson probably receives the fate he deserves for the story reveals him to be both incompetent and dishonest. As Lydgate was indebted to Bulstrode, so Charlson is indebted to Barnet, a well-to-do merchant, most unhappily married to a vulgar and demanding wife. Mrs Barnet appears to be drowned after a boat capsizes. Charlson attends to her, considers that he can do no more for her and greets Barnet somewhat mockingly with the words 'I sympathize with you in your bereavement' (*WT* 88). Barnet, however much he despises the woman, is not convinced that Charlson is right. From his dressing-room shelf he fetches a copy of 'Domestic Medicine', which had belonged to his mother who, like Hardy's maternal grandmother, 'had been an active practitioner of the healing art among her poorer neighbours' and peruses the section entitled 'Drowning': 'Exertions for the recovery of any person who has not been immersed for a longer period than half-an-hour should be continued for at least four hours ...' (*WT* 89).

Barnet carries out these instructions and his wife makes a full recovery. It seemed probable that Hardy lifted this quotation – the full version of which in the story runs to eight lines – verbatim from Graham; his book does not, however, have a separate section on drowning but deals with it collectively as part of 'suspended animation' (Graham 1864: 232), a topic which also includes hanging and poisoning by noxious gases. I was keen to identify the source of this citation – as likely to shed useful light on the origins of Hardy's medical information – it has, however, proved completely elusive, not appearing in any surviving *Domestic Medicine* volume. Most probably, Hardy wrote it himself. Unfortunately, Hardy's own copy of *Modern Domestic Medicine* is believed to have been lost in a warehouse fire in America.

Another doctor offers as a possible model for the older Fitzpiers. This is Dr St Cleeve, who, on first appearance, differs drastically from Fitzpiers in having being a lifelong bachelor and misogynist, but has, however:

> amassed a good professional fortune by long and extensive practice in the smoky, dreary manufacturing town in which he had lived and died. He was narrow, sarcastic and shrewd to unseemliness. That very shrewdness had enabled him, without much professional profundity, to establish his large and lucrative connexion, which lay almost entirely among a class which neither looked nor cared for drawing-room courtesies.
>
> (*TT* 112)

In short, he was a successful Middlemarch doctor. Very different from young Dr Lydgate and young Dr Fitzpiers, but financially successful – as Lydgate became – and practising in a Midland town, which is precisely where Dr and Mrs Fitzpiers are headed at the close of *The Woodlanders*.

5
Psychosomatic Illness and Death

Introduction

<u>No Crude</u> distinction of Mind & Body.

(Thomas Hardy 1876: *LN* 638)

The body and the mind are indivisible; that which affects one impinges on the other. Psyche & soma are indivisible but the presentation of illness may be placed more in one theatre than the other.

(Tessa Crowley 2004: *IPMJ* 13)

In the preceding chapters I have drawn attention to Hardy's consistent and continuous forefronting of psychological factors in the aetiology of illness. His fundamental belief, as a novelist and poet, in the primacy of the psyche over the soma becomes ever more apparent as one starts to analyse the causes of morbidity and mortality in Hardy's Wessex.

Hardy's approach to illness can be seen as a compound of a number of distinct and separate influences. During his formative years in rural Dorset, medicine was practised according to the traditional method, in which the patient's narrative formed the essence of the consultation. The doctor would spend a considerable amount of time delving into the patient's past history and then developing the story of the presenting illness; clinical examination would be perfunctory and diagnosis offered in the form of a description of symptoms (e.g., putrid malignant fever), linked to an assessment of the patient's constitution, according to Galenic principles. In addition, Hardy's childhood was steeped in the literature of Romanticism, which strongly promoted the unity of psyche and soma.

Over the 30-year period from 1868 onwards, during which Hardy wrote and published his major fiction, medicine underwent a metamorphosis – the healing art became a science based on the triad of clinical examination (using instruments such as the stethoscope pioneered by Laennec, see Plate 1), pathological anatomy and microbiology (both made possible by the widespread application of the microscope). Building on the foundations laid by Darwin, scientists theorised that not only all physical illness, but all human behaviour could be explained with exactitude in terms of the laws of patho-physiology. Huxley, thus, in 1874 proclaimed: 'all states of consciousness ... are immediately caused by molecular changes of brain substance' (Russett 1989: 111).

In lay terms this led to the popular view that man was no more than a machine, a 'conscious automaton' and that it was only a matter of time before doctors found a mechanical answer to all diseases. Most Victorian physicians, however, lacking effective therapeutic agents, interpreted these discoveries as a reinforcement of traditional attitudes on the unity of psyche and soma. Following the success of *Far From the Madding Crowd* (1875), Hardy was rapidly absorbed by London society, developing friendships with a number of eminent medical men, including Sir Clifford Allbutt whose blunt Yorkshire interpretation of Huxley's theories was that 'mind and body are one', and Sir Henry Maudsley who expanded on this topic in the 1873 Gulstonian lecture to the RCP:

> The metaphysician, may for the purposes of speculation, separate mind from body ... but the physician – who has to deal practically with the thoughts, feelings and conduct of men – must acknowledge the essential unity of body and mind.
>
> (Maudsley 1873: 109)

Robson Roose, another leading London physician, presented Hardy in 1891 with a copy of his *Nerve Prostration and Other Functional Disorders of Daily Life*, which is essentially a textbook of psychosomatic medicine. This accumulation of diverse influence is detectable in Hardy's approach to illness. I suspect, however, that Hardy's poetic intuition should be considered the primary motivating factor in his understanding of the intimate interweaving of psyche and soma in the human response to sickness and health. Flanders Dunbar, a twentieth-century New York physician, observed that 'psychosomatic case histories frequently sound like plagiarisms from best-selling novels', but realised that the explanation lay in the fact that: 'the writers of best sellers – the novelists and historians, who really know their business, know people as part of that business' (Dunbar 1947: 78).

Although Hardy's enduring popularity is based, like Shakespeare's, on the fact that he did notice such things, psychosomatic medicine as a specialty did not gain popular acceptance until the 1940s; highlighted in 1943 by the publication of two classic works on this subject – Dunbar's *Psychosomatic Diagnosis* and Weiss and English's *Psychosomatic Medicine* – but the medical roots of the subject extend back much further.

The Second World War brought psychosomatic medicine to the top of the medical agenda because of the large numbers of service personnel who were going sick with no obvious organic diagnosis – the more flamboyant shell shock of The Great War having been superseded in popular culture by subtler symptomatology. (Disease symptomatology being fundamentally a cultural dialogue between doctors and patients.) Weiss and English aver that:

> *Psychosomatic medicine* is a new term but it describes an approach to medicine as old as the art of healing itself. Physicians have always known that the *emotional life* had something to do with illness, but the structural concepts introduced by Virchow led to the separation of illness from the psyche of man and the consideration of disease as only a disorder of organs or cells.
>
> (Weiss and English 1943: 1)

Modern medicine was by this time moving a considerable distance away from the concepts of illness understood both by the eminent physicians of the late Victorian period and by Hardy in his fiction and poetry. However, because pharmacological options at this time were still so limited, the modern physician was therapeutically dependent on the psychological aspect of the doctor–patient relationship – to 'suggest' the patient into a cure. As Michael Balint, the pioneer proponent of the theory of this technique in the United Kingdom, stated on the first page of his first book: 'By far the most frequently used drug in General Practice is the doctor himself ...' (1964: 1).

Hardy, whose entire canon has been described as 'an investigation of the relationship between the mind and body' (Thurley 1975: 31), would have understood this well. Traditional medicine and folk healing, as instanced in his fiction, are based wholly on such psychosomatic concepts. Medicine, however, has moved on over the last half-century, into what Edward Shorter has aptly described as 'The Post-Modern Period', characterised by: 'an over-weaning confidence on the physician's part in medications which, for the first time in history, really do heal or ameliorate a vast range of disease conditions ...' (Bynum and Porter 1994: 792).

This pharmacological revolution, coupled with the rapid development of readily available surgical and micro-surgical techniques, plus the continued selection of medical students on the basis of academic achievement in science, and a political agenda founded on the collection of spurious statistical computer-generated measurements of well-being, effectively destroyed psychosomatic medicine by the early twenty-first century. The hallmark of postmodern medicine is reliance on the twin towers of laboratory investigation and potent therapeutic agents. The doctor no longer has time or inclination to take a detailed history or properly examine the patient. The patient, on the other hand, feels empowered by widespread media and Internet access to medical information. Ironically, the result of all this scientific wonder is a feeling of alienation on both sides of the doctor–patient relationship. Doctors are disillusioned by what they perceive as both patients' and politicians' unreasonable demands and, as Shorter has also observed: 'patients respond to what they perceive as the Physician's lack of interest with anger and withdrawal, ultimately with malpractice suits and recourse to alternative healers' (Brynum 792).

So the wheel has gone full circle and we are back to the eighteenth century, with a plethora of unlicensed and unregistered healers practising an extraordinary selection of 'complementary' therapies. These therapies often achieve significant success for the simple reason that the alternative practitioners take time and trouble with their patients. They listen to the patient and generate that feeling of confidence which is the most essential ingredient in achieving therapeutic change. What are these problems that patients take to alternative healers? They are the very psychosomatic problems that postmodern medicine prefers to ignore – because they don't respond to drugs, they take time to sort out and they are not the kind of symptoms that fit readily on to a computer database.

This has been a wide discursion from Thomas Hardy but it brings us right back to his understanding of illness, of the human psyche and its effect on the soma – a topic of crucial importance that he well understood but which postmodern medicine would rather forget. This is not the selfish plea by a member of a (somewhat dubious) profession trying to regain lost business, but a distress call to doctors in the twenty-first century on behalf of those patients who are suffering; and those being subjected to unnecessary, expensive and often dangerous procedures simply because an understanding of the psychosomatic is out of fashion. A more open-minded and sensitive approach:

> Wouldst heal the ills with quickest care
> Of me and all my kind.
>
> (*CP* 125).

I start by analysing causes of death in Hardy's fiction and poetry and comparing them with the Registrar General's national and local statistics for 1870, the year of publication of *Desperate Remedies* and also with the Registrar General's statistics for 1905, the year of publication of *The Dynasts Part II*. In addition, I compare them with statistics for causes of death in my own practice at Yalding, collected over a 24-year period – this longitudinal analysis giving some statistical validity to what is inevitably a small population. The current practice population is 5600; the mean over the 24-year period being 4190. It would have potentially been valuable to compare deaths in Hardy's fiction with those in the fiction of other late nineteenth-century novelists – but there appear to have been no such studies published.

Death in Hardy

> Death is the only grammatically correct full-stop.
>
> (Patten 1967: 27)

This is an analysis of the principal cause of death for 126 individuals whose deaths are described in his fiction and poetry (excluding *The*

Table 5.1 Principle causes of death in Hardy's fiction and poetry

Principle causes of death		
Psychological	Psychosomatic	41
	Mainly psychosomatic	25
	Suicide	20
		86
Violent	Murder/execution	17
	Manslaughter	6
	Accident	2
		25
'Natural'	Heart disease	2
	Obstetric	4
	Old Age	7
	Alcohol	2
		17
Total Deaths		*126*

Dynasts). This population comprises 78 men and 44 women. From this breakdown I have excluded still-births, neo-natal deaths and deaths in infancy and early childhood. These are the primary causes of death – thus John Durbeyfield's death is attributed to heart disease rather than alcohol, although drink and psychological factors were strong contributors to his demise.

The two deaths attributed solely to alcohol are those of Cartlett who died from Hepatic Cirrhosis and Sir George Drenghard who 'died of his convivialities' (*ND* 141). Where psychological factors are the principal reason why the person died, then the mechanism of death, which in seven further cases was heart disease, is not recorded as such above – examples being Mrs Yeobright, Uncle Benjy and Avice II.

Similarly, there are six further deaths principally due to alcohol but which appear under the actual cause of death; as in the case of the first husband who 'came home one midnight liquored deep' and was found dead in the morning, 'tightly laced in sheet and quilt and tick' – this I have attributed to manslaughter. The doctor here, like the unfortunate neighbours of Dr Shipman who recently appeared before the GMC, accepted the story offered at face value 'and thus 'twas shown to be a stroke' (*CP* 860). The total of eight alcohol-related deaths means that drink was a significant factor in just over 6 per cent of Hardyan deaths, which compares closely with my figure for my own practice of drink being a known major aetiological factor in 5 per cent of premature deaths.

Out of the total mortality of 126, if one excludes the 25 deaths due to murder, execution, manslaughter or accident (all of which are likely to have strongly psychosomatic aetiology) and the seven deaths due principally to old age, there remains a total of 94 deaths which can, by adding suicide and drink to the psychosomatic, be broken down as follows:

Deaths with a psychological cause	92.5 per cent
Deaths with a somatic cause	7.5 per cent
(Violent deaths	38 per cent)

In 19 (46 per cent) of the 41 cases where death is due to psychosomatic factors, Hardy offers no other explanation, no mechanism of death. Such cases include Elfride, Henchard, Lady Constantine, Lady Penelope and Edith Harman. At times, particularly in the Short Stories, Hardy does state that the cause of death was a broken heart – a diagnosis probably applicable to all this group – as for Lady Caroline:

> How long afterwards she lived I do not know with any exactness, but it was no great length of time. The anguish that is sharper than

a serpent's tooth soon wore her out ... and when the welcome end supervened ... a broken heart was the truest phrase in which to sum up its cause.

(*ND* 90)

Hardy's attitude to the satires of circumstance, to life and death, was in part innate, in part imbibed during his formative years, living in primitive conditions in rustic society on the edge of The Great Heath. The death of Farmer Broadford in *An Indiscretion* can be taken as the earliest death in Hardy's fiction – this tale being the rump of his first novel *The Poor Man & The Lady* written in 1867/8, abandoned unpublished, then resurrected for *The New Quarterly* magazine in 1878. Richard Broadford's death, true to what was later to become an established pattern, is purely psychosomatic, although ostensibly attributable to an accident.

There is much of the apparently autobiographical in this tale. Egbert, the *Poor Man*, lives with his amiable grandfather in the house in which the old man had been born and which 'was almost a part of himself; it had been built by his father's father' (*AI* 51). Squire Allenville, father of *The Lady*, wishes to demolish the house to enlarge his park. Egbert realises that moving his grandfather would 'affect his life to a degree out of all proportion'. The grandfather becomes so disturbed that 'he could scarcely eat or drink' (*AI* 52).

Hardy astutely observes that:

such was the responsiveness of the farmer's physical to his mental state that in the course of a week his usual health failed, and his gloominess of mind was followed by dimness of sight and giddiness.

(*AI* 60)

Whilst Egbert tries to negotiate with Geraldine Allenville, the old man's bent figure and facial expression clearly reveal 'a wish to sink under the earth, out of sight and out of trouble' (*AI* 62). On the following day, whilst Egbert is giving a geography lesson, a lad bursts in 'with the tidings that Farmer Broadford had fallen from a corn-stack' and 'hurt himself severely' (*AI* 63). Although Hardy tries to ameliorate the circumstances by stating that the ladder broke and quoting the surgeon's assessment that the external injuries 'were mere trifles', the grandfather is placed in his bed and on 'the next day the worn-out old farmer died' (*AI* 64–5). Dunbar investigated the nature of 'accidents' which she described as 'the major causer of human pain, suffering and disability' (Dunbar 1947: 97). She found that: 'only 10–20 per cent of these injuries, fatal or otherwise, are caused by really accidental accidents' (ibid.: 98).

The remaining 80–90 per cent can be attributed to the mental state or personality of the victim. There are resonances here of the 80–90 per cent of deaths in Hardy's fiction being attributable to the mental state or personality of the victim.

Richard Broadford's death I classify as psychosomatic. Geraldine Allenville's death from tubercular haemorrhage (effusion and fainting fit, in traditional medical terminology) falls into the category of deaths attributable to disease or accident, but where there are strong underlying psychological factors, for it is directly precipitated by the sudden abandonment of an unloved fiancé and elopement with her beloved Egbert. The pattern of deaths started in *The Poor Man and The Lady* continues in Hardy's immediately subsequent fiction. *Desperate Remedies*, being a mock-sensation novel, contains no less than seven deaths, the final one being Miss Aldclyffe's which is literally a rerun of Miss Allenville's (see Chapter 2). The first death is that of Cytherea Graye's father, who dramatically and absent-mindedly steps backward into the air off the scaffolding on top of a steeple, his mind being distracted by those same 'thoroughfares of stones' (*CP* 227).

The second death is that of Cytherea Aldclyffe's father; no cause is given and therefore it is excluded from my analysis. The next to go is Mrs Manston, murdered by fracture of her cervical spine, although the inquest comes to the erroneous conclusion that she had been incinerated. Next down – in a toll worthy of Agatha Christie – is Mr Brown who retreated to Cornwall to die of 'the rainy west winds they get there' (*DR* 313). The reputable railway porter, Joseph Chimney, cannot cope with the certain knowledge that Mrs Manston survived the fire and that Manston has therefore bigamously married Cytherea. He is the first of many Hardyan characters who would 'have my life unbe' (*CP* 177). Chimney 'got crazy-religious' with wishing he was dead so that 'he's almost out of his mind wi' wishen it so much' (*DR* 260). After counselling from Mr Raunham, the rector, Chimney decides that Wessex is too hot to hold him, and sets sail from Liverpool: 'intending to work his way to America, but on the passage he fell overboard and was drowned' (*DR* 337).

This is the first of 22 drownings in Hardy's fiction. As with the subsequent tragic death of Eustacia, Hardy gives no definitive answer as to whether this was an accident or suicide. But given Chimney's known pre-morbid state of mind, the latter seems the most likely verdict. This is the only death in *Desperate Remedies*, classified as purely psychosomatic in origin. The sixth and penultimate death is Manston's suicide by hanging in his cell at Casterbridge gaol (*DR* 388). In contrast, the three deaths in *A Pair of Blue Eyes* all belong in the purely psycho-

somatic category. Elfride's death is mysterious, unexpected and melodramatic, and perhaps also allegorical in terms of the death of

> the woman riding high above with bright hair flapping free –
> The woman whom I loved so, and who loyally loved me
>
> (*CP* 350)

to be brought about by Tom and Emma's impending marriage. Elfride,
psychologically destroyed by Knight's desertion, occurring on top of her
own abandonment of Stephen Smith, marries on the rebound 'my'
Lord Luxellian, 'not only handsome but a splendid courter'. Unfortunately: 'she fell off again afore they'd been married long, and my
lord took her abroad for a change of scene. They were coming home
... when she was taken very ill ... and died' (*BE* 379).

Although Hardy, in his 1912 revision of the text, expanded on the
'very ill' by adding the words 'with a miscarriage', this does not alter
the psychosomatic nature of her decline and demise. A similar fate has
already befallen Widow Jethway, who, bereft of both husband and son,
is described by Lord Luxellian as 'a desolate crazed woman' (*BE* 326).
She somehow manages to be crushed by the collapsing church tower as
she visits the tomb of her son; a grave, which incidentally, forms one
of Elfride's favourite courting places.

The girl, a true Hardyan heroine, is being a little more than perverse
in her liking for this spot, which naturally is a frequent haunt of the
distraught widow. Mrs Jethway, a governess before she married a
farmer, displays superior insight when she explains to Elfride that 'you
disturb my mind, and my mind is my whole life' (*BE* 271). Elfride
naïvely replies that she is sorry that Young Jethway died from consumption – to which the widow bitterly retorts:

> O, no, no! That word consumption covers a good deal. He died
> because you were his own well-agreed sweetheart, and then proved
> false – and it killed him. Yes, Miss Swancourt – you killed my son!
>
> (*BE* 271)

This accusation is not sufficient evidence to reclassify Jethway's death
as murder – it more safely remains psychosomatic. Elfride is one of
Hardy's heroines who, like Bathsheba, Avice II and Lady Penelope, has
a profound psychological need to work her way through a series
of suitors; it is the female equivalent of erotomania, which in the
Victorian world view was entirely a male condition. Hardy, of course,

knew better. The condition carries with it a form of dyslexia, or memory blindness, as an essential pathological prerequisite.

Although Elfride did not literally kill Jethway, the weight of accumulated scientific evidence entirely supports his mother's assertion. Pulmonary Tuberculosis was the biggest single cause of death in Britain in the nineteenth century, resulting in 50,000 deaths in England and Wales in 1870, with a further 20,000 deaths annually from non-pulmonary forms of the disease. As it was a chronic disease from which people slowly declined, there were at least four or five times this number of cases at any one time. Hardy had first-hand experience of this disease, for his Aunt Maria Sparks, mother of Tryphena, died slowly of phthisis in her crowded Piddle-side cottage in Puddletown. Dunbar questioning 'Why are the tissues of some well-nourished people so hospitable to TB?', found an answer in Sir William Osler's *The Principles and Practice of Medicine* (1891): 'The fate of the tubercular depends more on what they have in their heads than on what is in their chests', and then compared twentieth-century medical reactions to this truism with that of Hardy and colleagues:

> This idea remains difficult to those who think that a germ or a particular condition of body cells is the sum and substance of a disease. The Victorian novelists were more realistic than these sceptics ...
>
> (Dunbar 1947: 216)

Four further Hardyan characters succumb to consumption, two of whom are the unfortunate pair who fell under the spell of Sue Bridehead. Sue, for all her protestations of weakness is far too tough to fall prey to a mere bacterium, as in Heilman's incisive description of:

> La Belle Dame Sans Merci – of the three men who desire her, one finally has her as a shuddering sacrificial victim, and the other two die of 'consumption' which modern medical practice regards as predominantly of psychosomatic origin.
>
> (Draper 1991: 226)

It is wholly appropriate that Hardy's last novel *Jude* generated even more business for the fictional undertaker than did his first, *Desperate Remedies*, for Jude had a professional interest in gravestones just as his creator had a lifelong fascination with graveyards. It can also be said that *Jude* gave work to real undertakers, although *Jude* suicides never reached the epidemic proportions of those induced a century earlier by

Goethe's *Werther*. Of the 11 deaths in *Jude*, only the embittered Aunt Drusilla is allowed to die peacefully in her bed from old age. Jude's mother committed suicide by drowning in a pond, her estranged husband 'took with the shakings for death' and died, as a young man (*JO* 6–7); this may have been *delirium tremens* or stress-induced infection. Cartlett died from cirrhosis, Arabella's mother from dysentery in Australia; Jude and Sue's common ancestor was hung and gibbeted near the Brown House, Young Father Time murdered his siblings and then committed suicide by hanging; all of which history makes the deaths of the two consumptive young men seem quite a reasonable way out. Arabella's mother is one of a cluster of people who move away from Wessex in search of green pastures, but instead meet financial disaster and death from infection, induced by their broken spirits.

Another subgroup die shortly after getting married; medically, this makes perfect sense – getting married is a stressful process and as such will undoubtedly lower the body's resistance to infection as well as the subject's psychological resolve. In any case, it is now clearly understood in scientific terms that stress impairs the efficacy of the immune system, hence increasing the newly-wed's chance of developing infection. Whether the mechanism is regarded as wholly psychological or wholly physical, and in truth it represents a melding of the two, Hardy clearly understood the risks involved. There are also plentiful literary precedents for the concept of the marriage bed as deathbed, as exemplified by the successive deaths of Hindley's wife, Catherine and Young Linton in *Wuthering Heights*.

Marriage thus puts an end to Elfride (as above), to Ethelberta's first husband on their honeymoon (a chill), to Sweatley (fire and alcohol), Drenghard (alcohol), Mr Pine-Avon and Charles de la Feste (drowning). Bellston also drowns, on the eve of his wife's intended bigamous marriage to Nicholas; his body is not found for 17 years and when it is, it appears as a complete skeleton: 'extended on the grass, not a finger or toe-bone missing, so neatly had the aquatic operators done their work' (*CM* 81).

Death statistics

> Twenty years have gone with their livers and diers.
>
> (*CP* 490)

I have constructed these comparative death statistics (see Table 5.2) in an endeavour to place Hardy's fictional 'livers and diers' in overall context. Hardy possessed an exceptional understanding of the circumstances

Table 5.2 Overall annual death rates per 1000 of population

	All deaths	Aged 0–5 years
1870 (England & Wales)	22.9	94
1870 (Dorchester)	21.0	
1870 (Maidstone)	23.7	
1905 (England and Wales)	15.2	37
1905 ('Urban')	16.6	
1905 ('Rural')	13.2	
1905 (Kent)	13.1	
1905 (Dorset)	14.1	
1980–2004 (Yalding)	9.1	0.003

which commonly made people ill and commonly made them die. It was to his advantage that he had no medical training and was not trying to present these everyday events from a medically orthodox standpoint; his strength, therefore, to be unhandicapped by all the professional impedimenta, which a doctor acquires during his undergraduate training and postgraduate career.

Hardy was ever aware that 'a tale had to be worth the telling' and hence the experience of illness and death in his fiction is never going to be a duplicate of that in the real world. Inevitably there will be a surplus of violent, dramatic and horrifying happenings, but this does not invalidate the medical interpretation of the data thus provided.

The first and most striking feature of these figures is the dramatic reduction in the mortality rate for the first five years of life; in the year of the publication of *Desperate Remedies*, 41.1 per cent of all deaths occurred in children under the age of five. By 1905 when Hardy was 65 years old, this figure had fallen to 14.3 per cent of all deaths in Dorset and 19 per cent in Kent. In my practice in Yalding, the mean under-five mortality rate for the last 24 years has been 0.32 per cent; about average for a semi-rural practice with a fairly balanced demography. Our overall death rate is above average because the very elderly in residential homes form over 1.25 per cent of the practice population; these constitute an imported, mainly female population who come into the practice to die. If they are excluded from the statistics, our annual average mortality rate falls to 7.4 deaths per 1000. Hardy understood this problem, for as Egbert comments, when his grandfather is threatened with eviction: 'The transplanting of old people is like the transplanting of old trees; a twelvemonth sees them wither and die away' (*AI* 52).

I have already drawn attention to the high maternal mortality rate in Hardy's Wessex, which can be seen as a prime example of the need 'to intensify the expression of things' (*EL* 231–2). A total of 11 obstetric deaths occur, making obstetric causes responsible for 9 per cent of overall deaths and exactly 25 per cent of female mortality. The Registrar-General's statistics reveal that maternal mortality was responsible for 0.95 per cent of all deaths in 1870 and 0.84 per cent in 1905. The actual reduction in maternal death rate was significantly greater than it appears from these figures, which are skewed by the 60 per cent reduction in infant mortality during this time. When Joseph Poorgrass gives Bathsheba the sad news that Fanny Robin is 'dead in the union', his mistress enquires about the cause of death. Joseph does not know but speculates that it was due to 'general neshness of constitution' (*FM* 282). Whilst it is easy to dismiss this as rustic prattle, it is not far removed from the doctor's explanation of Geraldine's death (fainting fit and effusion) or the diagnosis given in 1914 by Dr Gowring in the early stages of Mary Hardy's terminal illness (extreme weakness of the stomach).

Indeed, the most striking difference between the Annual Reports of the Registrar-General for 1870 and 1905 is in the terminology used. In 1870 cause of death was generally expressed in terms that belonged to the traditional system of medicine; deaths being classified into five classes, each class being subdivided into orders – in a system which appears to be based on the Linnaean system of biological Phyla. The five classes were known as Zymotic, Constitutional, Local, Developmental and Violent Deaths. Zymotic, for example, then subdivided into four orders, namely miasmatic, enthetic, dietic and parasitic. Many of the causes of death listed appear to be light-years away from the twenty-first century, including 'mortification', 'glanders', 'thrush', 'atrophy and debility' and 'Phlegmon' – the latter two conditions being responsible for the deaths of 14,000 young boys in 1870. I suspect, however, that with adult deaths the nomenclature has changed more than the factors, physical or psychological, which kill people. By way of contrast, the *68th Report from the Registrar-General for 1905* appears securely anchored in the world of modern medicine with diseases being classified in three categories – General Diseases, Diseases of Particular Organs and Mortality in Infants and Young Children. A host of modern diagnostic categories now make their appearance, including diseases such as Diabetes Mellitus and Rheumatoid Arthritis and conditions such as Industrial Poisoning (79 deaths) and 'Opium, Morphia-habit' (13 deaths). Cancer, which was an uncommon diagnosis in 1870, had become a prominent and important cause of death by 1905 (see Table 5.3). It is doubtful whether this dramatic

Table 5.3   Proportion of deaths due to malignant disease

	Male	Female
1870	1.1%	2.7%
Hardy's Fiction	nil	nil
1905	22%	34%
Ca Breast 1905		5.7%
Ca Uterus 1905		7.8%
Ca Stomach 1905	4.8%	4.8%
Ca Liver 1905	2.9%	4.6%
Yalding 1980–2004		
(Patients aet < 70 years)		
Overall	26.3%	58.7%
Ca Bronchus	8%	12%
Ca Breast		12%
Ca Cervix		5.5%
Ca Ovary		5.5%
Ca Prostate	2.6%	
Cardiovascular Disease	47%	15%
(1980/6)	57%	22%
(1999–04)	42%	17%

change reflected a true increase in the prevalence of this type of disease.

It is more likely a reflection of change in medical practice – doctors were now fully examining their patients and hence were likely to detect visible or palpable tumours; in addition, advances in histopathology allowed diagnoses to be made routinely from tissue samples; a technique considered experimental only a generation before. A further factor to be born in mind is that the 60 per cent reduction in infant mortality between the two periods causes a significant increase in the overall proportion of deaths occurring in adult life and hence from diseases of maturity, such as cancer. The report for 1905 classifies 48 different types of cancer but there is no mention at all of carcinoma of the lung, which was to prove the leading cause of death from malignant disease in the twentieth century.

I analysed only those deaths in Yalding that might be considered premature, which I defined as occurring before the seventieth birthday. This equates with deaths in Hardy's time occurring before the age of 60; after the sixtieth birthday in the late nineteenth century, a person was considered old and thus eligible to die from old age. The figures above demonstrate a statistically significant fall in the number of men (and women) dying prematurely from vascular disease over the 24-year period – the result of improved diagnostic techniques and treatment. This reduction in mortality has unfortunately been counterbalanced over the last 12 years by an increase in premature deaths from hospital-acquired infections. There were no deaths from this cause prior to 1993. Between 1993 and 1998, 2.8 per cent of premature deaths in the practice were due to this cause – basically MRSA. The same figure for the most recent six-year period (1999–2004) stands at 6 per cent.

If 92.5 per cent of premature deaths in Wessex can be demonstrated as being primarily caused by psychosomatic factors, how does this compare with the real world? The Registrar-General is no help apart from giving figures for suicide, accidents and murder. I hoped that a close analysis of deaths in my practice might reveal something similar, many of these patients have been known personally to me over a considerable time span. As I travel around the practice, I am conscious that:

> So walked the dead and I together
> The quick among ...
>
> (*CP* 593)

Although I can recall several sad stories of linked deaths, it was immediately apparent that the overwhelming majority of premature deaths in the practice were due to nothing romantic or melodramatic, but were merely the demise of scores of prematurely aged people, frequently associated with preventable factors. In other words, nearly all the vascular disease and much of the cancer was smoking related; 5 per cent of deaths were directly alcohol related and a near similar proportion associated with gross obesity. From a psychosomatic viewpoint, these are different forms of addictive behaviour so it could be convincingly argued that most of these deaths can be attributed to psychosomatic factors. The incidence of AIDS-related mortality was 2 per cent of male deaths – none occurring in the last decade, since effective pharmacological agents have become available.

To confirm my belief in the extent of the psychosomatic workload, I analysed 152 consecutive surgery consultations (see Table 5.4) and found that the workload split almost evenly three ways between physical illness, psychological or psychiatric problems, and a third group of problems which really had nothing to do with illness at all. This last group would have been wholly alien to doctors in 1870. These patients attend for a variety of reasons – firstly, because the service is free and doctors, on

Table 5.4   Reasons for attending the family doctor, autumn 2004

Significant physical illness	7.0%
Minor physical illness	28.0%
	35.0%
Purely psychosomatic/psychiatric	22.0%
Psychosomatic with minor physical problem	10.5%
	32.5%
Iatrogenic/medicalised normality/administrative	32.5%

the whole, are friendly and willing to listen; secondly, because the NHS is top-heavy with administrators who need to invent spurious reasons for doctor–patient contacts; and thirdly, because the profession has been, and still is, heavily into empire-building, medicalising areas which have really nothing to do with sickness or health. The more I reflect on it, the more it appears that this category also falls under the psychosomatic umbrella; meaning that two-thirds of surgery attendances are for psychosomatic problems.

I must also have been feeling kindly disposed to those with minor physical illness when I recorded these figures. The majority of such consultations involve young children, brought by anxious parents – the child being the presentation of parental woe. The adults in this group are mainly 'the worried well' with viral illnesses. Taking this group to also be mainly psychosomatic reduces the physical illness figure to 7 per cent and increases the psychosomatic to 93 per cent – an almost perfect match with the figure of 92.5 per cent for psychosomatic causes of death in Hardy.

Hardy's friend, Clifford Allbutt carried out a similar exercise to assess the extent of psychosomatic illness in patients consulting him at his rooms in Park Square, Leeds. He presented his results to the RCP as Gulstonian Lecturer for 1884, in a series entitled *Visceral Neuroses*:

> On adding up the cases in my chamber note-book for 1883, I find that under the three heads of neuralgia, neurosis and neurasthenia – one hundred and fifty-one new cases were entered in that one year. What a tale of misery does this limited experience of mine indicate. This amongst the vigorous northern people in the West Riding ...
>
> (Allbuttt 1884: 20)

In this brilliant series of lectures, Sir Clifford makes a succession of impassioned pleas to his audience of eminent doctors. Firstly, he draws their attention to the high frequency of psychosomatic disease presentation. Secondly, he urges them to treat these patients seriously and to work together with the patient to overcome the illness, pre-empting Balint by 70 years. He then warns his colleagues against a plethora of unscrupulous practitioners, ready poised to prey upon such patients. He complains that in London: 'A smooth-tongued and audacious gentleman needs but six months' practice in the manipulation of some endoscope or other to become a dexterous specialist and a thriving tradesman' (ibid.: v–vi).

This brings to mind the image of Florence Hardy, hawking her symptoms of minor illness around a series of plush London consulting rooms, in the hope of finding a cure for her perpetual unhappiness. Allbutt closes his first lecture with a superb description of the neurotic patient. But it is not just a description; it is also a prescription, a rousing battle-cry to physicians to treat these patients seriously and to make them well:

> Such persons complain of globus, of palpitation which is never perceived by the stethoscope, of sleeplessness of which the nurse has no record, of dyspepsia which does not lessen the labours of the cook, of pains which never flush the cheek ... and if such persons have anaesthesia, unreal epilepsy, unreal syncope, unreal palsy – then set such a person down as hysterical but forget not, nevertheless, to cure her mind and body.
>
> (Allbutt 1884: 21–2)

This is a lecture of Shakespearean stature, delivered by the Yorkshire all-rounder: 120 years later, patients with these exact symptoms fill GP's waiting rooms and clog up Hospital Outpatient Departments seeking an explanation in physical terms for what is simply the somatic presentation of psychological distress. However radically the nomenclature on death certificates may have changed during that time, the causes of human distress remain unaltered.

The Great Outdoors

> The body is the chief source of idiom and metaphor for the expression of distress.
>
> (Kleinman 1985: 501)

A number of Hardy's characters express their distress with the world by wandering out of doors – often onto The Great Heath – and exposing themselves to the elements in the hope that they may then or there lay down and die. I examine five such case histories, starting with Hardy's most detailed study – the case of Mrs Yeobright.

'The burn of August'
(*CP* 336)

Hardy informs us of the exact date of Mrs Yeobright's last walk – Thursday 31 August. I consider that Carl Weber is, here, correct in his opinion that the action of *The Return of The Native*, which lasts one year and one day, took place in 1842–3. Mrs Yeobright was a woman in what, at that date, would be regarded as the later stages of middle-life – around 50 years old and almost certainly post-menopausal, for the menopause came earlier just as the menarche came later in those far-off times. She has been presented as a powerful character, a woman who stood up in church to object to the banns of her niece's marriage; but now has become a controlling woman who has lost anything to control. Her husband died, her niece married, away from home and against her wishes, her son has now done the same; she has just had a blazing row 'heat for heat' with her daughter-in-law whom she berates with the manipulative cut: 'I am only a poor woman who has lost her son' (*RN* 246). She withdraws to Bloomsend utterly defeated.

In this careworn depressed mood, she acquiesces to Venn's entreaties that she should visit Clym. She can see no future role for herself and lets the reddleman know that she is actively contemplating the grave: 'my life may be cut short and I should wish to die in peace' (*RN* 275). Throughout the narrative of her journey, Hardy keeps the reader in touch with two contradictory voices within the consciousness of this depressed woman. There is a positive voice, which seeks reconciliation with Clym and Eustacia and is bearing china as a gift; balancing this is a negative voice, which wishes the expedition to fail and her life to be over. This is the doppelgänger within us all, which comes to the fore in times of stress or distress. Her positive side had hoped 'to be well advanced in her walk before the heat of the day was at its highest' (*RN* 277). But the depressive negative voice held her back, making her set out too late in the day, without proper preparation and did not sanction turning around when she realised her mistake. In this low mood she plods slowly across an inferno, a hell on earth, branded by the torrid sun and populated by innumerable obscene creatures:

> independent worlds of ephemerons were passing their time in mad carousal, some in the air, some on the hot ground ... amid the

vaporous mud the maggoty shapes ... could be seen, heaving and wallowing with enjoyment.

(*RN* 278)

Mrs Yeobright sits down to rest and watch their happiness with 'the air around her pulsating silently' – in parallel with her sinking heart (cardio-vascular) – 'and oppressing the earth with lassitude' – in parallel with her sinking heart (psychological). A tremendous amount of transference is happening here. 'Her son appeared a mere parasite of the heath' – he too is a happy ephemeron 'heaving and wallowing with enjoyment'. It is not just all happiness but it is, particularly, sexual happiness that is denied Mrs Yeobright, as she 'throbbingly followed' her son to his home where Eustacia awaits his embrace. He's getting it, Eustacia's getting it, Thomasin's getting it, the insects are copulating madly but no one is offering anything – even a light touch – to this desperately over-heated perimenopausal woman, who is burning up inside.

Hardy's first *Literary Notebook*, which he compiled immediately before writing *The Return of the Native,* contains a number of references taken from the Reverend J. G. Wood's *Insects At Home* (1872). The word 'ephemeron' is used by Wood to describe the mayfly which has only 'one business, namely, to seek a mate, and provide a new generation' and die (Wood 1872: 268). What a credo for survival for Mrs Yeobright on this blasted heath where *Genesis* melds into *The Origin of Species*! The Reverend Wood also writes with that tremendous enthusiasm, typical of the Victorian amateur naturalist, about social insects, especially ants and in detail on the 'shining-tail' or glow-worm (ibid.: 135). Wood also, like Hardy, repeatedly draws attention to close parallels between insect life and the human world:

> Among the insects, too, we find not only instinct, but reason. We find that in the lesser creatures the passions and emotions of humanity have their counterparts. Love, for example, developes (sic) itself in many ways ...
>
> (Wood 1872: 2)

As Mrs Yeobright: follows her son towards his cottage she feels 'distressingly agitated, weary and unwell'; she sits down again at a 'singularly battered, rude and wild' place where 'the trees kept up a perpetual moan' – she has become the landscape or rather it has become an exaggerated expression of her innermost agonies. This is hell on earth. 'The place was called the Devil's Bellows' – Hardy is, quite appropriately, laying it on with a trowel. She approaches the gate – in the hot garden the satiated pussy sleeps in the sun and amongst the fallen apples wasps roll drunk or 'creep about the little caves in each fruit' which they had eaten out 'before being stupefied by its sweetness' (*RN* 280–1). All in this Eden is orgasmic, ecstatic and pulsating. She approaches the door weary, hot, sad, but sanguine that all her frustrations are about to be released – and nothing happens.

She sees a witch's face at the window and her insect son's tool on the ground. Nothing happens. This hell is the postmodern hell of Godot. She scuttles away like an insect to bury herself on the heath. Up until this moment the two voices have been balanced in her psyche, but now the negative force has assumed absolute control. She is suicidal. Her brain wishes to shut her body down. She speaks 'as one in a mesmeric sleep' – the depressive voice has induced a self-hypnosis. Little Johnny astutely asks: 'Have you seen a ooser?' (*RN* 288). She has; and she cannot cope with the subjoined 'beautiful body' without a heart inside. Clym, to whom she gave birth in an orgasm of suffering, has given his heart to this ooser with a beautiful body – her power is spent, her own heart must fail, she must die.

All alternative options are obliterated – she could have returned to the door, she could have called at the neighbour's house, she could have sent Johnny for help. The negative voice overrules all: 'Because I have a burden which is more than I can bear ... I hope to have a long, long sleep – very long' (*RN* 289). For this 'broken-hearted woman cast off by her son', the rest is mechanics – her exertions have 'well-nigh prostrated her' but she continues 'to creep along in short stages with long breaks between'. The western sun beats down upon her pallid and dyspnoeic body 'like some merciless incendiary, brand in hand, waiting to consume her' (*RN* 290). She is excluded from the garden – and it is a spurious Eden.

The ancient heath, rather, is subject to Darwinian laws: firstly, the survival of the fittest. Mrs Yeobright knows that she is not fit and that she cannot survive. Secondly, the adaptation of species: Mrs Yeobright senses that she belongs to a species that is poorly adapted; all around her is abundant evidence of the Insecta, the most successful and adaptable order of animals on the planet. She looks down upon 'an ant thoroughfare, which had been in progress for years at the same spot'; she hears 'the intermittent husky notes of the male grasshoppers' which show 'that the insect world was busy in all the fulness of life' (*RN* 290–1). In the sky above, a solitary heron flies away from her towards the sun. At this moment, like the blinded Pozzo '(s)he's all humanity' (Beckett 1965: 83). Like Lear on the heath, like Michael Henchard on the heath, she is broken down by filial ingratitude, which finds expression in the oppressive elements: for Lear the raging tempest, for Mrs Yeobright the raging heat.

Hardy's text is a masterful tapestry of interwoven themes as rich as the life of the heath itself. For now her only begotten son sets off through a cloud of 'white miller-moths' to visit his mother. He pauses to inhale 'a soft perfume' which 'wafted across his path' (*RN* 294) and discovers a female form comatose and moaning, collapsed on 'a bank where the wild thyme blows' (Shakespeare 1595: II.i.249). In heroic fashion he attempts to carry his moribund mother home across the darkened heath but eventually 'lays her down in a clod-built hut' and 'runs with all his might for help'. Once brandy is administered,'she became sufficiently conscious to signify that something was wrong with her foot' (*RN* 296). O Clym, the serpent did not just beguile me – it bit me also. In pursuit of a traditional remedy, Sam appears with three adders hanging from a stick – two dead and one living in a pastiche of the crucifixion. The Darwinian message is further rubbed home in a spine-chilling exchange of glances between the indignant but beautiful adder and the angry depressed Mrs Yeobright – they are both about to die but it is the adder who is triumphant. The doctor examines his patient and considers that she is dying from being overpowered by exhaustion on top of having a heart that 'was previously affected' (*RN* 305). The psyche has destroyed the soma; she is heartbroken mentally and physically. Hardy's doctor, being a local man, does not consider the adder bite to be particularly significant – the heath abounds with vipers in the summer. Hardy knew better than the medical textbook which he kept on his shelves, for Graham considers 'adder stings' to be frequently fatal (Graham 1864: 252). This is contrary to modern medical opinion which regards adder bites as merely a nuisance; but still in practice recommends a trip to hospital for anti-venom and observation. Adder bites can cause circulatory collapse and haemorrhage so the adder venom could have been the cause of Mrs Yeobright's death: but how did she come to be bitten? Because she lay down on the heath and hoped to die. To try to separate the soma from the psyche can be a perilous exercise.

Swithin St Cleeve is a flaxen haired Adonis, a strikingly beautiful young man in his late teens. He is, however, wholly unaware of these natural gifts, being obsessionally involved in the study of astronomy. He is pursued by an attractive, sexually desiring and frustrated older woman, Lady Constantine, whose husband has bigamously married an African princess and turned native on the dark continent, before choosing to blow his brains out with a revolver. Lady Constantine's great advantage is that, prior to being widowed, she has the money to fund Swithin's obsession.

Swithin, like Mrs Yeobright, lay down on the heath hoping to die. The story is somewhat disjointed in the novel because it is narrated in retrospect by Lady Constantine. Swithin has been overworking – up all night with his equatorial. Quite arbitrarily, Lady Constantine has already expressed the fear 'what should I do if my Astronomer Royal were to die?' (*TT* 59). The thought of imminent death is never far from the lips of many of Hardy's characters so, in context, this is not such an unusual question. Swithin, whose father died prematurely in a thunderstorm, becomes inordinately depressed on finding that he has been pre-empted by an American in his first great astronomical discovery. 'In a wild wish for annihilation', he flings himself down upon a patch of heather, 'and in this humid bed remained motionless' (*TT* 63). Ultimately he falls asleep, allowing the March rain to pelt him mercilessly until his clothing and hair are completely saturated.

On waking, he has all the symptoms of incipient pneumonia. Lady Constantine, when she eventually finds out what has happened, is extremely distressed by what she quite rightly describes as his suicide attempt. With Swithin, her kisses are no more efficacious than the doctor's potions. The doctor abandons hope as the young man lingers on the verge of extinction until suddenly the servant, 'Hannah tells the dying Swithin about a new comet' (*TT* 66). The pneumonic crisis, normally expected on the seventh day of the infection, occurs a week in arrears:

> The strenuous wish to live and behold the new phenomenon, supplanting the utter weariness of existence that he had heretofore experienced, lent him a new vitality. The crisis passed; there was a turn for the better; and after that he rapidly mended. The comet had in all probability saved his life.
>
> (*TT* 67)

Swithin suffers a psychosomatic near-miss; his para-suicide highlights the fact that Lady Constantine has no place in his inner being. To the young man she is a useful outlet for bodily functions – no more.

When Michael Henchard is first made bankrupt and has lost the will to live, he stands 'about the meads in damp weather' (*MC* 301). This piece of self-destructive behaviour leads to a secondary gain. The exposure to the cold and damp causes him to 'catch cold' and be confined to his room. Because he is ill, Elizabeth-Jane insists that she is allowed to care for him; the consequence of this attention is his rehabilitation into the town and the world of work, albeit it in a humble capacity. As Groddeck states: 'all diseases have a psychological function ... illness has a purpose, it has to resolve the conflict, to repress it ...' (Webster 1995: 545).

Ultimately, when Henchard's world has again come unstuck and he believes himself to be permanently rejected by Elizabeth-Jane, he wholly loses the will to live and wambles off into the Heath to die. In a passage with again strong resonances from *King Lear* Abel Whittle, the fool, finds him shelter in a hovel and makes him comfortable. But, as Whittle explains to Elizabeth-Jane: 'he didn't gain strength, for you see, ma'am, he couldn't eat – no, no appetite at all – and he got weaker: and today he died' (*MC* 409).

Giles Winterbourne, when he loses his home and his Grace, retreats similarly into the woodland, where his depressed mental state allows him to contract Typhoid. When Grace displaces him from One Chimney Hut, he lies down under a hurdle where, like Swithin, he becomes saturated by the rain, develops pneumonia and dies. Grace Melbury herself develops a psychosomatic illness after spending a night in the wood 'clasped closely' to Felice Charmond. The two young women breathed and heaved against each other 'while the funereal trees rocked, and chanted dirges unceasingly' (*TW* 240). In this lesbian variant of *A Midsummer Night's Dream*, the two women go into the wood estranged and emerge in the morning 'kissing each other' (*TW* 243). Grace has indeed returned to the Court changed – but changed and unwell: 'her illness being a feverish intermittent nervousness which had more to do with mind than body ...' (*TW* 259).

There is some justification for this state of ill-health: she does not love her absentee General Practitioner husband and knows that he has been having affairs with at least two of his patients, one of them Felice, to whom Grace became quite passionately attached during the night in the wood. Her well-intentioned buffoon of a father has meanwhile gone to London to try to obtain a quick divorce for her so that she can marry the second man of his choice. She has been given no chance to adapt psychologically to a series of quite major traumas or to reflect on her sexual orientation. Old Jones, her experienced family doctor, understood that what this 'elastic-nerved daughter of the woods' required was a reduction in levels of stress; when this remedy was applied in the form of a letter bearing good news: 'It soothed her perturbed spirit better than all the opiates in the pharmacopoeia. She slept unbrokenly a whole night and a day' (*TW* 278). A psychosomatic problem resolved – for the moment, at least.

As a sculptor, Jocelyn Pierston is a man supremely sensitive to the subtleties of the human form. As he prepares to court a woman 40 years his junior, he contemplates his face in this glass and becomes acutely conscious of the destructive effect which time allows the psyche to inflict upon the soma:

> it was not the blank page it had once been. He knew the origin of that line in his forehead ... He remembered the coming of this pale wiry hair ... brought by the illness ... when he had wished each night that he might never wake again. This wrinkled corner, that drawn bit of skin ... resulted from those months of despondency when all seemed going against his art, his strength, his happiness ...
> (*WB* 129–30, 300)

This passage is a prose precursor of the final poem in Hardy's first volume *Wessex Poems*, in the first stanza of which the poet prays for relief from emotional sensitivity:

> I look into my glass,
> And view my wasting skin,
> And say, 'Would God it came to pass
> My heart had shrunk as thin!'
> (*CP* 81)

Whilst there is no evidence that this ever happened to Hardy, who became hopelessly infatuated, as an octogenarian, with the beautiful Gertrude Bugler, this request was granted to Pierston after a protracted 'malignant fever' which started much like the illnesses of Mrs Yeobright and Giles Winterbourne. After Pierston's engagement to Avice III is abruptly terminated by her elopement with her young lover, Jocelyn decides that he has 'lived a day too long' and would rather be dead. In this negative frame of mind he attends the funeral of Avice II, held in 'the bleakest churchyard in Wessex': 'on one of those drenching afternoons of the autumn when the raw rain flies level as the missiles of the ancient inhabitants across the beaked promontory' (*WB* 328).

This exposure 'telling upon a distracted mental & bodily condition' (*WB* 329) causes him to develop a severe pneumonia on his return to London. His condition remains critical for weeks. As he eventually slowly recovers, he becomes 'conscious of a singular change within himself' (*WB* 330). The nature of this change slowly dawns upon him – he has lost his artistic sensitivity: 'his appreciativeness was capable of exercising itself only on utilitarian matters ...' (*WB* 330).

He subsequently discovers that 'I can no longer love' (*WB* 332). Pierston has suffered a somewhat complex sequence of illness. His depressed mental state and exposure to cold and wet precipitated the pneumonia, but then the physical illness damaged his mind, destroying his artistic sensibility. If this is so, then probably he suffered a localised CVA whilst seriously ill with the pneumonia. This has not caused any apparent physical sequelae, but just shut down that part of his brain which was of great benefit to him in giving him the sensitivity to become a successful sculptor; but which on the other hand caused him so much grief in his personal relationships as he pursued the elusive Well-Beloved. An alternative, and equally plausible, explanation is that his loss of artistic sensibility is entirely psychosomatic or, in other words, hysterical. The secondary gains are substantial – he is no longer capable of work and he is no longer doomed to pursue the Caro family. As Avice has now married, there is a substantial chance that Avice IV will appear over the horizon soon. The age gap would be similar to that between Hardy and Gertrude Bugler, that elusive daughter of Tess. For Pierston, therefore, the soma destroys the psyche after the psyche has nearly destroyed the soma.

Bewitchment

> The emerging fields of neurology, psychiatry and psychology were richly developing in the second half of the nineteenth century; they also sought to articulate modes of interaction between body and mind that figure so prominently in Victorian literature.
>
> (Vettros 14)

Farmer Lodge is 'a yeoman in the prime of life', in other words about 40 years old; a man who thinks 'so much of personal appearance' (*WT* 54). He is: 'cleanly shaven like an actor, his face being toned to that bluish-vermilion hue which so often graces a thriving farmers features ...' (*WT* 47).

He has a powerful mare and drives 'a handsome new gig'; he brings home as bride a 19-year-old girl, a lovely young woman with a face 'soft and evanescent, like the light under a heap of rose-petals' (*WT* 47). What fine prospects for the happy couple! But oh, 'the worm in th' bud!', for Farmer Lodge is a man with a past; a past of deep unresolved conflicts, of problems which no amount of ready cash or cans of bright smart paint will gloss over. He has already destroyed one woman, a 'thin fading' milkmaid of 30 who lives a twilight half-life on the edge of the Heath.

He is now on the verge of destroying himself, his young bride and his 12-year-old unacknowledged son. Lodge is a man who lives by outward appearances, a respectable and successful dairy farmer who has no use for the inner life. This story is a story of the triumph of the psyche over the soma. Lodge's cruelty to the beautiful young 17-year-old Rhoda, whom he impregnated, then abandoned, has crippled her inside. The accumulated hurt and anger has built up within her to the point where it can no longer be suppressed; it has to spread outwards to touch those around her and this it does – with a psychological intensity over which Rhoda has no control.

According to Hardy this story is based on real events that occurred in the first quarter of the nineteenth-century; the details being given to him by an 'aged friend who knew "Rhoda Brook" in person' (*WT* xxi). Although in the story, the visitation occurs at night whilst Rhoda is fast asleep and therefore can be classed as a dream, in reality the visitation occurred on a hot summer afternoon as Rhoda relaxed on her bed 'before falling asleep' (*WT* 50); the 'visitation' was therefore what is medically termed a hypnagogic phenomenon. As described in detail in that other tale of a wronged milkmaid, *Tess*, it was usual for milkmaids who rose before dawn to take a siesta on summer afternoons. In *Tess* Hardy wrote that 'the world is only a psychological phenomenon, and what they seemed they were' (*TD* 88), which is a helpful maxim to keep in mind when trying to understand *The Withered Arm*.

In waking reverie, Rhoda feels and sees the 'spectre' of Gertrude Lodge 'with features shockingly distorted and wrinkled' sitting on her chest, compressing her more and more, and thrusting forward her left hand, emblazoned with glittering wedding ring. Rhoda struggles with the 'incubus', which retreats to the foot of the bed, only to return and compress her once again. In a desperate effort Rhoda grasps the spectre by the 'obtrusive left arm' and whirls it to the ground. Rhoda starts up 'with a low cry'; Gertrude is there no more, but she can still 'feel her antagonist's arm within her grasp' (*WT* 50). Hypnagogic (at sleep onset) or hypnopompic (at sleep offset) hallucinations occur characteristically as part of the syndrome of Narcolepsy, first described medically in 1877:

Hallucinations are somesthetic, auditory or sometimes visual. The impression of a human presence in the room is frequent. Hypnagogic hallucinations are sometimes so frightening that the subject keeps a weapon on the bedside table or a dog in the room for reassurance.

(Gelder 2000: 1011)

It is possible that Hardy read the early medical accounts of this condition; it is more probable that he is describing a condition long understood in local folklore but, at that time, only just being 'discovered' by medical science. Organic condition or not, Hardy keeps the focus firmly on the psychological.

Psychologically, Gertrude, the supplanter, is compressing Rhoda's heart to the point where she can stand it no more. She is indeed 'maddened mentally and nearly suffocated by the pressure' (*WT* 50). Were the psychic forces thus generated so strong that Gertrude's arm withers as if grasped by a desperate hand? Psychologically this is certainly possible for 'there is nothing ... but thinking makes it so' (*TT* 100) and the basic principle of psychosomatic medicine is that: 'a pain is a pain, and it hurts just as much whether it is caused by an emotion or a club, a fear or a poison' (Dunbar 1947: 61).

Hysterical paralysis characteristically becomes progressively worse with time, which is exactly what happens to Gertrude, who experiences a 'gradual loss of her left arm' (*WT* 59). Hardy's use of the word incubus is somewhat idiosyncratic for an incubus is a male demon who sexually penetrates a sleeping woman; or is the implication that behind Gertrude lays the real demon, Lodge? Female nocturnal visitors are succubae but they exclusively confine their activities to arousing sleeping men. The story of Lodge's original relationship with Rhoda is not revealed; the inference may well be that he was an incubus; that this was rape. The name Lodge itself implies a parasite; he implants himself within Rhoda and slowly saps away her life-blood. A dozen or so years later, he repeats the process with Gertrude. Rhoda quite naturally becomes fascinated by the beautiful young girl who has supplanted her in Lodge's affections. Lodge, himself crippled inside, only has the power to inflict hurt.

Even before the marital discord produced by the withering arm, it is clear that Gertrude is unhappy in her marriage to a man more than twice her age. For from the beginning, she wanders the Heath alone on a daily basis, or as she rather pathetically confides in Rhoda: 'I walk a good deal' (*WT* 52). On this level, *The Withered Arm* is the story of an unhappy deteriorating marriage. In time, Gertrude sometimes whispers to herself 'six years of marriage and only a few months of love' (*WT* 60). Her husband is economical with the truth, with his money (*WT* 63) and with his love because having no inner life, he has no love to give. Conjuror

Trendle describes the injury to Gertrude's arm as being 'of the nature of a blight' (*WT* 61) which parallels Emma's posthumous voice trying to right her marital 'divisions dire and wry, / And long-drawn days of blight (*CP* 355). The arm is an obvious metaphor for all that is wrong in Lodge's relationships.

Gertrude's two visits to Conjuror Trendle are rooted on a firm psychological footing; that the hazy image in the egg fluid should resemble Rhoda is no surprise – because the mind always interprets images in line with preconceptions, subconscious or no. Trendle's high rate of therapeutic success also will come as no surprise to doctors, who understand the nature of the doctor–patient relationship. Trendle makes most judicious use of the 'drug doctor' (Balint 1964: 4). It is perfectly reasonable that laying a psychologically wounded arm across the neck of a recently hung man should 'turn the blood and change the constitution' (*WT* 61). Drastic diseases require drastic remedies. Hysterical symptoms characteristically disappear instantly once the correct psychological button is pressed. Dunbar rightly attributes the success of folk healers to the fact that they work 'on the patient's psychic trouble as well as on his bodily symptoms' and that they do not differentiate between the two (Dunbar 1947: viii). Maudsley came somewhat more laboriously to the same conclusion, when he wrote that:

> we do not, as Physicians, consider sufficiently the influence of mental states in the production of disease, and their importance as symptoms, or take all the advantage that we might take of them in our efforts to cure it. Quackery seems here to have got hold of a truth which legitimate medicine fails to appreciate and use adequately. Assuredly, the most successful physician is he who, inspiring the greatest of confidence in his remedies, strengthens and exalts the imagination of his patient: if he orders a few drops of peppermint-water with the confident air of curing the disease, will he not do more sometimes for the patient than one who treats him in the most approved scientific way, but without inspiring a conviction of recovery?
>
> (Maudsley 1873: 38)

In the twenty-first century, politicians and health-care administrators, who place irrational faith in computer-generated statistics and a scientific 'evidence-base', whilst failing to understand the fundamental realities of the healer–patient relationship, are constantly ignoring this essential truth. In both *The Withered Arm* and *The Fiddler of the Reels*, Hardy melds witchcraft and scientific medicine into the narrative to clearly demonstrate that they are but different facets of the same coin.

Gertrude's death from collapse 'under the double shock that followed the severe strain, physical and mental to which she had subjected herself during the previous twenty-four hours' (*WT* 69) is psychologically perfectly plausible after six years of marital abuse and neglect. It is a typical Hardyan irony that the villain of the story 'burdened at first with moodiness and remorse', which characteristically proves transient, should die peacefully in late middle-age of 'a painless decline' (*WT* 70). This man, who judged by superficial appearances, but who could no longer live with himself as a prosperous farmer once he had been given a glimpse of what lay below the surface. The leaving of his money to a reformatory for boys was, like Mr Featherstone's almshouses, just a means of buying his way into the kingdom of heaven.

Whilst *The Withered Arm* is the story of one man, two women and a child, *The Fiddler of the Reels* is the story of two men, one woman and a child. Car'line Aspent is engaged to be married to good, dull, 'measured and methodical' Ned, a hardworking but unimaginative mechanic. The name 'Aspent' itself has multiple resonances, suggesting the Aspen (populus tremula), a tree 'with especially tremulous leaves' (*COD* 73), 'aspend', an obsolete word meaning 'to spend, expend' (*OED* I: 493) and simply 'spend', the popular nineteenth-century term for sexual climax. Car'line (and where did the 'o' go?) rejects Ned because of an uncontrollable fascination with the music of a gypsy fiddler, a supreme 'woman's man', 'rather un-English' and smelling like 'boy's love' (*LI* 137–8); this infatuation extends from the music to the man himself.

The effect which his playing has on Car'line is ecstatic and orgasmic; he draws her soul from her body 'like a spider's web' until she feels 'as limp as withywind' and yearns for 'something to cling to' (*WT* 141). Her ear becomes so sensitive to this man that the mere sound of his footfall passing along the road, inaudible to the rest of the family, causes her to: 'start from her seat in the chimney corner as if she had received a galvanic shock and spring convulsively towards the ceiling ...' (*WT* 140).

Mop, who has a fiancée elsewhere, cannot resist 'a little by-play' with Car'line's 'too easily hurt heart' (*WT* 141). Car'line subsequently admits to being 'onlucky to be caught the first time he took advantage of me' (*WT* 146) although this may, of course, have been part of the psychosomatic syndrome – sex when 'overpowered with hysteric emotion' (*WT* 150) provoking spontaneous ovulation, as rape has been shown to do. Having impregnated Car'line, Mop vanishes; so, with babe in hand, she makes her way to Lambeth to join Ned who has been quietly caring for himself all the while 'with the facility of a woman' (*WT* 142). Somehow, to his surprise, Ned finds that Car'line resolves 'herself into a very good wife and companion' despite the fact that she had made herself cheap to him. He concludes that she is like 'another domestic article, a cheap tea-pot, which often brews better tea than a dear one' (*WT* 148).

Life as a domestic article proceeds peacefully for Car'line until the trio returns to Wessex, where Ned is seeking employment. At the Quiet Woman Inn on the southern edge of the Heath, the London wife is thrilled by the bewitching 'notes of that old violin', 'under which she used to lose her power of independent will' (*WT* 149). Her eyes filling with spontaneous tears, she is once more seized 'with a wild desire to glide airily in the mazes of an infinite dance' (*WT* 140). With his 'cunning instrument' Mop:

> projects through her nerves excruciating spasms, a sort of blissful torture. The room swam, the tune was endless ... Car'line would have given anything to leave off; but she had, or fancied she had, no power while Mop played such tunes ... Mop modulated into 'The Fairy Dance' – no less one of the foods of love which ... had always intoxicated her ... Car'line was left dancing alone ... slavishly and abjectly, subject to every wave of the melody, and probed by the gimlet-like gaze of her fascinator's open eye ...
>
> (*WT* 151–2)

Ultimately Car'line collapses, prone and motionless before being overtaken by 'convulsions, weeping violently' (*WT* 153). Next day she 'was calmer though the fits were still upon her' (*WT* 154). The sting in the tail of the tale is that Mop has abducted Carry, the little child, and vanished with her into 'the Dantesque gloom' of Egdon Heath. The housewifely Ned in a nympholeptic final twist is deeply distressed by the loss of the 'little maid' who was 'the whole world to me!', whilst her mother shows 'singularly little anxiety' (*WT* 154).

There are a number of interconnected medical and psychological themes in this story. Car'line's excessive sensitivity to music is a trait she shares with many of Hardy's heroines, most noticeably Tess, and also with Hardy himself who:

> was of ecstatic temperament, extraordinarily sensitive to music, and among the endless jigs, reels, waltzes, and country-dances that his father played of an evening ... there were three or four that always moved the child to tears ...
>
> (*EL* 18)

In Car'line's case this tendency has extended into what contemporary medicine branded 'hystero-epilepsy'. This is confirmed by the narrator's comment that 'it would require a neurologist' to explain Mop's influence over her; and her father 'knowing her hysterical tendencies' fears that her attacks are 'a species of epileptic fit' (*WT* 140). At the end of the nineteenth century, the boundaries between neurology and psychiatry and between hysteria and epilepsy were in the process of being defined.

Many patients with what is now recognised as epilepsy due to a structural brain lesion were labelled hysterical, but a still greater number of patients with psychosomatic symptoms were labelled as epileptic. Hysteroepilepsy was the specialty of Charcot, whose female patients would undergo prolonged and elaborate hysterical seizures, which were carefully 'photographed and interpreted using sexual imagery' (Showalter 1985: 148). Tears of any sort are not a part of organic epilepsy; attacks such as Car'line's, which involve 'violent weeping' and persist for hours, are invariably hysterical. The sexual element of hystero-epilepsy is self-evident in Car'line's case as Mop's 'cunning instrument' stirs her to an orgasmic musical rapture, which persists until she collapses in a state of postclimactic exhaustion. Loss of consciousness with protracted or persistent female orgasm remains a rare but recognised medical phenomenon.

But it is not just the music that took hold of Car'line, it was the musician himself. The sound of his footfall passing through Lower Mellstock caused a 'galvanic shock' to her oversensitive frame; when Mop starts to play she is 'intoxicated' by the 'acoustic magnetism' of the melody and 'probed by the gimlet-like gaze of her fascinator's open eye' (*WT* 151–2). Hardy piles on the possible explanations – and the full diagnosis may well be a blend of the three or four different strands. 'Weird and wizardly' Mop has the ability to mesmerise 'unsophisticated maidenhood' – this undoubtedly is part of the control which he exercises over Car'line. This links directly back to the 'drug doctor' (Balint 1964: 4) for Mesmer himself wrote: 'a magnetiser is the therapeutic agent of his cures: his power lies in himself. He must first establish a rapport with the patient …' (Ellenberger 1970: 69). Mesmer further elaborated that 'the magnetised person was oblivious to all but the magnetiser' (ibid.: 113) which concisely describes Car'line's condition when hypnotised by Mop and his music.

The text of this story is steeped in other allusions. Hardy suggests that Mop, if less indolent, could have been 'a second Paganini': the 'most famous of all violin virtuosi', the 'daemonic quality' of whose playing produced such an extraordinary effect on his audience, 'that it gave rise "to romantic talk about supernatural powers"' (Drabble 1995). Mop's playing was 'all fantastical', 'all were devil's tunes in his repertory' (*WT* 139) – this quality, coupled with his sexual potency, links him to Dionysus. His seductive music and abduction of Carry also connect him to 'The Pied Piper of Hamelin'; his 'ancient fiddle' indeed contains emotions: 'pent up within it ever since its banishment from some Italian or German city where it first took shape and sound' (*WT* 152).

The fiddle's continental origin points towards historical precedents for the instrument's effect on Car'line – namely the Dancing Mania, which spread through a large part of continental Europe in the fourteenth and fifteenth centuries:

> assemblages of men and women, united by one common delusion, exhibited to the public ... formed circles hand in hand, and appearing to have lost all control of their senses, continued dancing ... for hours together in wild delirium, until at length they fell to the ground in a state of exhaustion.
>
> (Carpenter 1875: 312–13)

This was the original St Vitus' dance, which in its fully developed form was associated with epileptic convulsions. There is a detailed description of this condition in Roose's *Nerve Prostration*, which was on the shelves at Max Gate, inscribed 'Thomas Hardy Esq. With the author's goodwill' (*DCM*).

Alicia's Diary, published by Hardy in 1887 in the provincial press but excluded by him from the Wessex edition, is the story of the bewitchment of a parson and his family by an enigmatic French landscape painter known as M. de la Feste. The record is Alicia's diary – she therefore acts as both narrator and interpreter – a technique that Hardy adapts to interpolate a quite risqué subtext. The story has two important psychosomatic aspects: M. de la Feste's mesmeric personality and its consequence – Caroline's anorexia nervosa. Alicia's mother and sister Caroline travel to France, leaving Alicia behind 'to attend to the calls' of her father's parishioners and 'to pour out his tea' (*CM* 88). Letters arrive from France, indicating in quick succession, firstly, that 'mother is so much interested' in M. de la Feste and then that Caroline 'is falling in love' with him. 'They are getting into close quarters obviously', for M. de la Feste lends some of his moustache gel to Caroline to smooth her wayward hair. This leaves Alicia speculating 'But my mother ... what can she be doing?' (*CM* 88–9). By the next post comes a letter to say that Caroline and M. de la Feste are engaged to 'my mother's entire satisfaction' (*CM* 90). Mother is then taken dangerously ill; Alicia notes, 'I don't [like] the sound of a haemorrhage at all in a woman of her full habit' (*CM* 92–3). Mother dies, having just had time to recommend M. de la Feste to Father.

Mother's body is brought home to lie in the family vault beside father's first wife, on which Alicia comments: 'I saw them side by side before the vault was closed – two women beloved by one man'. Alicia, who appears from the start to hold a more than sisterly affection for Caroline, then fantasises – still at her mother's funeral – 'that Caroline and I might also be beloved of one and lie like these together' (*CM* 94). This three-in-a-bed talk is consistent with the implication that it was the mother who fell first for M. de la Feste. Then, discovering that she had become pregnant, she planned to extricate herself from this debacle by arranging for Caroline to marry M. de la Feste. The trio could then pass the baby off as being Caroline's own – a not uncommon plot device in Victorian fiction. The dates conveniently provided by Alicia in her diary confirm that pregnancy was certainly feasible. Unfortunately, mother aborts and dies from the subsequent haemorrhage. It is left to the (subtext) reader to speculate whether this was a natural or an induced abortion. These women are abusing the poor parson in much the same way that Lady Constantine had abused Bishop Helmsdale.

Back in England, the girls and their father await M. de la Feste's promised visit to snatch up Caroline. Alicia confides to her diary that: 'it is odd that M. de la Feste should influence in his favour all those who come near him ... it is probably some sort of glamour or fascinating power' (*CM* 95). M. de la Feste, with a series of dubious excuses such as 'the sea is so turbulent' postpones his promised visit to his fiancée for over six months. When he does appear, Alicia is immediately smitten by him in the same way as her mother and sister had been before her. She admits to her diary 'I seem another woman for the effect of it' (*CM* 100).

Predictably, M. de la Feste forgets the sister he is engaged to and develops 'a wild passion' for Alicia, whom he woos in the Kitchen Garden, with the startling confession that she 'is the woman for whom my manhood has waited' (*CM* 104). He is without doubt 'one of the satyrs who populate the imaginative landscape of Hardy's fiction', who 'obey few laws outside their own need for immediate self-gratification' (Radford *THJ* 2.4: 56). These men such as Manston, Troy, Fitzpiers and d'Urberville are suffering from a Dissocial Personality Disorder (ICD-10),and characteristically come to a sticky end. M. de la Feste, undoubtedly another gallant in the Troy mould, on finding that neither Alicia nor Caroline are willing to allow a switch of fiancée, bolts back to the continent, where he forgets to reply to Caroline's letters. Like Mop, he is a mesmeric foreigner in the habit of vanishing without warning. The girls' father, over whom 'M. de la Feste has a sort of autocratic power' (*CM* 106) can offer no help or support. Caroline, who is unaware of the relationship between her sister and her fiancé, becomes anorexic:

> sinking by degrees into such extreme weakness as to make it doubtful if she can ever recover full vigour ... her position is critical. The doctor says plainly that she is dying of a broken heart ...
>
> (*CM* 107)

Caroline is one of three women in Hardy's fiction who develop anorexia nervosa. The first case is Fancy Day, who, happening to take shelter in a rainstorm at the house of Elizabeth Endorfield in Higher Mellstock, is given advice by this 'Deep Body' or 'witch' (*GT* 134) on how to make her father overcome his objections to Dick Dewy as a potential son-in-law. On Mrs Endorfield's instructions, Fancy deliberately starves herself until she is too weak to leave her bed. Her father succumbs to his daughter's manipulation, Fancy rapidly recovers and her courtship continues to a successful conclusion. *Under the Greenwood Tree* was published in 1872, more than a year before William Gull read his paper describing a new female nervous disorder, for which he coined the name anorexia nervosa. Hardy must therefore have been aware of the condition from folk knowledge – records of such women extend back as far as the Middle Ages, when they tended to be regarded as either 'Miraculous Maids', endowed by God with the ability to exist without food, or witches. Their witch-like appearance was in reality more the result rather than the cause of their self-starvation.

Clifford Allbutt, whom Gull had pre-empted in publication, was the first physician to note the unusual degree of control which self-starving girls were able to exercise over their parents, as his friend Hardy might well have pointed out to him! Anorexia nervosa was a very important condition in the history of psychosomatic medicine because it made the potential power of the psyche over the soma glaringly self-evident to sceptics in the medical profession. Here was a purely psychological condition, which not only produced profound physical changes but was also associated with a significant mortality rate.

Hardy's third anorexic and the only one to die from the condition was the beautiful Lady Penelope. Lady Penelope, like Bathsheba Everdene is the kind of woman, who in the words of Sergeant Troy 'a hundred men always covet' and whose 'eyes will bewitch scores on scores into an unavailing fancy' (*FM* 177). This is a magnetism of a quite different type from that described by Mesmer; most probably a form of autohypnosis. Lady Penelope was 'so perfect, and her manner so entrancing' that 'suitors seemed to spring out of the ground wherever she went' (*ND* 139). Like Bathsheba also, three men courted Lady Penelope in earnest. Tired of these three knighted suitors quarrelling over her, she separated them with the wisdom of Solomon but unfortunately then made a rash prediction: 'Have patience, have patience you foolish men! Only bide your time quietly, and, in faith, I will marry you all in turn!' (*ND* 140).

Like the convictions of people who believe that they are going to die on a particular day and then manage to do so (illustrated by Hardy in the true story of Pult P's husband who dies on the day foretold by Conjuror Mynterne) (*EL* 220–1), this careless declaration gradually came true. Lady Penelope first marries Sir George Drenghard, who quite rapidly succumbs to 'his convivialities' (*ND* 141), leaving her his ivy-clad manor house, Wolfeton. Without much enthusiasm, Lady Penelope then marries Sir John Gale, the only suitor still on the scene. He has a 'mean and meagre erection' (*ND* 142) and no satisfaction ensues from the marriage. After nearly three years of suffering, her husband falls ill 'of some slight ailment'. Whilst he is indisposed, the third suitor, Sir William Hervy, returns from abroad. His presence on the premises causes Sir John to work himself up into a great passion, 'which much increased his illness'. Within a fortnight Sir John is dead, psychological factors having led to the development of lethal complications (probably pneumonia) from what was initially trivial illness.

Lady Penelope ultimately weds Sir William, who, unfortunately, overhears gossiping workwomen falsely suggesting that his new wife had murdered her second husband. Sir William, 'a wanderer from his youth' (*ND* 146), rapidly disappears abroad, with dire effect on Lady Penelope:

> She dwindled thin in the face, and the veins in her temples could be distinctly traced. An inner fire seemed to be withering her away. Her rings fell off her fingers & her arms hung like flails of the threshers, though they had till lately been so round & so elastic.
>
> (*ND* 147)

She clearly had developed anorexia nervosa. She was already pregnant at the time of her husband's departure. The two conditions are not generally compatible. Severely malnourished, she gave birth to a stillborn child. Her errant husband, who had previously ignored all her letters, responded to a request from her mother to return immediately if he wished to see her alive: 'she was wasting away of some mysterious disease which seemed to be more mental than physical' (*ND* 147).

A scene of reconciliation is enacted but 'the worm had gnawed too far into her heart'; she dies from her anorexia. Her husband, 'stung with a dreadful remorse', returns abroad to die within a few years (*ND* 148). A sorry tale, which contains three psychosomatic deaths, one death from either cirrhosis or acute alcohol intoxication and one still-birth.

To return to *Alicia's Diary*: the news that Caroline, like Lady Penelope, is about to die from anorexia, leads to the reappearance of M. de la Feste, now known as Charles. He refuses point-blank to marry Caroline, but ultimately submits to a fake ceremony before bolting back across the channel. Predictably, Caroline, who believes the marriage to be genuine, makes a full and rapid recovery from her anorexia. Her strength restored, she flees to Venice in search of her errant 'husband', with the Vicar and Alicia in hot pursuit. They travel via Paris along the route taken by the Hardys on their recent holiday. At this point the plot stalls; the implication has been that Charles is a gigolo, the expectation that Caroline will surprise him in Venice, locked in the arms of an older woman. Instead, we are presented with a confused and melodramatic travelogue: Emma's Diary?

Once the cast return to England, Hardy appears to be in charge again but Charles has undergone a complete character change – he has switched overnight from a Troy to a Boldwood. He marries Caroline, complains of 'a slight headache' and disappears. Whilst Caroline waits patiently in the hall and Alicia confides to her diary that she is 'dreadfully afraid they will miss the train', Charles's body is being dragged from 'a pool in the water-meadows' (*CM* 123–4) where he has inconveniently decided to drown himself. Although Alicia knows that it is suicide, the Coroner's Jury returns a verdict of misadventure. Emma would not want anything unpleasant happening at a Vicarage in a story about their nice holiday abroad.

Violent death and suicide

> Medicine's truest state of mind: hopelessness.
>
> (Brynum and Porter 1994: 1531)

M. de la Feste is one of 20 definite suicides in Hardy's Wessex; I say definite because suicide remains significantly underreported. On the whole in fiction, it is possible to come to fairly clear conclusions about the cause of death in cases of *felos de se*, probably more so than in real life. Readers still may, however, want to give their fictional heroes or heroines the benefit of the doubt. There are, for instance, people who believe that Eustacia accidentally fell into the pool at Shadwater Weir in a state of distress on a wet and slippery night. This is not a wholly unreasonable belief, but Hardy has already produced abundant evidence that this woman is in a suicidal state and suicide by drowning is how Eustacia ended her unhappy existence.

When England was predominantly a Christian country there were strong reasons for avoiding the verdict of suicide: an afterlife of eternal damnation may seem attractive to a severely depressed person, but it is not, on the whole, a thought that appeals to the grieving family. Nor do relatives generally like the idea of the once-beloved being buried at a cross-roads with a stake through his heart, which was still standard practice in Dorset in the early nineteenth century. Hardy described this bitter end as being the fate of Old Sergeant Holoway; a fate that ultimately leads to the suicide of his son (*CM* 131, 141). Hardy was recognising here both family history and precedent as significant risk factors in suicide. Until the latter part of the twentieth century, suicide remained a criminal offence in England, which inevitably led to significant underreporting of suicide; and more particularly of failed suicide attempts and of para-suicide, for the police naturally were reluctant to press charges against a depressed person, now even more depressed because he had failed even to kill himself. Although most Christian sects in England abolished Hell in the late twentieth century, suicide remains underrecorded. Coroners will always prefer to opt for 'misadventure' – as in the case of M. de la Feste – unless the deceased has left a suicide note or given some other definite indication of intention.

I have, for example, recorded one road traffic accident (RTA) in my figures for Yalding (see Table 5.5) as being suicide because the patient had announced his intention beforehand; this is a type of suicide which undoubtedly is significantly underrecorded. The same applies to poisoning and drowning, but not to hanging. If a person sticks a rope around their neck and suspends themself, it is on the whole difficult to call this an accident. I have already drawn attention to research which clearly demonstrated that most 'accidents' are not accidents at all, but a psychosomatic expression of distress.

Self-poisoning is a gray area; not only is it frequently attributed to 'misadventure' but often it is missed altogether. This may occur in the elderly or chronically ill where carers can see no advantage in reporting the post-mortem discovery of a significant discrepancy in the patient's prescribed stock of potentially lethal medications. These deaths are certified as being due to natural causes and so they probably are. Philip Larkin's suggestion that 'Beneath it all, desire of oblivion runs' (Larkin 2003: 52) is clinically correct in the involutional melancholia associated with chronic disease.

At a conservative estimate, I would suspect that about half of actual suicides remain attributed to accidents or natural causes. A recent research project has investigated causes of death in nineteenth-century Massachusetts, the state that kept the most accurate records. The researchers predictably note that 'the recorded causes of death were often narratives, stories of symptoms' and comment on the high infant-mortality rate. The report concludes by drawing attention to the low incidence of suicide then compared to the present time, for in the twenty-first century: 'On the 11th slot in the CDC's mortal tally is a means of adieu quite rare among our forbears: suicide' (*New York Times* 25 May 2004).

Hardy had in 1895 anticipated this increasing incidence of suicide, which he defined as 'the beginning of the coming universal wish not to live' (*JO* 333).

Whilst violent death remains commoner in males, the sex difference has reduced from treble to double over the time studied. In Yalding, at least, the sex differential in suicide rates, which in 1870 was approximately 4:1 in 'favour' of men, has completely disappeared. Hardy being 'an advanced man', like the doctor who attended the triple hangings in the lodgings beside Sarcophagus College, has an even

Table 5.5   Violent deaths as a proportion of total deaths

Year / Place / Sex	Total	Suicide	Accidents	RTAs
1870 (E&W) Male	4.6%	0.4%		
1870 (E&W) Female	1.7%	0.15%		
1870 (Dorset) Male	4.8%	0.45	3.9%	
1870 (Dorset) Female	1.1%	0.1%	0.7%	
1870 (Kent) Male	4.1%	0.6%	3.3%	
1870 (Kent) Female	1.2%	0.15%	1.0%	
Hardy's Fiction Male	38.0%	14.6%	1.22%	
Hardy's Fiction Female	29.5%	18.2%	2.27%	
1905 (E&W) M & F	3.73%	0.68%	0.47%	
Yalding : Male	6.4%	1.4%	5.0%	3.0%
Yalding : Female	3.3%	1.4%	1.4%	1.4%

Note: In his statistics for 1905, the Registrar-General did not subdivide violent deaths by gender. The Yalding figures are for all deaths in the period 1980–2004, not just those aged under 70. Road Traffic Accidents (RTAs) were not recorded by the Registrar-General in 1870. The death of Prince was the only recorded fatality in an RTA in Hardy's Wessex.

higher incidence of suicide amongst his women than his men. Death by hanging from a clothes hook on the back of a door seems, at first appearances, to be merely a rather fantastical part of the overall horrific melodrama. There are, however, a number of contemporary accounts of actual suicides by this means. The most publicised case occurred in 1876 and also, coincidentally, in Oxford. One morning, Henry Rogers, the 17-year-old son of a history professor, did not appear for breakfast. His brother Bertram: 'went to his room to call him, and found him 'suspended by a strap from the hook on the door, quite dead' (Jalland 1996: 72).

Henry had appeared to be in a perfectly normal state of mind on the previous evening and had given no indication that he 'meditated self-destruction' nor had any cause to do so. The inquest was held in the dining-room where the family doctor stated that death was caused by mental derangement due to overwork, hoping to spare Henry's parents from a damning verdict. (As had happened in the case of Horace Moule, whose suicide was attributed to 'temporary insanity'.) The Oxford coroner, however, stating that no evidence was laid before the jury in support of the doctor's opinion, concluded that 'the deceased hanged himself' as a deliberate act of suicide. His brother, Bertram: 'felt sure Henry was happy at home, he was captain of Westminster School, and appeared to have good prospects at Oxford ...' (Jalland 1996: 72).

Henry appeared untroubled by any of the difficulties that bewildered Young Father Time and his too, too honest mother. Hardy could, indeed, interpret this case as an example of 'the coming universal wish not to live' (*JO* 333). Sally Shuttleworth has pointed out that Hardy took this doctor's statement: 'straight from Maudsley, who had argued that Goethe was right to make Werther commit suicide' (Mallett 2002: 147). Hardy had, I suspect, considerable sympathy for Maudsley's view that suicide, rather than being an aberration was for men like Werther, 'the natural and inevitable termination of the morbid sorrows of their nature' (Maudsley 1874: 272).

The high incidence of violent death in Wessex includes nine murders, eight executions and six deaths by manslaughter. The commonest mode of murder is stabbing, followed by a blow to the neck and hanging; Sergeant Troy is the only person to be murdered by shooting and Channing, the grocer, in 1705 the only person to be poisoned (*CP* 762). Channing's wife was 'strangled and burnt to dust' in public at Maumbury Ring six months later for his murder (*CP* 763). All other executions were by hanging, apart from Matthaus and Christoph, who were shot by firing squad. The Channings were real people and the tale of these *Melancholy Hussars* was based on a true story, so Hardy's fictional statistics have here – at least – crossed over into real life.

Execution was, in reality, extremely rare in England in Hardy's time. In 1870 only six men and one woman were executed in England and Wales (overall incidence 0.001 per cent). In 1905 there were 17 executions – all men (overall incidence 0.003 per cent). The rarity of female hangings highlights the significance of Tess's execution, and also of the hanging of Martha Brown, which so profoundly affected Hardy when he witnessed it as an impressionable sixteen year old.

Although any form of interpretation of these figures (see Table 5.6) must be extremely tentative, they do reflect some general trends – that drowning has always been more favoured by women than men who prefer more violent means of death, especially shooting themselves; and that poisoning is tending to replace drowning as the preferred method of self-slaughter for women. This reflects an increased availability of potent poisons and a reduction in the availability of quiet (unsafe) places where a woman may drown herself in peace. In fact, the only suicide by drowning that has occurred in my time at Yalding was a lady whom I had known for many years who managed to end it all in the bath. This is despite the fact that Yalding marks the confluence of three rivers. Drowning, however, accounts for 50 per cent of suicides in Wessex, which is not without precedent for in the late eighteenth century:

> The Humane Society taught life-saving techniques to resuscitate the drowned (because) the proverbially suicidal English were said to make a habit of drowning themselves.
>
> (Porter 1997: 299)

Shooting is the method of self-destruction preferred by such diverse characters as Sir Blount Constantine, Robert Trewe, the two Sergeants Holoway and that enigmatic character Baron Von Xanten, who suffers

Table 5.6 Methods of suicide

	Wessex		Yalding	
	Male	Female	Male	Female
Drowning	4	6	0	1
Shooting	6	0	0	0
Hanging	2	1	2	1
Poisoning	0	1	2	3
RTA	0	0	1	0
Total	*12*	*8*	*5*	*5*

from a chronic endogenous depression. Margery the milkmaid saves him from shooting himself on the occasion of their first encounter, for which she is rewarded with a fairy-tale trip to the Ball as a veritable Cinderella. She subsequently prevents his death from a psychosomatically induced pneumonia. It is, however, a truism that if someone is determined to end their life, they will eventually succeed for:

> In after years there was a report that another attempt on his life with a pistol, during one of those fits of moodiness to which he seemed constitutionally liable, had been effectual ...
>
> (CM 398–9)

Conclusions

In a late uncollected sonnet, 'Thoughts from Sophocles', Hardy wrote that:

> Death is the remedy that cures at call
> The doubtful jousts of black and white assays.
> What are song, laughter, what the footed maze,
> Beside the good of knowing no birth at all?
>
> (CP 936)

Whilst the final line of this stanza reiterates one of the most enduring tenets of Hardy's tentative philosophy, overall this poem represents but limited progress from Aeneas Manston's ante-suicide realist meditation on death in Hardy's first published novel, *Desperate Remedies*, where he reflects that:

> I am now about to pass into my normal condition. For people are almost always in their graves. When we survey the long race of men, it is strange and still more strange to find that they are mainly dead men, who have scarcely ever been otherwise.
>
> (DR 394)

This is indeed the man who 'hears it not now, but used to notice such things' (CP 553).

As well as being fascinated by the recent past, by death and by graveyards, Hardy maintained a lifelong interest in the power the psyche exercised over the soma, whether explained in the old terms of witchcraft and spells or in the new terminology of scientific medicine, which had not only been born but came fully of age during his long lifetime.

Both *The Early Life* and *The Later Years* bear detailed testimony to his deep interest in matters psychosomatic. He tells, for instance, the story 'of a farmer who was "overlooked" [malignly affected] by *himself*' to the great detriment of his livestock (*EL* 268) and also of two girls who were imprisoned in 1830 for casting spells over a young man, whom they fancied. The spells caused their victim to feel 'racking pains about the region of the heart'; rather than visiting his doctor to elucidate a physical or psychological explanation for his chest pains, this patient, who was obviously well-versed in witchcraft, went straight to the constable and had the unfortunate perpetrators arrested (*LY* 11). On the other side of the coin, Hardy describes how in 1907 he attended a dinner given by the Medico-Psychological Society in London, where 'he had scientific discussions with Sir James Crichton Browne and Sir Clifford Allbutt' (*LY* 126).

In his fiction and poetry, Hardy describes many aspects of sickness and of death from a viewpoint which melds the traditional pre-scientific folkloric approach with the scientific-psychological approach, developed during his lifetime as part of 'modern medicine'. The various examples which I have analysed have highlighted some of the lessons that must not be forgotten in this twenty-first-century age of 'postmodern medicine', regarding the importance of psychosomatic factors in the management of all forms of illness. Such an understanding represents, in reality, no more than a return to first principles, for:

Hippocrates observed that the physician only applies the splint; nature heals the broken bone. Since mind and body are one and indivisible, the same principle holds true in healing the breaks in the human emotional fabric.

Your mind is your body & vice versa and that is the meaning of psychosomatic medicine.

(Dunbar 1947: 260)

6
The Fitzpierston Syndrome

Introduction

> From all ills mine differs;
> It pleasures me; I rejoice in it;
> My illness is what I want
> And my pain is my health!
> I don't see, then, of what I complain,
> For my illness comes to me of my own will;
> It is my own wish that becomes my ill,
> But I find so much pleasure in wishing thus
> That I suffer agreeably.
> And so much joy within my pain
> That I am sick with delight
> (Johnson 1984: 146)

Words to warm a physician's heart – for here is a patient, who not only readily acknowledges the psychosomatic nature of his illness but also has no wish to get better – so the doctor's job is easily done! The words are those of Chretien de Troyes, one of the greatest poets of the age of troubadours and one of the earliest exponents of Romantic Love. In this poem he captures perfectly the passionate paradox whereby 'Love, and its ecstasy' (*CP* 475) is linked inexorably to sickness and suffering. Hardy, writing nearly 700 years later, expresses a very similar sentiment:

> Ache deep; but make no moans:
> Smile out; but stilly suffer:
> The paths of love are rougher
> Than thoroughfares of stones.
> (*CP* 227)

Lady Constantine, afflicted by 'an almost killing ennui', explores the eighteenth-century Tuscan column on her absent husband's estate, finds it to be 'a much more important erection' than she had expected, climbs the staircase and looking through the trap door is startled to see:

> sitting on a stool, his eye applied to the end of a large telescope ... a youth who was ... beautiful. The sun shone full in his face, and on his head he wore a black velvet skull-cap, leaving to view below it a curly margin of very light, shining hair ... As she continued to look at the pretty fellow before her ... a warmer wave of her warm temperament glowed visibly through her ...
>
> (*TT* 4–8)

Before the pair has exchanged a word, her Ladyship is hopelessly smitten; she retires to bed, dreaming that this young Adonis will be her 'Astronomer Royal'.

The village wryly observes, 'Lady Constantine had given up melancholy for astronomy, to the great advantage of all who came into contact with her' (*TT* 50). This beginning of love in secret watching is a pattern that recurs again and again in Hardy's fiction – in fact, Lady Constantine is just one example in an unbroken chain that extends from Edward Springrove in *Desperate Remedies* right through to Jocelyn Pierston in the book form of *The Well-Beloved*. It is an experience, which undoubtedly was close to Hardy's own heart. In a diary entry dated 26 August 1868, he records travelling with his sister Mary from Weymouth to Lulworth by steamboat. On board, he encounters:

> A woman on the paddle-box steps: all laughter: then part illness & the remainder laughter. M & I alighted at Lulth Cove: she did not, but went back to Weyth with the steamer. Saw her for the last time standing on deck as the boat moved off. White feather in hat, brown dress, Dorset dialect, Classic features, short upper lip. A woman I wd have married offhand, with probably disastrous results.
> (Millgate 1982: 112)

Hardy was 28 years old at the time; one wonders how many women he had already proposed to – as an opener to conversation – how many, fortunately for the young architect, had refused his somewhat impertinent offer. Gittings described this behaviour as 'Hardy's pathological habit of falling in love with each woman he encountered' (Gittings 1978: 145). Almost invariably, Hardy's characters are afflicted by a similar pathology – love beginning for them with the distant viewing of a person, never previously encountered: 'So susceptible are his lovers to the mysterious lure of another person that one glimpse is enough to cause an outpouring of bottled-up emotion' (Hillis-Miller 1970: 120).

Love never arises in Hardy from the direct meeting of one person with another but is always the result of fascination by a distant or unobserved visioning. It is very unlikely that Hardy actually exchanged a single word with the beautiful girl on the paddle-box steps. This problem is the root cause of almost all the tragedy in Hardy's fiction, for there is a fatal flaw in the character of almost all his main protagonists, namely: 'a catastrophic inability to accept that, for love to flourish, reality must sooner or later supplant the imaginary ideal' (Taylor 1982: 156).

It is only in the later fiction – from *The Woodlanders* onwards (*Tess* excepted) – that Hardy attempts to address this problem by giving his main characters an insight which their predecessors have lacked.

Hardy was now approaching 50, and on his own subsequent assessment, reaching the end of his protracted time as 'a young man' (*LY* 179). It seems likely that Hardy was trying to understand the nature of the affliction whereby:

> ... Love beckoned me,
> And I was bare,
> And poor, and starved, and dry,
> And fever-stricken.
> Too many times ablaze
> With fatuous fires,
> Enkindled by his wiles
> To new embraces ...
>
> (1883, *CP* 237)

As his spokesperson he chose Edred Fitzpiers, a young doctor nourished on a compound of English Romantic poetry and German metaphysics. To his sculptor, Jocelyn Pierston, he later gave even greater insight into the nature of the condition, but Pierston's self-knowledge was deep enough to prove disabling. It was left to the more cynical and self-interested General Practitioner to both expound and practise Hardy's theory of human love, with subsequent embellishments being provided by Pearston/Pierston. The two together form the basis of the condition, which I have labelled 'The Fitzpierston Syndrome'.

Appropriately, Dr Fitzpiers' arrival in Little Hintock is first signalled by a new and strange aurora, which under the gaze of the mesmerised

Grace, gradually migrates through the colours of the rainbow. His first personal appearance is a scene of multiple watching, where Giles, watching Grace on the road, observes Fitzpiers 'quizzing her through an eyeglass' (*TW* 65). A few days later, Fitzpiers is again cast in the role of a voyeur, 'abstractedly watching' (*TW* 111) how passing women cope with a newly painted gate – the men he ignores. That evening, on the way to a night-visit, he offers Giles a lift in his gig and quizzes him about the identity of the young lady, on whom he has been secretly spying. As Giles avoids giving a straight answer, Fitzpiers 'rhapsodises to the night' (*TW* 114) a stanza from Shelley's *The Revolt of Islam*. In response, Winterbourne suggests that Fitzpiers is 'mightily in love' (*TW* 115) with this unknown female.

The woodman's apparent discomposure encourages the doctor to expand further on the subject closest to his heart:

> Oh, no – I am not that, Winterbourne, people living insulated, as I do by the solitude of this place, get charged with emotive fluid like a Leyden jar with electric, for a want of some conductor at hand to disperse it. Human love is a subjective thing – the essence itself of man, as the great thinker Spinoza the philosopher says – *ipsa hominis essentia* – it is joy accompanied by an idea which we project against any suitable object in our line of vision, just as the rainbow iris is projected against the oak, ash or elm tree indifferently. So that if any other young lady had appeared instead of the one who did appear, I should have felt just the same interest in her, and have quoted precisely the same lines from Shelley about her, as about this one I saw. Such miserable creatures of circumstance are we all!
>
> (*TW* 115)

Giles stubbornly persists in his view that 'its what we call being in love down in these parts, whether or no'. Fitzpiers will only admit that he is in love with something in his own head, 'and no thing-in-itself outside it at all' (*TW* 115). Giles, who is quite rightly convinced that Fitzpiers is deliberately talking over him, ironically enquires whether it is 'part of a country Dr's duties to learn that view of things'? Not commonly so, anyway, for doctors who wish to avoid appearing before the GCMER, but it certainly falls within the remit of the poet, novelist or sculptor.

Fitzpiers' theorem partly fits the general experience of love in Hardy's Wessex but is predictably inaccurate and incomplete; for the doctor, currently preoccupied with abstract philosophy, is known for 'his keenly appreciative, modern, *unpractical* mind' (*TW* 124). His citation is an adaptation of Spinoza's definition of love as 'joy accompanied by the idea of an external cause', which philosophically is 'accurate only in a single instance – when the external cause is God' (De Rougemont 1983: 207). Five years later, in 1892, Hardy's sculptor, Pearston further developed these idiosyncratic views of human love in the serial publication *The Pursuit of The Well-Beloved*. Pearston's love is a 'migratory elusive idealisation' which ever since his boyhood had 'flitted from human shell to human shell an indefinite number of times' (*WB* 13, 182). He acknowledges that love is entirely a 'subjective phenomenon', essentially:

> of no tangible substance; a spirit, a dream, a frenzy, a conception, an aroma, an epitomised sex, a light of the eye, a parting of the lips ... He knew that he loved the Protean creature wherever he found her, whether with blue eyes, black eyes or brown; whether presenting herself as tall, fragile or plump. She was never in two places at once; but hitherto she had never been in one place long.
>
> (*WB* 16–17)

Combining these two experiences of Hardyan love with confirmatory evidence from the entire corpus of his fiction, it is possible to construct a clear picture of Love in Wessex or The Fitzpierston Syndrome. I have defined this syndrome in terms of eight major and ten minor diagnostic criteria.

The Fitzpierston Syndrome – diagnostic criteria

Major criteria

1. Principally an instantaneous visual fascination;
   - → Visual element strongly associated with voyeuristic behaviour
   - → Fascination occasionally auditory.
2. The afflicted subject is in love with an image – a product of the imagination:
   - → Love is greatest when reality is excluded i.e. when the process involves no actual contact with the beloved – other than visual engagement.
3. The process is instantaneous – a chemical reaction, precipitated by an electrical build-up, favoured by certain environmental factors, especially:
   - → Rural isolation
   - → Romantic location.

4. Just as the process starts instantaneously so it can end instantaneously:
   → Flash in/Flash out.
5. Alternatively it runs a standard course:
   → (i) Overwhelming infatuation (ii) Plateau phase (iii) Passion burnt out.
6. The first stage of this process can be extended indefinitely if:
   → (i) No actual contact occurs between the lover and the beloved or, preferably (ii) The beloved dies – in which case Love lasts forever.
7. Actual contact (personal interaction) with the beloved tends towards the gradual dissipation of the loving sentiments:
   → Marriage leads rapidly to the complete extinction of all love.
8. Afflicted subjects tend to suffer repeated attacks, as fascination transfers from one Well-Beloved to the next:
   → relapse almost inevitable
   → sufferers may be unjustly labelled 'serial philanderers'.

Minor criteria

1. Death of the beloved may result in the powerful reincarnation of a passion long since burnt out and forgotten.
2. Tendency to stalking of the Well-Beloved, in addition to voyeuristic espial.
3. Tendency to instant proposals of marriage = proposal at first sight:
   → I saw : I married.
4. Sex incidence: great male preponderance. Male to female ratio at least 10:1.
5. Condition has nympholeptic and age-phobic associations:
   → The younger, the more beautiful.
   → Link to concept of the extraordinarily beautiful woman whom 'a hundred men always covet' (*FM* 177).
6. Afflicted subjects capable of multiple simultaneous passions:
   → May also suffer from 'love within a love' – a temporary strong infatuation contained within a more enduring passion.
7. General denial of sexual element in the attraction:
   → Carried to its extreme logical conclusion in Bridehead variant (*JO* 142/3).
   → Sexual relationships arising from the syndrome tend to be short-lived and unsatisfactory.
8. Condition linked in some subjects with Obsessional Compulsive Disorder:
   → Associated tendency to Fetishistic behaviour (love tokens).

9. Suggested association of syndrome with persistent adolescent behaviour patterns, indicating immaturity of mental development.
10. Significant co-morbidity, both physical and psychiatric, particularly depression. Significant mortality rate also, especially suicide.

The next step in this analysis is to apply these diagnostic criteria to love in Hardy's fiction with the aim of: (1) confirming their validity; (2) obtaining a deeper understanding of human love, as interpreted by one of its greatest poetic advocates; and (3) assessing this understanding against nineteenth- and late twentieth-century theories of love – psychological, medical, scientific and literary. In this investigation no attempt is made to differentiate between love that is wholly platonic and love wholly driven by physical desire (lust), for these merely represent different points on the same spectrum, as indivisible as psyche and soma.

Visioning

In the diagnostic criteria I have twice used the rather ugly adjective 'voyeuristic'. Many esteemed Hardy critics including Beer, Wright and Millgate have used the term 'voyeur' to describe the activities of some of his observing characters. Charles Lock, indeed, recently described Hardy as 'one of the most scopophilic of novelists' (Mallett 2004: 25). Hardy is certainly a 'great visualizer' (Irwin 2000: ix), who repeatedly uses a cinematic technique to construct a scene from the safety of a great height and distance before focusing in on a solitary individual. His work is constructed of a series of such visual images; his characters behave much like their creator – watching each other through windows, over hedges, from behind trees and, at times, through peepholes. It is the latter behaviour, as exemplified by Oak, Troy and Dare, to name but three, which has led to the label 'voyeur'. I accept Irwin's view that this term is prejudicial and pejorative, with its definite implication of viewing for sexual satisfaction. In its place, I have adopted the gerund 'visioning', which adequately describes both the action itself and the transforming effect which the 'moment of vision' often has upon the observer.

Falling in love by instantaneous visual fascination has a long and distinguished pedigree, for in ancient Greek mythology the arrows of Eros are shot through the eyes of the lover. This process, described by Stendhal as 'a sudden sensation of recognition and hope' (Sternberg and Barnes 1988: 42), is the norm in Hardy's fiction, where one glimpse of another person releases a flood of bottled-up emotions. As the

Mellstock Quire watch a window in the snowy small hours of a Christmas morn, they nearly fall victim to collective infatuation:

> the blind went upward from before it, revealing to thirty concentrated eyes, a young girl framed as a picture by the window architrave ... she was wrapped in a white robe of some kind, whilst down her shoulders fell a twining profusion of marvellously rich hair in a wild disorder ... her bright eyes were looking into the gray world outside ...
>
> (*GT* 23)

Dick Dewy exclaims 'How pretty!'; his father, similarly smitten, describes the experience as 'as near a thing to a spiritual vision as ever *I* wish to see!'; but at the next (refreshment) stop, it is Dick who is missing; after some difficulty and alarm, the quire eventually locate him:

> opposite the window, leaning motionless against a beech tree, was the lost man, his arms folded, his head thrown back, his eyes fixed upon the illuminated lattice ...
>
> (*GT* 27)

Dick is one of the lucky ones for this electric emotive excitation leads to successful courtship and marriage. That solid man, Gabriel Oak also ultimately legally beds his woman, but only after three whole volumes full of watching, following and spying. A casual glance over a hedge brings that initial moment of vision as Gabriel espies a 'handsome girl' admiring and smiling at herself in 'a small swing looking-glass' (*FM* 4). A few nights later, alone on Norcombe Hill with his lambs, Oak is disturbed by an unexpected light; determining its source, involves for him 'putting his eye close to a hole' in the boarded wall of a shed and watching and listening to the occupants, namely Bathsheba and her aunt (*FM* 13). On the next morning, Gabriel is once more drawn towards the same spot, by unknown but irresistible forces. Unobserved himself, as always, he watches Bathsheba go through a series of erotic exercises astride a horse. She wears no riding habit and seated 'in the manner demanded by the saddle, though hardly expected of the woman' she trots out of his visual field. There are close links here with the pedestrian Tom, fascinated beyond measure by that accomplished equestrienne Emma bounding over the Boscastle hills on her beloved Fanny. After two brief episodes of direct contact with Miss Everdene, the second of which starts with Oak unconscious – a victim of carbon monoxide poisoning – he proposes marriage to her, in true Fitzpierston style. She declines his offer and leaves the area, this separation serving 'to idealise the removed object' and thus fuel his passion, ensuring that it flowed 'deep and long' (*FM* 33).

Once Gabriel re-establishes visual contact by taking employment as Bathsheba's shepherd, he resumes his old habits, 'watching her affairs as carefully as any specially appointed officer of surveillance could have done' (*FM* 163). This ritual is performed with a panting intensity that closely resembles his own dog watching his master whilst awaiting a meal – an analogy not lost on Oak himself who 'was quite struck with the resemblance, felt it lowering and would not look at the dog' (*FM* 23).

Ultimately the tables are turned, and it is Bathsheba who spies on Oak through his unshuttered cottage window; this episode is abortive, but her second attempt to seek out Oak results in their marriage, secured not by love in the Fitzpierston mould but by:-

> good-fellowship – *camaraderie* – usually occurring through similarity of pursuits ... a compounded feeling (that) proves itself to be the only love which is as strong as death – beside which the passion usually called by that name is evanescent as steam.
>
> (*FM* 407)

Hardy here is in an uncharacteristically upbeat mood – almost certainly because these lines were written shortly before his marriage to Emma, with whom he shared a *camaraderie*, based on their similarity of pursuits – both being up-and-coming novelists. An alternative analysis would be that Hardy penned this paragraph under Emma's directions; texturally it appears 'compounded' and not typically Hardyan – from here onward in Hardy's fiction, marriage is on a downward spiral.

Stalking

Oak's persistent patient pursuit of Bathsheba tends towards one of minor diagnostic criteria – namely stalking. Some psychologists, such as Frank Tallis, who describes 'compulsive following ... as one of the cardinal symptoms of love sickness' (Tallis 2004: 162), use the kinder epithet 'shadowing', but I will stick to stalking because this is the term in common usage for the type of behaviour exhibited by Hardy's more extreme infatuees. Diggory Venn, 'a radically more demonic version of Oak' (Morgan 1988: 71), definitely crosses the line between the acceptable observation of a person to protect their (supposed) interests (Oak to Bathsheba) and the following of a person with a view to interfering in their life, in pursuit of the stalker's self-interest. Although crimson in colour, the reddleman is an expert at secreting himself amongst the furze on the heath or creeping about under clods of earth in order to eaves-drop, with the overall aim of thwarting Wildeve's elusive pursuit of hap-piness. Venn, exceptionally, never spies on the woman with whom he is infatuated, but on those people whom he regards as her enemies.

Venn is the first of a number of characters in Hardy's fiction who take on a general watching brief – like the chorus in a Greek drama. Elizabeth-Jane and Giles Winterbourne spend much of their respective novels watching the other characters, like a form of supernumerary nar-rator, although both of these sympathetic individuals do also have a Well-Beloved in view. Jude, on first moving to Christminster, finds that:

> the emotion which had been accumulating in his breast as the bottled-up effect of solitude, and the poetised locality he dwelt in, insensibly began to precipitate itself on this half-visionary form ...
>
> (*JO* 84)

These are all highly significant symptoms on the diagnostic score-chart. The afflicted Jude, who only knows his cousin from a (well-kissed) photo-graph, decides 'to see her, and to be himself unseen and unknown was enough for him at present' (*JO* 85). He sets about a fairly comprehensive campaign of stalking the girl; this appears to keep him satisfied until, for-tunately perhaps for her, she becomes aware of his presence in the city and arranges to meet him. I say 'fortunately for her' because being stalked is not commonly regarded as a positive experience. However, in these cir-cumstances, it probably would have been for them both if Jude had remained only her stalker – for inaccessibility of the Beloved increases the desire and real physical contact is the fuel of tragedy.

Pierston, the protagonist of Hardy's final novel, engages in what he openly describes as 'professional beauty-chases', during the course of which he loiters on the streets of London until he spies an appropriate attractive female; then, once he has a victim in his sights, he relentlessly gives chase:

> like a detective; in omnibus, in cab, in steam-boat, through crowds, into shops, churches, theatres, public-houses, and slums – mostly, when at close quarters to be disappointed for his pains.
>
> (*WB* 212)

His normal pattern is 'to never exchange a word with her' and he believes that his victims are never conscious of his pursuit, or even of his existence. He knows that 'a ten minutes conversation' with the beautiful woman 'would send the elusive haunter scurrying fearfully away' in pursuit of some 'even less accessible' figure (*WB* 212).

This passage does perhaps make it easier to understand why D. H. Lawrence dismissed *The Well-Beloved* as 'sheer rubbish' (Wright 2003: 208) – this is certainly not his style! But might it not have been the style of the young poet from Wessex, alone in London in the 1860s – and still some years later willing to propose marriage on sight to a pretty girl visioned on a steam-boat? In terms of the Fitzpierston Syndrome, Jocelyn is following the process to its logical conclusion. If all personal contact with women leads to disaster, surely it is better just to remain a visionary and a stalker?

'Tommyrotics' (Ledger 1997: 13)

But if that is the case, there must be some psychological gain inherent in the process of watching. Freud described 'normal seeing' as involving both 'looking' and 'being looked at'. In what he described as a 'perversion' or abnormal seeing, the subject wishes to maintain 'visual mastery of the object' – to see without being seen and hence to watch from a place of concealment. Thus Freud believed that:

> the aim of voyeurism is to secure the viewer against pain to the ego that would come from being looked at – by being made an object.
>
> By turning the world into a permanent object, I become permanent subject, no longer threatened and now completely (if neurotically) in control.
>
> (Kincaid 1992: 227)

Like much of Freud's theorising, this statement has to be swallowed in slow gulps – but there may be some truth in his interpretation. It does not appear that most Hardyan protagonists are afraid of being looked at but it does appear that many, like Jude in Christminster, long for involvement, but are still wistfully aware of the potential hazards of allowing love to slip from the safety of the imagination into the cold harsh world of reality. This concept fits too with the image of the retiring poet, who had a life-long aversion to being touched. Martin Seymour-Smith made the, perhaps all too obvious, observation that: 'many of Hardy's characters live in circumstances which resemble his own and often share his psychological characteristics ...' (Seymour-Smith 1994: 84).

Seymour-Smith also considered, quite correctly, that Hardy's relationship with Emma prospered because 'most of the time they idealised each other at a distance' (Seymour-Smith 1994: 119). It was the separation of the lovers which allowed the relationship to proceed as far as marriage – unlike Hardy's relationships with his multiple previous Well-Beloveds, and despite his willingness to marry at first sight! Unfortunately for Emma – Hardy, Fitzpiers and Pierston are, in that order, progressively more insightful sufferers from the Fitzpierston Syndrome, which is really no more than a nineteenth-century reworking of Burton's pathological 'Heroical Love' – a condition which: 'will not contain itself within the union of marriage, or apply to one object, but is a wandering, extravagant, destructive passion ...' (Jackson 1986: 360).

Florence Hardy, who, unlike Emma, had the opportunity to study the entire corpus of Hardy's fiction before consenting to marry him, stated, somewhat wistfully perhaps, that there was more autobiographical detail in a single Hardy poem than in the whole of his fiction. The poetry certainly yields plentiful evidence of visioning and suggests that Hardy's view of love coincided closely with the Fitzpierston Syndrome:

Faintheart in a Railway Train

At nine in the morning there passed a church,
At ten there passed me by the sea,
At twelve a town of smoke and smirch,
At two a forest of oak, and birch,
And then, on a platform, she:

A radiant stranger, who saw not me.
I said, 'Get out to her do I dare?'
But I kept my seat in the search for a plea,
And the wheels moved on. O could it but be
That I had alighted there!

(*CP* 566)

It is reasonable to equate the listless traveller, who gazes through a train window as the world passes him by in cinematic procession, with the poet himself. This poem, which resonates into Larkin, was first published in 1922 in *Late Lyrics and Earlier* when Hardy was 82 years old; and therefore conjures up the image of an octogenarian poet stumbling on to a station platform to pay his addresses to some teenage tart, replete with 'feathers' and 'fine sweeping gown' (*CP* 158).

Many of his poems were, of course, written long before their date of publication and even then were referring back to episodes from his youth. He does, however, show himself here to be a true Fitzpierston – struck, like lightning, in a moment of fascination. 'A radiant stranger', an angelic female form on the platform before him – he fumbles for the correct introductory plea, just as Fitzpiers fumbles for the right hat when he sees Grace approaching the painted gate. Both by their procrastination lose their chance – in the poet's case for all eternity as the train carries him out of her life forever.

A by-product of the Fitzpierston Syndrome, to which Hardy was acutely sensitive, is the cumulative regret for all those missed opportunities. Hardy had met the artist Helen Paterson (later Allingham) briefly in 1874 to discuss the illustrations for *Far from the Madding Crowd*. Forty-eight years after this event, having had no contact with her in the interim, he published a poem entitled 'The Opportunity (For H.P.)' regretting that they had not 'clung close through all', concluding that:

> The tide of chance may bring
> Its offer; but nought avails it!
>
> (CP 621)

He was indeed a man 'in whose long vision they stand there fast.' (CP 319). A number of Hardy's poems are direct descriptions of love by visual fascination, for several of which there is definite extant evidence to confirm their autobiographical content – most particularly 'To Louisa in the Lane' (CP 839), published more than 70 years after the event and 'To Lizbie Brown' (CP 130).

In *A Laodicean*, Dare subjects Captain De Stancy to a 'sort of optical poem', which is also an experiment in the electrochemistry of the Fitzpierston Syndrome. De Stancy, being, like Hardy, a susceptible subject, is given a stiff drink and then made to peer through a peep-hole in the wall of the gymnasium. The poem is composed of:

> Paula, in a pink flannel costume ... bending, wheeling, and undulating in the air like a gold-fish in its globe ... absolutely abandoned to every muscular whim that could take possession of such a supple form ...
>
> (AL 152)

Dare, records the results of his experiment on De Stancy: that 'a fermentation is beginning within him ... a purely chemical process ...' (AL 153).

Electrochemistry

> It may be startling to realise that every thought & every feeling that we have, every action we undertake occurs only because of some form of biochemical activity in our brains – some electrical action along a nerve pathway, some chemical flux across the spaces between nerve cells. (Liebowitz 1983: 4)

Although Hardy's characters fall in love through an instantaneous visual fascination, the scientist in Fitzpiers believes that the mechanics of the process are entirely explicable in terms of biochemistry and internal electro-physiology. This approach had an impressive pedigree: at the beginning of the nineteenth century Goethe had published his novel *Die Wahlverwandtschaft* (1809), which was generally understood to be a demonstration of the chemical origin of love. The title itself was a technical term from eighteenth-century chemistry, but Goethe declined to publicly interpret his text. To state that love was due to a chemical process would at that time have been considered immoral and would have brought Goethe into conflict with the Weimar authorities.

In the second half of the nineteenth century, electric forces had been discovered to be responsible for all nervous and muscular activity within the body. In consequence, there arose a whole pseudo-science of 'electrotherapeutics' designed to treat every conceivable form of illness with electric currents – applied in a variety of different ways to the skin overlaying the symptomatic area. This treatment – which still survives into the twenty-first century in the hands of the physiotherapists – was particularly aimed at neurasthenics, who predictably found that 'the immediate effect of electricity ... is to produce a feeling of enlivenment and exhilaration' (Campbell 1873: 49). Also, it is no surprise to find that 'the genital organs are frequently corrected in their functions by general electrisation'! (ibid.:54). ECT was also a direct offshoot of electrotherapeutics, whose proponents believed that:

> The brain and nervous system bear a somewhat close resemblance to a galvanic battery in constant action, whose duty it is to provide a certain and continuous supply of its special fluid for consumption within a given time.
>
> (Campbell 1873: 6)

Victorian doctors were hot on 'special fluids', which enjoyed a mythology similar to that sported by serum cholesterol at the present time. Fitzpiers, however, had read his Campbell and understood that: 'every effort of the mind and every action of the body involves the necessity for a discharge of nervous force, much as a Leyden jar discharges its charge of electricity ...' (ibid.: 37–8).

Thus Tess has an 'electric' effect on Alec, when she re-encounters him in the role of Methodist ranter (*TD* 320), Trewe, the poet with whom Ella is hopeless enamoured, has 'a very electric flash in his eye' (*LI* 388) and Troy's sword play, 'as quick as electricity' in the hollow amid the ferns, rapidly overcame the susceptible Bathsheba (*FM* 189). Electricity was certainly the buzz term in physiology in the 1880s, when a woman's sexual excitement was considered 'the natural effect of electro-biology' and 'electric' aphrodisiacs were on sale (Marcus 1964: 250–1). Whilst the belief in the importance of electrical impulses in nerve conduction and muscle contraction has survived unscathed into the twenty-first century, the host of other magical powers ascribed to electricity barely survived to the end of the nineteenth. When Jude is suddenly confronted by Arabella, 'that complete and substantial female animal', he finds that:

> the unvoiced call of man to woman, which was uttered very distinctly by Arabella's personality, held him to the spot against his intention ... a dumb announcement of affinity *in posse*, between herself and him ... in common obedience to conjunctive orders from headquarters ...
>
> (*JO* 33–4)

He gazes at her and inhales a new atmosphere – as before the attraction is instantaneous, the fascination all-absorbing, but the implication is that a chemical reaction has occurred between Arabella and himself, rather than a unilateral electrical discharge. *Jude* was completed nearly a decade after *The Woodlanders* and this changed approach reflects Hardy's absorption of changes in scientific thinking over that time. The electric explanation for the biological mechanism of love was being succeeded by a chemical explanation – and that chemical explanation still holds sway in the twenty-first century.

An American psychiatrist, Michael Liebowitz, conducted extensive research into the psychobiology of love. The aim of his research was to explore 'the differences in how people react to positive or negative romantic experiences', 'why some people fall in love repeatedly and others do not' and 'why love does not last' (Liebowitz 1983: 4–5). Liebowitz identified an amphetamine-like compound called phenylethylamine (PEA) as being responsible for the mental stimulation and excitement of romantic love. PEA is produced in the body in a similar way to endorphins or enkepalins, which are the body's natural narcotics.

PEA works by attaching itself to neurochemical circuits in the 'pleasure centre in the brain's limbic system' (ibid.: 43), stimulation of which produces strong feelings of attraction and arousal. In susceptible subjects, visual fascination causes an outpouring of PEA, which: 'for many people happens very quickly ... sometimes it may even involve seeing someone from a distance and feeling you are suddenly smitten ...' (ibid.: 93).

'Joy accompanied by an idea' has given way to 'the limbic system, stimulated by PEA' but the outcome is the same. This form of visioning is to Liebowitz 'biologically like taking amphetamine' and is associated with a neurochemical inability to see the Well-Beloved 'realistically in the early phases of a heady romance'. *Quelle surprise!* Liebowitz also discovered that PEA is a biochemical precursor of norepinephrine and dopamine, high levels of which are responsible for the hypomanic phases of Bipolar Affective Disorder. He therefore speculates that falling in love is a form of hypomania, to which some people are genetically more susceptible than others.

> When in love they are giddy, energetic, optimistic and totally unable to view their 'Well-Beloved' realistically. When the romance ends they crash into real slumps ... and display symptoms ... which very much parallel amphetamine withdrawal.
>
> (Liebowitz 1983: 99)

He also considers that 'love addicts' and drug addicts have much in common; that the craving for romance is merely the craving for a PEA high. Another Californian researcher, Dr Donald Klein, has identified a condition called Hysteroid Dysphoria, sufferers from which fall continuously in and out of love.

There is undoubtedly a strong overlap between Hardy's Fitzpierston Syndrome and Klein's Hysteroid Dysphoria – they are most likely different descriptions of the same condition, which the psychiatrist Klein interestingly classifies as a form of depressive illness. Liebowitz also considers that the short duration of much Fitzpierston affection is due to a normal biological process, that is, the development of tolerance. He considers that tolerance to PEA develops in the same way as it does to an ingested amphetamine or narcotic. Fitzpierston sufferers are confronted by exactly the same problem as drug abusers, who have to continuously increase the dose to obtain the same effect, or else take 'drug holidays' so their brain becomes 'unused' to the abused substance, once more allowing small doses to get them high. This explains why Hardy's romance with Emma – conducted in small snatches – led to matrimony whilst all his previous, more temporally intense, relationships burnt out. Liebowitz dryly records that 'Tolerance is a real problem in romantic relationships, because it leads to people getting bored with each other' (Liebowitz 1983: 131):

> We were irked by the scene, by our own selves; yes,
> For I did not know, nor did she infer
> How much there was to read and guess
> By her in me, and to see and crown
> By me in her.
> Wasted were two souls in their prime,
> And great was the waste, that July time
> When the rain came down.
>
> (CP 429)

Liebowitz, whilst able to explain the biochemical mechanisms behind the Fitzpierston Syndrome, has no simple answer to the problem of tolerance, which he regards as a natural biological balancing process. He does, however, suggest drug treatment for Hysteroid Dysphoria and gives evidence of successful outcomes. The condition appears to respond well to anti-depressant medication, which will allow the sufferer to live a useful life *on their own* without being tempted to fall in love with other people or even come close to them. It is reassuring to know that in the twenty-first century the pharmaceutical multinationals have the capacity to drug the poetry out of the poet – just as readily as they can force an erection out of the old and impotent! Liebowitz's treatment actually reinforces one of the main characteristics of the Fitzpierston Syndrome – that it is better to avoid personal interaction with the Well-Beloved. 'O brave new world'! (Shakespeare 1611: V.i.183).

Imaginings

> You are right enough to admit that I am in love with something in my own head and no thing-in-itself outside it at all.
>
> (TW 115)

A pretty young lady crosses the good doctor's visual field and, as a result of an inborn error of cerebral metabolism, his brain pours out PEA, which latches on to his limbic system, and he is in love. Fitzpiers, as much a victim of this pathological process as the woman fixed in his sights, can merely respond, 'She's charming, every inch of her!' (TW 117); the PEA addict is once more happily fixated. Again and again in Wessex, men and women fall in love with the fantasy, which they have projected on to an attractive person, rather than with the person themselves, whom they often hardly know. Knight, a prototype Angel Clare, does not know and love Elfride, but rather an ideal abstraction, which he has constructed around her; Angel similarly loves a personalised image of Tess rather than Tess herself and tragedy again ensues. Novalis, whom Hardy misquoted in *The Mayor of Casterbridge*, wrote that 'the lover is alone with all he loves' (De Rougemont 1983:145). In psychological terms, men and women fall in love with a fantasy rather than the person they profess to love because: 'they have a great many disowned needs, disowned longings, disowned hurts, disowned desires which they are consciously unaware of ...' (Branden 1980: 132).

Love, when reciprocated, becomes a form of mutual selfishness – men and women do not actually *love* each other, but *use* each other as vehicles to have the intense passionate experiences, which are craved for by an amalgam of their subconscious needs and unresolved past traumas. Love in the Fitzpierston Syndrome:

> is not directed at a woman; it is directed at anima, at a man's ideal: his dream, his fantasy, his hope, his expectation, his passion for an inner being whom he superimposes over the external woman.
>
> (Johnson 1984: 141)

and thus:

> the woman walks and laughs somewhere at this very moment whose neck he'll be coling next year as he does her to-night; as he did Felice Charmond's last year; and Suke Damson's the year afore!
>
> (*TW* 363)

In *The Early Life*, Hardy admitted that Grace 'is doomed to an unhappy life with an inconstant husband', but that he could not accentuate this strongly in the book 'by reason of the conventions of libraries etc'; on the facing page, he records: 'July 9th. Love lives on propinquity, but dies of contact' (EL 288, 289).

With possession comes disillusion, for to consummate love is to destroy it. Hillis-Miller defined this as 'a law of life in Hardy's world' whereby:

> if someone seeks complete possession of another person he is doomed to be disappointed over and over, either by his failure to obtain the woman he loves or by the discovery that he does not have what he wants when he possesses her.
>
> (Hillis-Miller 1970: 149)

Pierston admits that he is 'faithful to what' he 'fancies each woman to be' until he comes 'into close quarters with her' (*WB* 35). A marriage ceremony is required before the innocent Angel can confront this painful reality and acknowledge 'the woman I have been loving is not you' but 'another woman in your shape' (*TD* 239). A marriage ceremony also brings enlightenment to Wildeve:

> To be yearning for the difficult, to be weary of what offered; to care for the remote, to dislike the near; it was Wildeve's nature always. This is the true mark of the man of sentiment.
>
> (*RN* 216)

This statement, which as near as Hardy ever comes to a poetic credo, applies equally well to the poet himself, to Fitzpiers, to Pierston and most of the leading protagonists on the landscape of Hardy's Wessex. Hardy fully appreciated all the difficulties inherent in the Fitzpierston Syndrome, but his fiction, like life, being 'a series of seemings' could not offer any ready answers. In the poem 'The Minute before Meeting', he explores one possible solution – namely to 'live in close expectance never closed' as a substitute for 'far expectance closed at last' (*CP* 236). In other words, never meet the beloved in person, then life is less messy and love can last forever. Neither the problem nor the solution are novel. Ermengau, an early fourteenth-century troubadour, believed that 'The pleasure of love is destroyed when desire finds its fulfilment'; whilst in the Arab world 'refusal to fulfil desire completely is the most refined way to make it eternal' (De Rougemont 1983: 349).

This leads into one aspect of the Fitzpierston Syndrome which I have not included in my diagnostic criteria, that is, the masochistic element. Hardy does not overemphasise this, and few of his characters appear to gain much pleasure from their sufferings in love. The poet himself, however, despite his undoubted affliction by the Fitzpierston Syndrome, lived in reality into a ripe old age – a fate on offer to very few of his protagonists. Does the syndrome actually offer positive benefits in the form of masochistic gain – as well as pain? Following the syndrome back to its literary roots in the world of courtly love and, in particular, the Legend of Tristan and Iseult, one uncovers a deep mine of masochism for: 'The more Tristan loves, the more he wants to be parted from the beloved. This means that the more he loves, the more he wants to be rejected by love' (De Rougemont 1983: 148).

The masochistic element, the revelling in sorrow, is also very much the theme of the poem by Chretien de Troyes with which I started this chapter. Florence Hardy writing to Sydney Cockerell on Boxing Day

1920 complained, firstly, that her husband had 'lost his heart to Gertrude Bugler entirely' and, secondly, that: 'Hardy is now – this after-noon – writing a poem with great spirit … Needless to say it is an intensely dismal poem' (*LH* 171).

This letter from Florence gives a pointer towards a neuro-physiological explanation of the see-saw nature of the Fitzpierston Syndrome. In Lie-bowitz's biochemical terms, the sequence runs like this: Fitzpierston spies a beautiful woman, instantaneous visual fascination, outpouring of PEA – he is now on a high – Hardy writing a poem to Gertrude – time passes – love plateaus – PEA levels drop – relationship falters – 'The pangs of dispriz'd love' (Shakespeare 1599: III.i.72) – PAIN – outpouring of endorphins to counteract pain – Fitzpiers on an endorphin high – happy being unhappy – the joy of a miserable poem – endorphin levels drop – Fitzpierston peer-ing out for another woman – cycle about to repeat itself.

This cycle of alternating PEA (natural amphetamine) and endorphin (natural narcotic) highs fits the symptoms of both the Fitzpierston Syn-drome and Romantic Love very well and is at least as plausible as Lie-bowitz's evidence about tolerance. Hillis Miller, who describes this cycle as 'The Dance of Desire', carefully documented the repetitive nature of attacks of the Fitzpierston Syndrome:

> From proximity to distance and back to proximity without ever yield-ing to the lure of unmediated closeness, Jude and Sue perform their version of the dance of desire. All Hardy's loves must move in this dance, and their approach or withdrawal is motivated as much by the presence of other people as by the natural rhythm of their love.
>
> (Hillis Miller 1970: 167)

Not to yield – if at all possible – to 'the lure of unmediated closeness' is absolutely characteristic of love in Wessex. Fitzpiers, having long lost all interest in Grace, unexpectedly discovers that distance increases desire when Grace misleads him into believing that she had enjoyed a sexual relationship with Giles. Immediately, Fitzpiers's PEA levels rocket, his behaviour begins to resemble that of dogged Gabriel and doggy George, and he now proclaims to the bemused Grace that: 'I have never loved any woman alive or dead as I love, respect and honour you – at this present moment' (*TW* 335).

Fitzpiers does at least have sufficient insight to add the qualifying clause at the end. Pierston in conversation with his friend Somers is even more frank about lack of control: he is willing 'faithful to what I fancy each woman to be till I come to close quarters with her', but

admits that 'her flitting from each to each individual has been anything but a pleasure' – 'the divinity which has informed her' turns
'from flame to ashes, from a radiant vitality to a corpse' (*WB* 35).
Rosemary Sumner linked this loss of control with Jungian theories of
'the irrational nature of the anima – the female in the man' (Sumner
1981: 38). The change from divinity to corpse is the change from PEA-
stimulated to endorphin-seeking man.

The Queen of Cornwall

> The sprite resumed: 'Thou has transferred
> To her dull form awhile
> My beauty, fame, and deed, and word,
> My gestures and my smile.'
>
> 'O fatuous man, this truth infer
> Brides are not what they seem;
> Thou lovest what thou dreamest her;
> I am thy very dream!'
>> ('The Well-Beloved' *CP* 134)

The concept of Romantic Love arose from the Courtly Love of the
Middle Ages; tales of Romantic Love were promulgated and disseminated by troubadour poets, subsequently becoming absorbed into
Western culture. The greatest and the most enduring of these tales
is the myth of Iseult and Tristan, of which five different medieval
versions survive. The myth is centred on the court of King Mark of
Cornwall – at Tintagel. Hardy visited the ruins of Tintagel Castle with
Emma in the early days of their romance, subsequently describing her
as 'an Iseult of my own – mixed in the vision of the other' (Pinion
1968: 116). Hardy had a copy of the popular contemporary version
of this tale, *Le Roman de Tristan et Iseult: Renouvelle par Joseph Bedier*,
in English translation on his shelf in the study at Max Gate. In 1923
he published a drama, entitled *The Famous Tragedy of the Queen of
Cornwall*; predictably, Hardy's version is somewhat idiosyncratic and
does not accord directly with any of the five originals.

In brief, King Mark of Lyonnesse sends his trusted knight Tristram to
fetch his bride Iseult the Fair from Ireland. On the return voyage, they
accidentally drink a love-potion and fall deeply and irretrievably in love
with each other. Iseult marries Mark, leaving her beloved Tristram
to dejectedly wander the world (Cornwall and Brittany). He ultimately
marries the daughter of the King of Brittany, Iseult the Whitehanded,

but is still deeply in love with Iseult the Fair and refuses to consummate his marriage. He is taken prisoner by King Mark, but escapes to snatch a brief moment of 'matchless joy' with Iseult the Fair. They both return to their respective spouses but whilst Mark is away on a hunting trip, Iseult the Fair sails to Brittany only to be told the false news that Tristram (ill from love-sickness) is dead. Ultimately, they all return to Tintagel where King Mark stabs Tristram – as he slowly dies, Iseult the Fair stabs Mark to death and then commits suicide by leaping over the cliff. The unloved Iseult the Whitehanded returns grieving to Brittany. Such is Romantic Love – this dance of desire could quite easily be seen to form the plot framework for *Jude the Obscure*. Here also, undoubtedly, lie the literary origins of the Fitzpierston Syndrome. There are a number of very specific links, which are worthy of brief consideration:

1. Courtly Love – this was based on three characteristics: firstly, that it was an idealised spiritual relationship; there was no sexual involvement between the knight and his lady. Secondly, that they were not married to each other; the lady was usually married to another nobleman. Thirdly, the courtly lovers keep themselves aflame with passion yet strive to spiritualise their desire for each other. These characteristics make it a consenting relationship between a pair of Pierstons. The whole process is designed to nicely maintain PEA levels with no mess and no traumatic fall-out.

2. 'A man believes that he must always search for Iseult the Fair and always reject Iseult of the White Hands; he must seek the divine world that he projects onto a woman but never relate to that woman as an individual person' (Johnson 1984: 138); this is classic Fitzpierston Syndrome.

3. 'Romantic Love never produces human relationships as long as it stays romantic' (Johnson 1984: 133). The Fitzpierston Syndrome does not produce lasting relationships, which is a central aspect of the next point:

4. 'Tristan and Iseult do not love one another. What they love is being in love.' (De Rougemont 1983: 41). Whatever obstructs their love consolidates it as they aim towards the ultimate annihilating passion – death. This again is characteristic of the Fitzpierston Syndrome, where no love can be more enduring and unalterable than love for a dead person. It is no coincidence that the most enduring romances of Western literature occur between lovers who, through untimely death, are never granted the opportunity to remain together.

5. Tristan states that 'the love of Love consumeth me, I am united with Love, intoxicated by Love' (De Rougemont 1983: 159). The drug, Love, passionately intoxicates him; he is on a PEA high. It is interesting to note that in these texts – as in Hardy's poetry, Love is frequently spelt with a capital L, as God used to be. There is a convincing argument that over the last 200 years Romantic Love has replaced Christianity as the principal religion in Western society. Literature, especially the novel, and subsequently films and television have played a major part in promoting 'the idealised eroticism that pervades our culture' (ibid.: 16).

6. During his wanderings, Tristan is trapped in Morois Wood alone with the projection of his anima – an image 'radiant to his eye yet phantasmal' which 'fades even as he holds her in his arms, only to reappear half hidden among the trees, behind the rock, or in the mists above the waters' (Johnson 1984: 107). This passage echoes through Mr Rochester's search for his 'ideal of a woman':

> Sometimes ... I thought I caught a glance, heard a tone, beheld a form ... but I was presently undeceived ...
>
> (Brontë 1967: 335–6)

to closely resemble Hardy's description of Pierston's ideal form which flits away:

> to reappear in an at first unnoticed lady ... to flit from her and stand as some graceful shop-girl ... then she would forsake this figure and rediscloses herself in the guise of ... a piano-player, at whose shrine he would worship.
>
> (*WB* 212)

Both excerpts are strongly influenced by Tristan and Iseult, whose legend forms the basis of the mythology of The Well-Beloved. Current psycho-sociological classifications of love acknowledge just two broad categories: passionate and companionate love. Both Romantic Love, and its specific nineteenth-century variant the Fitzpierston Syndrome fit comfortably under the umbrella of passionate love. By contrast, companionate love appears to be an artifice constructed to cushion the psychological trauma of enduring marriage – the result of falling adult mortality rates in the nineteenth century.

Love-sickness

> There ain't no cure for love
> There ain't no cure for love
> All the rocket ships are climbing through the sky
> The holy books are open wide
> The doctors working day and night
> But they'll never ever find
> That cure for love
> There ain't no drink, no drug
> There's nothing pure enough
> To be a cure for love
>
> (Leonard Cohen 1988)

Love is 'a common fallacy of the sound mind' (Maudsley 1897: 73):

When is love a form of mental illness?
What is the relationship between the Fitzpierston Syndrome and mental ill-health?
Did Hardy see love as sickness?
What has the medical profession to offer as a cure for love in the twenty-first century?

Chretien de Troyes was proud to wallow in his love-sickness. In this he was not alone, for the sickness metaphor has been one of the most consistent features of love songs and poetry throughout the ages. From ancient Greece until the seventeenth century, doctors regarded love sickness as a legitimate and viable diagnosis. With the gradual absorption of science into medicine, doctors – with a few notable exceptions, Dr Fitzpiers included – appear to have been keen to withdraw from this field which was altogether too irrational and illogical to fit scientific classification; perhaps also – for reasons given below – too hot to handle. At the beginning of the 1860s, the decade in which Hardy started to write fiction, there had been a flurry of interest in love-mad women – particularly Dickens's Miss Havisham, who followed closely on the heels of Wilkie Collins's *The Woman in White*. These women, in turn, were direct descendants of Charlotte Brontë's Bertha Mason.

Although Hardy's first published novel *Desperate Remedies* was, on Meredith's advice, a sensation novel in the Wilkie Collins mode, he avoided being drawn into this melodramatic presentation of female distress. All Hardy's female characterisation was far more realistic and his portrayal of love was in what would now be seen as the mainstream of European literary tradition.

Looking into contemporary medical texts, Graham has no references at all to love, marriage, sex or erotomania. The closest it comes to considering human relationships is in a section entitled 'Passions, command of, how to gain it'. Recommended treatment 'Fervent prayer and resolute effort, through Jesus Christ, are the ordained means of cure' (Graham 1864: 227). During the Victorian period, there appears to have been a moratorium on the publication of medical textbooks on love, marriage and related topics. After Henry Allbutt was struck off by the GCMER in November 1887 for publishing *The Wife's Handbook*, which contained 'matters of importance necessary to be known by married women' (Allbutt, H. 1988: 1), it is not surprising that other doctors feared to venture into this field. The fact that there appear to be no surviving medical books on love or marriage published in the preceding three decades can be seen as an indication that the profession was developing the kind of attitude that lead to Dr Allbutt's erasure. Alternatively, such books may have been published, but were subsequently suppressed or destroyed in the post-Allbutt fall-out.

The closest extant example of a medical textbook on this subject is *The Philosophy of Marriage* (1843), 'part of a course of obstetric lectures' by Michael Ryan, Consulting Physician at the North London School of Medicine. He starts by informing his students that 'the ideas which most young persons entertain of LOVE are both romantic and foolish' (ibid.: 3) and then, after complaining that parish relief offers a financial incentive for women to raise bastard children rather than get married, states that 'love is implanted by the Deity in human beings' (ibid.: 61); we are back in the same territory as Graham. It is odd that as society became increasingly materialistic and love began to supplant religion as the central spiritual focus in people's lives, the medical profession should wash its hands of this area and pass patients back to the church.

I suspect that this is part of the same dual standard whereby the medical profession, whose leaders vigorously condemned the use of contraception, had the 'smallest family size of all occupational groups' in Britain (McLaren 1978: 134). *The Family Physician* published by 'Physicians and Surgeons of the London Hospitals' in 1884, predictably, makes absolutely no reference to love or sexual or marital relationships. This lacuna persists into the twenty-first century: Kumar and Clark's *Clinical Medicine* (2002) avoids all such issues in its 1446 pages and *The New Oxford Textbook of Psychiatry* (2000) in its 2432 pages makes no direct references to love or marital pathology, limiting its concern to the effects of divorce on mental health. This is all quite bizarre considering the high consultation rate in General Practitioners' surgeries for marital and relationship problems and the tremendous amount of suffering in the community at large which can be directly attributed to the pathological complications of human relationships.

Tallis points out that up until the late eighteenth century 'love' was an acceptable medical diagnosis for 'it was assumed that love and sickness were virtually inseparable' (Tallis 2004: 31). He considers that:

> In terms of durability, love sickness has proved itself to be one of the most successful of all diagnoses. Most diagnostic terms used by contemporary psychiatrists are less than a hundred years old. Compared to love sickness, their clinical utility has hardly been tested.
>
> (Tallis 2004: 31).

Tallis, a practising clinical psychologist, argues that considering the controversy surrounding psychiatric diagnosis, the exclusion of love-sickness does not mean very much. He argues with conviction that the syndrome of love-sickness is more clearly defined than are many of the conditions that appear in psychiatry's two diagnostic bibles – the ICD and the DSM. These systems work on the principle of the addition of symptoms to make a sufficient count to reach a definite diagnosis, the model that I have used in my table of diagnostic criteria for the Fitzpierston Syndrome.

Dr Tallis, although approaching the problem from the opposite end of the spectrum to Liebowitz – from the psychological rather than the biochemical standpoint – quite surprisingly comes to the same conclusion, that 'Bipolar Affective Disorder is the most accurate psychiatric analogue of love' (Tallis 2004: 58). It is generally recognised that both being in love and BAD are associated with an increase in artistic creativity. This certainly appears to have been Hardy's personal experience and it was definitely that of his sculptor Pierston, who after a protracted 'malignant fever' (*WB* 330), finds that not only is he at last rid of the curse of the Fitzpierston Syndrome but that his artistic sensitivity has departed also. Tallis has also drawn attention to the links between love and Obsessional Compulsive Disorder; as exemplified *par excellence* by Pierston's pursuit of his Well-Beloved. For Pierston, and probably Hardy as well, love was addictive behaviour, presumably mediated through PEA-dependence. Psychologist Brenda Schaeffer, who has written extensively on this subject, considers that love is a biological dependency based on the deeply ingrained human 'need to be close to other people – the yearning to be special to someone' (Schaeffer 1997: 19). She has identified 20 separate 'Characteristics of Addictive Love'; number three on her list being 'exhibit sado-masochism' (ibid.: 51), thus linking directly with my speculations on why certain individuals seem to thrive on this potentially destructive condition.

Hardy's most detailed account of love as an obsessional compulsive disorder is, however, his sensitive portrayal of the agonies suffered by Farmer Boldwood. Bathsheba's thoughtless valentine throws a switch in the neuro-electrics of the brain of this man 'trained to repression' (*FM* 212) and opens the floodgates (with a torrent of PEA?) to an intense obsessional infatuation. Here the Fitzpierston Syndrome is pre-cipitated as usual by a visual stimulus but it is a stimulus by proxy – not the woman herself but a letter – a letter with a large red seal which 'became as a blot of blood on the retina of his eye' as he sat in the quiet of his parlour 'where the atmosphere was that of a Puritan Sunday lasting all the week' (*FM* 100). Because there is no consistent contact with, or encouragement from, the Well-Beloved, PEA levels remain high and Boldwood stays in a state of perpetual listless obsessional fascination.

Driven by a 'fevered feeling' as 'strong as death' (*FM* 212, 206), he wholly neglects his agricultural duties in the single-minded pursuit of his obsession. As the tale progresses, Boldwood's 'fond madness' spills over into the physical symptoms of love-sickness – he looks thin and drawn and develops a tremor sufficiently severe to prevent him tying his own neckerchief. When the Christmas party, which should have been his moment of triumph, turns into a disaster, he commits murder but is prevented from suicide. As he languishes in Casterbridge gaol: 'in a locked closet were now discovered an extraordinary collection of articles ... somewhat pathetic evidences of a mind crazed with care and love' (*FM* 395).

This fetishistic accumulation of female clothing and jewellery, coupled with his 'unprecedented neglect of his corn stacks' were recognised 'as unequivocal symptoms of mental derangement' (*FM* 395–6). Thus, his symptoms of severe Obsessional Compulsive Love-Sickness, were accepted by the Home Secretary as proof of insanity and he was spared the hangman's noose. People in love – who frequently indulge in extensive washing and cleaning rituals before meeting and often exhibit a superstitious tendency to invest chance circumstances with special significance – commonly display multiple symptoms of obsessive-compulsive behaviour.

The Fitzpierston Syndrome, in general, is associated with a high mortality rate; an association that carries over into the real world and into the twenty-first century, for as Tallis notes: 'contemporary suicide statistics suggest that the ancient physicians were correct in considering love sickness a potentially fatal illness' (2004: 56). This is a potent argument in favour of the formal re-recognition by the medical profession in general, and by psychiatrists in particular, of the significance of the psychopathology of love. Tallis bases his main case in favour of the acknowledgement of love-sickness as a psychiatric illness on two straight-forward observations. Firstly, that: 'when people fall in love, they reliably describe four core symptoms – preoccupation (with the loved one), episodes of melancholy, episodes of rapture and general instability of mood' (ibid.: 54).

He points out that these symptoms, as displayed by Boldwood, correspond closely with the conventional diagnoses of OCD, depression and BAD. Secondly, that as PEA levels fall and:

> lovers part, they exhibit a number of symptoms usually attributed to depression – depressed mood, diminished interest or pleasure in activities, loss of appetite, insomnia, fatigue and inability to concentrate. Exhibiting only five of these six symptoms for a mere two weeks is sufficient to merit a diagnosis of major depressive episode according to DSM-IV criteria.
>
> (Tallis 2004: 56)

Tallis's interpretation leads to conclusions very similar to those reached by Liebowitz 20 years earlier: namely that where love is resulting in significant psychiatric symptomatology, its excesses – both highs and lows – should respond to antidepressant medication. Liebowitz had discovered that the older antidepressants, particularly the MAOIs inhibit the breakdown of PEA and thus can be used to successfully cushion Fitzpierston Syndrome sufferers from the worst effects of their most extreme symptoms. Tallis favours the prescription of SSRIs on the basis of Italian research, which demonstrated reduced levels of Serotonin in the acute phases of love. So where is the cure for love? In severe cases of the Fitzpierston Syndrome, it would seem reasonable to prescribe Lithium or another mood stabiliser such as Sodium Val-proate, for the symptoms resemble those of BAD and such therapy should successfully prevent both the extreme highs and lows of love-sickness. Once stabilised on Lithium, Jocelyn Pierston could safely proclaim:

> No more will now rate I
> The common rare,
> The midnight drizzle dew,
> The gray hour golden,
> The wind a yearning cry,
> The faulty fair,
> Things dreamt, of comelier hue
> Than things beholden!...
>
> (*CP* 237)

and then reach for the Viagra as he approaches his 'once queenly creature' reduced to a white-haired 'wrinkled crone' (*WB* 167, 168).

Eight Other Aspects of Love/Minor Diagnostic Criteria for The Fitzpierston Syndrome

1 *Necrophilia*

In this context, necrophilia does not mean sexual intercourse with a dead person – physical contact never being high on the agenda for suf-ferers from the Fitzpierston Syndrome. Instead, it means the passionate love of a deceased person. Always for Hardy's lovers inaccessibility increases the desire and there is no person more permanently excluded or unavailable than a dead person. Death has an unprecedented power to renew love, for the imagination can run riot without any unfortunate impingement of reality. Pierston had never been sure whether he loved Avice I, but immediately on the news of her death:

> He loved the woman dead and inaccessible as he had never loved her in life. The flesh was absent altogether, it was love rarefied and refined to its highest attar. He had felt nothing like it before.
>
> (*WB* 58, 231)

Pierston's intense mixture of grief and adoration parallels that already experienced by Troy on the death of Fanny Robin and Marty South over Giles, who became her personal possession only in death. The most remarkable aspect of this passage from *The Well-Beloved* is how 20 years later it became a self-fulfilling prophesy in the devastating grief felt by Hardy on the loss of Emma and the immediate rekindling of a love which had been wholly dormant if not stone-cold dead for decades. Several of the poems indicate that he felt a similarly intense grief on the death of Tryphena Gale (née Sparks) in 1890 – two years before he wrote this passage for *The Pursuit of The Well-Beloved*, which was therefore probably rooted in recent experience rather than being so wholly theoretical and prophetic. The power of death to send love soaring to previously unattainable heights is a classic symptom of the Fitzpierston Syndrome – and was recognised as such by Hardy for it forms a recurring theme in his poetry from 'She at his Funeral' (*CP* 12) to 'In the Moonlight':

> 'Nay she was the woman I did not love,
> Whom all the others were ranked above
> Whom during her life I thought nothing of.'
> (*CP* 423)

It is a common experience for bereaved individuals in the early stages of their loss to be recurrently conscious of the presence of their dead partner, and frequently experience both visual and auditory hallucinations of that person. 'This strange necromancy' (*CP* 348), which is a normal stage of the bereavement process, was turned by Hardy into the most profound and intense sequence of love lyrics ever written in the English language. In 'Thoughts of Phena', the poet has to 'urge my unsight / To conceive my lost prize' (*CP* 62), direct visual fascination no longer being possible. This poem, along with 'When I Set out for Lyonnesse / With magic in my eyes!' (*CP* 312), forms a prelude to the 'Poems of 1912–13'.

For the first seven poems of the 21-poem sequence *Veteris vestigia flammae*, the bereaved Hardy does not experience any hallucinations, then in the eighth poem 'The Haunter' he becomes aware of Emma's 'faithful phantom' (*CP* 345), in the ninth poem 'The Voice' (*CP* 346), the hallucination has become auditory rather than visual. His hallucinations became more intense when in March 1913 he revisited the scene of his initial infatuation with Emma: 'Hereto I come to view, a voiceless ghost: / Whither, O whither will its whim now draw me?' (*CP* 349).

The ghost leads him on, just as Emma originally led him on 43 years earlier; whilst he remains in Cornwall he is haunted by the 'ghost-girl-rider' who he sees 'as an instant thing / More clear than today' (*CP* 354). As the 'love-led man' (*FM* 144) leaves Boscastle:

> one phantom figure
> Remains on the slope, as when that night
> Saw us alight.
>
> (*CP* 352)

he knows that this visual hallucination is 'shrinking, shrinking', to disappear completely by the time he has travelled on to Plymouth – and never return.

2 Sex incidence

It is self-evident that the Fitzpierston Syndrome much more commonly afflicts men than women. In terms of natural selection, it is important that a male mates with as many females as possible in order to keep 'the Darwinian wheel of variation, differential survival and reproduction turning in our favour' (Tallis 2004: 70). Love can thus be seen as an adaptive 'psychological lubricant'. Alfred Kinsey in his detailed research into human sexual behaviour found that males are much more sensitive than females to 'the charms of fantasy' (Robinson 1976: 111) and hence more prone to the Fitzpierston Syndrome.

However, the sensitive man locked up in some women will come out! Hardy recorded in his Literary Notebooks one such real case (*LN* 1688) and produced a number of examples in his fiction. Fitzpiers gazed in 'undisguised admiration' at Felice Charmond when he discovered her to be a similar love-addict or 'soul of souls!' (*TW* 190). Avice II may be only a 'little laundress', but she is another Pierston at heart:

> I get tired of my lovers as soon as I get to know them well. What I see in one young man for a while soon leaves him and goes into another yonder, and I follow ... I've loved fifteen already. Of course it's really to *me* the same one all through, only I can't catch him!
>
> (*WB* 83, 253)

Arabella also has a touch of the syndrome about her 'always wanting another man than her own' (*JO* 289) and, for example, eyeing up the 'nice gentlemanly' clergyman at her remarriage to Jude (*JO* 379). Nevertheless, it remains the lot of the male to be primarily afflicted – to 'ache deep ... but stilly suffer' (*CP* 227).

3   Flash in/Flash out

Pierston has already amply demonstrated this symptom but there are a number of other examples in Hardy's fiction. Eustacia Vye has the capacity to switch intense emotions on and off at will – presumably by being able to control PEA release. For Wildeve, the signing of the marriage register with Thomasin is the 'natural signal to his heart to return to its first quarters' (*RN* 264) – in other words to switch off his love for Thomasin, now his wife, and reignite his passion for Eustacia. Hardy confirms that *The Well-Beloved* has a strong autobiographical element by the multiple examples of his tendency to fall instantly in love, described in *The Life*: 'with a pretty girl who passed him on horseback' (*EL* 32), with an equestrienne at a circus (*EL* 217) and with 'That girl on the omnibus' who had a face of 'marvellous beauty' (*EL* 288). Not only did Hardy remember in detail these casual visionings of an attractive female, but he felt them to be of sufficient importance to be recorded for posterity in his (auto)biography. He truly believed that 'Love lures life on' (*CP* 458). To Gittings, Hardy was 'a perpetual adolescent, even into his eighties' who 'was out of love only shortly after he was in it' (Gittings 1978: 96).

4   An immature behaviour pattern

This is a somewhat thorny issue, which again Hardy tackles in *The Well-Beloved*. Human biology has demonstrated that man's sexual capacity peaks in mid-adolescence – in Darwinian terms this is the time when he has the strongest drive to go out and rut – an activity which should be promoted by the instantaneous visual fascination of the Fitzpierston Syndrome – the lack of personal interaction, other than impregnation, would be completely appropriate for the survival of the species. Psychologists confirm that 'love at first sight' is a phenomenon, which occurs most 'especially among teenagers' (Tallis 2004: 128) and that 'Romantic Love' is 'a normal and healthy emotional state ... for young adults' (Liebowitz 1983: 195). Pierston was aware that nearly all his contemporaries: 'had got past the distracting currents of passionateness and were in the calm waters of middle-aged philosophy' (*WB* 74: 245) as exemplified by his friend Somers who, artistic sensibility long since dead, turns out marketable paintings to cover drawing-room walls. Somers chooses a wife as casually as most men might buy a loaf of bread. Pierston's 'standing misfortune' was that 'hitch in his development' which made him emotionally no more mature than the young Avice II. He felt the curse of 'his heart not aging' (*WB* 106, 276):

> I look into my glass
> And view my wasting skin,
> And say 'Would God it came to pass
> My heart had shrunk as thin!'
>
> (*CP* 81)

Hardy's own life appears to be inextricably interwoven into the text of *The Well-Beloved*. He recorded that 'I was a child till I was 16; a youth till I was 25; a young man till I was 40 or 50' (*EL* 408) – a summary of the gradual development of his emotional life which coincides with the three stages of *The Well-Beloved*. Millgate confirms that at 45 'Hardy's emotional susceptibility was as naive and adolescent as it had ever been' (Millgate 1970: 243); a comment subsequently adapted by Gittings into Hardy's 'perpetual adolescence'; adolescent love, in any case, bears strong resemblances to courtly love – a chaste all absorbing passion. G. K. Chesterton shrewdly remarked that 'nothing is more characteristically juvenile than contempt for juvenility'. Hardy was locked in a protracted adolescent behaviour pattern, but it was this emotional immaturity that gave him his creative sensitivity. Had it ever left him, he would have ended up like Pierston – artistically and emotionally bankrupt. We should praise rather than condemn men whose 'fragile frame at eve' still shakes 'with throbbings of noontide' (*CP* 81). It was this persistent adolescent sensibility that allowed him to publish his first book of poetry at nearly 60 years of age and produce seven further volumes over the next 30 years plus his *magnum opus*, *The Dynasts*.

5 Multiple simultaneous passions

Hardy undoubtedly experienced these at times; for example, when he was overwhelmed by Lady Portsmouth and her daughters (*MB* 242–3). Florence wryly commented, 'I say there's safety in numbers' (*LH* 172) when she realised that her husband was infatuated simultaneously with both Gertrude Bugler and Mrs Clement Shorter. Once more Hardy allowed Fitzpiers to be his surrogate:

> the love of men, like Fitzpiers is unquestionably of such quality to bear division and transference. He had indeed once declared ... that

on one occasion he had noticed himself to be possessed by five distinct infatuations at the same time.

(*TW* 209)

Hardy's use of the words *quality* and *infatuations* are revealing in terms of how he saw his own restless heart. Wildeve demonstrates a variation on this phenomenon when trying to explain to Eustacia how he came to marry Thomasin: 'Men are given to the trick of having a passing fancy for somebody else in the midst of a permanent love, which re-asserts itself afterwards just as before' (*RN* 284).

6   Nympholepsy

Nympholepsy, according to the definition given in the end-notes of *The Well-Beloved*, could well be used as an alternative name for the Fitzpierston Syndrome – 'ecstasy or frenzy, especially one inspired by the unattainable' (*WB* 345). My meaning is yearning for, or infatuation with, a nymph or beautiful young woman. What distinguishes this from mainstream Fitzpierstonism is that the girl is of more tender years than might normally be considered appropriate as a target for such visioning. This bears no relationship to that quite extraordinary late twentieth-century neurosis labelled paedophilia, which we appear to have adopted lock, stock and barrel from across the Atlantic. For centuries, Britain had followed Roman law, 'according to which a man may marry at 14 and a woman at the age of twelve' (Westermarck 1925: 1. 387). Nympholepsy was not therefore a practical problem until the age of consent became a matter of public concern in the late Victorian period – finally being fixed at 16 for both sexes according to the Age of Marriage Act 1929.

It is a logical extension of the idealism of the Fitzpierston Syndrome that, as Hardy saw it, 'the most perfect essences were to be found in the most youthful bodies' (Seymour-Smith 1994: 37). Nympholepsy is an ongoing theme in *The Hand of Ethelberta* – introduced initially by an urban milkman who considers that it is 'a natural taste' for an old man to pounce 'upon young flesh like a carrion crow' (*HE* 34). This occupation of watching Ethelberta is common to most male characters in the novel, especially Lord Mountclere, a lover of 'nymph-like shapes' (*HE* 361), who ultimately manages to legally pounce upon the nymph in question. Hardy gives a number of loving descriptions of Tess, from her charming schoolgirl persona onwards (*TD* 32–3), some of which he repeats, almost verbatim, in his tale of that other milkmaid Margery (*CM* 300). Tess, like Ethelberta, is the subject of ongoing male visioning:

> From the passing strangers at the beginning of the novel to the sixteen patient policemen at Stonehenge, Tess is the object of erotic male gaze which 'never innocently alights on its object' but 'constructs in it the image of its own desires' ...
>
> (Wright 1989: 109)

In a similar vein, Hardy focuses in on a group of pretty schoolgirls 'eyed' 'from the road outside' in the poem 'The High-School Lawn' (*CP* 812).

As Pearston/Pierston grows older, the targets of his affection do not follow suit – his Well-Beloveds remain young nubile women, resulting in an ever-increasing age gap so that by the time Pearston marries Avice III, he is three times the age of his bride. The closely interbred nature of the population of the Isle of Slingers suggests that any relationship between two children of the island is a kind of incest. Psychological theory suggests that a person in love is actually seeking his or her own 'self in the person of another' (Branden 1980: 71) – on Slingers, where everyone is a blood relation, this theoretical concept becomes a practical reality. Avice II, 20 years younger than Pierston, realises that she is pregnant after she has been living alone with Pierston in his flat in London. The pregnancy is attributed to her estranged husband, now in Australia. A close reading of the text of this novel 'with its three sequential versions of the same story ... and four possible endings' (Hillis-Miller 1982: 155) leaves open the option that it was Pierston who impregnated his beloved Avice II and that the baby whom he married 20 years later (Pearston and Avice III) was actually his own daughter. This would be a kind of nympholeptic triply incestuous bigamy with the granddaughter of his childhood sweetheart – small wonder that Hardy abandoned fiction at this point!

There can be no doubt that the marriage was bigamous, for Pearston in his infatuation with the third incarnation of Avice had conveniently forgotten that he was still married to Marcia, who also happens to be the mother of Avice III's lover. Pearston had long since dismissed mentally the 'ill-matched junction' with Marcia, in a phrase that echoed into *Jude*, as 'a legal marriage ... but not a true marriage' (*WB* 39).

7   *The extraordinarily beautiful woman*

This theory is expounded in detail by Troy to Bathsheba:

> Such women as you a hundred men always covet – your eyes will
> bewitch scores on scores into an unavailing fancy for you.
>
> (*FM* 177)

Troy waxes lyrical on the miserable fate of all the unfortunate men
who will be Fitzpierstoned by her, but have no outlet for their passion.
Hardy is dealing here with a real phenomenon, which has stood the
test of subsequent scientific research. For beauty is not in the eye of the
beholder. Both men and women have very clear and very similar ideas
about who is and who isn't beautiful. Experiments have shown that:
'the brain is sensitive to feature arrangements within 1mm; the tiniest
alteration to a computer-generated facial image will alter attractiveness
ratings ...' (Tallis 2004: 132–3).

These studies also revealed that the more symmetrical a man, the
more he is perceived as beautiful and the more likely his partner is to
experience orgasm during intercourse! More interesting than that piece
of statistical nonsense is that the study doesn't report similar findings
for women.

8   *A la recherche du temps perdu*

> 'Love is an incurable disease: love secretes a permanent pain'.
>
> (Proust 2002 : 2. 157; De Botton 1997: 59)

Proust, in his *magnum opus*, expounds a theory of love which overlaps
considerably with the Fitzpierston Syndrome. Love for Proust is 'within
us and not outside us' (Proust 2002: 4. 518), 'a projection of our pleasure' (ibid. 5: 463), which inevitably died on contact: 'When you come
to live with a woman, you will soon cease to see anything of what
made you love her; though it is true that the two sundered elements
can be reunited by jealousy' (De Botton 1997: 186).

Proust's theory of involuntary memory also overlaps considerably
with Hardy's concept of moments of vision, for in the imagination of
both men: 'the beloved is by the strength of the lover's emotions
identified inextricably with a characteristic scene, so the two are ever
afterward associated in his mind' (Hillis-Miller 1970: 138).

A prime example of this association in Hardy is the way in which the
dairy-house at Talbothays becomes inextricably linked in Angel's mind

with Tess herself as he falls progressively more deeply in love with her. Hardy acknowledged that Proust had been strongly influenced by his theory 'of the transmigration of the ideal beloved one, who only exists in the lover' from 'material woman to material woman' (*LL* 59), which Marcel Proust developed 'still further' (*LL* 248). Proust, who was born 31 years after Hardy but died almost six years before him, often wrote in a vein which corresponded with Hardy's bleaker side, stating for instance that 'there are few things humans are more dedicated to than unhappiness' (De Botton 1997: 2).

This attitude held considerable appeal for the next generation of writers, particularly Samuel Beckett. Hardy can be seen not only as a proto-modernist in style but also as a postmodernist in his philosophy, such as it was – 'a series of seemings' (*JO* xix) – no more. Proust there-fore forms an important bridge between Hardy and Beckett, two men who share much common ground. Beckett in 1931 wrote a critical monograph on Proust, interpreting his work in characteristically dra-matic fashion:

> Habit is the ballast that chains the dog to its vomit. Breathing is habit. Life is habit. Or rather life is a succession of habits, since the individual is a succession of individuals; the world being a projec-tion of the individual's consciousness ...
>
> (Beckett 1931: 19)

The Fitzpierston Syndrome is certainly a succession of repetitive habits: the outside world no more than a projection from the individual's con-sciousness: marriage can be seen as the ballast that chains the dog to its vomit. Proust differed from Hardy in that he considered jealousy, to which Hardy pays limited attention, to be one of the two main drives to love – as here summarised by Beckett:

> Love ... can only exist with a state of dissatisfaction, whether born of jealousy or its predecessor – desire. It represents our demand for a whole. Its inception and continuance imply the consciousness that something is lacking. 'One only loves that which one does not possess entirely.'
>
> (Beckett 1931: 55)

> How great my grief, my joys how few,
> Since first it was my fate to know thee!
> (*CP* 137).

Marriage

'All Romances end at marriage.'

(*FM* 277)

These encouraging words were spoken by Troy to Bathsheba as they argued over money – just two months into their marriage; *Far From the Madding Crowd* was first published in two-volume form in November 1874, which, coincidentally, happened to be exactly two months into Hardy's marriage to Emma. Two months appears to be about the expected duration of marital harmony for Hardy's characters. Fitzpiers, after only two months of marriage, is overtaken by 'an indescribable oppressiveness' (*TW* 179). Clym and Eustacia, in the absolute solitude of their cottage at Alderworth, consume 'their mutual affections at a fearfully prodigal rate' (*RN* 241) so that after two months of marriage, Eustacia declares 'Two wasted lives – his, and mine' (*RN* 259), a line which Hardy subsequently recycled into the poem 'We Sat at the Window': 'Wasted were two souls in their prime' (*CP* 429), describing his early married life with Emma. Two months into his marriage with Arabella, Jude was regretting that there was: 'something wrong in a social ritual which made necessary a cancelling of well-formed schemes ... because of a momentary surprise by a new and transitory instinct ...' (*JO* 56).

Some marriages fare worse – such as that of Tess and Angel, who become estranged on the first evening and separate a few days later – but two months seems to be about the average time for the persistence of some semblance of happiness in marriages in Hardy's Wessex. This is not altogether surprising because admission to marriage is almost exclusively through the Fitzpierston Syndrome, which survives on a distance visioning of the beloved and deteriorates rapidly on personal contact.

This problem is characteristic of all Romantic love, which can 'overcome no matter how many obstacles' but 'almost always fails at one – the obstacle constituted by time' (De Rougemont 1983: 292). The Fitzpierston Syndrome, unfortunately, tends to lead not only to disastrous marriages but, as indicated in my original diagnostic criteria, quite frequently to the death of one or more of the parties involved. An analysis of the outcomes of marriage in Hardy's novels makes sober reading. Such analysis is complicated by the fact that *The Well-Beloved* exists in two different forms with different marriages in each and a choice of endings; also by the repeated cycles of coupling, uncoupling and re-coupling which occur in that novel of railway timetables, *Jude the Obscure*. If one temporarily excludes these two 'problem novels', then a total of 20 marriages occur in the first 12 novels. Eight of these 20 marriages are concluding marriages and the reader is left to assume that all live happily ever after, apart from Elfride, who dies, and Ethelberta, who has married an old man for his money.

I have included here the marriage of Venn and Thomasin – an optional extra, included to satisfy the reading public contrary to the tenets of artistic purity. Thomasin, like Elizabeth-Jane is a survivor who 'never expected much' (*CP* 886), so both will probably ride the vicissitudes of marriage fairly well.

Once Hardy was married himself, happy marriages almost disappeared from his fiction but it is reasonable to assume that Cytherea and Springrove, Dick and Fancy, Bathsheba and Oak, and Somerset and Paula managed to be at least as happy as was Tom himself.

On the down side of the equation of the 12 marriages which occur during the course of these novels, nine end in the deaths of one of the participants and there are four deaths which are the direct result of the marriage but involve a third party – as, for example, the death of Henchard, which can be directly attributed to the marriage of Farfrae and Elizabeth-Jane. So a dozen marriages lead to 13 deaths (foetuses not included). If one adds in Hardy's final 2.5 novels (counting as 3), we acquire a further eight marriages, occurring during the course of these novels, two deaths of participants and three marriage-related deaths. The overall statistics therefore are 19 deaths out of 20 marriages, excluding the concluding unions of the un/happily-ever-after variety. Obviously this is fiction and Hardy believed that 'a tale had to be worth the telling', but it makes a grim point none the less about the risks of matrimony in Wessex.

Jude the Obscure

> We don't need no piece of paper from the city hall,
> Keeping us tied and true.
>
> (Joni Mitchell 1971)

Jude is the story of one man's three disastrous marriages to two women and of one woman's three disastrous marriages to two men. It is also the story of Arabella's three marriages to two men – but it would not be appropriate to describe her marriage to Cartlett as 'disastrous'. As marriages go, it was fairly average – she originally married him bigamously, then abandoned him in Australia to be subsequently reunited with him as a publican in a heavy gin-drinking district of Lambeth, where he dies fairly rapidly from hepatic cirrhosis. Hardy recorded that:

> Marriage is a survival from the custom of capture and purchase, propped up by theological superstition.
>
> (*CL* 2: 92)

> In *Jude*, the marriage question is a vehicle of the tragedy; a bad marriage is one of the direst and cruellest things on earth ...
>
> (*CL* 2:98)

These two excerpts are from letters written by Hardy as *Jude* was appearing in serial form, by which time he had himself been married 21 years. There can be little doubt that he regarded his own marriage as 'dire and cruel'. He was, however, fully occupied not only in earning his living through writing but also in pursuing, Pierston-style, a number of beautiful ladies during the London season; in between times fascinating himself with shop-girls, parlour-maids, 'the girl on the omnibus' (*EL* 229) or, in her absence, other 'young women in fluffy blouses' (Millgate 1982: 454). During this time he was also deeply committed in a safely Fitzpierston way with that 'rare fair woman' Mrs Florence Henniker: 'I enter her mind and another thought succeeds me that she prefers; Yet my love for her in its fulness she herself even did not know' (*CP* 320).

It does not appear that he ever seriously considered ending his own marriage, however viciously he might write about marriage in general. He was, no doubt, conscious that domestic suffering was beneficial to artistic creativity, and by this time had enough insight into the Fitzpierston Syndrome to know that personal happiness would ever prove elusive for a man of his temperament. Hardy's personal marital difficulties, which were probably at least 15 years old by the 1890s, coincided in that decade with a time of pan-European concern about 'The Marriage Question', divorce and 'The New Woman'.

After the considerable financial success of *Tess*, Hardy was in a strong position to write a bitter and extreme novel on these topical issues, at the same time, venting some of the frustrations which were the result of his deeply ingrained Fitzpierstonism. He always had a shrewd eye for the market, and if a bishop were to end up burning his book, that could only ultimately boost his sales. Marriage was in trouble in the 1890s for a variety of reasons, not least of which were the falling adult

– and maternal – mortality rates; the result of widespread improvements in public health. There had always been a more than even chance that infectious disease or obstetric disaster would bring an end to the marriage within a decade or so; marriage had never in general, therefore, been regarded as a lifelong commitment for both parties. The second problem was Romanticism:

> The concept of romantic love as a widely accepted cultural value and as the ideal basis of marriage was a product of the nineteenth century. It arose in the context of a culture that was predominantly secular and individualistic; a culture that specifically valued life on earth and recognised the importance of individual happiness.
>
> (Branden 1980: 38)

Branden identifies Shelley as the ring-leader of the radicals who proposed free love as superior to the institution of marriage. It is no coincidence that Hardy used Shelley's poetry as a vehicle for his arguments in both *The Woodlanders* and *The Well-Beloved*. In *Jude*, Hardy absorbed much of the material which abounded in the contemporary radical atmosphere from J. S. Mill, quoted by Sue, who back in 1865 had written: 'Marriage is the only actual bondage known to our law. There are no legal slaves, except the mistress of every house', (Gibson, C. 1994: 701) to George Egerton who wrote in the short story *Virgin Soil* that marriage for many women was 'a legal prostitution, a nightly degradation, a hateful yoke' (Egerton 2003: 131).

This sentiment echoed Tolstoy, who, in *The Kreutzer Sonata*, wrote, 'prostitutes for the short term are usually despised, while prostitutes for the long term are accepted' (Tolstoy 1997: 102). In this novella, which was on the shelf at Max Gate, Pozdnyshev, a man who murdered his once-beloved, but now adulterous, wife, describes a married couple as being 'like two convicts hating each other and chained together' (ibid.: 126). In the same year Mona Caird in *The Westminster Review* deplored how 'the chain of marriage chafes the flesh', and then portrayed the ideal relationship in terms which are pure Sue Bridehead: 'The ideal marriage ... should be *free*. So long as love and trust and friendship remain, no bonds are necessary to bind two people together' (Caird 1888: 197).

Caird subsequently argued against the foolishness of allowing 'two people, when they are beginning to form their characters', to pretend that they were 'sure of their sentiments for the rest of their days'

(Cunningham 1973/4: 183). This is exactly the tone taken by Hardy in his description of Jude and Arabella's first marriage:

> standing before the aforesaid officiator, the two swore that at every time of their lives till death took them, they would assuredly believe, feel and desire precisely as they had believed, felt and desired during the few preceding weeks. What was as remarkable as the undertaking itself was the fact that nobody seemed at all surprised at what they swore.
>
> (*JO* 52)

When Jude and Sue subsequently attempt the same process, the sensitive Sue cannot cope with the squalid idea of 'being licensed to be loved on the premises' (*JO* 255). She fully understands 'the true mark of the man of sentiment' (*RN* 216), for such men are much more likely to continue in love if unfettered by a 'sordid contract, based on material convenience' (*JO* 205). Once bound by such a legal obligation, they will inevitably 'cease loving from that day forward' (*JO* 255).

The Fawleys' ostracism from 'the society of Spring Street' (*JO* 294) because of their failure to be branded by 'a Government stamp' (*JO* 255) has parallels in other Victorian literature. Walter in *My Secret Life* accosts two young women in Leicester Square; he finds that this pair of 'Ruined Maids' (*CP* 158) are country girls who had to leave their village because 'both had been caught fucking without a license' (Marcus 1964: 121). Walter considers that the more voluptuous of the pair, Sophy, 'must have been reared like a pig'. Like Arabella, who was raised with pigs, Sophy is a 'complete and substantial female animal' (*JO* 33) or as Walter expresses it 'a magnificent bit of fucking flesh but nothing more' (Marcus 1964: 122, 124). Like Jude, Walter 'was sick of the sight of her directly our bodies unjoined' (ibid.: 122). The plot thickens further because Mrs Oliphant, in her diatribe against Hardy entitled 'The Anti-Marriage League' published in *Blackwood's Magazine* in January 1896, describes Arabella as 'a human pig' (Oliphant 1896: 258). Was Mrs Oliphant a secret reader of *My Secret Life*?

Jude the Obscure contains six different marriages between five different participants, each of the three main protagonists marrying three times (counting Sue and Jude's cohabitation which produced three pregnancies as a 'marriage'). None of these relationships produces any happiness for those involved and all offspring die in early childhood. Sue's final marriage is a 'fanatic prostitution' (*JO* 356) to a 'reptile' of a man (Lawrence 1936: 502) who makes her flesh creep. Arabella's final marriage is only achieved by maintaining Jude in an inebriated state until the ceremony is completed; once sober he takes his revenge on her by committing slow suicide. All is not well in the state of matrimony.

The pioneer sexologist, Havelock Ellis was, however, full of praise for Hardy, stating that *Jude* 'exposed the reality of marriage ... for the first time in our literature' (Wright 2003: 198). Other male authors were writing in a similar vein, particularly Grant Allen, who though lacking Hardy's expressive and imaginative genius, produced in Herminia, the protagonist of *The Woman Who Did*, a recognisable prototype for Sue Bridehead:

> I know what marriage is – from what vile slavery it has sprung up; on what unseen horrors for my sister women it is reared and buttressed; by what unholy sacrifices it is sustained and made possible.
>
> (Allen 1908: 36)

Jude sold well, despite causing the expected outcry. Hardy then produced a revised version of *The Pursuit of The Well-Beloved*, in which he toned down the anti-marriage sentiments present in the serial version, as if he had worked that obsession out of his system by writing *Jude*. He was now approaching 60 and financially secure enough to abandon novel-writing, which he did in favour of his original vocation, poetry.

He continued to periodically express strong views against the state of matrimony, but when Emma suddenly died in November 1912, he had no compunctions about remarrying, after a respectable interval of 16 months. His bride Florence was nearly 39 years his junior and was motivated to accept his offer through a strange admixture of chronic depression and literary hero-worship, coupled to a definite masochistic streak. She had read his novels and known Emma, so she cannot have expected marriage to be a positive experience. On the other hand as an unemployed (and unemployable, through ill-health) 35-year-old spinster schoolteacher, her marital retail value was low. Hardy had no illusions, for not long after his second marriage he wrote: 'If I were a woman, I'd think twice before entering matrimony' (*CL* 5: 283). A second marriage at nearly 74, not surprisingly, does not appear to have altered Hardy's views. In response to a question in 1905, he wrote, somewhat petulantly:

> I have already said many times during the last twenty or thirty years that I regard marriage as a union whose terms should be regulated

entirely by the happiness of the community, including primarily, that of the parties themselves. As the present marriage laws are ... the gratuitous cause of at least half the misery of the community.

(Millgate 2001: 332)

What exactly does he mean by 'the community'? Which 'community' did he consult before marrying Florence? It was in fact absolutely right and proper than an old man, the most eminent figure in English literature at the time, should remarry so that he might be properly cared for in his final years. Howard Jacobson in his wonderful parodic romp *Peeping Tom* neatly summarises the whole issue of the Fitzpierston Syndrome and marriage:

> Just because a loving wife could not, by definition, provide me with the form of gratification I most craved – namely, the sensation of being with a woman who wasn't loving – there was no reason to discard all the other pleasures and obligations which marriage exists to confer.

(Jacobson 1986: 237)

The poetry, which Hardy continued to write and publish right up until the time of his death, in general showed the same cynical attitude towards the married state, as in 'The Curate's Kindness' where it is the man, not the woman, who bitterly regrets 'this forty years' chain' (*CP* 209). One of his finest lyrics about marriage is the gently ironic poem, entitled 'The Christening'; the baby's father is a typical Fitzpierston, who lives 'in the woods afar' and would happily meet the baby's mother:

> 'To clasp me in lovelike weather,
> Wish fixing when,
> He says: To be together
> At will, just now and then,
> Makes him the blest of men;
>
> 'But chained and doomed for life
> To slovening
> As vulgar man and wife,
> He says, is another thing:
> Yea: sweet Love's sepulchring!

(*CP* 261)

Divorce

The marriage contract is a product of man's fiction-making powers.

(Scarry 1983: 99)

Public opinion in Europe is pre-occupied with the question of divorce.

(Tolstoy 1997: 87)

Divorce doesn't happen much in Hardy. George Melbury tries unsuccessfully to obtain one on his daughter's behalf. Both Jude Fawley and Sue Phillotson manage to obtain divorces quite readily and inexpensively, but they then display the same contempt for divorce, which they display for legal marriage by remarrying their original spouses as they step through their strange dance of desire. Apart from the death of your spouse, the most effective way to end your marriage in Wessex was to auction off your wife as Henchard did at Weydon-Priors fair. Not only did he make five guineas out of the transaction but it was a clean break arrangement, there were no legal fees to pay and no maintenance costs. Research has revealed that this was by no means a rare occurrence; written records survive of almost 300 wife sales in England between the mid-eighteenth and mid-nineteenth centuries.

The Times commented humorously in 1799 that the country was becoming more civilised for at Smithfield Market 'the price of wives had risen ... from half a guinea to three guineas and a half' (Gibson, C. 1994: 51). Hardy conducted his own research for *The Mayor of Casterbridge*, copying the following entry into his *'Facts' Notebook*: 'Sale of wife at Brighton market – transaction entered by clerk in market book and toll and auctioneer's fee paid' (*FN* 51).

Up until 1857, divorce was only possible in England by private Act of Parliament. The Matrimonial Causes Act of 1857 was about procedure and process only – the substantive divorce laws remained unchanged:

For a wife to divorce her husband, he had to be proved to be guilty of adultery plus either bigamy, rape, sodomy, bestiality, incest, cruelty or desertion for two years or more.

(Gibson, C, 1994: 58).

It was not until the Matrimonial Causes Act of 1923 that wives were given equality with husbands in terms of grounds for divorce. Beaucock was undoubtedly deceiving Melbury when he told him of a new law and: 'a new court established last year, and under the new statute ... unmarrying is as easy as marrying. No more Acts of Parliament necessary: no longer one law for the rich and another for the poor' (*TW* 271).

It hardly seems likely that Hardy was ignorant on this point. Beaucock's intervention must therefore just be seen as a plot device. Weber dates the action of *The Woodlanders* to 1876–9 so the law referred to by Beaucock was already 20 years old. Hardy/Beaucock might have had in mind the Matrimonial Causes Act of 1878, but this merely allowed a wife whose husband was convicted of assault against her to obtain a separation order, together with maintenance, in the magistrates court. No further divorce legislation was enacted until 1920.

On the other hand, all was not at all well at Max Gate and Hardy could have just been sending a covert message to Emma who was extremely bitter about their marriage: 'Thomas Hardy understands only the women he <u>invents</u> – the others not at all' (*LH* 6, Emma to Mary Haweis 13/11/1994).

The state of the divorce laws in the 1880s would therefore have made it impossible for Sue to divorce Phillotson. Under the 1857 legislation, which allowed a husband to divorce his wife for a single act of misconduct, Jude could readily have divorced Arabella and might even have obtained damages from Cartlett for trespass. However, the proceedings would have been complicated by Arabella's bigamy and by the fact that Jude had technically condoned her adultery by having intercourse with her after she had been living with Cartlett. In reality: 'the divorce laws in England severely restricted the availability of divorce both to the poor and their wives' (Gibson C. 1994: 69).

Jude as a jobbing stone-mason would not have been able to afford to divorce Arabella. Why did Hardy introduce these quick divorces – if he knew that they were not possible? I think it unlikely that he was ignorant of the law; it seems more probable that he was trying to show solidarity with the New Woman movement. Ultimately, it is important to remember that, despite the whole 'Wessex' industry that arose from the marketing of his novels, Hardy was not writing realist fiction.

Conclusions

On 1 June 1896, Hardy wrote to his beloved Mrs Florence Henniker:

> seriously I don't see any possible scheme for the union of the sexes that would be satisfactory.

> (Blake 1983: 164)

Despite the outpouring of deeply intense and personal love lyrics which was precipitated by the death of Emma, there is no evidence that Hardy came to any more definite conclusion on love and marriage by the time of his own death in 1928.

The Fitzpierston Syndrome itself appears to confer evolutionary advantages in encouraging males to mate with as many different females as possible. A successful mating once a year is all that a female requires to keep reproducing satisfactorily. This arrangement does not encourage home-making or child-rearing – an activity which is presumably best left to the female. The male in any case would be too busy listlessly peering down from a vantage point, over a bush or through a peephole, waiting to espy his next victim, to have time to pay any attention to children. It is a simple cycle: Listlessness → fascination → brief contact → disillusion/listlessness once more. It is a behaviour pattern more common in sensitive men of an artistic temperament: thinkers, dreamers, men with time on their hands – Hardy, Fitzpiers, Pierston. In his detailed descriptions of the Fitzpierston Syndrome, Hardy has painted a clear picture of his own personality – and of what he understands by human love.

On the 'Marriage Question' Hardy could offer no answers. Much of the debate in the 1890s had its origins in Romanticism; the same debate remains current today, although the efforts of Hardy and his contemporaries have produced woman's emancipation and much freer divorce. Despite, or perhaps because of, the ready availability of divorce – which tends to leave men in financial chains but women free – marriage has never been so popular as it is in the twenty-first century – is a strange reality in an age where 'irregular cohabiting arrangements' such as those pioneered by Sue and Jude have become almost the norm. The Californian concept of the 'take-out' throwaway marriage has gained influence in an ever-more materialistic age. Emma Bovary killed herself because she rediscovered 'in adultery nothing but the banality of the marriage bed' (Flaubert 1998: 267). She had not learnt the fundamental lesson of the Fitzpierston Syndrome – that 'whatever turns into reality is no longer love' (De Rougemont 1983: 34).

This is the grim truth at the heart of the 'Marriage Question' – if matrimony is to be based on Romantic love, then it is based on the very thing that destroys the happiness of the married couple. Havelock Ellis, echoing Sue Bridehead, was a fierce critic of the need to transfer a private relationship into a legal contract. He considered that marriage should never be legally binding for the 'simple reason that no law can command two individuals to love one another' (Robinson 1976: 30).

Romantic Love, as practised in the Middle Ages, was a spiritual discipline. Like the Fitzpierston Syndrome, in its purest form it was a spiritual visioning, not designed for carnal fulfilment. Romanticism by making this ideal the basis of marital relationships has: 'sentenced us to a seemingly endless cycle of impossible expectations, followed by bitter disappointments' (Johnson 1984: 147).

Goethe, whose writings were most influential in bringing about changes which occurred at the turn of the eighteenth century, suggested that marriages should only be contracted for a fixed term of five years because: 'they ruin the tenderest relationships, and the only real reason they exist is so that at any rate one of the parties may pride himself on a cruel sense of security' (Goethe 1971: 96).

At the time of expressing these views, Goethe was quite content to live as if married without actually being so but he, like many great artists, was a sufferer from the Fitzpierston Syndrome. Like Hardy also, his life began to fulfil the pattern of his fiction. Having lived quite happily with his partner for many years, he was eventually forced into matrimony. Predictably, within a year of being 'licensed to be loved on the premises', the 58-year-old Goethe had fallen hopelessly in love with a girl of 18.

Goethe's idea of a temporary marriage contract has recently been taken up in one European country at least. Since 1999 in France, couples can sign up to a Pacs ('*Pacte civil de solidarite*', *The Times* 12.5.2004) – this is a legally binding registered partnership between two people who wish to live together – it is taken out in court and entitles the couple to the same property and inheritance rights as marriage, but can be cancelled by either party on giving three months notice to the other individual and to the court. The legislation was originally intended to provide legal security for homosexual couples but when enacted was extended to all adult couples.

It might not appeal to the Romantics but it seems a practical way of reconciling the socio-economic requirements for marriage with the needs for freedom and flexibility inherent in the Fitzpierston Syndrome. Of course, had Tom and Emma been able to sign up for Pacs, we would never have had the 'Poems of 1912–13'. On the other hand, if both parties to a union know that their partner can dissolve it at any time on three months notice, then they might become more tolerant of each other:

> *Gabriel*: and at home by the fire, whenever you look up, there I shall be – and whenever I look up, there you will be.

Bathsheba: I shouldn't mind to be a bride at a wedding, if I could be one without having a husband.

Gabriel: I shall do one thing in this life – one thing certain – that is love you, and long for you – and keep wanting you till I die.

(*FM* 30)

> About my path there flits a Fair,
> Who throws me not a word or sign;
> I'll charm me with her ignoring air,
> And laud the lips not meant for mine.
>
> (*CP* 238)

7
The Mind Diseased

The lunatic, the lover and the poet

> The lunatic, the lover and the poet,
> Are of imagination all compact.
>   (Shakespeare 1595: V.i.7)

My investigations of the Fitzpierston syndrome led to the conclusion that there are strong links between this personality trait and Bipolar Affective Disorder (Manic-Depressive Illness). These connections are demonstrable both in terms of behaviour patterns and brain bio-chemistry. In *A Midsummer Night's Dream*, Theseus similarly links the lover with the madman but constructs a triad by including the poet, the common denominator being 'strong imagination'. Shakespeare's exploration of the boundaries between madness, eroticism and creativity is part of an ongoing dialectic which can be traced back to Aristotle, who questioned why 'all men, outstanding in poetry and the arts are melancholic?' (Jamison 1993: 51).

Over the last 30 years, a considerable amount of scientific research has been directed at answering this question. Inevitably, there is not unanimous accord, but most authorities agree that: 'the manic-depressive and artistic temperaments are, in many ways, overlapping ones; and that the two temperaments are causally related to one another' (Jamison 1993: 237).

If this research is coupled with the evidence linking the Fitzpierston Syndrome to Bipolar Affective Disorder, we can conclude that the tendency to fall in love dramatically and repetitively is linked to the tendency to creativity – and that both are connected with a propensity to Manic-Depressive Illness or BAD. This is not to say that all writers or artists are mentally ill or that they all suffer from the Fitzpierston

Syndrome, but just that a disproportionate number of them are so afflicted. Scientific investigation has therefore confirmed what Shakespeare had surmised – and Hardy had suspected, when Pierston's 'curse is removed' (*WB* 333) by the severe illness which 'cures' both his creative sensibility and his manic pursuit of the Well-Beloved.

Kay Jamison, Professor of Psychiatry at Johns Hopkins, observed that 'the fiery aspects of thought and feeling that initially compel the artistic voyage' were commonly accompanied by 'the capacity for vastly darker moods, grimmer energies' and occasionally 'bouts of madness' (Jamison 1993: 2). These fluctuating mental states bore a close similarity to the syndrome of Manic Depressive Illness (MDI). Jamison utilised historical, biographical, literary and psychiatric evidence to confirm this suspected connection. Initial acceptance of her work was hindered by ignorance of the true nature of MDI for:-

Many are unaware of the milder, temperamental expressions of the disease or do not know that most people who have manic depressive illness are ... without symptoms most of the time.

(Jamison 1993: 5)

These 'milder temperamental expressions of the disease' include the condition known as cyclothymia – 'a persistent fluctuating mood disturbance including numerous periods of depressive symptoms' (Gelder 2000: 687). It is a subsyndromal mood disorder, the depressive episodes of which are insufficiently severe to warrant inclusion in the psychiatric diagnostic classifications: DSM-IV and ICD-10. Jamison argues that the distinction between full-blown MDI and cyclothymia is purely arbitrary and that 'the evidence supports the inclusion of cyclothymia as an integral part of the spectrum of MDI' (Jamison 1993: 15). The relevance of cyclothymia is that it appears to be an extremely common condition amongst writers and poets, including Thomas Hardy – and Georges Simenon, who despite being one of the most prolific and financially successful authors of all time, argued that: 'Writing is not a profession but a vocation of unhappiness. I don't think an artist can ever be happy' (Storr 1972: 1).

At the other end of the spectrum stands 'mad, bad and dangerous to know' Lord Byron, who displayed the full-blown MDI in textbook manner, showing: 'frequent and pronounced fluctuations in mood, energy, weight, sleep patterns, sexual behaviour, alcohol and other drug use' (Steptoe 1998: 197). Despite being so afflicted, Byron was clinically normal most of the time. Typically, he experienced bouts of energy during which he wrote poetry at breakneck speed and was financially extravagant, alternating with episodes of weariness and depression, during which he recurrently expressed suicidal thoughts. His chaotic pattern of personal relationships and intense and impulsive romantic and sexual liaisons are not only characteristic of hypomania but also link directly back to the Shakespearean triad of 'the lunatic, the lover and the poet'. Byron was one of the subjects of Jamison's initial investigation, in which she took biographical evidence to determine the frequency of mental illness amongst major British and Irish poets born between 1705 and 1805. Making retrospective diagnoses on individuals who had all died before the advent of modern psychiatry, she demonstrated a strikingly high disease incidence:

> Six of the 36 poets were committed to lunatic asylums. Another two committed suicide. Over 50 per cent showed strong evidence of mood disorder ... including overtly psychotic symptoms ... to be a poet in Britain in the eighteenth century was to run a risk of BAD 10-30 times the national average, suicide 5 times and incarceration in a madhouse at least 20 times the national average.
>
> (Nettle 2001: 142)

Jamison next extended her research to a cohort of 47 prize-winning living poets, writers and visual artists. With their cooperation, she was able to use diagnoses made by their own medical attendants, prior to the study. She found that:

> 38 per cent of the subjects had received treatment for an affective disorder.
> 29 per cent had had antidepressants or lithium or been hospitalised.
> 55 per cent of the poets and 63 per cent of the playwrights had a diagnosis of mood disorder.
> 20 per cent of novelists, biographers and artists had mood disorders.
>
> (Nettle 2001: 142–3)

The incidence of mood disorder in the general population, using the same diagnostic criteria is less than 6 per cent. A subsequent similar study in Iowa of living professional writers against matched controls revealed a highly statistically significant difference between the two groups, with 40 per cent of the writers having suffered from major depressive illness and 45 per cent having a diagnosis of BAD. Jamison published the cumulative results of seven research projects on the link between manic depressive illness and creativity in *Scientific American*, demonstrating: 'that artists experience up to 18 times the rate of suicide seen in the general population, 8–10 times the rate of depression and 10–20 times the rate of manic depression and cyclothymia' (Jamison 1995: 49).

Jamison believes that the altered cognitive state in hypomania may well 'facilitate the formation of unique ideas and associations'. MDI and creativity also share certain non-cognitive features, such as 'the ability to function well on a few hours sleep', 'bold and restless attitudes', and 'an ability to experience a profound depth and variety of emotions':

> The manic-depressive temperament is, in a biological sense, an alert sensitive system that reacts strongly and swiftly ... depression is a view of the world through a dark glass, and mania is that seen through a kaleidoscope – often brilliant but fractured.
>
> (*SA* 2.95: 50–1)

Jamison suffers herself from MDI and might therefore be expected to have a particular personal viewpoint to expound. By way of supporting evidence, there has been a recent plethora of independent publications on this subject, most of which come down firmly in her favour. Rothenberg (1990) accepted the evidence for the link between BAD and creativity over his (preferred) traditional model of the artist as schizophrenic. Post in London, concluded that: 'certain pathological personality characteristics, as well as tendencies towards depression and alcoholism, are causally linked to some kinds of valuable creativity' (1994: 22).

Steptoe edited a text which in general supported Jamison, but still aired his preferred view that the 'artistic personality' is a twentieth-century invention, which celebrates artists for 'their behaviour and way of living' more than their creativity (1998: 268–9). Nettle wholly endorsed Jamison's findings: 'These results are very clear. There is an increased risk of psychosis and related disorders in those who become eminent in the creative arts ...' (Nettle 2001: 147). Nettle argues that the scientific evidence supports Shakespeare's premise – that madness and creativity do indeed share a common root in an inherited type of temperament.

Thomas Hardy and depression

> Nov. 17th–19th (1885) In a fit of depression, as if enveloped in a leaden cloud.
>
> (*EL* 230)

> 'depression comes down like a cloud'
>
> (Jamison 1995: 130)

Letter to Edmund Gosse Aug 30.1887
As to despondency, I have known the very depths of it – you would
be quite shocked if I were to tell you how many weeks and months
in bygone years I have gone to bed never wishing to see daylight
again.

(*CL* 1: 167)

There can be no reasonable doubt that Hardy suffered from ongoing
recurrent bouts of quite severe depression. In recent years there has
been considerable critico-biographical debate over the image of 'miserable little Thomas Hardy'; the general consensus being that the
poet who could write *Great Things* (*CP* 474) could not have been a
depressive. Suggestions that he suffered from a depressive illness are
dismissed as the invention of hostile early critics or part of the
Florence–Purdy axis' ongoing battle to discredit Emma. Unfortunately
these analysts of Hardy – eminent men amongst them – have failed to
properly assess the evidence.

They have also failed to acknowledge one fact of vital importance
– that most of the evidence we have was left for us by Hardy himself.
His ghosted autobiographies *The Early Life* and *The Later Years* contain
multiple references to his depression. The same applies to his correspondence. These are items which were written by Hardy himself
– the autobiographies – with full intention that they would be published; the letters in full knowledge that they were liable for eventual
publication. If Hardy did not consider that his depression formed an
important part of his life (and, most likely, of his creativity) why did
he take the trouble to repeatedly include references to it (often in the
form of resurrected diary entries) in the reconstructed story of his life?
The presumption must be that Hardy realised the importance of his
depressive tendency in the formation not only of his outlook(s) on the
world but also of his creative capacity.

The early critic and biographer Pierre D'Exideuil, who met Hardy at
Max Gate, clearly understood this important personality trait which he
described as Hardy's 'inborn sadness', resulting in a 'bitter despair' –
'the child of negation, hanging over the world like a dark shadow'
(D'Exideuil 1929: 48, 44).

In *The Early Life*, Hardy tells us that before the age of eight he had
already concluded that life was not worth living and greatly upset his
mother in telling her so, 'considering she had been near death's door
in bringing him forth' (*EL* 19). The references to depressed feelings are
ongoing and continuous – more in *The Early Life* than *The Later Years* –

but from this stage the correspondence takes over, indicating a steady unchanging process. In fact, the longest gap without a reference to personal depression occurs during the war years 1915–19, which may be in part because the tragedy in Europe distracted his mind from his more personal misery. But it is also a reflection of how deeply despondent he became as the carnage dragged on – the shattering of his melioristic hopes left him inert and withdrawn, for once disinclined to express his sorrow. Florence told Cockerell that Hardy 'feels the horror of it so keenly that he loses all interest in life' (Millgate 2004: 458) and Hardy writing also to Cockerell stated that the brutality of modern warfare 'does not inspire one to write ... but simply make one sit still in apathy, & watch the clock spinning backwards ...' (*CL* 5: 45).

Looking at the 60 years of Hardy's mature adult life – from 1867 to 1927 – there are no less than 40 references to him as suffering from depression. These break down as follows – ten in *The Early Life*, five in *The Later Years*, 19 in *The Collected Letters* as published by Millgate and Purdy, and six from other first-hand sources – mainly Florence's correspondence. Each of these references is to a separate individual attack of depression – 40 such attacks over 60 years cannot be ignored – at the very least it means that Hardy suffered from a depression that he felt it worthwhile writing about once every 18 months; but this is of course not a comprehensive study – these letters survived by chance. No one set out to prospectively document his illness.

J. M. Barrie described Hardy as, at times, 'the most unhappy man I had ever known'. (Roberts *THYB* 1997: 9–8). Dr Marguerite Roberts states that 'Hardy seems to have assumed that unhappiness accompanied writing', adding that:

Acute depression had been characteristic of Hardy for many years. Expressions like 'sick headache' and 'in a fit of depression' run through his *Notebooks* and letters ... He confessed to T. P. O'Connor, 'that I didn't think there was anybody in the world that could be so depressed as I can be?'

(*THYB* 9–8)

This pattern is confirmed by Hardy's entries in *The Early Life*. In January 1867 his relationship with Eliza Nicholls had disintegrated, prompting that most bleakly beautiful of all poems – 'Neutral Tones'. Back at work in London, he fell ill with pallor and increasing languor, which may in retrospect be safely diagnosed as somatised depression (Turner 1998: 14). He consulted his then new copy of Graham's *Modern*

Domestic Medicine and prescribed himself a bottle of milk stout a day (*EL* 70). This tonic did not prove of lasting benefit because in July of the following year, 'in all likelihood after a time of mental depression', he lists three 'cures for despair' namely:

> To read Wordsworth's 'Resolution and Independence'.
> "   "   Stuart Mill's 'Individuality' (in *Liberty*).
> "   "   Carlyle's 'Jean Paul Richter'.
>
> (*EL* 76)

Reading these works appears to have been at best a temporary solution, for two years later, during the early stages of his courtship of Emma, he is quoting Hamlet: 'Thou wouldst not think how ill all's here about the heart' (*EL* 109) and the following summer, a similar passage from *Macbeth*. Hardy is particularly prone to noting down a depressive birthday or New Year message. On 1 January 1879, he is troubled by 'a perception of the FAILURE of THINGS to be what they were meant to be' (*EL* 163). New Year's Eve 1885 found him 'sadder than many previous New Year's Eves had done' – he felt depressed by the building of Max Gate, which seemed an unwise 'expenditure of energy' (*EL* 231). He describes 2 June 1887 as the '47th Birthday of Thomas the Unworthy' (*EL* 262) – a theme which continues right through to his final birthday 40 years later, where he describes himself as 'in a sad mood by the end of the day' (*LY* 254).

Hardy repeatedly feels 'so deep in the dumps' because 'this planet does not supply the materials for happiness', he has very little 'zest for life', suffers 'dreadful languor' / 'lassitude' / 'depression'; by June 1909 he is 'very much depressed with London and with life in general' so that he is 'ready to die' (*CL* 4: 35). Over the next two years he describes life in his correspondence as 'most depressing' / 'deeply miserable' / 'deeply depressing' / 'most miserable' (*CL* 4: 1909–11). Despite the international recognition and honours that came his way in the early years of the twentieth century, Hardy continued to be plagued by negative thoughts concerning his creative abilities. In 1902, he admitted that his 'zest for production' was destroyed by the belief that 'there is nobody to address, no public that knows' (Turner 1998: 177).

In July 1921, he wrote in a similar vein to Walter de la Mare: 'I have just corrected the proof of a wretchedly bad poem, that nobody wanted me to write, nobody wants to read and nobody will remember' (*CL* 6: 95). The poem in question was the sonnet *Barthelemon at*

Vauxhall – still publicly read and anthologised to this day – number 519 in a total published output of 947 poems. Hardy was 81 years old at this time: combined statistics which suggest a considerable discrepancy between his expressed and actual states of mind.

Florence was herself aware of this duplicity, describing Hardy in a letter to Cockerell dated 26 December 1920 as now 'writing a poem with great spirit', adding the proviso 'needless to say it is an intensely dismal poem' (*LH* 171). Part of the attraction that Florence held for Hardy – apart from the 40-year age gap – was a similarity of temperament. This he readily acknowledged:-

> That the union of two rather melancholy temperaments may result in cheerfulness, as the junction of two negatives forms a positive, is our modest hope. It may seem odd to you ...
>
> (*CL* 5: 16)

There is intentional humour here, for the letter was addressed to Frederic Harrison, the leading English positivist. In reality, two depressives don't tend to have a ball! But a gloomy atmosphere at Max Gate may well have been exactly what Hardy was seeking – as being most conducive to his particular brand of creativity. That he got a gloomy atmosphere is in little doubt, for Florence in her correspondence describes Max Gate as a place 'lonely beyond words' where staff cannot be retained, because it is 'like living in a dungeon' (*LH* 75, 181). Her husband increasingly frequently 'doesn't care about seeing anyone' and is happy not to speak to 'anyone outside the house' for days on end (*LH* 169, 195).

Florence subsequently confided to Cockerell that after a bout of 'flu' eight years into their marriage, Hardy told her that 'he had never felt so despondent in his life'. Hardy, as depicted by Florence, was becoming increasingly dependent, for he added as a rider that if anything happened to her, 'he would go out and drown himself' – this she took as a compliment (*LH* 194). The link between this cyclothymic depression and the Fitzpierston Syndrome is highlighted in a contemporary comment by Hardy's parlour-maid: 'Mr Hardy seemed to come out of his shell when talking to younger women as if a light were suddenly breaking through ...' (Titterington 1974: 342).

In the following year (1923) the ever-indiscrete Florence told Marie Stopes that Hardy was 'far more nervous and highly strung than he appears to anyone outside the household' (*LH* 203). This was the year also of the visit of the Prince of Wales to Max Gate. Millgate is

2   The Hardys at Max Gate *c.*1920

'Yea, to such rashness, ratheness, rareness, ripeness, richness
Love lures life on.'

(*CP* 459)

Source: Courtesy of the Thomas Hardy Memorial Collection, Dorset County Museum.

probably right in his analysis of the only surviving evidence of this occasion: photographs, in which Florence displays her 'habitual melancholy' and where 'the Prince seems equally oppressed and Hardy only slightly less so' (Millgate 1982: 549). It would inevitably take more than a royal visit to lift the gloom of that establishment, the matrimonial home of a poet who acknowledged:

> How great my grief, my joys how few,
> Since first it was my fate to know thee!
>
> (*CP* 101)

Cyclothymia

> One of the most extraordinary things about him is the rapidity of his changes of mood ...
>
> (Gibson, J. 1999: 118)

This comment, dated 13 August 1919, is from the journal of Elliott Felkin, a Cambridge-educated officer at Dorchester Prisoner of War camp. Felkin, who had literary interests, struck up an easy rapport with Hardy, taking tea at Max Gate quite regularly and keeping a contemporaneous record of each visit. In other words, he was a reliable witness. Prior to their marriage, Florence also was conscious of the volatility of Hardy's moods. A letter to Clodd, dated 11 December 1911, includes the following paragraph:

> He is very well and seems quite gay. Mrs Henniker told me yesterday that she had never known him in better spirits than when she was in Dorset, so his passing moods of depression do not signify much perhaps.
> P.S. This morning I hear from Mr T.H. that he is 'most miserable' ...
>
> (*LH* 73–4)

It is this rapidity of mood change that can be seen as the root cause of much of the confusion regarding Hardy's affective well-being. So many contradictory interpretations have arisen because his episodes of deep depression were often interspersed at short intervals with joyful light-hearted and energetic moods. Without doubt, Hardy was suffering from the mood disorder which would today be classified

as cyclothymia. Cyclothymia is a temperamental disposition characterised by rapid changes of mood, in which 'patients suffer short
cycles of depression and hypomania' which fail to meet 'the sustained duration criteria for major affective disorder' (Gelder 2000:
742). These natural cycles of opposing emotional mood states generate the force which drives the creative tension in cyclothymic
individuals. During the negative, or dysthymic, phases such
patients:

> complain of gloominess, lethargy and self-doubt; they typically
> work hard but do not enjoy their work; if married they are dead-
> locked in bitter and unhappy marriages which lead neither to recon-
> ciliation nor separation; their entire existence is a burden ... they
> brood about the uselessness of existence ...
>
> (Gelder 2000: 737)

This is a surprisingly accurate description of life at Max Gate – at
least up until November 1912. Millgate gave a detailed account
of Hardy's cyclothymia, without actually using a diagnostic label,
directly linking these mood swings to Hardy's creativity, particularly to his presentation of his work as 'a series of seemings':

> Though extraordinarily consistent and persistent at the deepest
> levels of personality and purpose, at more superficial levels
> Hardy was capable of rapid changes of mood. His frequent
> acknowledgment of the inconsistencies in the views expressed
> in his work was a direct result of his personal shifts in feeling
> and outlook. His darkest depressions were thus capable not
> only of coexisting with outward geniality, but also of alter-
> nating with periods of actual cheerfulness.
>
> (Millgate 1982: 381)

Millgate, recognising that Hardy's darker moods 'were conducive
to creative activity' thought Hardy capable 'if not of deliberately
generating depression', at least of 'surrendering to it willingly and
without resistance' (ibid.: 381). Jamison shares Millgate's assessment of the potential creative value of Hardy's ever-fluctuating
outlook on life, for: 'ultimately these fluxings and yokings may
reflect truth in humanity and nature more accurately than could a
fixed viewpoint ...' (Jamison 1995: 51).

Felix Post

Post, Consultant Psychiatrist at Bethlem, conducted a study of world-famous men, in which he sought to determine the prevalence of various psychopathologies in outstandingly creative individuals to test the 'widely accepted' belief in a 'causal nexus between creativity and psychopathology' (1994: 22). This was a retrospective study based on his own analysis of biographical data, transformed into DSM-III-R criteria, where appropriate. He classified his subjects into six groups – Scientists, Politicians, Thinkers, Composers, Artists and Writers. He compared and contrasted the incidence of psychopathology between and within the different groups by classifying each of his 291 subjects into one of four diagnostic categories:

1. No Psychopathology
2. Mild Psychopathology
3. Marked Psychopathology
4. Severe Psychopathology

To merit inclusion in the Writers group, a man had to be internationally pre-eminent as a novelist or playwright. Poets *per se* were excluded but: 'many of playwrights and novelists were also notable poets ... to give a few examples, Boris Pasternak and Thomas Hardy were outstanding poets ...' (Post 1994: 23).

Post had difficulty with the exclusion of cyclothymic or dysthymic personality from DSM-III because he found that many of his subjects were 'afflicted with an undue tendency to brief mood swings' and had to employ 'the controversial concept of borderline personality disorder' (1994: 24). These men would be classified by Jamison as suffering from MDI – extending her umbrella somewhat wider than DSM. This problem of taxonomy affected Post's conclusions because those subjects with cyclothymia and dysthymia, whom Jamison and others diagnosed as suffering from MDI, were, according to the strict application of DSM-III-R, suffering from a personality disorder. He therefore found that: 'Only the following kinds of psychopathology had a higher prevalence than in ordinary people: disabling personality deviations (visual arts and prose writers), largely subjective personality problems (especially writers) and depressions (markedly only in writers and playwrights)' (ibid.: 33).

Predictably the highest incidence of psychopathology was amongst writers and the lowest incidence amongst scientists. Overall Post concluded that 'certain pathological personality characteristics' are 'causally linked to some kinds of valuable creativity' (Post 1994: 22). Amongst his other findings were that:

1. Far above average, 90 per cent of creative writers exhibited some traits of DSM personality disorders.
2. Seventy-two per cent of novelists and playwrights suffered from depressive conditions.
3. All the depressions of writers were of more than 2 weeks duration.
4. The sexual and marital histories of the writers were the least normal of the six categories studied.
5. Compared with the role of husband's infidelities, wives caused marital problems far more often on account of mental instabilities.

(Post 1994: 27–31)

All of these findings relate directly to Hardy, his depressions, his outlook on life and his marital difficulties. Most importantly, in Post's diagnostic classification of subjects into no/mild /marked or severe psychopathology, he classed Thomas Hardy as suffering from Marked Psychopathology. This independent psychiatric opinion reinforces my own diagnostic conclusions regarding Hardy's mental well-being.

Hardy suffered from cyclothymia, which according to Post's strict application of DSM counts as a Borderline Personality Disorder, but according to Jamison counts as the mild end of the MDI/BAD spectrum. Hardy described himself as displaying from early childhood a mixture of 'ecstatic temperament' ('Great Things') and brooding melancholy (*EL* 19). For like Little Father Time in *Jude*:

> Hardy is already as old as the hills when he is born, foresees the vanity of every wish, and knows that death is the end of life. To see the world this clearly is to see the folly of any involvement in it.
>
> (Hillis-Miller 1970: 13)

Biographico-critical opinion

Hardy biographers and critics have been engaged, over the last 30 years, in a protracted debate regarding his depressive tendencies – the most recent vogue (1990s) being to deny them completely. Having made a firm diagnosis myself, it would seem reasonable to evaluate the varied opinions of these respected Hardy scholars.

Robert Gittings (1978 and1979) was the first of the modern Hardy biographers; he pays scant attention to Hardy's depressions and offers no interpretative opinion. He was followed by Millgate (1982 and 2004), whom I have already cited in support of my diagnosis of Hardy's cyclothymia.

Michael Millgate is an extremely painstaking and thorough researcher; because he has made full and balanced use of the available material – especially *The Early Life* and *The Later Years* and *The Collected Letters* – his text contains multiple references to Hardy's depression, a total of 22 separate episodes being recorded. He acknowledges the link between Hardy's frequent complaint of lack of energy and his underlying depression (Millgate 1982: 239). He also analyses both the endogenous elements in Hardy's mood disorder, particularly in the context of the bleak despairing poetry of 1896 ('In Tenebris I, II & III' and 'Wessex Heights') (Millgate 1982: 381), and the reactive elements arising particularly from Hardy's marriage to Emma (Millgate 1982: 399). Millgate overall presents an accurate account of Hardy's troubles.

Martin Seymour-Smith (1994) set out to redress what he saw as the imbalance in Millgate's and Gittings' accounts. On the positive side Seymour-Smith acknowledges Hardy's cyclothymia as a 'temperament ... both ecstatic and melancholy' (Seymour-Smith 1994: 15, 18). He also draws attention to May O'Rourke, Hardy's secretary's description of Max Gate as: 'the solidification in brick of Hardy's intermittent moods of helplessness at the ugliness of life ...' (ibid.: 311) which again supports my diagnosis. However, he loses credibility in his repeated attempts to explain away Hardy's depression with nebulous terms such as 'creative illness' and 'comic hypochondria' (Seymour-Smith 1994: 78, 737). He attacks Millgate for accepting 'the Florence-inspired, and male-centred, thesis, first filtered through Purdy', but then himself makes use of Florence to back his assertion that Hardy's depression should 'not be taken too seriously' (ibid.: 350, 737); to add to the confusion, he then follows Purdy in blaming Emma for Hardy's negativity (ibid.: 748, 751). In his consideration of the despairing poems of 1896 Seymour-Smith also manages to defeat his own argument. But one can, however, draw from his description of these 'periods of great gloom', which do not constitute 'clinical depression', the clear conclusion that Hardy was suffering from cyclothymia (ibid.: 571–4). Another major limitation of Seymour-Smith's work is the complete lack of references. On the positive side, his biography is a charming Fieldingesque romp through the Hardy story, which perhaps should itself 'not be taken too seriously' (ibid.: 737).

The late James Gibson (1996 and 1999) set out with the specific intention of proving that Hardy was:

> anything but the miserly, miserable, reclusive man portrayed by some biographers. Most of those who actually knew him personally were charmed by his kindness, his hospitality, his vitality, his sense of humour, his modesty and his intense curiosity about life ...
>
> (Gibson 1999: xi)

There is no doubt that Jim Gibson was a very sincere man, but the second sentence of this citation is more an uncannily accurate self-portrait than an evidence-based analysis of Hardy. The central issue here is to do with approach – those who feel the need to defend Hardy see mental illness as a dirty word – any mention of misery or depression as a slur on a good man's character. They fail to acknowledge the positive benefits of cyclothymia or mild BAD. They do not appreciate that locking yourself away in your room, refusing to see visitors and refusing to answer letters may all be essential elements of the creative personality. They do not appreciate that Hardy's misery and reclusiveness were part of the psychological make-up which gave him his creative genius, even if they pay lip-service to his profound belief 'that if way to the better there be, it exacts a full look at the Worst' (*CP* 168). With the singular exception perhaps of John Betjeman, the poet is very seldom a 'good chap'.

In *Thomas Hardy: A Literary Life* Gibson acknowledges the contradictions within Hardy's personality both in the context of the poem 'So Various' and Elliott Felkin's description of Hardy's cyclothymic mood changes (Gibson 1996: 134, 172–3). It is in the introduction to Gibson's companion volume *Interviews & Recollections* (1999) that he declares his personal interest in disproving allegations of Hardy's miserable tendencies. This book is a collection of previously unpublished research material concerning Hardy's life. On dispassionate analysis it fails to fulfil its author's intentions, for it contains no less than six new major pieces of evidence in support of a diagnosis of depression/cyclothymia – evidence, which was unavailable to Millgate in 1982.

Paul Turner's biography (1998), unlike most of its predecessors, is text – rather than life – centred. Like Gittings, Turner records facts, but does not offer detailed interpretations. He does, however, make a number of relevant connections. He sees Trewe, the poet in *An Imaginative Woman*, as a Hardyan self-portrait – 'a pessimist ... with an unlimited capacity for misery' (Turner 1998: 136). He considers that Hardy's 'world-weariness' found expression in *The Dynasts*, making it overall 'a depressing work' (ibid.: 181, 193) which may be a partial explanation for the persistent unpopularity of the book, which Hardy considered his *magnum opus*. Through the mouth of Josephine (ex-Jemima), Hardy expresses his simple philosophy: 'Yet all joy is but sorrow waived awhile' (ibid.: 193) – a most appropriate axiom for a cyclothymic personality.

The publication of two further biographies came in 2006: Claire Tomalin's is a cosy coffee-table read, which acknowledges Hardy's cyclothymic tendencies but offers no new insights, apart perhaps from her connection of the poem 'The Dead Man Walking' with Hardy's blackest moods (2006: 225). She also offers a wonderful description of 'the shifting feelings in a marriage' as being 'as complex and unpredictable as cloud formations' (ibid.: 183). Unlike Tomalin, Ralph Pite rejects much of Millgate's research, identifying Horace Moule's suicide and the First World War as the most important factors in the aetiology of Hardy's depression. He fails, however, to grasp the depth of Hardy's melancholia, noting in a simplistic and dismissive understatement that 'Hardy was evidently a moody person' (Pite 2006: 227).

So Various

1
You may have met a man – quite young –
A brisk-eyed youth, and highly strung:
One who desires
And inner fires
Moved him as wires.

2
And you may have met one stiff and old,
If not in years; of manner cold;
Who seemed as stone,
And never had known
Of mirth or moan.

3
And there may have crossed your path a lover,
In whose clear depths you could discover
A staunch, robust,
And tender trust,
Through storm and gust.

4
And you have also known one fickle,
Whose fancies changed as the silver sickle
Of yonder moon,
Which shapes so soon
To demilune!

5
You entertained a person once
Whom you internally deemed a dunce:-
As he sat in view
Just facing you
You saw him through.

6
You came to know a learned seer
Of whom you read the surface mere;
Your soul quite sank;
Brain of such rank
Dubbed yours a blank.

7
Anon you quizzed a man of sadness,
Who never could have known true gladness:
Just for a whim
You pitied him
In his sore trim.

8
You journeyed with a man so glad
You never could conceive him sad:
He proved to be
Indubitably
Good company.

9

You lit on an unadventurous slow man,
Who, said you, need be feared by no man;
That his slack deeds
And sloth must needs
Produce but weeds.

10

A man of enterprise, shrewd and swift,
Who never suffered affairs to drift,
You eyed for a time
Just in his prime
And judged he might climb.

11

You smoked beside one who forgot
All that you said, or grasped it not.
Quite a poor thing,
Not worth a sting
By satirizing!

12

Next year you nearly lost for ever
Goodwill from one who forgot slights never;
And, with unease,
Felt you must seize
Occasion to please ...

13

Now ... All these specimens of man,
So various in their pith and plan,
Curious to say
Were *one* man. Yea,
I was all they.

(*CP* 870–1)

This poem was first published posthumously in *The Daily Telegraph* on 22 March 1928. It represents Hardy's most unequivocal statement about his lifelong 'rapid cycling disorder' (Gelder 2000: 687). Critics have linked the poem to an observation in *The Early Life*:

> I am more than ever convinced that persons are successively various persons, according as each special strand in their characters is brought uppermost by circumstances.
>
> (*EL* 301)

Yes, but ... it warrants closer analysis. The poem is conventionally printed with the 13 stanzas unnumbered, succeeding each other in lineal fashion. I have reproduced it differently to illustrate the fact that it is composed of six pairs of stanzas, plus a concluding thirteenth stanza, which in the last line of the poem reveals that the poet is writing about himself. Each pair contains one negative verse and one positive verse. The first two pairs start with the positive side of the coin, which is then reflected in the negative by the subsequent stanza. From verse 4 onwards the process is reversed – the final four pairs all starting with the negative stanza, which is followed by its positive reflection. The only arguable exception to this is stanza 12, which hovers just on the positive side of neutral.

The crucial stanza comes at the breakpoint – stanza 7, which is Hardy in his usual dysthymic mood, 'a man of sadness / Who never could have known true gladness'. This pairs with stanza 8, which is Hardy in euphoric state – the poet of *Great Things*, 'a man so glad / You never could conceive him sad'. Although in the other stanzas Hardy is looking at various aspects of the human condition – youth versus age, fidelity versus faithlessness, enterprise versus sloth – in each pairing the negative is overshadowed by the grim grey inertia of depression,whilst the positive has the light touch of those 'joy-jaunts' (*CP* 475). It is a most revealing poem, straight from the soul.

The poet of 'So Various' bears a striking similarity to Lord Byron, famed for his 'chameleon-like qualities' whereby at different hours of the same day, 'he metamorphosed himself into four or more individuals', each possessed 'of the most opposite qualities'. Byron himself remarked that: 'I am so changeable, being everything by turns and nothing long, – I am such a strange *melange* of good and evil, that it would be difficult to describe me' (Steptoe 1998: 195–6).

There is no simple answer as to why this manic-depressive tendency is of benefit to the poet but there are some proven positive associations. Studies of the speech of hypomanic patients have shown that they 'tend to rhyme and use other sound associations, such as alliteration' far more frequently than do unaffected individuals. Such patients also 'use idiosyncratic words nearly three times more often' than do normal controls (Jamison 1995: 50). This immediately brings to mind Hardy's extended use of alliteration, his frequent resort to neologisms and his obsessive rhyming.

Nettle concludes his account of '*Strong Imagination*' with the idea that although 'madness is the antithesis of good mood' and productive thought, it is 'a state with paradoxical underpinnings':

> Those underpinnings are oxymoronic; the superior mental order which leads to mental chaos, and the overwhelming joy which leads to overwhelming despair. Within the capacity for madness dwell some positive qualities which help make people more creative ...
>
> (Nettle 2001: 212)

or to quote Henry Maudsley, writing in 1871:

> I have long had a suspicion ... that mankind is indebted for much of its individuality and for certain forms of genius to individuals with some predisposition to insanity.
>
> (cited in Nettle 2001: 135)

'My mind to me a Kingdom is' (*RN* 169)

> The unequivocal identification of the heath with the unconscious at the beginning of the book establishes its significance in Hardy's portrayal of the human psyche.
>
> (Sumner 1981: 100)

> Or on that loneliest of eves when afar and benighted we stood,
> She who upheld me and I, in the midmost of Egdon together,
> Confident I in her watching and ward through the blackening heather,
> Deeming her matchless in might and with measureless scope endued.
>
> (*In Tenebris III CP* 169)

The Return of The Native is a novel of darkness, set on the black and benighted heath; it is a novel of depression and despair, of sorrow, bereavement and suicide; it is a novel of passion and pain, of failure and futility where all is ultimately absorbed into the encompassing night. The encompassing night, the enclosing heath – they are one and the same – for all is darkness, death, depression and despair. The heath is Hardy and Hardy is the heath. All the characters come from Hardy and to Hardy they return. All the characters are fragments – offshoots – wastings of his own self. The heath comes from his mind and the heath is his mind. The heath is blackness, darkness, death, depression, despair. The heath is Hardy.

> the universe only exists as perceived by our eyes and registered by our brains.
>
> (Irwin 2000: 161)

> depression is a view of the world through a dark glass.
>
> (Jamison 1995: 51)

In the opening chapter of *The Return of The Native*, the heath is presented to the reader as the physical embodiment of depressive symptoms. Like depression 'it could best be felt when it could not be clearly seen'; it is 'a near relation of night' which meets 'the evening gloom in pure sympathy' and 'exhales darkness ... in a black fraternization'. It is a 'home of strange phantoms' which can:

> retard the dawn, sadden noon, anticipate the frowning of storms scarcely generated, and intensify the opacity of a moonless midnight to a cause of shaking and dread ... the hitherto unrecognised

original of those wild regions of obscurity which are vaguely felt to
be compassing us about in midnight dreams of flight and disaster ...

(*RN* 3–5)

The heath, like depression, blackens the outlook of the observer, causes
morbid thoughts, irrational fears and anxieties, sleep disturbance and
early morning waking. Like depression, it is associated with psychomotor retardation and generates pervading feelings of inadequacy, leading to suicidal ideation. To Hardy, it is 'a place perfectly accordant with
man's nature', like him 'slighted and enduring' (*RN* 5). Also to Hardy,
this was his home. The cottage where he was born, and where his
parents were still living at the time of the publication of the novel,
appears bottom-centre of the sketch map, which faced the frontispiece
in the first edition of the novel. 'Clym (Hardy) had been so interwoven
with the heath in his boyhood that hardly anybody could look upon it
without thinking of him ...' (*RN* 170).

It is known that Hardy, having published five novels in the preceding five years, deliberately stopped in 1876 to take stock of his position, paused and thought carefully prior to commencing work on *The
Return of the Native*. He was much more deliberate than ever before, or
ever again, in his planning of this carefully structured novel which
observes the classical unities of place and time; albeit the latter
extended from one day to one year and a day.

How can one reconcile this careful conventional artistic scheming
with the fact that the book appears to be flagrantly autobiographical
and with my contention that despite outward appearances, *The Return
of the Native* is actually a proto-modernist novel written directly from
the depths of Hardy's subconscious? Hardy provided a partial answer
to this problem in a letter written to John Addington Symonds in
1889:

The tragical conditions of life imperfectly denoted in *The Return of
the Native* & some other stories of mine I am less and less able to
keep out of my work. I often begin a story with the intention of
making it brighter & gayer than usual; but the question of con-
science soon comes in; & it does not seem right, even in novels, to
wilfully belie one's own views. All comedy is tragedy, if you only
look deep enough into it. A question which used to trouble me was
whether we ought to write sad stories, considering how much
sadness there is in this world already. But of late I have come to the
conclusion that, the first step towards cure of, or even relief from,

any disease being to understand it, the study of tragedy in fiction may possibly here & there be the means of showing how to escape the worst forms of it ...

(CL 1: 190)

There are a number of answers in this letter. Firstly, Hardy admits that he is using the structure of classical tragedy to contain the contemporary unstructured tragedy of his own life. Secondly, the tendency to always see the tragedy beneath the comedy is a cardinal symptom of depression – a mind that always paints it black. The depressed person will unvaryingly see the negative in the environment and discount the positive. Thirdly, this is an admission of his cyclothymic cycling – in his mind gay intentions are always rapidly superseded by black thoughts. Fourthly, any creative genius – be it Hardy, Shakespeare or Pasternak – will rationalise these continuous intrusive thoughts into a pessimistic if not tragic world view. Fifthly, the disease metaphor is most revealing on a personal level – he is writing through his depression in the hope that he may come to better understand it and thus be able to better cope with it.

It is also revealing that in the first edition of the novel, Eustacia's vantage point was appropriately known as Black-Barrow – only subsequently Wessexified to Rainbarrow by Hardy in the 1890s. The classical unity of place in this novel, where a spectator standing on Black-Barrow could observe all the action, means that all the characters were retained within the oppressive heath. This is a precise metaphor for the disabling effects of depression, which prevent the sufferer from escaping either physically or psychologically from the restraints imposed by the disease. As D. H. Lawrence acknowledged: 'In Hardy's novels, there exists a great background, which matters more than the people who move upon it ...' (Lawrence 1936: 419).

Many early critics, lacking Lawrence's insight, picked up the depression but nothing else:

> the movement is uncommonly slow, the personages are uncommonly uninteresting, the action is uncommonly poor, the conclusion is uncommonly flat ... (*Illustrated London News*).

(quoted in Blunden 1967: 43)

It is hardly surprising that it was at the end of this year that Hardy recorded his 'perception of the FAILURE of THINGS to be what they were meant to be' (*EL* 163). Later and more perceptive critics, such as

W. L. Phelps writing in the *Atlantic Monthly* in 1910, understood Hardy's intentions in his apt description of *The Return of the Native* as 'a masterpiece of despair' (Cox 1970: 399).

The autobiographical nature of this 'most depressing of Hardy's novels' (Sherman 1976: 134) is confirmed as night closes in on the heath, its depressive near relation, and the archetypal romantic figure is displaced from Black Barrow by faggot-bearing heathens (heath-men) who dance their 'jumbled druidical rites' (*RN* 15) in the embers of their fire and discuss those issues uppermost in Hardy's mind – the failure of human projects, the effects of aging, the melancholy outcome of most marriages, depression, anxiety and sexual impotence, here exemplified by Christian, the eponymous representative of an obsolete religion, whose rituals Hardy still held dear.

'Humanity appears upon the Scene, Hand in Hand with Trouble' (*RN* 7)

> After marrying Emma in September 1874, Hardy did not return to Bockhampton until Christmas 1876 … using this visit to gather materials for *The Return of the Native* whose hero returns to his native heath and imperious mother on a Christmas Eve.
>
> (Casagrande 1982: 32)

The result is an intensely autobiographical novel, in which each of the three male protagonists bears a close resemblance to Hardy. In addition, both Eustacia and Thomasin display aspects of Hardy's personality – and the final member of this sextet, Mrs Yeobright is a thinly disguised psychological portrait of Jemima – or more accurately, a portrait of the psychological effect this powerful woman had upon her son. At different stages in the text, each of these six main characters resembles their creator, in displaying significant depressive symptomatology.

Two commit suicide, one drowns accidentally (see Chapter 5 on the nature of 'accidents') and Clym, the character most closely identified with Hardy, only just survives the depressive maelstrom, deeply wounded both physically and psychologically. 'All these specimens of man, / So various in pith and plan' can be identified with an aspect of Hardy's personality described in 'So Various' (*CP* 870/1).

Diggory Venn, a picaresque precursor of Tess and Jude, has 'relinquished his proper station in life for want of interest in it' (RN 75). Like Hardy, a returning native, who has to face the probing questions of the Bloomsend mother figure: 'What made you change from that nice little business your father left you?' (RN 37). A career as a novelist does not offer the same security as architect to a well-established family firm of builders. Presumably out of lost love for Thomasin, he has adopted the mark of Cain, the blood-coloured disfigurement 'that was the sublimation of all horrid dreams' (RN 74). From this disguise of frightening red vagabond, he converses in 'sad and occupied tones' (RN 8). To underachieve, to be indecisive, to be careless of personal appearance and to experience feelings of guilt and worthlessness are all cardinal symptoms of depression. He is the 'man of sadness' but as a lover offers 'staunch, robust, / And tender trust, / Through storm and gust' (stanza 3). Like Hardy, he is also an instinctive voyeur, a manipulator and, ultimately, a survivor.

Damon Wildeve, of the three men, is the closest in character to Hardy himself. Although Clym might superficially appear to be nearer to Hardy, it is Wildeve who shares his most fundamental characteristics. Hardy, indeed, admitted that 'Clym is the nicest of all my heroes, and not a bit like me' (Gibson 1996: 76). Wildeve follows the pattern of returning to the heath, having abandoned the profession to which he was trained, as here described by the rustic chorus:

> To give him his due he's a clever learned fellow in his way – He was brought up to better things than keeping the Quiet Woman. An Engineer – that's what the man was ... but he threw away his chance, and so 'a took a public house to live'. His learning was no use to him at all.
>
> *(RN 21)*

Like Hardy, Damon was driven by the Fitzpierston Syndrome, a representative of stanza 4, 'one fickle, / Whose fancies changed as the silver sickle / Of yonder moon'. There are elements of both Troy and Alec d'Urberville about him; he is capable of remaining consistently faithful to Eustacia, provided she is unavailable to him. Like Hardy in the early 1870s, he nearly falls between two lovers: 'To lose the two women – he who had been the well-beloved of both – was too ironical an issue to be endured ...' (RN 155).

Like Hardy, he is described as 'a nervous and excitable man', the recurrent subject of 'evident depression', 'exquisite misery' and gloomy 'oppression of spirits'. To Wildeve, Hardy applies the epithet which justly is Tom's own: The Rousseau of Egdon Heath: 'To be yearning for the difficult, to be weary of what offered; to care for the remote, to dislike the near' (RN 216) it was Hardy's nature always.

Wildeve shared Hardy's cyclothymic personality trait; to drown by 'accident' is an unfortunate psychosomatic ending for a 'man of sadness' who never knew 'true gladness' (*CP* 871).

Clym Yeobright, although in personality less close to Hardy than Wildeve, represents Hardy's most detailed and comprehensive portrait of a young man suffering from depression. Many of Clym's life circumstances closely resemble Hardy's and there is good evidence that much of his detailed symptomatology came from the author's own experience. Much about Clym has to be autobiographical, for he was born and raised on the same heath as Hardy, living in the very cottage which is to this day preserved in Hardy's memory by the National Trust. When Clym is first introduced into the novel, his countenance clearly shows that 'thought is a disease of the flesh' and his facial expression is of 'a natural cheerfulness striving against depression ... and not quite succeeding' (*RN* 139–40). Hardy, it seems, conceived Clym as a kind of Hamlet:'a superior mind and sensibility ravaged by that disease, thought and misunderstood by the cruder world ...' (Draper 1991: 126).

In fact, Hardy probably saw himself as a kind of Hamlet, sent away from Elsinore to a great seat of learning, ultimately returning as a dissatisfied and depressed perpetual student. In December 1870, whilst courting Emma, Hardy marked the following passage in his copy of *Hamlet*: 'Thou wouldst not think how ill all's here about my heart; / But it is no matter!' This quotation is accompanied by the comment that: 'Hardy was far from being in bright spirits about his book, himself and his future at this time' (*EL* 109).

Clym, like Hardy, 'had been a lad of whom something was expected'; also, like Hardy, he had shown an early interest in the Napoleonic Wars and, in a biblical image, by the age of 12 his fame 'as an artist and scholar' had spread 'at least two miles around' (*RN* 170–1). The evolutionary 'result of a long line of disillusive centuries', Hardy's 'New Man' had returned home because he could be 'a trifle less useless here than anywhere else'. In 'very depressing' Paris, Clym woke every morning to 'see the whole creation groaning and travailing in pain' (*RN* 173, 177) – a faithful replication of Hardy's own experiences as an apprentice architect in that London of 'Four million forlorn hopes' (*EL* 285). Hardy then asks the question:

Was Yeobright's mind well-proportioned? No. A well-proportioned mind is one which shows no particular bias; one of which we may safely say that it will never cause its owner to be confined as a madman … its usual blessings are happiness and mediocrity …

(*RN* 175)

This passage is wholly autobiographical – Hardy has good insight into his own mind – that of the cyclothymic, manic-depressive creative personality. In his ghosted autobiographies, Hardy recurrently refers to his own lack of social ambition. Clym, similarly 'had no desires of that sort'. Like Hamlet, returned to Elsinore, like Hardy in London in his late twenties, Clym had: 'reached the stage in a young man's life when the general grimness of the human situation first becomes clear … in France it is not uncustomary to commit suicide at this stage …' (*RN* 189). But Clym came home from Paris to avoid this eventuality to join Hardy in England where: 'we do much better or much worse as the case may be. The love between the young man and his mother was strangely invisible now' (*RN* 189–90).

This juxtaposition in the text of reactive depression, suicidal thoughts and love for the mother cannot be seen as coincidental. Albeit a subconscious connection, Hardy has unearthed the Oedipal root of the problem. Clym has filled his mental vacuum by falling in love, in the process of which he becomes irretrievably alienated from his mother; he then marries in anger and in haste. His mother does not attend the wedding just as Hardy's parents were not invited to his marriage ceremony. From here onward, Clym's life becomes a leisurely repentance as disease half-blinds him and his mother and wife, in turn, die in tragic circumstances. Both deaths contained multiple preventable elements; a depressed person is frequently a tragedy not just for themselves but for all those close to them as well.

His mother's untimely death provokes a morbid grief reaction with psychotic features including auditory hallucinations. During the course of this illness, which compounds his already depressed state, Clym becomes overtly suicidal, longing 'for death as a field-labourer longs for the shade' (*RN* 312); such thoughts are common currency on grim Egdon. Clym recovers to a limited extent, but remains mentally stultified and unable to build the necessary bridges to repair his relationship with Eustacia. Separated from his wife and lodging alone back at Blooms-end, Clym continues to express suicidal ideation but uses humdrum physical activity as 'a screen between himself and despair' (*RN* 347). Depressed, deeply introspective and mentally inert, he obtains a masochistic pleasure in labelling himself a double-murderer on Eustacia's suicide: 'She is the second woman I have killed this year.

I was a great cause of my mother's death and I am the chief cause of hers' (*RN* 380).

The widowed Clym, like the widowed Hardy grieving for Emma, seems 'but a dead man held on end / To sink down soon' (*CP* 339). Despite, or perhaps because of his own near death experience, his grief at the loss of Eustacia appears to be no more than a passing formality. Clym's Acute Opthalmia, which turns him into a 'pur-blind prank'ster (*CP* 538), is a powerful image of his psychological impairment.

At the end of the novel, the 'undead' Clym, 'the mere corpse of a lover' (*RN* 398), ekes out his days visiting the graves of the two women, whom he once loved. Like Pierston at the conclusion of *The Well-Beloved*, Clym's emotions are perpetually anaesthetised as he ritual-istically acts out his guilt in the graveyards and on the selection of dangerous places so carefully listed by Hardy in his new role as: 'a lonely and misunderstood preacher – perhaps rather like Hardy himself' (Williams 1978: 145).

In *So Various*, Clym, like Hardy, mainly inhabits stanza 7 as 'a man of sadness' with occasional excursions, like Hardy in the preceding stanza as 'a learned seer' (*CP* 871). Clym shares all Hardy's cyclothymic personality characteristics, but does this amount to Clinical Depression? And, if so, does that tell us anything reliable about Hardy himself? The checklists, ICD-10 and DSM-IV, act as score-cards in the process of trying to standardise the diagnosis of a condition which is not yet accessible to biochemical or electrophysiological measurement. In order to diagnose a 'Major Depressive Episode' at least five of the listed criteria should have been present for at least two weeks and either numbers 1 or 2 must be present:

Acute Depression as defined in ICD-10 and DSM-IV
1. Depressed mood most of the day, nearly every day.
2. Markedly diminished interest or pleasure in all or almost all activities, most of the day, nearly every day.
3. Loss of energy or fatigue nearly every day.
4. Loss of confidence or self-esteem.*
5. Unreasonable feelings of self-reproach or excessive or inappropriate guilt, nearly every day.
6. Recurrent thoughts of death or suicide, or any suicidal behaviour.
7. Diminished ability to think or concentrate, or indecisiveness, nearly every day.
8. Psychomotor agitation or retardation, nearly every day.

9. Insomnia or hypersomnia nearly every day.
10. Change in appetite (decrease or increase with corresponding weight change).
   (*This criteria excluded from DSM-IV)

(Gelder 2000: 683)

Altogether there are 15 separate textual references to Clym suffering from depression – scattered throughout *The Return of The Native* in a similar fashion to the scattering of references to Hardy's depression in *The Early Life* and *The Later Years*. Clym in Paris found it 'very depressing' 'trying to be like people who had very little in common with myself' (*RN* 172) but this echoes Hardy – and there is no evidence that he was failing to function on a day-to-day basis in Paris any more than Hardy failed to cope in London. After his mother's death, he scores ten out of ten and this illness was of more than two weeks duration. However, some authorities consider that recent bereavement excludes a diagnosis of Major Depression – so this really takes us back to square one. Diagnosis – a dysthymic individual who suffers recurrent depressive episodes of insufficient duration to be classified as Depression under DSM-IV.

Thomasin is the most stable of the six main characters in the novel. Her initial abortive attempt at marriage and subsequent mistreatment by Wildeve naturally result in some reactive tearfulness and sorrow, but no serious depression. Thomasin has been seen by some critics as an expression of the female side of Hardy's character – the deliberate clue being in her name. It has also been suggested that this is a portrait of his sister Mary. She is certainly a resilient woman with many of the personality characteristics of Mrs Yeobright / Jemima. I think that the clue does lie in her name, but this does not make her a female Thomas. Her name should be correctly read as 'Thomas-in' or even 'Thomas-sin', for the person she bears most resemblance to, Hardy's cousin, Tryphena Sparks. Don't forget that Thomasin is Clym's cousin.

There is strong evidence to support the view that at the time Hardy took up with Emma, he was engaged to be married to Tryphena. The label 'Thomas-in' is the equivalent of the ram's reddle brand on the ewe. Hardy dallied with Tryphena's affections just as Wildeve dallied with Thomasin – but Tryphena was tougher than the idealised fictional cousin. In the real world, Tom was offered no second chance, for Tryphena left Dorset to become Headmistress of a girls' elementary school in Plymouth and within three years was married to a local publican, named Gale rather than Wildeve! Success at the altar for Thomasin, in typical Hardyan fashion, brings no happiness but instead casts 'a shadow of sadness' over her 'pure sweet face' (*RN* 268).

Eustacia, Queen of Night is at first sight a complex and confusing character. This is almost certainly a reflection of the way in which she developed within Hardy's creative consciousness. In his original scheme for the novel, Eustacia was to have been a 'malign witch' named Avice (Woodcock 1978: 28). History does not relate why his plans changed so radically, but this original scheme must surely connect with 'that wild weird western shore' (*CP* 351), a land populated by heathens (heath men) who had never fully accepted Christianity, a land where witchcraft was rife and where he had himself been bewitched by 'the swan-necked one who rode / Along the beetling Beeny Crest' (*CP* 338) – a woman who was a non-Christian at the time of their courtship, if not a witch herself. From these quite tumultuous beginnings, the malign Avice was translated into the beautiful but miserable Eustacia, who nevertheless retained some of her original black attributes.

But black magic was transformed into black moods as Eustacia evolved into a wholly human and increasingly unhappy young woman. This change either reflected or anticipated a change, which was to occur in Emma on displacement eastward – from unbeliever to obsessionally devout Christian. Eustacia, 'the raw material of a divinity', was 'a girl of some forwardness of mind', just as Emma had been when Hardy first met her; a girl who 'hated Sundays' but would read her bible on a weekday 'that she might be unoppressed with a sense of doing her duty' (*RN* 67). Her prayers, however, were more Romantic than Christian: 'O deliver my heart from this fearful gloom and loneliness; send me great love from somewhere, else I shall die' (*RN* 67).

Eustacia, 'full of nocturnal mysteries' (*RN* 63), is not only the character most closely allied with the heath but also the person most consistently depressed, with no less than 28 separate textural references to her sorrowful state of mind. Hardy's initial description reveals her wandering in 'a desponding reverie' (*RN* 54); we are next informed that 'she suffered much from depression of spirits' and, in company with Clym and Hardy himself, had arrived 'at that stage of enlightenment which feels that nothing is worthwhile' (*RN* 68). 'To be loved to madness – such was her great desire' but, like Hardy the poet, 'she concluded that love was but a doleful joy' (*RN* 67). Like Emma Bovary and Grace Melbury, an ambitious father had over-educated her for a secluded rural existence. Like Emma, her mind was full of Paris and adolescent fantasies, which lead only to suicide.

In her first recorded conversation with Wildeve, Eustacia identifies two separate causes for her intractable gloominess. Firstly, there is a reactive element due to her isolation on the wild heath coupled with her lover's vacillations and his typical Romantic unreliability. Secondly, she is conscious of an endogenous element in her depression: 'It was in my nature to feel like that. It was born in my blood I suppose' (*RN* 60–1). Wildeve somewhat unhelpfully labels this 'hypochondriasis', but the narrator confirms the depressing effect of this bleak environment on the girl with pagan eyes by stating that 'Egdon was her Hades' and that 'she had imbibed much of what was dark in its tone' (*RN* 64). Blooms-end indeed becomes Hell's-gate. In Darwinian terms she was a creature unadapted to her environment, for she dwelt on the Heath without studying its meanings, the equivalent of 'wedding a foreigner without learning his tongue' (*RN* 68). This 'strange sense of isolation' (*RN* 68), generated by immigration into a hostile and alien environment, is a potent cause of depression. Eustacia's experience here is paralleled in *The Woodlanders* where depression does not afflict the native woodmen, but strikes the urban outsiders deposited down in that dark Darwinian wilderness, where they fail to take root and thus fall prey to the 'Unfulfilled Intention which makes life what it is' (*TW* 52), with fatal consequences for Felice Charmond and near-fatal consequences for Fitzpiers.

At this early stage in the novel, Eustacia perceptively acknowledges that the heath is 'my cross, my misery and will be my death' (*RN* 82). As with many depressives who ultimately commit suicide, her thoughts recurrently return to the prospect of her own death. When Venn tries to arrange for her to move to Budmouth to act as companion to an old lady, her languor and inertia are such that she is unwilling to consider it, even though it would give her direct access to the social world for which she ostensibly longs. This response to Venn's offer gives adequate clinical information to definitely diagnose Eustacia Vye as suffering from a Major Depressive Episode in Book the First of this tragedy. She has an ongoing positive score for at least five of the criteria in ICD-10. Namely: (1) Depressed mood; (2) Markedly diminished interest or pleasure; (3) Loss of energy or fatigue; (4) Loss of confidence and self-esteem; (5) Recurrent thoughts of death.

Eustacia's depression ties in with manic-depressive aspects of the Fitzpierston Syndrome for she believes that:

Love was ... the one cordial which could drive away the eating loneliness of her days. And she seemed to long for that abstraction called passionate love rather than any particular lover ... she desired love as one in a desert would be thankful for brackish water.

(*RN* 66–7)

It is inevitable therefore that the idea of Clym, the glamorous Parisian outsider, should act as a temporary antidote to Eustacia's depression. True to their creator, however, the first words of conversation between the pair comprise an agreement that life is 'a cause of depression a good many have to put up with', followed by a lapse into silence (*RN* 145). During the brief spring and foreshortened summer of their courtship and early marriage, Eustacia's native melancholia is somewhat suppressed, but it is never far from her consciousness. As Clym kisses her on Blackbarrow by the suppressed light of a lunar eclipse, he questions her gloomy fancies. She replies: 'it is my general way of looking. I think it arises from my feeling sometimes an agonising pity for myself that I ever was born' (*RN* 197).

The married state accentuates rather than alleviates her depression because it highlights all the dreams than can now never be realised. 'The Closed Door' can be interpreted as referring equally to the ending of all hope of happiness for Eustacia by marriage to Clym, as much as to the exclusion of his mother on the hostile heath. The door of the cottage is the door to the coffin for Eustacia and Clym and probably Wildeve also. Newly wed, Eustacia's mood sinks more and more into a mournful groove; she hides herself away from Clym in the garden to 'weep despairing tears' (*RN* 251). Meanwhile, her purblind prankster of a husband sings gay Parisian songs in his ophthalmic affliction, steadfastly refusing to acknowledge her consummate need to escape the overwhelmingly oppressive heath. The odds are stacked increasingly against Eustacia – her husband's partial sight may give him vision enough to chop furze, but it allows him no insight at all into her mental state.

Despite this lack of support, Eustacia 'goes out to battle against Depression'; to do her best to 'be bitterly merry', albeit acknowledging that death offered 'the only door of relief if the satire of heaven should go much further' (*RN* 258–9). In her determination not to succumb to the depression, the increasingly desperate girl self-prescribes CBT, in line with the best current evidence-based medicine. She initiates this 'new system' by going to a dance (*RN* 285). In the process she does, however, admit to herself: 'Two wasted lives – his, and mine' (*RN* 259) in a direct echo of Hardy's poem 'We

Sat at the Window', written just ten months into his marriage with Emma:

> We were irked by the scene, by our own selves; yes,
> …
> Wasted were two souls in their prime,
> And great was the waste, that July time
> When the rain came down.
>
> (CP 429)

A similar state of non-communication exists in the cottage at Alderworth, where Eustacia is left alone and 'considerably depressed' (*RN* 300). Mrs Yeobright dies and the 'pale tragical' girl has to nurse, in solitary confinement, her distracted, mentally disturbed husband. With her tender care, Clym recovers sufficiently to accuse her, with his customary lack of insight, of being his mother's murderer. Eustacia, who has never placed much value on her own life, echoes Hamlet as she invites him to reciprocate for 'the place will serve as well as any other – as somewhere to pass from – into my grave' (*RN* 330, 333).

This altercation drives her away from Alderworth forever – back to her grandfather's house where, isolated and deeply depressed, she would have blown her brains out with the old man's pistols but for Charley's timely intervention. She is thoroughly worn down by 'the heavy and the weary weight / Of all this unintelligible world' (Wordsworth 1991: 114) and asks tremulously 'Why should I not die if I wish?' (*RN* 340). Characteristically, for an ongoing severe depressive illness, her thoughts return recurrently – and in her own mind quite logically – to suicide. With an alienated husband and an indifferent grandfather, Charley's loving ministrations are insufficient to counter her recurrent major depression. At this stage she scores nine or ten out of ten on ICD-10/DSM-IV.

By the second 5 November, Eustacia is weeping openly beside Charley's bonfire. Here at last, Wildeve acknowledges what the others have been blind to – that 'it has been pushed too far – it is killing you' (*RN* 344). But his misguided attempts to remove her from the overpowering darkness of the heath and the overpowering bleakness of her own mind are no match for the suicidal intent of a woman whose soul is 'in an abyss of desolation' (*RN* 362). As is often the case in severe depression, a small amount of recovered motivation turns an inert patient into a high suicide risk. On that dark stormy night she heads across the wind-swept heath towards the dubious comfort of Wildeve's gig, but instead finds eternal comfort in the inviting flood-swollen waters of Shadwater Weir. Quite appropriately, Hardy reveals no details of Eustacia's final journey beyond the fact that Venn heard a sobbing woman pushing through the heath past his van. The last moments of a successful suicide are seldom public property.

With Eustacia dead, the darkened heath with which her pagan personality was so entwined loses all its malignancy; it becomes a bland pallid background upon which children Maypole dance and from which Thomasin can gather flowers.

*   *   *

The Return of The Native can therefore be read as a detailed treatise on depressive illness. The heath itself can be taken both as an image of the author's own mind and as a complex metaphor for depression. The text contains several detailed case histories as well as the author's own (thinly veiled) testimony to his personal experience of depressive symptoms. In addition, Hardy recurrently rationalises depression in this novel as a post-Darwinian philosophic stance on the futility of existence, whilst simultaneously showing it to be the natural expression of native Egdon melancholia – rendered in the local dialect as the wish to 'have my life unbe' (*CP* 177). Eustacia Vye, whose case history he develops the most fully, declares in her last rally before her final suicidal decline that: 'I'll be bitterly merry and ironically gay, and I'll laugh in derision' (*RN* 259).

On his native heath, Hardy goes back to the future. For here, a tragedy which observes the classical unities of time and place divides into two opposing dead-ends – or recurrent acts: death that is meaningless, and life that is futile. At this point Hardy connects directly into Samuel Beckett. For Clym and Eustacia, read Vladimir and Estragon.

The Wessex Lament or *Taedium Vitae* (Prichard 19)

It wears me out to think of it,
To think of it:
I cannot bear my fate as writ,
I'd have my life unbe;
Would turn my memory to a blot,

> Make every relic of me rot,
> My doings be as they were not,
> And gone all trace of me!
>
> (*CP* 177)

Hardy attributed these words to Tess, but Eustacia, or any of the other 20 successful suicides in Hardy's Wessex, could equally well have spoken them.

Aeneas Manston, Hardy's first self-slaughterer, leaves behind him a lengthy confessional suicide note which reveals not only an immense supportive sympathy between the author and the supposed villain of this melodrama, but also shows Hardy's nihilistic 'life unbe' philosophy to be already fully developed in *Desperate Remedies*. Manston begins his note in Hamlet tones, by renouncing 'man's life' as a 'wretchedly conceived scheme' (*DR* 388) and logically concludes that: 'I am about to pass into my normal condition. For people are almost always in their graves' (*DR* 394).

Despite Hardy's declared intention to make *Desperate Remedies* a sensation novel, his deep human sympathies cannot help breaking through, with the result that Manston emerges more as a victim than a villain. Fortunately, Hardy abandoned his attempts at the genre and from here on there can be no such doubts. Hardy's *Literary Notebooks* reveal a continuing interest in suicide; in particular he recorded numerous excerpts from an essay entitled 'The Ethics of Suicide' which had appeared in *The Saturday Review* in 1876, just before he started work on *The Return of The Native*. There is good evidence that Hardy was deeply affected by the suicide of his friend and mentor Horace Moule. Moule, who appears to have been suffering from MDI, slit his throat with a razor in his rooms at Cambridge. Moule had significant alcohol problems, a common concomitant of MDI/BAD. Hardy wrote several poems about the death of his friend, the first of which begins simply 'You died, and made but little of it!' (*CP* 861) – an echo of Moule's final words 'So easy to die!' (Turner 1998: 266).

Clym, the returning native, had reached the stage 'in a young man's life' where 'in France it was not uncustomary to commit suicide' (*RN* 189). In the event it was not Clym, but his young wife who took this path. Other writers at this time expressed similar views, as in Mary Elizabeth Braddon's somewhat Romantic assertion that 'the youthful mind hankers naturally after suicide' (Braddon 1998: 225). Hardy's studies on this subject were in line with modern research which has revealed that:

1. Fifty per cent of adolescents have suicidal thoughts almost once a week
2. Ten per cent of people who suffer an episode of severe depression, ultimately commit suicide
3. At least five people are influenced by each case of suicidal behaviour.

(Wolpert 1999: 64–8)

Hardy had done his research well, for not only is Eustacia suffering from a recurrent depressive illness but also she comes from just the kind of unsupportive background that greatly increases suicide risk. We are not told her exact age, only that she is three years older than Charley who is described as a youth; one whose voice is less 'juvenile and fluty' than her own (*RN* 126, 131). This probably makes Eustacia 18 or 19 years old, a calculation that undermines those critics who condemn her for 'adolescent behaviour'. She is an orphan whose musician father throve until 'her mother's death'. then 'left off thriving, drank and died also' (*RN* 65). We are not told the cause of his death, but we know 'that his pockets were as light as his occupation'. It is likely that Eustacia inherited her depressive tendency (probable BAD) from her father. Such a diagnosis would fit with his rapid professional failure, alcohol abuse and death so soon after the loss of his wife. Hardy does not reveal whether this was direct or indirect suicide.

The orphaned Eustacia is transported to the 'loneliest of lonely houses on these thinly populated slopes' (*RN* 69), where her wholly unsupportive grandfather neglects her. As when first seen on Blackbarrow, she remains a solitary figure who cuts herself off from her neighbours, whom she disdainfully describes as 'a parcel of cottagers' (*RN* 89). She does not love Wildeve and she falls in love with a dream of Paris rather than the man known as Clym. Her youth, her isolation, her genetic make-up, her family history and the total absence of any form of support network make her a prime candidate for suicide.

Para-suicide

Eustacia's successful attempt at suicide followed an initial failure when Charley removed the pistols. This represents one of ten thwarted suicide attempts in Hardy's fiction. As in Eustacia's case, nearly all the others manage to achieve premature death within a year or so of the initial unsuccessful attempt. Suicide is commuted to life imprisonment as 'a timely blow from Samway' (*FM* 388) sends the contents of the second barrel of Boldwood's shotgun into a beam rather than the unfortunate farmer's skull. Lady Constantine fails in her intention to leap from the tower, but instead dies from 'sudden joy after despair' (*TT* 262) on Swithin's return – always beware the returning native!

Michael Henchard is another man who has much of his creator in his make-up. He is a man subject to 'gloomy fits', 'moody depressions' (*MC* 128, 264), violent mood swings and strong emotions. These rapid emotional fluctuations, which strongly suggest a cyclothymic disposition, make it difficult for him to form any stable relationship. Ian Gregor noted similarities between Eustacia's duality and Henchard's divided self, which cause 'his very energies to be directed towards self-destruction' (Gregor 1974: 115). Just as Eustacia inhabited the heath of Hardy's early childhood, so Henchard inhabited the Dorchester of Hardy's boyhood. Both Henchard and Hardy work their way up from rural obscurity to positions of prominence, both, like Tess, are extremely susceptible to music, and both sat as Magistrates in Dorchester – Hardy being appointed to the bench whilst he was writing *The Mayor of Casterbridge*. The connections are multiple and as Rosemary Sumner observed:

> Henchard's behaviour pattern is repetitive, but with a fitful downward movement. Hardy shows his awareness that there is no clear dividing line between mental health and illness. The aggressive-depressive nature of Henchard's personality makes him very vulnerable ...
>
> (Sumner 1981: 63)

This aggressive-depressive cycle means that when outward circumstances are favourable, 'his practical largeness of view' (*MC* 264) has the upper hand, but when events turn against him (bad corn, bad critics), he has no reserve and gravitates towards 'the miserables' on 'the remoter bridge' (*MC* 297). Ultimately, he 'took off his coat and hat' and 'stood on the bank of the stream with his hands clasped in front of him', but is prevented from falling into 'the pool he was intending to make his deathbed' (*MC* 372) by the fortuitous appearance of his skimmity doppelgänger. Like Clym, he then bitterly regrets that 'that performance of theirs killed her, but kept me alive!' (*MC* 374). His health declines, he becomes 'morbidly sensitive' (*MC* 384), he expresses recurrent suicidal thoughts, he is completely anorexic but fortunate in that 'the very heaviness of his soul causes him to sleep profoundly' (*MC* 393). At this point his cyclothymia has transformed into a major depressive illness. Having been thwarted in suicide, he bides his time and nature runs its course.

On Tess's marriage, her companion Retty, who has previously expressed suicidal thoughts, nearly succeeds in her intention but for the waterman who spies something floating in the Great Pool: 'He and another man brought her home, thinking 'a was dead; but she fetched round by degrees' (*TD* 232).

Tess's offer to follow suit receives a derisory response from her husband, so she then plans to hang herself under the mistletoe, but suffers a failure of will and has to wait until she can be officially hung by the due processes of law in Wintoncester gaol. Tess, like Eustacia, Henchard and Hardy, is prone to rapidly alternating states of depression and elation, which in this novel – as in *The Return of The Native* – are characterised by bright shafts of sunlight suddenly breaking through the gloom. The darkness rather than the light was picked up by an early critic in *The Saturday Review*, who could see 'not a gleam of sunshine anywhere' except among the cows at Talbothays (Abbott and Bell 2001: 65).

Tess, like Eustacia, has a background that gives her a high risk of both depressive illness and suicide on this 'blighted planet' where 'the daylight has nothing to show' (*TD* 354). Hardy's 'Pure Woman' is raised in poverty, prostituted by her inadequate and alcoholic parents, raped by her employer, bereaved of her infant daughter, then courted, married and immediately deserted by a man with a severe personality disorder. It is hard for a girl in these circumstances to stay in contact with reality so, feeling 'like a fugitive in a dream' (TD 397), she murders the man who raped her and thus, as stated, commits suicide by proxy, achieving her enduring ambition to 'have my life unbe' (*CP* 177).

Jude, the next in Hardy's catalogue of failed suicides, is an orphan who comes from an equally disturbed background as Tess and Eustacia, and also displays the same tendency to cyclothymia. He is brought up by his great-aunt who repeatedly tells him, 'poor useless boy!' (*JO* 7), that he would be better off dead. Jude has a family history of suicide, for his mother drowned herself in a pond after separating from his father. Once Jude's own hasty marriage has disintegrated, he walks on a frosty night into the middle of a large round pond, he then jumps up and down in the centre of the pond but the ice holds firm: 'He supposed he was not a sufficiently dignified person for suicide. Peaceful death abhorred him as a subject, and would not take him' (*JO* 65).

The President of the Immortals has yet to finish his sport with Jude, who must suffer more and pass that suffering on to Young Father Time and his two siblings. Once this trio have been crucified, Jude manages at last to reach Manston's much courted 'normal condition' by combining the effects of a 'driving rain' and 'the coldest of winds' on a body already consumptive and psychologically broken (*JO* 382, 386).

As he crawls home to 'put an end to a feverish life which ought never to have been begun', he experiences auditory hallucinations for the voices of phantom Alumni have:

> ... a way of whispering to me – fellow-wight who yet abide
> In the muted, measured note
> Of a ripple under archways, or a lone cave's stillicide.
>
> (*CP* 60)

In particular, Jude hears the voice of Robert Burton 'the great Dissector of Melancholy' (*JO* 387/8), the propounder of the view that 'melancholy madness was the only reasonable response of an intelligent man to a crazy world' (Berrios and Porter 1995: 417). Pearston in *The Pursuit of The Well-Beloved* also fails in his attempt to commit suicide by drowning, drifting Rousseau-like in a rowing boat, not on the calm surface of the Lac de Biel but in the torrential currents of the 'Southern', tearing between 'the Beal and the Race' (*WB* 164). Like Jude, he is not allowed to drown – just to sustain a severe head injury that destroys his artistic sensibility – and thus enables him to enjoy a peaceful retirement with 'a wrinkled crone' for 'The Juno of that day was the Witch of Endor of this' (*WB* 167).

Other failed suicides include Matthaus, the Melancholy Hussar, who ultimately succeeds in being shot by firing squad, arguably because his beloved Phyllis suffers such cognitive impairment that she is unable to adhere to her decision to elope with him. Her clinical depression is the result of living in a world of 'indescribable dreariness' (*WT* 32) with an equally depressed and withdrawn father – both endogenous and reactive factors are in operation here. The outcome for Phyllis is similar to that experienced by Clym – a severe bereavement reaction during which 'they despaired of her reason', followed by a cataleptic half-life tending two graves whilst awaiting her own (*WT* 43–4). The final character in this series is the mysterious Baron Von Xanten, whose suicidal persistence in the novella, *The Romantic Adventures of a Milkmaid*, is ultimately rewarded. In this updated fairy-tale, Prince Charming recurrently attempts suicide in preference to marrying Cinderella. Life in Hardy's Wessex is tough, futile and best terminated prematurely.

However much Hardy's characters extolled the virtues of *felo de se*, and however much he bitterly complained of depression and the futility of existence, there is no evidence that he ever attempted to end his own life. Amongst his fellow creative artists and poets, this makes him almost the exception rather than the rule. Despite his cyclothymia, Hardy was well enough mentally balanced that any suicidal tendencies could be dissipated through his literary creations rather than his own body. Jamison's research endorses Hardy's fictional case histories for she found that:

> The overwhelming majority of all adolescents and adults who commit suicide have been determined, through post-mortem investigations, to have suffered either bipolar manic-depressive or unipolar depressive illness.
>
> (Jamison 1993:16)

'The passion for destruction is also a creative passion' (Bakunin in Alvarez 1971: 41)

Jamison considered that the following eighteenth-century poets suffered from MDI – Cowper, Chatterton, Blake, Coleridge, Byron, Shelley and Clare, whilst Goldsmith, Burns and Keats suffered like Hardy from cyclothymia and Wordsworth merely 'probable recurrent depression' (Jamison 1993: 63–71). Tennyson, with a family history of severe psychiatric illness, also receives a retrospective diagnosis of MDI. Two of these poets were certified insane and two committed suicide, apart from those who died prematurely from the indirect effects of their illness/creative impulse.

In 'An Imaginative Woman' (1893) Hardy wrote a fictional account of his own suicide. Ella Marchmill, a thinly disguised portrait of Hardy's 'rare fair woman' (*CP* 320) Florence Henniker, is locked in a loveless marriage. She writes poetry 'to let flow her painfully embayed emotions' (*LI* 11). but her dissatisfaction with the inadequacy (real or imagined) of her writing reinforces her depressive tendency. Trewe, the object of Ella's fanciful infatuation, is a self-portrait of the young Hardy – a man, 'dreamy, solitary, rather melancholy', a pessimist 'who looks at the worst contingencies as well as the best in the human condition (*LI* 9, 11). Mrs Marchmill twice arranges to meet this dark-eyed mustachioed man for whom she lusts both in body and poetic mind.

Unfortunately, the depressed poet prefers to write his 'Lyrics to a Woman Unknown' rather than meet Ella in the flesh. Trewe, also like Hardy, is a man morbidly sensitive to adverse critical reviews. Unable to cope with the 'ferocious criticism' of his new volume, he commits suicide with a revolver, quite probably one manufactured by Ella's husband. Grieving and pregnant once more, for Marchmill, atypically for a Hardyan character, is an adept manufacturer of children, as well as lethal weapons, Ella's depression deteriorates. She develops a morbid conviction that she will die in childbirth and promptly does so – all for the sake of another 'unnecessary life' (*LI* 31).

Jamison has shown that prior to the availability of lithium and other agents for the effective treatment of MDI/BAD, one in five of those affected committed suicide. As far as poetry and literary creativity is concerned, this creates an awkward dilemma. Should the medical profession cure the poet of his poetry in order to ensure that he survives, like Thomas Hardy, to a ripe old age? If Emma had dragged her reluctant Tom along to the doctor in the early years of their marriage complaining about his intractable depressive tendencies, would a suitable prescription have allowed him to resume a comfortable career as a local architect, with no compulsion to record the tragic nature of the human condition? In these days of evidence-based medicine, this would be a wholly reasonable way to proceed for: 'a meta-analysis of 15 controlled trials in dysthymia showed that 55 per cent of patients responded well to antidepressant drugs' (Stott 6).

We 'fellow-wights who yet abide' (*CP* 60) must be eternally grateful for the fact that Hardy was born in 1840 not 1940! Similarly, if Eustacia, Henchard, Tess or Jude had sought medical help, or been sectioned under the Mental Health Act when overtly suicidal, and then prescribed the appropriate chemical agent, would they each have survived into a discontented old age, tolerating the side-effects of their medications, their emotional excesses pharmacologically suppressed? There is, however, a sting in the tale of this argument, for in reality: 'Doctors do much to facilitate suicide by providing patients with the appropriate medications with which to carry it out' (Clare 1976: 351).

Many patients in any case refuse treatment for BAD because the medications prescribed impair both alertness and sensitivity. The overall prognosis is by no means rosy; figures from the United Sales indicate a tenfold increase in the diagnosis rate for depression between 1900 and 2000. There could be many variables in this kind of startling statistic; more concrete is the fact that: 'In the past thirty-five years, the suicide rate amongst American college [students] has tripled' (Schwarz 2005: 209).

As in Hardy's time, adolescents and young adults remain extremely vulnerable to self-slaughter. In the twentieth century, the tendency to suicide amongst female creative writers appeared to have become endemic – if not epidemic. These sorrowful women exemplify Hardy's predicted 'coming universal wish not to live' (*JO* 333), sharing in both 'Tess's Lament':

> I cannot bear my fate as writ
> I'd have my life unbe;
> Would turn my memory to a blot,
> Make every relic of me rot,
> My doings be as they were not,
> And gone all trace of me!
>
> (*CP* 177)

and her considered opinion that 'birth itself was an ordeal of degrading personal compulsion, whose gratuitousness nothing in the result seemed to justify' (*TD* 376). This leads us full circle back to the beginning of this book – to Obsextrics and Hardy's instructions 'To an Unborn Pauper Child':

> Breathe not, hid heart: cease silently,
> And though thy birth-hour beckons thee,
> Sleep the long sleep.
>
> (*CP* 127).

8
Afterwords

'The persistence of the unforeseen' (*MC* 411)

... from Yalbury to Yalding

In the final chapter, I explored the links between Bipolar Affective Disorder (BAD, an MDI), its milder variant, Cyclothymia, and both literary creativity and the Fitzpierston Syndrome. I also examined the way in which Thomas Hardy's creative impulses were inextricably linked with his depressive tendency, arguing that he suffered from a cyclothymic tendency, which he repeatedly recreated in his protagonists, as illustrated by Tess and Henchard – but demonstrated in greatest detail in *The Return of The Native*, which can be read as a complex treatise on depression. What is quite extraordinary about this text is the way in which Hardy produces a detailed portrait of Clinical Depression far superior to anything available in medical textbooks of that time. In fact, it was not until the second half of the twentieth century that doctors began to understand, and psychiatric textbooks began to describe, Clinical Depression with anything approaching the depth of knowledge displayed by Hardy in this novel published in 1878.

In this book, I have in general tried to illustrate how Hardy may be used as a two-way window, both for backward visioning into the pre-scientific medical world of mid-nineteenth-century Dorset and forward viewing into the post-scientific medical world of mid-twenty-first-century England. The similarities will be more striking than the differences, for human nature does not change – medical, political, social fashions wax and wane, but the human response, that complex psychosomatic bundle – the beast at core – remains unaltered. This is why Hardy, with his exact observing eye and responsive sympathetic pen, will, like Shakespeare, remain a source of both knowledge and excitement for as long as the English language survives as a means of communication.

Hardy's texts, like any narrative, medical or literary, are a complex interweaving of fiction and reality – of the subjective impulse and the objective interpretation. His patients – if they recover – do so despite, rather than because of, the interventions offered by their General Practitioners.

These doctors develop in parallel with their creator, from the sensationally inept surgeons in *Desperate Remedies* to the bleak postmodern practitioner in *Jude*, who predicts 'the universal wish not to live' (*JO* 323). Hardy's one detailed medical portrait, Edred Fitzpiers, is of a man whose strengths as a doctor lie more in poetic intuition than in scientific knowledge. This love-led man, a Shelleyan self-portrait, an individual untroubled by the petty restrictions of government-sponsored regulatory bodies, is a doctor who understands that the doctor–patient relationship is a two-way process. Dr Fitzpiers, who represents a development from Eliot's Lydgate and Kingsley's Thurnall, is the vehicle for Hardy's most detailed exploration of the nature of poetic love, medically reconstructed as The Fitzpierston Syndrome. This is wholly appropriate for Hardy understands the true relationship between the psyche and the soma – always accentuating the former – whether in the medical consultation or in the amatory relationship.

Hardy's understanding of 'the persistence of the unforeseen' (*MC* 411) is the gel that binds together the disparate medico-literary themes of this thesis. Scientific medicine, the post-Darwinian religion, that 'struggle to transcend the thought of dying' (Larkin 2003: 131), represents, like literature, an attempt to break life down into comprehensible, controllable components. These constituent parts – mainly psychological in the case of literature and mainly physical in the case of medicine – might then be amenable to repair, replacement or revision – like the mechanism of a motor-car. This is the hollow thinking behind the Department of Health's current drive to 'save lives' by lowering blood pressure, cholesterol, weight, glucose – and any other parameter they happen to seize upon – as if man would thereby become immortal. But this is not the nature of reality, and never will be; however many billions of pounds are spent on pharmacological agents and micro-surgical techniques. Hardy, like the great Physicians of his day (Allbutt, Maudsley, Crichton-Browne) knew that such intervention was both futile and irrelevant.

Man is not a machine; the human response, like all natural mechanisms, will always remain unpredictable: a minor illness kills, love does not last, a baby is stillborn, meningitis strikes, Bathsheba falls for

Troy, a wife is barren ... 'happiness is but an occasional episode in a continuing drama of pain' (*MC* 411). Life is constructed of a series of chance events, coincidences, unpredictable happenings – any attempt by medicine to impose order upon the chaos is doomed to failure. 'That's how it is on this bitch of an earth' (Beckett 1965: 38). In Wessex, the answer is simple but grim – avoid expectations and steer away from tragedy by accepting things as they are.

The unforeseen is part of the fabric of daily life. Hardy, the physician, acknowledged through the eyes of that wise-woman Elizabeth-Jane that survival was based on:

> the secret of making limited opportunities endurable ... in the cunning enlargement of those minute forms of satisfaction that offer themselves to everybody not in positive pain ...
>
> (*MC* 411)

This closely parallels the mission of the doctor, who should 'cure sometimes, relieve often but comfort always' as he helps his patients endure 'the doubtful honour of a brief transit through a sorry world' (*MC* 411). This takes us to the core of Hardy's tentative philosophy, which he expressed with greatest clarity in a poem written on his eighty-sixth birthday:

He Never Expected Much

Well, World, you have kept faith with me,
Kept faith with me;
Upon the whole you have proved to be
Much as you said you were.
Since as a child I used to lie
Upon the leaze and watch the sky,
Never, I own, expected I
That life would all be fair.

'Twas then you said, and since have said,
Times since have said,
In that mysterious voice you shed
From clouds and hills around:
'Many have loved me desperately,
Many with smooth serenity,
While some have shown contempt of me
Till they dropped underground.

'I do not promise overmuch,
Child; overmuch;
Just neutral-tinted haps and such,'
You said to minds like mine.
Wise warning for your credit's sake!
Which I for one failed not to take,
And hence could stem such strain and ache
As each year might assign.

                              (*CP* 886)

Glossary

abortion a miscarriage.

BAD abbreviation for Bipolar Affective Disorder.

CBT Cognitive Behavioural Therapy, the form of psychotherapy currently recommended for treating depression.

COD *Concise Oxford Dictionary.*

CVA abbreviation for Cerebrovascular Accident, that is, a stroke.

DCL Dorset County Library.

DCM Dorset County Museum.

DSM abbreviation for Diagnostic and Statistical Manual of Mental Disorders – produced by the American Psychiatric Association. Current version is DSM-IV (1994).

eclampsia a serious complication of late pregnancy, associated with convulsions and a significant foetal and maternal mortality rate.

GCMER abbreviation for the General Council for Medical Education and Registration – the regulatory body for medicine, created by the Medical Act of 1858. Name abbreviated to GMC (General Medical Council) in 1951.

Graham Dr Thomas Graham FRCP (Edin.), whose 'Popular Treatise' *Modern Domestic Medicine* 13th edition (1864), was kept by Hardy as his standard medical reference work. On the dispersal of his library, Hardy's copy of this book was sold to an American dealer. It is believed to have been subsequently destroyed in a warehouse fire.

ICD International Classification of Diseases – produced by the WHO. Currently on ICD-10.

IPM(J) Institute of Psychosexual Medicine (Journal).

LSA Licentiate of The Society of Apothecaries.

MAOIs abbreviation for Monoamine oxidase inhibitors: the earliest group of pharmacological antidepressant drugs – now largely superseded.

MDI Manic Depressive Illness.

(M)RCP (Member of) The Royal College of Physicians.

(M)RCS (Member of) The Royal College of Surgeons.

NIGP National Institute of General Practitioners.

OCD Obsessive Compulsive Disorder.

Personality Disorder an inherent tendency to antisocial and immoral behaviour; usually with minimal insight and usually considered untreatable.

primigravida a woman pregnant for the first time.

RCGP Royal College of General Practitioners.

Works Cited

Abbott, Ron and Bell, Charlie, *Thomas Hardy: A Beginner's Guide*, Hodder & Stoughton, Abingdon 2001.

Allbutt, Clifford T., *On Visceral Neuroses*, Blakiston, Philadelphia 1884.

Allbutt, H. A., *The Wife's Handbook*, Ramsey, London 1886.

Allen, Grant, *The Woman Who Did*, Grant Richards, London 1908.

Alvarez, Al, *The Savage God*, Bloomsbury, London 1971.

Ashton, Rosemary, *George Eliot : A Life*, Hamish Hamilton, London 1996.

Ashton, Rosemary, *George Eliot*, Oxford University Press, Oxford 1983.

Aston, J. N., *Textbook of Orthopaedics*, Hodder & Stoughton, London 1967.

Bailey, J. O., *The Poetry of Thomas Hardy*, University of North Carolina, Chapel Hill 1970.

Ed. Bailey, J. O. (ed.), *Poems and Religious Effusions by Emma Lavinia Hardy*, Toucan, Guernsey 1966.

Balint, Michael, *The Doctor, His Patient and The Illness*, Pitman, London 1964.

Barnes, Robert, *A System of Obstetric Medicine & Surgery*, Smith Elder, London 1884.

Beckett, Samuel, *Proust & Three Dialogues*, John Calder, London 1931.

Beckett, Samuel, *Waiting for Godot*, Faber, London 1965.

Berrios, G. and Porter, M. (eds), *A History of Clinical Psychiatry*, Athlone, London 1995.

Blake, Kathleen, *Love and the Woman Question*, Harvester, Brighton 1983.

Blunden, Edmund, *Thomas Hardy*, Macmillan, London 1967.

Boswell, James, *Boswell's London Journal 1762–1763*, Macmillan, London 1966.

Braddon, Mary Elizabeth, *The Doctor's Wife*, Oxford University Press, Oxford 1998.

Branden, Nathaniel, *The Psychology of Romantic Love*, Tarcher, Los Angeles 1980.

Brontë, Charlotte, *Jane Eyre*, Pan, London 1967.

Bynum, W. and Porter, R. (eds), *Encyclopaedia of the History of Medicine*, Routledge, London 1994.

Caird, Mona, 'Marriage', *Westminster Review* 130:2, 1888, pp. 186–201.

Campbell, Hugh, *Nervous Exhaustion*, Longmans, London 1873.

Carpenter, William B., *Principles of Mental Physiology*, Henry King, London 1875.

Casagrande, Peter, *Unity in Hardy's Novels*, Macmillan, Basingstoke 1982.

Clare, Anthony, *Psychiatry in Dissent*, Tavistock, London 1976.

Clouston, Thomas, *Clinical Lectures on Mental Diseases*, Churchill, London 1887.

Collins, Vere, *Talks With Thomas Hardy*, Duckworth, London 1928.

Conan-Doyle, A., *The Hound of the Baskervilles*, Jonathan Cape, London 1976.

Conan-Doyle, A., *The Stark Munro Letters*, John Murray, London 1912.

Cope, Zachary, *The Versatile Victorian*, Harvey & Blythe, London 1951.

Copland, James, *A Dictionary of Practical Medicine*, Longmans, London 1866.

Cox, R. (ed.), *Thomas Hardy: The Critical Heritage*, Routledge, London 1970.

Cronin, A., *Adventures in Two Worlds*, NEL, Holborn 1977.

Cunningham, A., 'The "New Woman Fiction" of the 1890s', *Victorian Studies* 17, 1973/4.

Cumberlege, J., *Changing Childbirth*, HMSO, London, 1993.

De Botton, Alain, *How Proust Can Change Your Life*, Picador, London 1997.

De Rougemont, Denis, *Love in the Western World*, Princeton University Press, New Jersey 1983.

Drabble, Margaret, *Oxford Companion to English Literature*, Oxford University Press, Oxford 1995.

Draper, R. (ed.), *Thomas Hardy – The Tragic Novels*, Macmillan, Basingstoke 1991.

D'Exudeuil, Pierre, *The Human Pair in the Work of Thomas Hardy*, Toulmin, London 1929.

Drysdale, George, *The Elements of Social or Physical, Sexual and Natural Religion*, E. Truelove, London 1875.

Dunbar, Flanders, *Mind & Body: Psychosomatic Medicine*, Random House, New York 1947.

Egerton, George, *Keynotes & Discords*, Birmingham University Press 2003.

Eliot, George, *Middlemarch*, Zodiac, London 1987.

Ellenberger, Henri, *The Discovery of the Unconscious*, Allen Lane, London 1970.

Flaubert, Gustave, *Madame Bovary*, Oxford University Press, Oxford 1998.

Foucault, Michel, *The History of Sexuality*, Penguin, Harmondsworth 1979.

Gale, Dolly, *I Was Emma Lavinia's Personal Maid*, THYB 1973/4, rptToucan Press, Guernsey 1974.

Garson, Marjorie, *Hardy's Fables of Integrity*, Clarendon, Oxford 1991.

GCMER Minutes Volume XXIV 1887, Spottiswoode, London 1888.

GCMER Minutes Volume XXXVIII 1901, Spottiswoode, London 1902.

Gelder, M. (ed.), *New Oxford Textbook of Psychiatry*, Oxford University Press, Oxford 2000.

Gibson, Colin, *Dissolving Wedlock*, Routledge, London 1994.

Gibson, James, *Thomas Hardy: A Literary Life*, Macmillan, Basingstoke 1996.

Gibson, James (ed.), *Interviews & Recollections*, Macmillan, Basingstoke 1999.

Gittings, Robert, *Young Thomas Hardy*, Penguin, Harmondsworth 1975.

Gittings, Robert, *The Older Hardy*, Penguin, Harmondsworth 1978.

Gittings, Robert, *The Second Mrs Hardy*, Heinemann, London 1979.

Goethe, Johann, *Elective Affinities*, Penguin, Harmondsworth 1971.

Graham, Thomas, *On The Diseases of Females*, London 1861.

Graham, Thomas, MD, *Modern Domestic Medicine*, Simpkin, London 1864.

Gregor, Ian, *The Great Web*, Faber, London 1974.

Heath, Stephen, *The Sexual Fix*, Macmillan, London 1982.

Helman, Cecil (ed.), *Doctors & Patients*, Radcliffe, Oxford 2003.

Hillis-Miller, James, *Distance and Desire*, Oxford University Press, London 1970.

Hillis-Miller, James *Fiction and Repetition*, Blackwell, Oxford 1982.

Houston, J. C., Joiner, C. L. and Trounce, J. R., *A Short Textbook of Medicine*, Edinburgh University Press, London 1975.

Irwin, Michael, *Reading Hardy's Landscapes*, Macmillan, Basingstoke 2000.

Jackson, Stanley, *Melancholia & Depression*, Yale University Press, New Haven, CT 1986.

Jacobson, Howard, *Peeping Tom*, Vintage, London 1999.

Jalland, Pat, *Death in the Victorian Family*, Oxford University Press, Oxford 1996.

Jamison, Kay, *Touched With Fire*, Macmillan, New York 1993.

Jamison, Kay, 'Manic-Depressive Illness & Creativity', *Scientific American* 2, 1995, pp. 46–51.

Johnson, Robert, *The Psychology of Romantic Love*, Routledge, London 1984.

Junior Practitioner, *A letter to Henry Warburton MP*, Churchill, London 1834.

Kay-Robinson, Denys, *The First Mrs Thomas Hardy*, Macmillan, London 1979.

Kidd, J., *Observations on Medical Reform*, Churchill, London 1842.

Kincaid, James, *Child-Loving*, Routledge, London 1992.

Kingsley, Charles, *Two Years Ago*, Macmillan, London 1866.

Ed. Kleinman, Arthur (ed.), *Culture and Depression*, California University Press, Berkeley 1985.

von Krafft-Ebing, R., *Psychopathia Sexualis*, Davis, Philadelphia 1924.

Kramer, Dale (ed.), *Critical Approaches to Thomas Hardy*, Macmillan, London 1979.

Kumar, Parveen and Clark, Michael, *Clinical Medicine*, Saunders, Edinburgh 2002.

Laqueur, Thomas, *Making Sex*, Harvard University Press, Massachusetts 1990.

Larkin, Philip, *Collected Poems*, Faber, London 2003.

Lawrence, D. H., *Study of Thomas Hardy*, Heinemann, London 1936.

Ledger, Sally, *The New Woman*, Manchester University Press 1997.

Liebowitz, Michael, *The Chemistry of Love*, Little, Boston 1983.

Logan, Peter, *Nerves & Narratives*, California University Press, Berkeley 1997.

Longmate, Norman, *King Cholera*, Hamish Hamilton, London 1966.

Mallett, Phillip (ed.), *Thomas Hardy Texts & Contexts*, Palgrave Macmillan, Basingstoke 2002.

Mallett, Phillip (ed.), *Thomas Hardy Studies*, Palgrave Macmillan, Basingstoke 2004.

Marcus, Steven, *The Other Victorians*, Weidenfield, London 1964.

Mason, Michael, *The Making of Victorian Sexuality*, Oxford University Press, Oxford 1994.

Maudsley, Henry, *Body And Mind*, Macmillan, London 1873.

Maudsley, Henry, *Responsibility in Mental Disease*, Henry King, London 1874.

Maudsley, Henry, *Natural Causes & Supernatural Seemings*, Kegan Paul, London 1897.

McLaren, Angus, *Birth Control in Nineteenth-Century England*, Croom Helm, London 1978.

Merrimum, Dr, *The Validity of 'Thoughts on Medical Reform'*, Longman, London 1833.

Millgate, Michael, *Thomas Hardy; A Biography*, Oxford University Press, Oxford 1982.

Millgate, Michael (ed.), *The Life & Work of Thomas Hardy*, Macmillan, London 1984.

Millgate, Michael (ed.), *Thomas Hardy's Public Voice*, Clarendon, Oxford 2001.

Millgate, Michael, *Thomas Hardy: A Biography Revisited*, Oxford University Press, Oxford 2004.

Morgan, Rosemarie, *Women and Sexuality in Thomas Hardy*, Routledge, London 1988.

Moscucci, Ornella, *The Science of Woman*, Cambridge University Press, Cambridge 1900.

Moule, Henry, *Paupers, Criminals & Cholera*, Toucan, Guernsey 1968.

NIGP, *Medical Reform*, Davy, London 1848.

Nettle, David, *Strong Imagination*, Oxford University Press, Oxford 2001.

Oliphant, Mrs, 'The Anti-Marriage League', *Blackwood's Magazine* 1, 1896, pp. 135–49.

Patten, Brian, *Little Johnny's Confession*, George Allen, London 1967.

Peterson, Jeanne, *The Medical Profession in Mid-Victorian London*, California University Press, Berkeley 1978.

Physicians & Surgeons, *The Family Physician*, Cassel, London 1883/4.

Pike, Royston, *Human Documents of The Victorian Golden Age*, Allen, London 1967.

Pite, Ralph, *Thomas Hardy: The Guarded Life*, Picador, London 2006.

Pinion, F., *A Hardy Companion*, Macmillan, London 1968.

Pope, Alexander, *Poetical Works*, Oxford University Press, Oxford 1966.

Porter, Roy, *The Greatest Benefit to Mankind*, Harper Collins, London 1997.

Porter, Roy, *Gout – The Patrician Malady*, Yale University Press, New Haven, CT 1998.

Post, Felix, 'Creativity & Psychopathology', *British Journal of Psychiatry* 165, 1994, pp. 22–34.

Prichard, James, *A Treatise on Insanity*, Sherwood, London 1835.

Proust, Marcel, *A la Recherche du Temps Perdu*, Penguin, Harmondsworth 2002.

Robinson, Paul, *The Modernization of Sex*, Paul Elek, London 1976.

Rolleston, Humphry, *Sir Thomas Clifford Allbutt*, Macmillan, London 1929.

Rothenberg, Albert, *Creativity & Madness*, Johns Hopkins University Press, Baltimore, MD 1990.

Rothfield, Lawrence, *Vital Signs*, Princetown University Press, New Jersey 1992.

Russett , Cynthia, *Sexual Science*, Harvard University Press, Cambridge, MA 1989.

Ryan, Michael, *Philosophy of Marriage*, Bailliere, London 1843.

Scarry, Elaine, 'Work and the Body in Hardy', *Representations* 3, 1983.

Schaeffer, Brenda, *Is it Love or is it Addiction?*, Hazelden, Minnesota 1997.

Schwartz, Barry, *The Paradox of Choice*, HarperCollins, New York 2005.

Seymour-Smith, Martin, *Hardy*, Bloomsbury, London 1994.

Shakespeare, William, *A Midsummer Night's Dream* (1595), Routledge, London 1994.

Shakespeare, William, *Hamlet* (1599), Routledge, London 1982.

Shakespeare, William, *The Tempest* (1611), Thomas Nelson, Walton-on-Thames 1997.

Shaw, Bernard, *The Doctor's Dilemma*, Penguin, Harmondsworth 1946.

Sherman, G. W., *The Pessimism of Thomas Hardy*, Associated University Press, London 1976.

Shorter, Edward, *From Paralysis to Fatigue*, Macmillan, New York 1992.

Showalter, Elaine, *The Female Malady*, Virago, London 1985.

Smith, Russell, *Medical Discipline*, Clarendon, Oxford 1994.

Steptoe, Andrew (ed.), *Genius & the Mind*, Oxford University Press, Oxford 1998.

Sternberg, Robert and Barnes, Michael, (eds), *The Psychology of Love*, Yale University Press, New Haven, CT 1988.

Sterne, Laurence, *Tristram Shandy*, Penguin, Harmondsworth 1985.

Storr, Anthony, *The Dynamics of Creation*, Secker & Warburg, London 1972.

Stott, Peter (ed.), *Options in Depression*, Medicom, Esher 2001.

Sturgis, Matthew, *Passionate Attitudes*, Macmillan, Basingstoke 1995.

Sumner, Rosemary, *Thomas Hardy-Psychological Novelist*, Macmillan, Basingstoke 1981.
Tallis, Frank, *Love Sick*, Century, London 2004.
Taylor, Richard, *The Neglected Hardy*, Macmillan, London 1982.
Thompson, Henry, *Diseases of the Urinary Organs*, Churchill, London 1879.
Thompson, Henry, *Modern Cremation*, Smith Elder, London 1901.
Thurley, Geoffrey, *The Psychology of Hardy's Novels*, Queensland University Press 1975.
Titterington, Ellen, *Afterthoughts of Max Gate*, Toucan, Guernsey 1974.
Tolstoy, Leo, *The Kreutzer Sonata*, Oxford University Press, Oxford 1997.
Tomalin, Claire, *Thomas Hardy: The Time-Torn Man*, Viking, London 2006.
Trevor-Roper, Patrick, *Lecture Notes on Ophthalmology*, Blackwell, Oxford 1974.
Turner, Paul, *The Life of Thomas Hardy*, Blackwell, Oxford 1998.
Tyler Smith, W., *A Manual of Obstetrics*, Churchill, London 1858.
Various, *Medical Reforms 1833–1854* (Canterbury Cathedral Library).
Various, *The Holy Bible*, SPCK, London 1934.
Vrettos, Athena, *Somatic Fictions*, Stanford University Press, California 1995.
Weber, Carl, *Hardy of Wessex*, Routledge, London 1965.
Webster, Richard, *Why Freud Was Wrong*, HarperCollins, London 1995.
Weiss, Edward and English, O. Spurgeon, *Psychosomatic Medicine*, Saunders, Philadelphia 1943.
Westermarck, Edward, *The History of Human Marriage*, Macmillan, London 1925.
Williams, Merryn, *A Preface to Hardy*, Longman, London 1978.
Wolpert, Lewis, *Malignant Sadness*, Faber, London 1999.
Wood, Rev. J. G., *Insects At Home*, Longmans, London 1872.
Wood-Homer, Christine, *Thomas Hardy and His Two Wives*, Toucan, Beaminster 1964.
Woodcock, George (ed.), *The Return of The Native*, Penguin, Harmondsworth 1978.
Worboys, Michael, *Spreading Germs*, Cambridge University Press, Cambridge 2000.
Wordsworth, William and Coleridge, Samuel Taylor, *Lyrical Ballads*, Routledge, London 1991.
Wright, T. R., *Hardy And The Erotic*, Macmillan, Basingstoke 1989.
Wright, T. R., *Hardy And His Readers*, Palgrave Macmillan, Basingstoke 2003.
Youngson, A. J., *The Scientific Revolution in Victorian Medicine*, Croom-Helm, London 1979.

Songs

Cohen, Leonard, 'Ain't no Cure for Love', from *I'm Your Man*, CBS 1988.
Mitchell, Joni, 'My Old Man', from *Blue*, Warner Bros 1971.

Index